MIRRORS KILL

DATE DUE

5/8/97		
9/-4-/c		
3/14 - Rco		

Demco, Inc. 38-293

MIRRORS KILL

JACK CURTIS

G.K. Hall & Co. • **Chivers Press**
Thorndike, Maine USA   Bath, Avon, England

This Large Print edition is published by G.K. Hall & Co., USA
and by Chivers Press, England.

Published in 1995 in the U.S. by arrangement with Crown Publishers, Inc.
Member of the Crown Publishing Group.

Published in 1995 in the U.K. by arrangement with Orion, an imprint of
Orion Books Ltd.

U.S.   Hardcover   0-7838-1298-1 (Core Collection Edition)
U.K.   Hardcover   0-7451-7871-5 (Windsor Large Print)

The text of this Large Print edition is unabridged.
Other aspects of the book may vary from the original edition.

Set in 16 pt. News Serif by Minnie B. Raven.

Printed in the United States on permanent paper.

British Library Cataloguing in Publication Data available

Library of Congress Cataloging in Publication Data

Curtis, Jack, 1942–
    Mirrors kill / Jack Curtis.
        p.   cm.
    ISBN 0-7838-1298-1 (lg. print : hc)
    1. Large type books.   I. Title.
    [PR6053.U775M57   1995b]
    823'.914—dc20   95-13855

To Barnaby

Show not an evil man his image in a glass: suchlike are mirrors for the blind.

Show not that first man's image to a virtuous man: such mirrors kill.

A
WEDDING
IN
AMERICA

1

At noon that day, a hawk flew across the sun, small and fast and nimble; its eye had found prey in the paddocks beyond the perfect two-acre lawn. The little killer was no more than a dozen feet above the heads of the wedding guests, and her shadow licked faces or flickered on crisp white linen and fine glassware. For a fraction of a moment, it striped the bride's dress of oyster-colored slubbed silk.

Sonia Bishop was the only person who noticed the hawk. Among the guests, she was friend not family — she and the bride had been close during their school days, but now were little more than acquaintances. Sonia had gone along for the champagne and the food . . . and out of curiosity. The family was inexpressibly rich, and Sonia wanted to see what that looked like up close.

After the ceremony, the speeches, the first three courses, Sonia had taken a full glass and started to wander through the twenty-room New England mansion. Enough of talking to fools, fending off passes, exchanging trivial histories. She got to one of the third-floor bathrooms, locked herself in, and rested her elbows on the sill of the open window. She was looking out over the lawn: the tables arranged along three sides of a rectangle, the guests, the waiters, the string quartet. It was a flawless day — the sun warm,

9

the sky cloudless. A one-man enterprise called Memories was filming a video of the occasion.

That was when Sonia saw the hawk, below her, lower than treetop height, its wings flashing like knives as it crossed the open space between woodland and paddock.

That was when she saw the latecomer.

A short man, maybe five five, wearing the wedding day's uniform of cream tuxedo and bow tie. In one hand, he carried the gift that would be added to the laden table in the larger drawing room. Sunlight ran on the silver gift wrapping. He was neither hurrying nor strolling — making for the top table, so that he could offer his apologies to the bride and groom, to the bride's parents. Sonia was too far off to see him clearly; even so, she noticed the little, flat, puglike face and pale skin. Closer-to, she'd have seen the mottled look of his lips, and the darkness, like bruising, that lay beneath the translucent skin around his eyes.

She wedged herself along the sill, back against the casement on one side, a foot braced against the window frame on the other, and lifted her champagne to her lips. Sunlight flooded the glass, blinding her for a moment. When she looked again, the latecomer had reached the top table.

The bride and bridegroom were standing, just returned from a tour of the tables, saying hello and thanks to people they half knew. The latecomer lifted a hand, as if in greeting, then seemed to hold the wedding gift forward, as if to say, "Sorry I'm late," or, "Here it is," or, "Happy life."

Sonia saw a strange thing happen. The bride raised her arms, as if delighted to see the man, as if she might lean across the table and embrace him. But instead of moving forward she went back.

Then several things occurred at once, fast enough to cheat the eye; and the sound of automatic gunfire was almost too loud and too shocking to be understood.

The bride's backward movement was extended with a violent and savage grace. The front of her oyster-colored dress opened, red and wet, as if something had burst. She rose like a diver, arms up, and made a long back flip. The groom danced over toward her, legs jerking, body jazzing to and fro with the push-pull of the bullets.

Sonia was stock-still; the glass tilted in her hand, letting a thin stream of champagne drizzle into her lap. She looked down on what was happening like a child engrossed by a story.

The bride's mother was motionless, too. She sat in her chair, back straight and strangely regal, like a queen listening to petitions. A cluster of bullets had taken her over the heart, and she wore the fist-sized wound like an exotic brooch.

The bride's father leapt to his feet, arm extended, as if accusing the new guest of a breach of good manners. It wasn't obvious to Sonia, but he was pointing a small gun. As she watched, a piece of his face flew off, then another.

They weren't the only ones to die. An automatic

assault weapon is more random, more comprehensive than that. In all, six people were killed and four wounded. It all happened very quickly; guests were eating and drinking and talking — they barely had time to turn, to register shock, to become afraid. At first, nothing was happening but the killing; as if it had been wonderfully stage-managed and was holding the audience enthralled. Then everything caved in.

You could hear the screams and the yells. You could see people running to either side or back toward the house — no one moving toward the latecomer, his eyes everywhere as he backed off toward the paddock. He glanced up and Sonia winced, as if he were seeking her out, but he was looking beyond her, higher, above the rooftop. In the same moment she heard the sound of helicopter rotor blades.

Sonia saw the two-seater pod set down, its under-carriage barely touching the grass. The latecomer threw his gun in, then yanked himself aboard. The helicopter tilted forward as it rose again, getting to rooftop height, and Sonia watched as the killer's face floated up toward her like something in a dream.

As in a dream, she couldn't move. The transparent dome sat at her eye level, rotor blades chattering. The man was laughing; Sonia could see that it was a nervous, savage laughter born of excitement and wild energy — it wouldn't stop. In the same moment, he turned his head and looked Sonia full in the face. He was taken aback to see someone almost peering over his shoulder, then the laughter seemed to grow more fierce, as if Sonia's being there were a terrific joke. In the same instant the helicopter banked and slid sideways, traveling away from the house at full speed.

The sound of its blades had all but deafened Sonia; she could hear nothing of the chaos beneath her. The wetness of the spilled champagne had seeped through to her thighs. She felt it, but didn't move. All she could think was how odd it was to be alone at such a time — nothing to say, nothing to do. Her pulse was like gunfire.

The Memories man was among the dead. His body was a little farther back than the rest — he'd been focusing wide to take in everyone at the tables. His camera was still switched on; the viewfinder framed the bride's face where she lay, eyes wide, face stippled with blood from chin to brow, hair perfect under its sheen of lacquer. The groom's hand rested possessively on her neck.

Sonia knew she would have to do something but couldn't imagine what it might be.

A fast, dark flicker arrived at the corner of her vision and the hawk returned, flying lower this time, as if it had caught the smell of fear. It traveled against the sun towing its splinter of shadow, thin and dark as the wing of the angel of death.

After a wedding, good cheer . . . He was laughing as he came out of the bathroom, laughing as if he had never stopped. He stood in front of a mirror to comb his hair, wet from the shower. In the corner of the glass was the image of a woman, half-naked, with her back turned on him. She continued to dress, wordlessly, hurriedly, and he barely gave her a second glance. He didn't know her name and she didn't know his; as she crossed the room, she gave him a tight little smile that her face in the mirror scarcely registered. "Okay, honey? I gotta go." She waited. "Okay?" There was a rough edge to her voice, husky, as if she were nervous.

He turned and licked his lips at her, then looked away. She went out, closing the door behind her with too much of a bang, but he just grinned and went back to his reflection.

"Shoulda seen the look on their faces when I started shooting," he said, "like someone stuck a pig," and the laughter frothed up again. With the whore gone, there was no one to talk to but himself. *The goddamn look on their goddamn faces!"*

His expression grew pensive. He reached out and touched his reflection, fingertips to cheek, to mouth, to eyes. "What a moment that was," he whispered. He put his forehead against the mirror and rested it there a moment, then he kissed the glass. His breath left a damp smudge.

He went to the bed and sat naked to dial a number. The phone was lifted on the second ring.

"Shoulda seen the look on their goddamn faces," he said.

A

FUNERAL

IN

FRANCE

2

There were flags and torches and drums.

The little Breton churchyard stood close to the sea, its foundations bedded in the granite of the cliff top. The cluster of birch trees that stood on a rise just beyond the church was crooked and leaned inland, their thin branches reaching out along the prevailing wind.

It was a raw afternoon. You could see whitecaps to the horizon; the torch flames whickered and flattened. The beat of the drums was echoed by a strange seismic *boom* as the sea barreled into caves two hundred feet below.

The drummers, the standard-bearers, the torchbearers — all had the look of recruits, enlisted but not yet in uniform, so they'd invented a uniform of their own: jeans, boots, leather, hair shorn to the scalp. There were eight of them in all: not much of a phalanx. They had assembled close to the churchyard, then stepped out to the drumbeat, following the coffin in military slow step. Behind them, twenty or so mourners, older men, no women. Two in particular seemed to bear the weight of authority. On the approach to the graveside, they had walked slightly ahead of their fellows: one a tall man in a belted greatcoat, the other slighter, more dapper, narrow faced and thin lipped.

Now they all stood in a semicircle around the grave,

yellow flames leaking a thin, black smoke into the wind, banners crackling, the drums silent. The priest muttered pieties and tossed a handful of damp earth down onto the lid of the casket. The thin-lipped man stepped forward and stooped to collect his own token handful: *Man that is born of woman . . . earth to earth, ashes to ashes . . .*

Others were there. A dozen or so people from the nearby village stood along the narrow path that led to the church porch; they had come out of curiosity, or because they had known the dead man, or because they had hated him. Closer, but somehow more withdrawn, were a few journalists and a TV camera crew, cold and impatient, some angry, some bored, but all there to do a job.

There was also the uninvited guest.

He came out of the birch grove and started downhill with no more than sixty yards to cover before he arrived at the graveyard. No one noticed him. Just before he reached the stone wall he lengthened his stride as if he were about to break into a run, but slapped his hands down on the top and used the impetus to hoist himself up and over, coming down on the other side and stepping away as if he'd never broken stride. A short man, the tails of his unbuttoned raincoat lifting in the wind like a cape.

The gun was slung around his body on a strap and hidden by his coat. When he came opposite the funeral party he drew the strap around, bringing the gun to hand, and fired a long burst that started low and left, then climbed right, curving like a scimitar.

The thin-lipped man died, and the tall man in the greatcoat. The priest died. One of the standard-bearers died, taken in the throat. He pitched forward, bridging the open grave.

It took eight seconds. Some people found cover — gravestones, the church porch, the church itself; others stood still, as if waiting to be selected. The uninvited guest went back to the wall, gun up and visible to threaten everyone. He smiled for the camera: little, flat face, dark eyes, lips livid like salami. The smile became a laugh — *yip-yip-yip-yip-yip* — shrill with nervous energy. Twenty yards light of the wall, he turned and ran to the birch grove.

The TV cameraman kept filming. He'd been taken too much by surprise to find proper cover. He lost the gunman among the birches, then shifted position and went in close on the dead. They lay alone amid guttering torches and a single fallen flag — black with a white circle and inside the circle a black swastika.

Now that it was too late, now that it was pointless, people were running and shouting. Two of the young men with shaven heads sprinted halfway to the birch grove, then stopped and began to tell each other why it was a bad move. Others paced to and fro in the churchyard, like dogs on a chain.

A villager, an old man, went to look at the lumber of corpses. He bent over, peering, as if he might recognize someone among the dead, then spat on the flag. After a moment, he spat on it again.

19

Only the camera saw him.

After a funeral, fond memories . . . The flight was proving rocky — clear-air turbulence was bouncing the plane around the sky and those passengers who weren't throwing up seemed stranded between mild anxiety and outright panic. All except the ugly little bastard in club who was drinking scotch and plain water and chuckling at some private joke. The stewardess jostled and jounced down the aisle to bring him another drink and he gave her a big grin, his lips mottled and glistening like salami carrying a sweat of oil.

Ugly little bastard. It was how she'd thought of him since he stepped aboard; and because he knew that, his grin broadened.

He said, "You're very kind," an old-fashioned Southern gentleman, and contrived to brush the back of her hand with his fingertips as she set the glass down.

He drank the scotch slowly, looking out at the port wing as it trembled and wagged. The window held a faint reflection of his face, seeming to be suspended beyond the glass as if he were looking in at himself. He raised his scotch like someone giving a toast and whispered, "Here's to us."

He finished the drink and called for another. The plane banged around the sky. He felt pleasantly tired so he rested his head close to the darkening glass, close to his floating image. His breath made a tiny decal of mist like the last damp trace of a kiss.

Tom Bullen was roping down eighty feet or more into what looked like deep water; there was so little light that the depth was anyone's guess, but even in daylight the surface would have been slick and dark with minerals. Bullen paid out rope through the rappel rack connected to his chest harness and went fifteen feet closer to the water. The light from his helmet ran across a great, fluted scroll of limestone that fell to the surface of the pool like a loose curtain.

The sound of water was everywhere. In front of his face, the rock was streaming. Echoes of falls rang in the bowl of the cavern, as if some vast sluice system were at work washing down the world.

Earlier, Bullen had ascended a couple hundred feet from the deepest part of the cave. He'd heard the water before he'd seen it. At first he thought he had found a fast stream underground, or a waterfall. Nothing like that was charted, but then he'd been in unknown terrain for better than an hour. After a short while he realized that the cave was flooding.

People who go down into the dark from a cave's entrance to the maze of tunnels hundreds of feet below go in groups for the most part. They take a lot of back-up equipment, too. It's easy to get lost underground, and it's easy to die. There had been a time when Bullen had gone underground as part of a team

21

of geologists. His role had been that of pathfinder rather than scientist. To Bullen, caving was mountaineering in reverse.

If he ever went underground now, it was simply to test himself against the darkness.

He had started from the deep cavern and climbed up out of a narrow limestone gallery, making for the surface as the water rose, and somewhere he'd taken a wrong turn. Now he was retreating, going deeper, searching for an alternate way out. The water looked fast and cold.

He went in up to his waist and felt the breath leave his body as if it had been siphoned off. His helmet light showed him an arch at one end of the chamber; it bristled with tiny stalactites. He guessed that two-thirds of it was underwater, like a doorway in a drowning house. The back end of the gallery was a vast boss of solid stone that gave him nowhere to go.

Bullen waded forward with the flood against him. The arch was narrow and seemed to let into a second chamber. He paused a moment, then pushed through against the flow. Immediately he felt his feet lift, borne up by water as he stepped over the edge.

The fall took seconds but seemed to last all day. He thought, *I hope I'm killed;* and then he went his length, stretched like a diver, rolled as a seal rolls to get his balance, and stood up in the dark vault of the second chamber.

He could hear the rush and rumble of a waterfall as more of the flood fell in somewhere to his left. He was immersed to his chest now, and getting colder. The chamber sloped up to a narrow corridor, five feet or so above the waterline and no more than a couple of feet wide. Bullen pushed off and made a clumsy breaststroke that took him closer to the tunnel.

Because the slope was in his favor, the water fell away to his thighs as he waded forward and peered into the mouth of the passageway. It was as tight as a tile drain and limitlessly dark. He took a purchase on the rock, then hoisted himself out of the water and went in headfirst.

He traveled twice his body's length, working with elbows and knees, then paused. The cone of light from his lamp showed him fossils and nubby bedrock. Nothing. He was as sure as he could be that he was edging into a dead end. His shoulders brushed the sides.

He crawled another coffin's length and stopped again. The tunnel sloped upward, rising some three feet perhaps, then seemed to level out — a vertical dogleg. Bullen turned onto his back like someone turning inside his own clothing and began to feed his body around the tunnel's contour, the palms of his hands on the tunnel roof, his heels digging to give him traction. He got his torso into the upper part of the tunnel and arched his back to bring it over the angle. Then he couldn't move; and he couldn't breathe.

He thought, It's just panic, the not breathing is just panic. There came a swell of dizziness, like music you could feel but not hear, and all at once his body was incredibly light. He fought it hard for a couple of minutes, then blacked out.

When he came to he was breathing almost normally and his heartbeat was no longer savage enough to make him nod. He rocked his shoulders, making the movements slight, until the small of his back came up over the ridge to the second level, then turned onto his belly once more and continued with elbows and toes, making a few inches with each shove.

For a moment the panic returned. He felt the weight of thousands of tons of rock above him and darkness everywhere; darkness lapping him; darkness like something solid that he must push through.

He broke out into a wider funnel, then a little gallery that he could half stand up in, then a walkway that allowed him to stand upright if he bowed his head like a penitent. He was happy to bow his head.

On the floor of the walkway were pools, ankle-deep. They were cluttered with detritus from the world outside: twigs, a frond of fern, a bedraggled hank of rosebay willow herb, a Budweiser can half sunk in mud. He could still hear water falling far back in the cave, like some terrible machine taking its cargo too far into the earth for imagination to guess at.

He emerged into saturated woodland, deep green, and birdsong everywhere. The rain had passed, leaving a sky livid with emerging sunlight, gray and yellow like an old bruise.

Not dead then, he thought.

He trekked the mile and a half to where he'd left his four-wheel-drive. When he got back to the cottage,

Paul Shelley was waiting for him.

Before he went into the place Bullen knew someone was there, and knew that meant trouble. The cottage stood amid woodland, a mile from the road, and he'd rented it only two weeks before through an agency picked at random. "Somewhere in the Neath Valley," he'd said. "Somewhere on its own." If you looked out from Bullen's front door on a day when there was no mist, no scribble of fine rain twitching back and forth in the wind, you could see evidence of two other houses — the chimneys of one, the tile ridge of another. Neither had occupants. Bullen had left no messages, no address, not even with Anne. She wouldn't have expected it. Their relationship wasn't about possession or keeping track of each other: Anne knew this because Bullen told her so.

He backheeled the door and threw his caving gear into a corner. He didn't speak, though he gave Shelley a look that said, "I'm not going to like this." It was the first time the men had seen each other in two years.

Shelley glanced at Bullen as he peeled off his sodden clothing, leaving it where it fell, then walked naked to a sideboard and half filled a tumbler with scotch. He was lithe and long muscled like a distance runner, dark hair a little overlong, a narrow, intense face that bore a little cluster of scars on the left temple from a caving accident.

Shelley couldn't have been more than five or six years older than Bullen — forty-two, perhaps — but he had a tight, rounded paunch that sat just under his

25

rib cage, and the line of his jaw was beginning to dissolve. His thin, blond hair showed the scalp. He watched Bullen walk naked to the stairway and said, "I used to look like that. Women passing in the street would hand me their panties." When Bullen didn't react, he continued: "I thought you never went underground these days."

"I never go underground publicly or with anyone else."

"Isn't that dangerous?" Shelley could tell that Bullen wasn't going to offer him a drink. He crossed to the sideboard and got it himself. He said, "Are you going to make me work for everything, Tom?"

"I've got a small amount of money," Bullen told him. "Came to me when my father died. Not a spectacular sum, but I can live on it. I don't need to go to the office, I don't have to listen while someone tells me what to do, I don't have to kiss ass, or look for a promotion, or worry about losing my job. I don't need work."

"This isn't work."

"Sure it is. What else would it be?"

Bullen drank off half the whiskey, then took the glass with him as he went upstairs.

Bullen showered in a couple of minutes and went back downstairs feeling less angry but more tricky. He stood at Shelley's shoulder, the whiskey bottle in his hand, and topped up both their glasses. "My friend," he said. "Aren't you my friend?" Shelley smiled, but said nothing. "Do you always know where I am?"

"What are friends for?"

At one time, Bullen had been the foremost British organizer of caving expeditions. He'd traveled to most countries in the world.

Sometime in the late eighties, before the death of Communism, before the death of certainties, Paul Shelley had arranged a meeting with Bullen. He'd suggested that expeditions were expensive to fund, and he'd suggested a solution. It was that Bullen carry things across borders now and then; leave messages; exchange bits of merchandise. Shelley's people — the Friends, they called themselves; sometimes the Firm — had even designed a piece of caving equipment that would house certain items.

Bullen had said okay; he was trying to fund an expedition at the time. A month later he'd carried something into East Germany during an exploration of the gypsum caves in the Harz mountain range.

"There's something I want to show you," Shelley said. "A piece of film."

"I came up here for two weeks," Bullen told him. "Five days to go."

Shelley shook his head. It was difficult to tell whether the gesture meant "No days to go," or whether it reflected his astonishment at Bullen's foolish pastime. Finally, he said: "What happened today?"

"Happened . . . ?"

"You were soaked. You looked wet to the bone."

"The cave flooded. Part of the cave."

"Were you frightened?"

Bullen took a mouthful of his drink, shaking his

head at the same time. Shelley saw the confusion of signals and knew the truth at once. Bullen swallowed the whiskey and said, "Nothing to be frightened of. I just climbed out. Fell into a cave pool on the way."

"What do you look for," Shelley asked, "down there in the dark?"

"Dark gods."

Shelley laughed at Bullen's joke as if he understood it.

4

There is a building on the south bank of the Thames that doesn't exist. It stands on the water's edge close to Vauxhall Bridge, a massive structure of crenellations, buttresses, domes, and towers, all balanced symmetrically and rearing hundreds of feet into the dirty London air. Its colors are gray and a slubby matte green. It's a new building, so it hasn't yet taken on that used-up, broken-down, busted-facade appearance. It has conical trees and two protective moats, one of which pretends to be a fountain. It's made of concrete and the first two floors are completely windowless.

The Friends live there, and it doesn't exist.

Stuart Cochrane shook Bullen by the hand, smiling, apparently reluctant to let go. He said, "Paul tells me you were on holiday. I'm sorry." The handshake continued; Cochrane continued to smile. "Don't

28

worry; there's just something that we want you to help us out with. Probably won't take too long." Cochrane had met Bullen and Shelley by an elevator bank, turning up at just the right moment, as if he'd been timing the event for weeks. He was a tall man in his midforties. His hair was brown with touches of gray and had a slight curl which took some of the severity from his narrow face and thin nose. His cheeks had the smooth shine of a close shave. When the elevator arrived, he ushered Bullen in, still holding his hand, letting go only to press a button low on the selector plate. They were in a glassine bullet; it dropped into darkness.

The viewing theater was in the uttermost depths of the nonexistent building and at least a hundred and fifty feet from any natural light source. Shelley and Cochrane sat a row behind Bullen, like latecomers. Someone out of sight started the tape and the first images flowed over the screen: a slow procession, flags and drums, a church, an open grave.

Bullen watched what the cameraman had recorded. He saw the cropped heads of the young Nazis and the two older mourners following — the man in the belted greatcoat, the dapper, thin-lipped man. The priest stepped forward with a handful of dust.

Bullen said, "What is he — ?" but Cochrane tapped him briefly on the shoulder and whispered: "Later . . . later . . ." The uninvited guest seemed to shoulder his way into the frame, arriving lopsided and full of mad energy, the automatic weapon already in action and swinging through a wide arc, so fast and fluent that the killer's hands seemed to be chasing it.

29

The camera was doing cartwheels. People were running. There was a moment when the screen showed nothing but cuts of sky, treetops, the grainy blur of a gravestone. Then the cameraman found cover and focused in time to show the killer going over the cemetery wall. There was nothing much else that Cochrane wanted Bullen to see, but he let the tape run on to find the moment when the old man spat on the flag.

They sat in the dark, all facing the blank screen. Bullen said, "I've been away for ten days. No newspapers, no TV, no radio."

"Very Spartan." Cochrane was one of the old school: stylish; he liked games.

"When did this happen?"

"Yesterday," Shelley told him. "I'm sorry, Tom. Were you fond of him?"

"He was famous in the family when I was a child. MP at twenty-three, junior minister eight years later. Beyond that, I didn't really know him. My mother was very proud of him."

"Brother and sister," Cochrane said. "They looked alike, didn't they? Aristocratic chins, flaxen hair." He spoke the word *flaxen* as if it meant something more: Aryan, perhaps. *Ubermensch*. "It's a pity that he chose to fuck it all up. You can't cavort about the place in swastika armbands saying that the Holocaust was a trick of the light without putting your career at risk."

"He never did that."

"No," Cochrane agreed. "Might as well have." Without raising his voice, he said: "Put the bloody

30

light on," and at once a pale neon flicker started up around the room.

Bullen turned in his seat. "Who killed him?"

Shelley shrugged. "We don't know."

"Politics or vengeance?"

"No, really — we don't know; it's why you're here."

Cochrane said, "They were burying a man named Claude Riboud" — Bullen shook his head — "no, why should you? Friend of Le Pen, hence the turnout. Very active in the French neofascist movement, until God decided to give him rectal cancer. The presence of your uncle, along with a similarly outspoken French politician and the Neanderthal flag bearers, was designed to get the movement some news coverage." He laughed. "Certainly succeeded, didn't they?"

The glassine tube took them back into an atrium filled with murky daylight. Cochrane handed Bullen a videocassette. "Thought you might find it useful to have the chance of seeing it again."

Bullen wondered if anyone had told his mother — warned her. He asked, "The film's been shown, has it? On television . . ."

"Several times," Cochrane said. After a pause, he laughed loudly, as if the punchline of some subtle joke had just become clear. "Several times, yes. I'll bet that cameraman couldn't believe his luck."

Shelley walked Bullen out of the building, then, as if it was what they had always intended, kept him company until they came to a *tapas* bar on the river-front.

The place was raucous with bad flamenco and young men in business suits. The stubby aerials of mobile phones bristled from their pockets like the masts of a sunken fleet. Bullen and Shelley ordered beer and two dishes apiece, then shouldered through to a couple of high stools that faced a window.

"You knew he was a Nazi though?" Shelley spoke as if they were in midconversation.

"Everyone knew."

"But no one much minded."

A little gusher of anger rose in Bullen; a sourness in the throat. "I fucking minded."

Shelley smiled. "No one in the party."

The beer came. Shelley drank while Bullen looked out at the river traffic. He was thinking about his mother. Her brother had been murdered on television for all to see. He said, "Roland Cecil was a minor politician; no one special. People who hated him — who hated his opinions — thought him largely power-less. People who approved of him thought the same."

"Not the case now." Shelley rolled the base of his beer glass in a pool of spillage. "The tabloids are having a terrific time. There's suddenly a very lively debate about British neo-Nazism, and the PM is screaming to have the whole issue capped and smoth-ered like a torched oil rig. It's a hell of an embarrass-ment. Everywhere you look in Europe there are narrow-browed cretins making Nazi salutes and throwing firebombs at some poor bastard immigrant who thought he'd reached a place of safety."

"Who are you worried about?" Bullen asked. "The PM or the poor bastard immigrant?"

"If I told you," Shelley said, "you wouldn't believe me." He leaned sideways to allow the waitress to set down their dishes. "Anyway, there's more to it than newspaper headlines about the spawn of Hitler. Cecil wasn't some sordid little prick with a room full of yellowing propaganda; he was a Tory MP and some-one shot the shit out of him on prime-time TV." He put a forkful of *patatas* in his mouth and said, "Give my condolences to your mother." Then, "You will be seeing your mother . . . ?"

"Why ask?" Bullen said. "That's what you want."

"She might know" — Shelley shrugged — "some-thing."

He ate some sausage, took a gulp of beer. Bullen's plates remained untouched. Shelley said, "Because she's a Jew hater, too, isn't that right?"

5

When Anne Warbeck woke up, she was in motion. She had risen from the armchair, moving in a crouch, and taken an awkward tumble across a coffee table laden with objects. Bullen heard the *clatter-smash* and Anne's yell. When he came through from the kitchen, he saw Anne lying amid the jumble, holding her arm and looking bewildered. He picked her up and put her back into the armchair.

"Snipers' alley," she said. "I was in snipers' alley." Anne worked for a national newspaper; she had been back from Sarajevo for ten days.

Bullen retreated to the kitchen for a moment, then came back with two vodka-tonics. Anne took hers and held the dewy glass to her brow. "There came a time," she said, "when people simply stopped running. Defiance, I suppose. Before that, if you came to a cross street you got low and moved fast. Old ladies, bent double and moving in a sort of sideways galloping shuffle. I could never figure out why, but the old people all seemed to put a hand to their heads when they ran — a flat palm on the top of the head."

"Hat memories," Bullen suggested. "There was a time when everyone wore hats. If you ran, you held your hat on."

"The cross streets were perfect for the snipers," Anne said.

She drank some of the vodka, then set it down and began to pick up the bits and pieces she'd sent flying; among them were her Dictaphone and a tiny wash-leather pouch that contained a flint arrowhead — her lucky piece. Bullen watched her as she collated a fan of photographs. She was beautiful in an unconventional way: nose a little out of true, mouth a little too generous, jawline a little too strong, fair, tousled hair that fell into her eyes as she flipped through the photos. It added up to something strong and attractive. He thought she was terrific and brave and couldn't work out why in hell he wasn't in love with her. In love with her *enough*.

The photographs were of dead bodies. Anne put the

drawstring of the wash-leather bag round her neck. "When are you going?" she asked.

Bullen walked back to the kitchen and answered from there. "I don't know."

"She's your mother." Bullen had told Anne he was going to pay his mother a visit. Anne had seen the killings on TV like everyone else, but had no idea Bullen was Roland Cecil's nephew. All she knew was his mother was crazy and lived alone and Bullen never went near her.

"I can tell that's an accusation, but I don't really know what you're accusing me of."

"You don't feel you owe her something?"

Bullen came back with two plates of food: corned beef hash, flageolet beans in salsa on the side. Anne opened a bottle of Villera. They ate in silence for a while; Anne seemed lost in her thoughts. After a while she said: "It's none of my —"

"No, I don't," Bullen said. "I don't think I owe her shit. She's just a mad old woman who fucked up my life."

Cochrane's office had windows that faced downstream. Paul Shelley was looking out of them as he spoke, not so much out of interest in the river traffic, but because Cochrane was lying on a massage table with a small towel over his bare ass while a young woman in a T-shirt and jogging pants took her thumbs up and down his spine. She had long blond hair that swung as she worked, falling over her face in a discreet curtain. Shelley knew all about power plays and the value of positional tactics. He stood in Cochrane's office in a dark blue suit and a striped tie while his immediate boss lay naked. Naked but clothed in power, Shelley thought, and studied his reflection in the glass for any sign of movement about the mouth. In truth, Shelley wasn't facing away from Cochrane because he was embarrassed or threatened. He was afraid that he might laugh. He said, "No, he hasn't been to see her yet."

"It's more than a week, for Christ's sake." Cochrane grunted as the young woman added oil to her hands and started work on his triceps. "Has he called her?"

"No."

"Then what the Christly fuck is going on?"

"I'm not sure."

"Have you asked him?" Cochrane's head was pillowed on his hands. He raised it for a moment, staring angrily at Shelley's back, then dropped it so that the young woman could get at his neck. "Why not ask him?"

"I will. I don't want to push too hard."

"His mother's brother was murdered, just about everyone in Europe must have seen the newscast, it got national newspaper coverage, and what's he doing?"

Shelley took the question to be rhetorical until Cochrane repeated it. He said, "I don't know."

"Aren't we watching him?"

"Why should we?"

The blonde was pushing deep into the small of Cochrane's back, her thumbs getting just under the towel before traveling up to his rib cage. "What about the mother?'' he asked. ''What's happening there?''

''She never goes out, makes no phone calls, sees no one. If you mean: Has she made any effort to get in touch with her son? then the answer's no.''

''I thought we were setting up a bear trap,'' Cochrane said. ''Isn't that what we're trying to do?''

''He'll go. He'll go eventually.''

''What kind of a son is he?'' Cochrane wanted to know. ''Uncle dead, mother alone in some dripping manor house in Yorkshire, he stays in London — what? Doing what?'' Cochrane's indignation seemed to be on behalf of ill-treated mothers everywhere.

''He's got a girlfriend,'' Shelley said. ''Anne Warbeck. He's staying with her.''

Cochrane's head came up sharply. He looked like an animal suddenly alerted to prey. ''So you have been watching him.''

''Just a glance or two,'' Shelley said, ''to stay in touch.''

''Okay. With her — but doing what?'' Cochrane's laugh was muffled by the pillow. ''Screwing aside.''

''They listen to music a lot, send out for food or go to a local Italian place, talk about nothing in particular.''

''What kind of music?''

''Opera. *Bohème*, *Fidelio*, bit of Wagner sometimes.'' Shelley was enjoying himself now.

Cochrane said, ''Give him two more days, then haul him in again and kick his ass.''

''He doesn't work for us, Stuart, not really. It isn't like the old days.''

"He signed the Official Secrets Act didn't he?"

"I expect so."

"Two days," Cochrane said.

Shelley left his reflection in the window and went to the door. He risked saying, "I know him better than you, Stuart. Best not to push." Cochrane averted his head like a petulant lover.

The blonde turned him over and began to loosen the joints of his shoulders and the muscles in his neck. Little tracers of electricity raced across Cochrane's skull. She said, "What's a bear trap?"

"What's a honey trap?"

"I am," she said. "Target the man, get him into bed, be a good listener. And make sure his dick is pointing at the hidden camera."

"A bear trap uses the same theory of infiltration. You find someone with an axe to grind —"

"This Bullen," she observed.

"And make sure he keeps on grinding. The idea is to stir things up."

"Will it work?"

"In this instance?" Cochrane gave a horizontal shrug. "Maybe. His mother's brother was assassinated; he must at least be curious. The best bear traps are when the trapper doesn't know he's being used. That's true in this case. It's also a help if he's dispensable."

"Is he?"

"Most people are," Cochrane said.

The young woman was giving his biceps a last slap and pummel. She stopped and reached for a roll of paper towel, tearing some off to wipe her hands. "Okay," she said, "I'm finished."

Cochrane shook his head. "No you're not."

The girl sighed very slightly and looked toward the window, as if waiting for him to change his mind. Cochrane said, "Okay?"

She dug into the pocket of her jogging pants and came up with an elastic band. She scooped her long hair back and held it at the nape of her neck while she fixed it into a ponytail, then twitched the towel off Cochrane's hips.

He said, "Honey trap, honeycomb, sweetness, sweetlips."

6

Sonia Bishop was running it again in her mind. The hawk, the sunlight flashing on the silverware, the uninvited guest. She saw him crossing the lawn with his gift at the ready. She saw the deaths and the chaos.

Some of the images in her mind's eye came from the tape filmed by the Memories man. The nation had shared those with her. Others were exclusively her own: the moment when she had seen the killer, puglike and pale, looking at her from the pod of the helicopter and laughing himself bug-eyed.

"What's happening?" There was weariness in Larry Reed's tone, but a lick of anger too. He took his hands off Sonia's body and propped himself on an elbow. She could feel his erection petering out against her thigh.

"Nothing's happening. I'm fine."

"No, no." Larry flopped onto his back. "I mean, what's happening in the action replay? Has he gotten across the lawn yet? Has he shot them? Is he in the chopper — what? Where are we?"

Sonia turned to look at him in the hope that a show of frankness would cover the lie: "I wasn't thinking about that." She had meant to put a hand on him as she spoke, but somehow the gesture hadn't emerged.

Larry sighed. "Sure you were."

Sonia and Larry were supposed to be on the mend. Their relationship was a year old; they'd been out to a neighborhood restaurant to celebrate: the best Chinese food in Brooklyn. Larry remembered how he and Sonia used to talk about the logistics of moving in together. Would he transfer to Brooklyn, or would she go over to Queens? They hadn't talked about such things in a long time.

"It's not the wedding," Larry said. "Not *just* the wedding. The wedding makes things worse, that's all."

Sonia felt a little electric *zip* of anger. I watched some people die, she thought. One minute a wedding party, flowers, wine, cake, happiness everywhere like something passing from hand to hand, people in love promising each other their bodies, their wealth, their lives . . . The next minute gunfire, blood hosing the linen, bodies. She remembered the way the groom jived and shook as the bullets struck, and how the bride's dress broke open, full and red.

"What's happening now?" Larry asked again.

40

"Are they all dead yet?"

"Jesus Christ!" Sonia said. "If you want to fuck me, why not fuck me?" She yanked the duvet onto the floor and grabbed her own ankles.

"Sonia . . ." He couldn't think of a thing to say.

She tucked her heels up to her ass and spread her knees. "You want some of this, or not?"

Her anger was making it worse for him; making him horny. He faked some anger of his own — "Okay. Why not?" — and scrambled onto her, pressing his hands down on her shoulders as if he thought she might change her mind. He whacked at her, hips thumping, and kept his eyes on her face as if to check for errant thoughts. She looked right back at him.

After a while he saw a flush of red start down from her throat to touch the slopes of her breasts. She said, "I'm coming," in a tone that was both intrigued and matter-of-fact, then closed her eyes to shut him out. She gritted her teeth — *"Ahhh!"* — and her mouth stayed wide until the sensation died away; then she licked her lips and opened her eyes and laughed. Larry thought, Why did that happen? And in the same moment, he knew the answer: it was never going to happen again, not with him.

Sonia let the tension go from her arms and legs. She said, "Your turn. How do you want it? Any way you like . . ."

"No . . . no, this is fine." He sounded foolish. He sounded like a considerate guest, or else like someone in too much of a hurry to care.

Larry dressed with his back to her. When his cab

41

arrived, he said: "I can come back . . ."

Sonia nodded. She knew that the sentence ended: ". . . for my things." She closed her eyes and immediately guessed what he'd say as he was leaving.

"What's happening?" The door opened. "Are they all dead yet?"

"No," Sonia told him. "The little pug-faced man is walking across the lawn."

The door rapped twice against the frame before Larry managed to get it closed.

The little pug-faced man was walking across the lawn. The Memories man's film showed him there in the background. At the top table, the bride's father leaned toward his wife, getting close in order to say something no one else ought to hear. She pretended to look affronted, then laughed at the joke.

Sonia knew that there was something she was missing, but didn't know whether it was on the tape or in her memory. It nagged at her. It was one of the reasons she played the tape again and again — on the video and in her head. She tried to think through the arrivals, the ceremony, the moments before people took their places at the wedding breakfast table. It teased her. She thought it must be a person, but couldn't make whoever it was step out of her memory's shadows and into the light. She rewound the tape, going back to the point where the newsreader began to reprise the item, then hit Play and watched the edited slaughter one more time.

No one much cared, now. It was old news — twelve days old. Since then the president had ordered troops into downtown L.A. for the second time that summer, a man arrested in Missouri for a traffic violation had shown the police where he'd buried eight of his nineteen victims, and the Braves were leading the NL East.

Sonia had been one of many wedding guests to be interviewed by the police. She'd given them a description that had resulted in a likeness of the killer so accurate that she hated to look at it. She was told that an investigation was in progress, but so far as she could tell the dead members of the Duval family were rapidly changing from people to statistics.

Sonia hit the Rewind button until she got to a moment the TV news had used as an establishing shot: the happy couple in close-up as they gave their vows, then guests chatting on the lawn, glasses of champagne in their hands. Bride, groom, parents of the bride — all smiling and blessed with sunlight. Everything was going according to plan. Unless an ugly little man with a gun arrived, it was always going to be a wonderful day.

7

The Calder Valley was all grays and greens. Gray skies, gray rain, the pale green of tree canopies. And on the high moor it was grayness again: granite, huddled sheep, dry stone walls. The greens up there had worn thin — a pelt of turf on thin topsoil.

Constance Bullen's house was built of gray stone blocks, so streaked and weathered now that the place seemed a part of the landscape. A small manor house — mullioned windows, oak and ironwork doors, tall chimneys that had withstood the winter blow for a hundred and fifty years — it stood on the outer edge of a village, aloof from other buildings and cut off from the single road by two acres of paddocks.

At one time there had been horses in the paddocks; now there were nettles and poppies and chickweed. Behind the house was an apple orchard. No fruit had been harvested there in a decade. The trees bore their crop each year and shed it to rot.

Bullen watched his mother nudge a cigarette out of its pack. It was three years since he'd seen her, and she seemed to have aged ten. Her arms were stringy sinew under loose folds of dark, dappled skin. Her face was mottled and so heavily lined that when she pursed her lips around the tip of the cigarette, her mouth fell into soft crenellations, like a ruff. Bullen felt little itches running across his skin.

Her hair was corn colored and she wore a flower-patterned skirt, together with a pale blue silk blouse open to the cleavage.

The whole valley was under a steady fall of rain; Bullen could hear it drumming on the yellowing glass of the conservatory at the back of the house.

Constance said, "I saw him die. They shot Roland next to an open grave. There were torchbearers and drummers."

"I saw it too."

44

"The Jews got him in the end." Constance thumbed an old flint-and-wick lighter and drew on the cigarette until she was out of breath. The tip left her mouth with a moist smack, glossy with plum red lipstick, and she hauled a pillar of smoke down into her lungs. "The Jews, wasn't it?"

They were sitting at either end of the dining room table; Bullen could see fluorescent specks of viridian mold dappling the wood. The whole place smelled musty — a mix of food waste, rotting wood, and unwashed clothing.

"No one knows who it was," Bullen told her. "The French police are investigating. They seem to be reaching the conclusion that the assassin was deranged — a madman acting on impulse. No political motive, they say. Just one of those people who like to kill the famous." He paused to let Constance absorb this information, then asked: "When did you see Roland last?"

She sat and smoked her cigarette in silence, drawing on it so deeply that the coal hissed raggedly down the paper. There was a chill on the place that had sunk into the walls and floors. Bullen guessed that the fires hadn't been lit for months. There was no central heating. A small electric fan heater stood on the brick floor of the fireplace, but wasn't switched on. The yellow dye on his mother's hair shone more brightly as the light began to fail.

She got up and went to the door, little feet, a geisha's staccato walk. "Later, Desmond," she said. "We'll talk about it later."

Desmond was Tom Bullen's father; he'd been

dead for fifteen years.

The house was cobwebs and stale air; fungi growing in closets. Bullen found her in an upstairs room turning the pages of a photograph album. Beside her was a large blanket chest, the lid thrown back on papers, letters, damp documents.

He said: "You evil old bitch. Why the fuck aren't you dead?"

There was a brandy decanter on the floor and an empty tumbler. Constance poured herself a drink and lit a new cigarette. "Roland," she said. "Roland, Roland, Roland . . . A handsome boy from golden summers of my youth." She laughed, a sound so thick with despair that Bullen was startled into speech.

"He came here from time to time? Is that right?"

"This was his," Constance said, pointing at the blanket chest. "Is it mine now he's dead? What's mine?"

"I'll let you know. I expect so. There was a funeral in London a few days ago."

"They told me."

"You were next of kin."

"They told me."

"Someone took care of things," Bullen said. "They cremated him."

Constance lifted her glass. There was a double bow of magenta lipstick on the glass. "I wish I were," she said. "I wish I *were* dead. We used to own the world."

Bullen lay fully clothed on the damp mattress of an unmade bed and listened to the night sounds: the roof

46

beams shifting, a barn owl's shriek, the bark of a vixen.

He knew what she was talking about. A memory came back to him of a warm evening, still twilight at ten-thirty, lamps hanging in the orchard, music, the house full of people. The men were wearing white tie, the women long dresses that rustled in the grass. The evening stood outside time, as if it could go on forever, and the people who went to and fro in that soft dusk were the country's elect. You could see that nothing would ever change. You could see that the world would behave.

It wasn't Bullen's memory. His mother had told him those stories when he was a child; they were all stories of loss and death. Bullen hadn't wanted to listen because in many of them he was the thief, the murderer.

He remembered . . . Constance's bedroom. Bullen was six years old; he'd walked in to find her, to ask some question, and she was standing naked in front of her cheval glass. He'd said, "Oh!" but was too curious and shocked to move; all he knew of his mother was elegance, beautiful clothes, perfect hair. She was a distant figure: others cared for him, others fed him and bathed him, others shared his life. He knew that his mother disliked him, but he didn't know why. It made him crave her love.

Constance had turned and looked at him, making no attempt to cover herself, an expression on her face of terrible loathing. "Look," she had said, and turned to face him. It had meant nothing to the boy that her breasts drooped, that her stomach was striped with

47

broad, pale stretch marks. "You wrecked me," she'd said. "You fed off me, like a leech. You brought your mess into the world." Her mouth had made an ugly little **O**. "I could feel you eating me from the inside." She'd walked close to the child and looked down at him. A hiccup had escaped her, as if she might retch, and she'd slapped him hard across the face.

Later that same night, she had come to his bedroom. The child had been awake but had pretended to sleep. He'd wanted her forgiveness for what he'd done, though he had no idea what it was. Maybe she'll wake me, he'd thought, to say it's all right. He'd summoned up a vision of his mother gathering him into her arms for the first time, stroking his hair, talking to him in a low voice. "I love you. Don't worry, I love you." The thought had been so seductive that the child had felt a scald of tears behind his closed eyelids.

Constance had been drunk. She'd stood in the doorway, letting a shaft of light from the hall strike across his bed. She'd said, "You almost died. Did you know that?" From the child's breathing, from his stillness, she couldn't have known whether he was asleep or awake. "I thought I was going to die, but that was just the pain. You really were going to die. But they saved you, they helped you to live." Her voice had sunk, weighed down with hatred and regret. "My God, I wish you had. I wish you'd died. Nine months of misery and sickness and being *unattractive*." She'd made the word sound like *leprous*, like *deformed*. "And now here you are, cluttering up my life with your stupid whining voice, your mess, your noise. I wish you had died, you filthy little shit."

The child had heard the pause as she took a long drink from her glass. He'd heard the violent exclamation she'd made before she'd turned from the door and stumbled downstairs. It was the sound of raw revulsion and disgust.

Bullen went to the room where Constance had sat with her brandy. The blanket box was still open. Bullen removed the papers one by one and read them.

He learned who you have to kill to purify the earth.

The telephone rang in the middle of the night. Bullen woke to complete darkness. His clothes felt limp and sticky and there was a mossy coating on his teeth. He lumbered around in the dark, cracking his legs against the bed until he found the wall light.

Pretty soon, he thought, the damn thing will stop. By the time I'm halfway there, it'll stop. But the ringing continued as he pushed his shoes on and went out into the hallway, then followed the sound downstairs to the hall. Bullen was curious, now — the phone had been ringing for some minutes. He sat on the bottom step and slowly laced his shoes before going to the hall table and lifting the receiver.

"Hello?" he said, and listened to the silence, which was what he'd expected.

On his way back to his room, he saw the reflection of a light in a hallway window on the opposite side of the stairwell. His mother was sitting up in bed drinking brandy. She was naked apart from the bandanna that

49

bound her golden hair.

She said, "I adored Roland. You always knew that, Desmond. He laid down his life for us."

Bullen had taken what he wanted from the blanket box. Among the photos he had found his father and Roland Cecil, both aged about eighteen, dressed in black shirts and riding breeches. Between them stood his mother, her arms linked in theirs and smiling for all the world to see.

8

Although it was midmorning when he woke, his mother was not yet up. Sleeping it off, he thought. She'll have a hangover that could crack cement. It occurred to him to wonder whether that happened most mornings.

He found some coffee and drank three cups to get the film off his teeth, then went outside, wanting the wind on his face. It was a warm morning, but overcast. Slow streams of ground mist flowed on the hillsides and pooled in the well of the valley.

Bullen set off from the house, taking a route that led from the paddocks across to the valley's lip. He found a downhill track and walked over the remains of old packman routes that followed the ridge. It wasn't a planned walk. After fifteen minutes or so he cut across country, making a slow circle through woodland on a path that would take him back to his mother's house.

He saw the smoke as he started back across the paddocks: a thin, dark haze against paler gray. By the time he'd covered half the distance, running through long, wet grasses that dragged at his shins, it had become a plume, hanging heavily above the rooftop. He ran with his head up, looking for the source of the smoke, waiting for the first mix of dull red among the darkness. Everything seemed suddenly still; the wind had dropped and there was no birdsong. It was like the moment before an explosion.

Bullen was through the first paddock and climbing the fence rails into the next when he caught a flicker at the corner of his eye. A man was moving along the path Bullen had taken earlier, toward the valley. He was running, but not going flat out — an easy lope that ought to be sustainable for a couple of miles if the man was fit. He wasn't looking in Bullen's direction; he might have been a jogger taking the scenic route, except for the fact that he was wearing jeans and a leather jacket. Except for the fact that he was running away from the house.

Bullen changed direction, taking an angle that would cut the corner of the second paddock and bring him into the fringe of the trees where they bordered the property. He lengthened his stride, wondering how long it would be before the man turned and saw him. But the man didn't look around. He simply maintained his easy pace, disappearing into the tree cover ten seconds or so before Bullen arrived and followed him in.

There was a mossy stillness in the wood and the light dimmed, as if a storm had suddenly gathered.

Bullen stood motionless and listened for the noise of a runner going through brush. There was nothing. Somewhere deeper in, a thrush gave a hysterical *chip-chip-chip*. Bullen went another twenty paces and stopped again amid silence; a shiver twitched his shoulders and ran to the small of his back, as if someone had pulled a thread in his spine, and he turned fast but saw no one.

The wood was small, little more than a spinney — mostly dwarf oaks and silver birch, spindly and scarved in dull, blue-green lichens. He looked among them for a straighter, heavier figure, but saw nothing.

Through and out the other side, Bullen thought. Had there been time for that? He knew there hadn't. Either the man was standing still, just as Bullen was doing, and waiting for the first mistake, or else he was moving so skillfully that only a bird would pick him up. Bullen walked forward a couple of paces, started a slow trot, then as if confirming a decision, picked up the pace until he was going too fast for caution, clattering through the underbrush, weaving between the trunks of trees.

Something snagged his foot and he fell heavily. When he landed, he felt a pain in his left arm and realized that he must have flung out a hand to break the fall. He tried to draw himself up, but whatever had made him fall still had a hold. In the moment that he turned to look at what gripped him, the man released Bullen's ankle and leapt forward.

Bullen had just enough time to half turn, presenting a lifted shoulder to his attacker. The man's hands closed on Bullen's head and banged it on the ground three times, like someone bouncing a ball but forgetting to let go. Bullen felt twigs and stones and a wetness that might have been dew. He kicked out, but didn't make contact. The man shifted position with a little crouching jump that brought both his knees down on Bullen's chest. Bullen grunted, an ugly, hurt, bass sound, way below his normal range. His head was lifted again and struck the ground again. He tried to lay a hand on the man, to find flesh, but he couldn't even see him —fingers pressed at his eyes and a broad palm was crushing his nose. His head rose and fell and he was less and less able to struggle. When the man got to his feet, Bullen stared up at him through a red-black drizzle, thick as static on an old movie.

Then the wood was full of sounds and Bullen was on his own. He remembered the moment when he blacked out, and after a second or two he remembered the pain because it came back at him like a tide wash. He sat up and watched the trees doing a slow revolve, rising and falling, then gradually settling back onto their roots. He sat very still, elbows on knees, his head lowered. He was taking shallow breaths because breathing hurt him.

He thought the house must be ablaze; if he listened hard he could hear the dull tumble of flames and billowing explosions as roof beams fell into the furnace.

When he emerged from the wood, the house was still standing; the smoke had drifted off on the wind, leaving a sky that was clearing and brightening. Bullen got himself up to a slow, shambling trot, as if a couple of minutes could still make a difference. He thought, If she's dead I won't know who to thank, and laughed as he ran, half-in, half-out of a dreamworld where hands still held his skull as if it were a delicate bowl and tried to smash it.

She was sitting on the doorstep flanked by the two ugly little stone griffins that were always there in Bullen's memories of childhood. In one hand, a large old-fashioned compact case, the lid open to reveal a mirror; in the other, a soft stick of magenta lipstick. Bullen passed her and went upstairs toward the hot, sour smell of charred wood.

The blanket box was still smoldering slightly — embers glowing on the edges — and there was a thin mist of smoke in the air that reamed his sinuses. On one side, the box was burned through to a thin, charcoal patch. The room was full of ash, the remnants of the papers that had been in the box, some still page-sized, some flimsy fragments, some just wisps and flakes. They were skimming the ceiling, climbing on updrafts by the open window, floating and turning in the air, flocking like exotic and delicate birds. Bullen watched, spellbound, as they alighted on chairs, on the mantelpiece, on windowsills, their dark plumage soundless as they settled.

He dragged the blanket box out into the orchard. The room was untouched apart from the floorboards beneath the box and some scorch marks to ceiling and walls. Because the floorboards felt hot, he doused them with water, but the flames hadn't ever taken hold there. When he bent to swill water from his bucket, pain clanged in his head and he went down onto his knees to recover.

His mother was eating bread and cheese in the dining room; she had set the table for one. She said, "There was someone in here, Thomas — a man. He ran off across the lower paddock."

Bullen said, "Will you be all right?"

"What do you mean?"

"I don't know . . . have you got enough food, things like that?"

She looked at the bread and cheese. "I've got food. Of course I have." She had added a little blusher to her cheeks, and Bullen wondered if she'd done it for him. Every hair was in place, gold to the roots.

He went to the bathroom and looked at his reflection. A line of blood had run from somewhere on his scalp and dried on his cheek. He sponged it off, then tracked down the wound just over his left ear. It stung when he cleaned it, and a hank of hair came free, but the bleeding didn't start up again. There was a bruise on his forehead and another alongside his eye. He ran a basin of water, then stripped off his shirt and dunked his head a few times.

Constance was helping the bread and cheese down with a little brandy. He said, "I'll have to go pretty soon, okay?"

She smiled at him. "Did you find what you wanted?"

Bullen said, "I'll have to go now." Last evening he had taken certain papers from the blanket box and laid them beneath the mattress in his room; now they were distributed around his pockets, heavy ballast, and he felt ridiculous, like a thief in a department store trying to waddle out with five suits on.

His mother picked a crumb of cheese up from the verdigris of the tabletop and slipped it into her mouth. She said, "This house isn't what it was."

Of all the papers in the blanket box, only one set might have ended Roland Cecil's career: a series of letters to a Mississippi chapter of the Ku Klux Klan, written after Cecil had visited America ten years before. He had kept a copy of each, written in his own hand. Of the rest, Bullen had left the speeches, the letters to senior politicians and ministers, the drafts of manuscripts started then abandoned. They had one theme — the common enemy: Jews, blacks, Asians, homosexuals, left-wingers of all persuasions. There were a few notebooks and diaries; these Bullen had brought away with him.

He drove for an hour, making reasonable time until he joined the highway and hit the first traffic jam. The sun broke through, suddenly revealing the haze of exhaust fumes that shimmered along the five-mile line of cars and trucks. The drivers leaned on their horns for a while, then got tired and simply sat back to swelter, edging up a few feet every five minutes and turning their sound systems up as if they wanted to close their senses down by wrapping themselves in music.

Bullen's head throbbed. A thin tinnitus, like a trapped mosquito, sang in his ear, and every so often his vision shifted a touch, then back, as if someone were adjusting reality for him.

He got out one of Cecil's diaries and started to flip through it. The writing slid in and out of focus. Bullen rubbed his eyes and lobbed the book onto the passenger seat. The sun was singing off the car's roof. Free-flowing traffic on the opposite side of the highway flung rhomboids of white light from windshields, their slipstreams loud as cannon fire.

Bullen got out of his car and walked across two lanes to the hard shoulder, where he knelt and threw up among oil slicks and blackened grass and the torn corpses of birds.

9

There were people moving among the trees in the orchard, men in evening dress, women in elegant, low-cut gowns of satin and silk. From each of the lower branches hung a lamp; each lamp shed a pale, luminous globe in the blue-black half light. Low voices and a moment's laughter mixed with music from the open French windows.

A woman approached him, smiling. As she got closer, all else fell away — the lights and voices and music growing dimmer until they were all one and very distant. The woman loosened her dress and let it slip. Her breasts were globes of light; a shadow lay in the cleft of her legs. Bullen knew from the waist-long corn yellow hair that it was his mother.

Anne said, "Are you awake?" There were a dozen or so candles in glass holders, some on the dressing table, some by the bed. Anne stood in front of him, her breasts and flank lit by the buttery glow of the candles, face and legs in darkness. She said: "Am I boring you?"

"I dozed off."

"Terrific. I go to the trouble of making the place look like a whore's boudoir, slither out of my clothes like a snake in heat, and Tom Bullen goes to sleep."

"It looks more like Dracula's tomb to me."

"It does? All right," she said, "eat me."

"What happened to your face?" She was touring the room, putting fresh candles into the stubs of the old.

"She was smoking in bed. The cigarette end set fire to a trunk full of papers. I was towing it out into the garden and fell on the stairs."

"No — *really* happened."

"She was smoking in bed," Bullen said gamely. "The cigarette end —"

Anne put a hand over his mouth, stooped to kiss him, then replaced two of the bedside candles. She said, "Was she okay when you left her?"

"Fine," he said. He thought of the hands that had clutched his head and deafened him with a beating. That man had been in his mother's house; now she was up there alone, drinking her brandy, checking her makeup in the mirror, tying her hair up in a bandanna for the night.

I won't know who to thank . . .

58

"Yes, she was fine."

"That's good." Anne seemed to believe it. She climbed astride him and bent low, so that her hair trailed on his face, and whispered, "What dangerous games are these?"

She rolled onto her back and spread her knees. Bullen lowered himself gently, feeling the ache in his chest.

Anne laughed. "We should do this more often."

It was a good relationship, friendship and terrific sex and no one making demands. Anne knew this because Bullen had told her so.

He winced as he fucked her. She thought, What in hell does that mean?

When the candles had guttered out and Anne was asleep, Bullen went into the kitchen and drank a beer. He took Roland Cecil's diaries from the drawer of a Welsh dresser and started to read.

Sleeping, Anne spread her limbs into the vacant space on Bullen's side of the bed. Her legs flexed and drew back and flexed again, dragging the bedclothes into a knot.

She was running one of the cross streets in Sarajevo.

›

10

Joe Chesnik's idea of a good night was to go to a friend's house where a small group of people known to each other would play some poker. "Texas hold 'em" was Joe's taste. While he was at the table, he'd drink branch water; if he took a break, he might have a Jack Daniels on the rocks, but that was the extent of his risk. He could never understand players who would do a line of coke between check and raise.

To make a good evening great, the game should end at about midnight, with Joe a few thousand up. Then, if his host had been thoughtful, some girls would arrive and everyone would watch some pornographic movies and get pretty hot. Maybe a couple of the girls would put on a show, or one of the players would fuck his choice right there in the room. Joe had seen that happen and he liked it a lot.

Then Joe would take his girl to a room and collect what she'd been paid for. Collect it all and a little extra, maybe. There were things a hooker would take that you couldn't ask for at home.

Finally, Joe's great evening would end with some reminiscing and the rest of that bottle of bourbon now that it wouldn't take the edge off poker and sex. Joe would get home at about 3 A.M. He would have been driven there by one of his bodyguards, while another accompanied him in the back of the limo; nothing more than a precaution, but he took them along as part of the feel-good factor. From time to time he'd wondered whether he shouldn't get his host to draft in some snatch for the bodyguards — bimbos for the Rambos — but then he'd think, The hell with it, how can they watch my ass and some hooker's at the same time?

That was Joe's perfect evening. Tonight he was attending a performance of *Oklahoma!* at a theater off Times Square. This represented a perfect evening for his wife, Billy-Jean. Joe was hating every minute of it. So were the Rambos. Joe hated the music, hated the plot, and thought Curly and Laurey were the biggest pains in the ass he'd ever encountered. He wished fervently that the whole bunch of crap would end with Curly and Laurey getting caught up in a threshing machine while screwing amid the high-as-an-elephant's-eye corn.

The only consolation was that during the intermission he could send one of the Rambos for a triple Daniels straight up. Loss of concentration would be a godsend; unconsciousness would be better.

Billy-Jean asked him if he was enjoying himself and he assured her that he was having the time of his life. There was a crush in the lobby, people jostling one another as they passed to and fro. After the first call to say the second half of the show was about to begin, a girl knocked shoulders with Billy-Jean and lost her balance for a moment. Her cup of coffee pretty much emptied out over Joe Chesnik.

The girl was desolate. She was also beautiful, which helped take the sting out of Joe's anger. She stood close to him as she made lame attempts to sponge him down with a tiny rag of tissue. She had long blond hair and a terrific figure, a lot of which was visible above her dress.

Joe did his best to smile, consoled himself by looking down the girl's cleavage as she bent toward him, then went to the bathroom to make a better job of things. The Rambos went with him. Joe sent one of them back to get the blond girl's phone number. He had already told Billy-Jean that his shirt was soaked and he'd probably have to go home. The evening was beginning to look up.

The second call was sending people back to their seats. Joe and the bodyguard went into the bathroom and Joe stripped off his shirt. "Dry it there." He was pointing toward the electric hot-air hand dryer. Two guys hurried in and stood at the urinals. They were talking about the show.

"Are you liking this?"

"It's shit."

"Me, too. My wife just nagged the hell out of me until I got the tickets."

The other guy shook and zipped up. "It's our wedding anniversary. Jesus, if I don't get laid tonight, there'll be trouble."

They walked to the door. The first man said: "Anyone in mind?"

After they'd gone, Joe laughed. He was still laughing when a man stepped out of one of the stalls and shot him through the left eye.

The bodyguard didn't react immediately. The gun

was fitted with a silencer and the roar from the hot-air dryer was enough to almost mask the sound; but he heard something that might have been the door of the men's room closing. It half alerted him, so he looked up to catch Chesnik's reflection in the long mirror that fronted the washbasins; he wanted to reassure himself.

A fist-sized chunk of Chesnik's skull had hit the mirror — bone and brain — and blood was geysering out of the crater and onto the glass. The bodyguard half turned, getting a hand to his jacket lapel: that was the best he could do before the killer shot him twice, high in the chest, then stepped back as the bodyguard crashed down onto his knees. In that position he was only a little shorter than the killer. He took the next bullet in the throat and pitched back onto the floor.

The lobby of the theater was almost empty. A few people were still hurrying to their seats. The killer hastened through without really being noticed, though if someone had been able to give a description that would make a police sketch, you'd have seen a little, pug-faced man with pale skin and full, red, mottled lips. You'd have noticed that his eyes had a bruised look, as if he hadn't slept for days, and he was laughing noiselessly, teeth bared, his shoulders shaking with merriment.

Chester Birkin was also having a bad night; not as bad as Joe Chesnik's, but bad all the same. Chester was a waiter at a classy restaurant on Chicago's North Side. The view of the lake was nice, but people came for the food and the service, both of which were legendary. That night, a guy had come in with a reservation for two, but the girl hadn't shown up. Maybe that was the reason for the guy being such an asshole, but Chester wasn't inclined to take that into account.

The water wasn't chilled, and no he didn't want ice in it, he wanted it *chilled* for Christ's sake. Was that too tough? The wine was cool, when it should have been at room temperature. Chester knew that the wine was exactly right, but he took it away and warmed it. The guy's fork had stale food on one of the tines. This was invisible stale food, but Chester listened while the guy complained loudly about the standards of cleanliness in the restaurant. Most of the other diners in the restaurant listened, too.

It continued throughout the meal: prawns not fresh, veal underdone, salad dressing too sharp, coffee too weak. The bell captain came over and offered a free brandy on the house. This was bribery, it seemed. In the end Chester and the bell captain simply rode out the storm, consoling themselves by each letting go a little *zip* of piss into the pot of now very strong coffee before Chester took it back to the man's table.

Chester wasn't alone; other people were in for a bad evening. After he left the restaurant, the man took a cab ride and offered no tip. The cab dropped him at a bar close to the Loop, where he picked up a hooker and accused the bartender of shortchanging him. The bartender was unimpressed, even when the man threatened to call the cops. A closed-circuit camera recorded the argument; it showed the bartender reaching for a gun close to the spill tray, then deciding he didn't need it. Later, it recorded a sequence that showed the angry customer, hooker in tow, leaving the bar at a backward walk, so that he could call the bartender a cocksucker.

Given the hour time difference between Chicago and New York, this would have been about the time that a fountain of blood from Joe Chesnik's cranium was hitting the mirror and falling like a slow curtain on *Oklahoma!*

The hooker was beginning to think that she might be taking a risk she didn't have to take. In the taxi, the angry customer became suddenly docile. He laughed and opened his wallet to show her a wad of high denomination bills. He said, "How much of this do you think you can earn?"

She laughed. "How much can you take?"

Maybe he'd sensed her edginess, who knows? But all of a sudden he was Mr. Nice.

He was Mr. Nice all the way back to his hotel. He was Mr. Nice as he poured drinks for them both. He was Mr. Nice as he put out the Don't Disturb sign and locked the door. He was Mr. Nice when he laughed and said, "Okay, honey, let's see what you've got to sell."

The hooker did a little strip for him; he hadn't ordered it, but what the hell — this guy was loaded and a little extra might do the trick for this trick. She looked through her legs at him as she rolled her panties down over her thighs. "See anything you care for, honey?"

She shimmied over to join him on the bed and

offered one of the usual lies — they also came free: "Hey, that's some stand for a little fella."

He took her wrist and pulled her sharply toward him. His eyes changed and he wasn't Mr. Nice anymore. He said: "Baby, you're gonna *limp* out of here."

He was telling the truth. When the hooker walked through the hotel lobby an hour later, the desk clerk thought she must have lost the heel from one of her shoes.

A few days later she told her roommate about the guy, just in case he cruised any of the bars her friend worked. He was a little guy, she said, flat faced, a snub nose, and lips like bratwurst.

11

We met at a friend's house," Timothy Adams said. "A dinner party. He leaned over and whispered in my ear as he passed the port. It was all very middle-aged — the company, I mean. No screamers." Adams was sifting through Roland Cecil's possessions. He was holding a little notebook with a patterned cover, and a gilt fountain pen.

"What did he say?" Bullen asked.

"He offered me money to sleep with him." Adams smiled. "It happens a lot; I'm pretty." As he spoke, he was standing in front of a sketch in a heavy gilt frame. "Matisse," Adams said, "just a couple of lines of charcoal, but look what he does with them. We

66

bought it together; I've got the receipt."

"It's not a family matter," Bullen told him.

"What?" Adams stopped cataloging for a moment and looked at Bullen suspiciously.

"I'm not here to make any claims on his property. The solicitors will take care of that."

Adams only heard one word. "I was with Roland for six years. Most of what you see here was jointly owned. Your mother will get the bloody money; she'll probably get this flat. Isn't that enough?"

Bullen smiled. "If you asked her for the money, I expect she'd give it to you; the flat as well. She wouldn't have any use for them."

"No?" Adams looked dubious.

"She doesn't care about possessions. She's floating back into the past."

The news seemed to cheer Adams a little. Nonetheless, he said: "Six years. We bought a lot of stuff." Then, as if holding a train of thought, "So why are you here?"

"Aren't you curious," Bullen asked, "about why he was murdered?"

"A crazy," Adams said. "The French police think it was a mad person." He made a note of a porcelain shepherdess with lamb and crook. "It wasn't your mother, I suppose?"

Bullen smiled. "You don't seem to mind."

"Mind . . ." Adams seemed to think the matter through for a few seconds. "No, I do mind, but I think it was time — for us, I mean. Roland and me. We'd just about run out of relationship. I'm sorry he's dead, but I won't miss him. Do you see? I'd already started to think of life without him." He jotted down a tiny bronze of a ballet dancer and Lartigue photograph of a bowler-hatted man leaning into the wind. "How did you know about me? Am I common knowledge?"

"I read his diaries."

Adams gave a little laugh, which did nothing to conceal his unease. "So that's it."

"No," Bullen said, "it's not. I couldn't care less about Roland's sex life. I want to know why he died."

"I just told you — a mad person."

"You believe that?"

Adams remained silent. Bullen said, "Tell me about the Party for British Unity."

Adams sighed. "Yes, Roland did have his tedious side. We used to go to meetings — they usually took place in some atrocious little house in the East End. People turned up in black leather." He smiled. "I quite liked the camp aspect of it. Once they were off the streets, they'd all put on their swastikas and SS flashes and Gestapo daggers, like a group of closet queens at a drag party. Then they'd talk for hours, and finally we'd leave. I used to make Roland take me to the Caprice as compensation."

"You didn't mind?" Bullen asked him.

"Mind what?"

Bullen paused to allow Adams to make a start on a row of first editions. "What did they talk about?"

"Jews, blacks, Asians, Irish, gays, Britain for the British, how the concentration camps were all propaganda, links with like-minded groups in other countries . . ."

"Gays?"

68

"Roland was particularly loud on that subject. It was very funny."

"Didn't they know?"

"Apparently not."

"Who did they think you were?"

"A convert, I suppose. A baby Nazi."

Bullen tried again. "And you didn't mind?"

Adams closed his notebook. "You probably think that this all sounds rather decadent, and you're right, but life is all about give and take. Roland gave me a good life, and I took it in the ass for him. It can bring tears to your eyes, dear, but then so can a charcoal sketch by Matisse."

"Who's Arthur Seacourt?" Bullen asked.

"He used to phone here and leave a message if Roland wasn't in. Just 'call back'; nothing interesting."

Some entries in Cecil's diaries had hidden nothing — entries that included Timothy Adams for instance; others were much more cryptic. Arthur Seacourt was among the cryptic. "Who is he?"

Adams turned from Bullen's question. "I really don't know. I didn't care much about Roland's business and political contacts. He never came here, I can tell you that much. Roland's dinner parties were either political or gay; either way you might get fucked. There was something going on, though. I mean, this Seacourt used to call a lot — more so recently. At one point, I wondered whether he was someone Roland had picked up."

"You wouldn't have minded?"

"You mean would I have been jealous?" Adams

laughed. "Did you ever see Roland with his clothes off?"

Bullen got up to leave. "Send me a list of what you want," he said, "I'll see you get it."

Adams looked stung. "I'm not a wife," he said. "Nothing's mine by right. I'm simply being careful."

"Don't apologize. Whatever you want . . ."

Adams said, "We lived together for years, Roland and I. You can't help forming an attachment to things."

12

The room was in darkness apart from the projector beam and a hundred dots of light from burning cigarettes. Bullen's throat was sore from inhaling second-stream smoke. It seemed that everyone there had a cigarette except for himself. Out of the corner of his eye he could see that Anne was smoking, though she had given up for good a year before. He felt she was doing it as an act of solidarity.

Bullen couldn't understand the voice-over, but the images on the screen needed no explanation.

A muted explosion was a shell falling somewhere nearby. A group of people crossing a street seemed fixed by the sound — four men and two women — until you realized that things were starting in slow motion. The six were still for a beat or two, then balked like a group of gazelles, their bodies making a slow

70

revolve as they checked and changed direction and moved from the blast frame by frame. It was clever — an agony — that they seemed to go at such a slow pace, clever to compose their actions in such a balletic way. You could read everything — panic on their faces, crease by crease; terror in their flight, inch by inch; risk in every foot of ground they had to cross in order to find cover. The rest came thick and fast.

A man quaking with shock as others lifted him, his gut dragging out of the cavernous hole in his belly like wet, red, tangled sheeting.

Ordinary people loading other ordinary people into a makeshift ambulance. Except they were no longer ordinary. The living had no expressions. The dead had no faces, no legs, no tops to their skulls, no heads at all.

It continued for about an hour. Someone passed Bullen a bottle; he took a great gulp and was almost knocked backward by the fierceness of the liquor. He took a second swallow and passed the bottle on. A young woman was on-screen, talking to an off-camera interviewer. You could see only her outline because she was being shot with a light bias that would mask her features in darkness. Bullen thought she was slender and long haired; her voice was mellifluous and low. He leaned toward Anne and asked, "What's she saying?"

Anne shook her head briefly. After a while the interview ended and there were panning shots of urban devastation — smoldering houses, burned-out trucks, broken minarets. When the lights went up, a man stood in front of the screen and said, "So here is

Sarajevo in this time. Is Sarajevo of war. We show you this to ask help, yes, but more to make aware the people of other countries. If there are questions I will speak to them."

Anne turned to Bullen and spoke in a low voice. "She was telling how she and other women were raped over several days by fifty men. They were kept for that — for rape. Among those regularly raped were girls aged from six to ten years old. The soldiers shot some of them; they were all beaten, and a pregnant woman was disemboweled. There was more, but it was all like that."

The bottle came back, a thick, oily spirit. Anne said, "Slivovic," and took a slug before handing it to Bullen. She said, "Come on, let's go; I interviewed this guy in Bosnia. I know what he thinks. I know what I think."

"What's that?"

"I think he's a brave man and doesn't have a prayer."

He went into the bathroom as she was stepping out of the shower. It was the fourth night they had spent together in a week and Bullen was feeling a little jumpy about that. So was Anne. As if separation were the real issue between them, he said: "When do you go back?"

"I'll be there this time next week."

"That won't be a problem?"

"It's never a problem getting the press into a city under siege. It'll be dangerous." She paused slightly, as if surprised by the candor of her own remark. It was the first time she'd said it out loud.

She had long legs topped by a thin taper of pubic hair, shaved like a swimmer's. Water trickled from her shoulders into the dip of her back. Bullen wanted to put his lips there and wait to be fed, like a creature that lives on dew.

She asked, "What is it that you want?"

"You know me — a drink, a fuck, a simple meal . . ."

She smiled at him. "How long has this relationship got, Tom?"

He wanted to say, "You know how difficult commitment is for me. What you don't know is why." He wanted to say, "I'm scared of it; help me." He wanted to say, "How long? As long as you like. As long as we can hold on." The words stuck in his jaw. "Arthur Seacourt?" he asked her. "Does that name mean anything to you?"

"Yes," she said. "Tell me why you want to know."

"Roland Cecil was my uncle."

"Roland Cecil." It wasn't a question; she was taken aback. There was a mirror over the sink, and she looked at her own reflection before looking at him, as if observing her surprise.

"My mother's brother."

"What else don't I know?"

He shrugged. "Nothing. It's my family, not me. We never think our own families are very remarkable, do we?" Nothing, he thought. I used to carry this and that for the Friends; I was a bit of a spook. Not much of one. They paid me, and with the money I funded expeditions and by that means found my way under-

73

ground — where I most wanted to be. Nothing.

"Arthur Seacourt . . ." This time it was a question.

"When I went back, I found his diaries — Roland's. Seacourt is mentioned." Bullen had made an abstract of the entries that were puzzling — names, dates, times — entering them into a small, spiral-bound notebook. Now he took the notebook out and checked the mentions of Seacourt: more than a dozen meetings.

Anne shed the towel and walked past him to fetch a robe from the back of the bathroom door. He was leaning against the wall just inside the room, and she went close enough to knock his hip with her own, as if inviting him to touch. When he did, she brushed past him, smiling, as if the caress had been an accident, and went into the kitchen. She said, "Vodka, or not?"

"Vodka."

"Seacourt runs an organization called Light. It's interesting because it likes to be exclusive. Most neo-Nazi groups will take anyone — the sweepings of the slum estates, the urban psychopaths; they like to pretend they'll be the movement's shock troops when the day for action arrives. Light is an elite. They're the political philosophy wing rather than the gouge-your-eyes-out-with-a-blunt-bayonet wing. Strong links with French and German groups. They're planners, not perpetrators; generals, not foot soldiers. Got the picture? I did the basic research on them but got diverted by Operation Babylon — the Iranian super-gun story. The paper gave it to someone else." She had found a tray of ice in the freezer; now she poured vodka over it slowly, to prolong the welcoming sound it made. "I'm not surprised Roland Cecil knew him.

I'm not surprised he wanted to keep it a secret, either."

She handed a drink to Bullen and looked at him over the rim of her glass. "You didn't answer my question."

"What?"

"How long — us?"

"If you don't get killed in Bosnia," he said, "I'll be here when you get back."

"A romantic through and through."

They lay side by side drinking vodka over ice, and she suffered him to unfasten her robe and peel it back as if he were flaying her.

She said, "What do you need to fight a war?"

"Tell me."

"Guns and ammunition, hatred — basic ingredients. Both easy to come by, had you noticed that?"

"What?"

"See a film like one we saw tonight. What it tells you is that if people want to fight, there'll always be the means. You want guns? Here are some guns. You want tanks? Okay, tanks. Grenade launchers, mortars, fieldpieces, shells — no problem at all."

She drew the robe back around her body. "Fuck me later, Tom. I'm working out a line of approach."

"What will it be?"

"From manufacturer to supplier, from supplier to soldier . . . then victim — the real subject of the piece."

He grazed on her body, lips and tongue, a meat eater disguised as some gentle herbivore.

She lay in the crook of his arm. His chest and arm

muscles were hard with use — lowering himself into darkness, dragging himself out.

She said, "I don't care what you do. Just give me a little warning, okay?"

"Why do you keep rehearsing the end of things?"

"I'd like to be word-perfect when the time comes."

He said, "Don't get shot in the cross streets."

"Tom . . . do you know what else you need to fight a war?"

He was dozing, his mother's gaudy smile aimed at no one, paper smuts floating in a room like darkness reassembling. "I don't know. What?"

"Men."

13

Three girls stood in a row, a little production line, one stacking, one packing, one sticking labels. They were mailing a magazine called *Godhead*. Two of the girls wore studded leather jackets and ripped-up Levis, the third a denim blouse and skin-thin tights; they all wore clusters of stud and loop earrings that went from the lobe to the tip.

Godhead wasn't a journal that promoted Christian fellowship. In its pages people lay in chains, were crucified, flogged, displayed slit noses and pierced genitals. The current issue led with an article on methods of suicide and step-by-step instructions on how to videotape your own death. The final few pages were closely printed ads selling computer pornography, autopsy videos, war footage, portfolios of homemade pain.

Bullen leafed through and found a woman spiked onto a donkey; next to it, a carefully set up parody of Piero della Francesca's *The Flagellation of Christ*. The girls stacked and packed and stuck, three in a row: hear no evil, see no evil, speak no evil.

Arthur Seacourt was standing behind Bullen as he read through the small ads. Bullen hadn't noticed his arrival. "We have lots of advertisers who offer snuff movies," Seacourt said. "God knows what they supply. It's an urban myth. No such thing ever existed. Let's go through to the back." He padded away between metal filing cabinets and tables cluttered with packing materials. Bullen followed. There was a sweet smell of cigar smoke and damp paper.

Seacourt's office had no windows. The air was thick and pearly. Seacourt sat at his desk behind a little array of mechanical support systems — three phones, fax, desktop copier, computer, laser printer. He was fifty or so, overweight, and had a swatch of thin, sandy hair. His shirtsleeves hung unfastened under his jacket cuffs — his wrists were too plump to allow button and buttonhole to meet. Like all fat men, he leaned back in his chair and put his legs out straight, as if he were trying to stand up sitting down; the idea was to make room for his paunch.

"This New Age material," he said, "lot of demand for it. Weirdiana. We carry everything — occult, sex, death fantasy, cannibalism. It's a philosophy, you know? A way of seeing the world."

"A way of raising funds," Bullen said.

Seacourt's diary was open in front of him. Even so he asked, "Let's see Mr. Bullen, you're from —"

Bullen gave the name of Anne's paper and a contact number — Anne's private line.

Seacourt said, "I remember. It's not a paper I'd expect to be sympathetic."

"I'm not going to write an article saying we ought to shoot all the niggers and Jews," Bullen told him. "The idea would be to present Light as an organization with a point of view that might have something to recommend it. We need respectability as much as we need recruits."

"You're a sympathizer, then."

"Yes."

"You said 'we.' "

"I'd show you the copy before I submitted it. The important thing is to get the right tone. Yes I said 'we.' I meant like-minded people."

"Why haven't I heard of you before, Mr. Bullen? I thought I knew everyone in the media who'd be likely to have a kind word for me."

"Times change. Circumstances change. I've always believed what you believe; I never felt a need to act on my beliefs before. Now I must. There's a movement, an international movement — people fighting to preserve their nationality, their way of life, their racial identity. I want to be part of it."

Seacourt shrugged as if still waiting to be impressed. "You'll go public — support us openly?"

"I can help more if I don't do that."

Bullen's answer seemed to convince Seacourt. He offered a wry smile and said, "Of course." See No Evil came in and presented him with a set of page proofs. She had a chalk white skin, black eye shadow, black mascara; a small ruby was hooked into the flare of her right nostril.

Seacourt said, "Turn up on Saturday." He pushed a photostated broadsheet across the desk — on the back, a page from a street map together with instructions. "Part of your research, if you like. Try not to look like the press."

The girls were still at work. As Bullen left, he skimmed a paper off the top of the pile. None of the three spoke or looked at him. Speak No Evil was bent to her task. A shaky needle-and-ink tattoo of a swastika adorned the side of her neck, like a purple nevus.

Stuart Cochrane was looking at the woman and donkey. He said, "Trick photo, don't you think?" sounding like someone expecting to be disappointed.

Paul Shelley wandered over and looked, but didn't offer an opinion. He spoke to Bullen: "Things are going along fine," he said, "what's the problem?"

"No problem," Bullen told him, "I just can't see a reason for going much further."

"We need you to. Okay?" Cochrane's tone was a drawl, lazy, but the question flicked like a whip.

"Threaten me," Bullen suggested. "Take away my company car; cancel my pension scheme."

"What happened to your face?" Cochrane asked.

The swelling had gone, leaving just a trace of a bruise, as if Bullen had spent a few nights without sleep. "I fell down a flight of stairs at my mother's house. I was drunk."

Next to *Godhead* on Cochrane's desk were Roland Cecil's diaries. Chasing down a train of thought, Cochrane asked, "You don't feel it's a family matter?"

"There's not much of my family left," Bullen replied, "and in any case, I'm not very good at belonging to things."

"Do this for us," Shelley asked. "This — and go to France."

"I've contacted Seacourt. I'll follow that through. Send someone else to France."

"You've taken things this far; if there are connections to Seacourt and his bloody Nazis, you'd be the likeliest person to spot them. One thing points to another, you know that. Links in a chain." Shelley's tone was coercive as he tried to make the shoe fit. "The French have had to abandon the lone assassin theory since the press got onto the fact that he left the scene in a helicopter. God knows why they ever thought it would be believed. But apart from knowing that it wasn't some lunatic, we're none the wiser. Bullen" — he shrugged as if to say, "What difference?" — "go to France for us. We'll talk to them, see that they cooperate."

"Do I owe you anything?" Bullen asked. "Anything at all?"

Cochrane said, "Do it because you've got nothing better to do."

Bullen handed in his security-clearance tag and walked across Vauxhall Bridge looking for a taxi. He was light-footed, and when he paused to look at the river a million silver chips of sunlight cascaded toward him, as if he had already stepped off the parapet and was falling toward the water.

What's this? he thought. The smell of river mud and exhaust fumes bloomed in his nose; he felt heady. What's this? It was an adrenaline rush, clean and hot as liquor in the vein. It was abseiling down a hundred feet into the dark.

Don't get to like it, he thought. There are lots of ways to wind up trapped. To wind up dead.

Shelley said, "It's strange. I thought once he'd got started . . ." Phones were ringing on Cochrane's desk. Both men ignored the sound until it stopped. "It really doesn't seem likely that he'll want to help us beyond poking around in France for a while."

Cochrane was still glancing through the pages of *Godhead*; now he looked up as if focusing a thought. "I wonder what it would take? We need him."

"Do we?" Shelley wondered.

"There's something here, Paul. I can smell it. Can't you smell it?"

"You mean money . . ."

"I mean opportunity. There's something going on, a deal, something . . . These guys weren't killed for love, they were killed for profit. Who knows what kind of profit?"

"You'd like to find out?"

"I'm going to find out."

The blonde came in and placed a signature folder in front of him. He showed her the picture of the woman bending over for the donkey. He said, "Could you do this?"

"Of course," she said, "with a clever photographer."

After she'd left, Cochrane said: "It's not personal for Bullen, is it? Not a personal issue. We thought it would be, but it's not." As if asking the question for the first time, he said, "I wonder what it would take to put him on the hook."

14

They met in a park near Jamaica Road. There were banners and drums, just as there had been at the funeral in France. There was chanting. There were speeches. There were young men who were sober and hard eyed and wanted someone to kill. Bullen heard a *whick-whick-whick* overhead as a surveillance helicopter made a pass.

Seacourt was making a speech through a bullhorn, his words borne on whistling gusts of feedback. What he was saying seemed to make his audience angrier and angrier. When he'd finished a forest of arms went up to him, palms flat. A long banner with the word LIGHT on it shook out as two men hoisted the poles to leather supports and the march began to weave out of the park and up through Southwark; they were taking the news to the people.

Bullen stayed in the thick of it until Seacourt found

him. "Not a good place to be," he said, "if there's trouble."

"Will there be?"

"Who knows?" Bullen thought Seacourt looked hopeful.

The uniform was work denims, T-shirts, boots, hair cropped to the bone. They chanted like soldiers, in unison, hard voiced, and three men carrying bass drums struck in time with the response. It made Bullen think of the Roman turtle — men moving behind a carapace of shields, striking the leather with the flat of their spears. The thickness in their voices was blood.

A sparse line of police marched on either side like kids keeping up with the band.

First, there were a few people at an intersection shouting "Nazi scum." A phalanx of ten men from the march peeled off and feinted toward them. The police closed ranks to shut them out. Lapel radios squawked like exotic birds put to flight by the sudden disturbance. It came to nothing.

Next, there were a hundred of them, cordoned off by police barriers, with bullhorns and banners of their own: Anti-Nazi League, miners' unions, Workers' Revolutionary Party. A group of about sixty Asian boys stood on their own — a little apart, a little forward, as if deliberately showing themselves. Everyone yelled at the marchers, a deep single syllable echoing the drumbeat: *"Scum, scum, scum, scum, scum."*

Then came an arrowhead — twenty men breaking

83

the police line and plowing into the march. They struck out with fists and feet, then dispersed and regrouped behind the cordon.

The march was reaching an area of open ground between two apartment buildings — scrub trees, garbage and dog shit over an acre of patchy grass; it had all the utilitarian bleakness of a battlefield. Bullen looked around for Seacourt but couldn't find him; then he saw a car pulling away and passing through the police line. A bottle smashed at Bullen's feet, though he hadn't seen it coming; a second hit someone close to him, splintering as it struck. Bullen felt a lick of blood on his own face as the man screamed and went down.

For a moment the police line held. The helicopter was right overhead now, the sound of its blades whacking off the gray cliff face of each building. Then somewhere someone made a decision and the line broke as the police fell back, giving the two groups up to one another.

Bullen was doing pretty well. Everyone there wanted to kill someone else. He didn't. Apart from having to sidestep and weave, he was making good progress across the battlefield; he wasn't crop headed and tattooed, he wasn't wearing an ANL badge, and he wasn't Asian. Around him was a continual roar of human voices, screaming with fury, screaming with pain.

Images emerged from the chaos, blurred snapshots. One man on the ground, six men kicking him; they moved in and out to give each other room. The man who was down hopped and rolled, trying to get clear, but the circle moved with him as the men picked him off, standing back one by one, then taking little runs to help the kick.

A woman sprinting for the barren spaces under one of the apartment buildings, three men behind her. It didn't look as if she could outrun them.

One man felling another with a banner pole, then standing above him to smash the pole down again and again, aiming carefully, following the face as a man thrusting a spear into the water follows the fish.

Bullen was jogging now, staying aware, cutting a line between the nearest apartment building and the road; that way he would avoid the spearhead of the march, which had passed the wasteland and hit the roadway before the fighting began. Now Bullen could see a couple of hundred people slugging it out up and down the street while people in motionless cars and buses sat utterly still. They looked to him like prey that hasn't yet been noticed.

As he thought that, he heard the first breaking of glass and saw the first car being rocked. The people inside swam around the car's interior in panic, their hands going out to the windows as if they could steady the car from inside. Rows of white, terrified faces stared out from other vehicles.

The fight flowed along the pavements and across the street. Men clambered over cars as if they were boulders; they used them for cover. As Bullen went into the gloom of the cavern under the apartment building, he saw the pale flicker against the sky that signaled the first gas bomb.

Bullen ran through like a man moving from a clearing into jungle.

He glanced sideways, his attention drawn by a noise and sudden movement, and there was another snapshot, this one murky and underdeveloped. A woman was moving backward as three men advanced. She was swinging a camera at them, as if it might make a difference. Her features were smudged by twilight, but something about her brought Bullen to a standstill. A moment later he knew who it was, and for a moment he was dizzy with fear.

The men were laughing, taking their time; every now and then one of them would snake out a hand to touch her somewhere — face, breast, hair. One skipped behind her and slapped her ass. When she turned, another wrapped his arms around her, lifting her off the ground a moment, then dumping her full-length. The men gathered over her, their hands busy. She yelled: not "Help me" or "Leave me" — she was cursing the men, damning them to hell. Bullen ran toward her, looking for a weapon. He picked up the front fork of a bicycle, ran on, then threw it away in favor of a three-foot length of brass piping. He wondered why the men couldn't hear him, then he saw that Anne was already naked to the waist; the men were preoccupied — working at getting her jeans off, cuffing her as she struggled and kicked out. One of them was already unbuckling his belt.

Bullen took him out first, swinging the pipe in a short, crisp arc that struck just at the base of the skull.

The man twisted at the knee and stayed poised for a moment, as if looking over his shoulder to see what had happened. His eyes showed only the white. He let a sudden gush of blood from the mouth where he'd bitten through his tongue, then fell forward, landing next to Anne.

The second man had sensed the disturbance behind him and had straightened up. He was turning, moving backward, as Bullen stepped in to him, jabbing the pipe as if delivering a spear thrust. It took him in the mouth, then over the eye, doing damage, but he rode the blows like a boxer. Bullen felt the third man at his back and turned, ducking at the same time, but ducking only brought him down onto his attacker's kick. The boot took him on the upper arm and chest, right-hand side, and Bullen felt a weakness flow into the arm. He switched the pipe from right hand to left and jabbed. The man laughed. He was wearing several gaudy ropes of chain around his neck; they glinted in the half dark. Bullen jabbed again, but the man knocked the pipe aside and kept coming; in the same moment, Bullen felt an explosion at the base of his spine as a kick came in from the man at his back.

Anne had got up and retrieved her camera. No one noticed; rape was more fun than most things, but now the men were doing what they did best. Bullen was on his knees, still holding the pipe, though the men were inside its range and kicking hard. Anne swung the camera once around her head, then measured off and pulled like a hammer thrower, putting her weight into the trajectory.

The camera body struck just over the ear. The man

went sideways a couple of paces, then stopped as if a thought had come to him. He tried to put a hand to the place, but couldn't coordinate the movement and his fingers plucked a moment at the chains around his neck. He walked away, his feet crossing and tangling, like someone trying a complicated dance step, then paused; his knees were bent, as if he were about to pick something up from the ground. He went a few paces farther to a cluster of garbage bags and sat down with his back to them.

Bullen had rolled into the space left him when the man with the chains suddenly stepped away. He came up swinging the pipe backhanded and managed a lucky blow to the neck. His attacker was moving in as the pipe struck; now he started to choke. He put his hands to his throat, fingers locked like a strangler. Bullen backed off. Anne was pulling her shirt back on, getting her arms into the sleeves of a denim jacket.

She said, "Are you all right?" He nodded, unable to speak, and looked around. The man with the chains was still leaning against the garbage bags; he had begun to shake, arms loose, head nodding, his eyes blank and fixed on the ground. She said, "Have I killed him?"

Bullen managed, "Not yet," then he took her hand and they walked backward for a few yards. He said, "I can't run." They walked to the far end of the building, through the strewn urban tidewrack, then out into the daylight. The fighting was on the other side of the apartment building — they could hear the roar of voices, car horns, sirens. Busloads of police in riot gear were moving into the area, but the side streets were clear and empty; the houses had drawn curtains and locked doors.

They walked for a mile or so without speaking. When they came close to Blackfriars, Bullen flagged a taxi. As soon as he sat down, Bullen closed his eyes and slept. When he opened them the taxi was on the Embankment near Chelsea Wharf. There was a wind pushing furrows across the water and the pavements were suddenly wet.

She smiled at him, a shaky smile, and said, "Your place or mine?" She had put the camera on the floor and some way away from her because stuck to it was a hank of bloody hair, like a scalp.

He said: "Your place, because you are definitely buying the drinks."

The bedroom was a clutter of clothes and documents and equipment. She had been packing as much as she could carry in a knapsack. Hanging from the bedpost was a light cotton fisherman's vest with about twenty pockets inside and out. Among other things it would carry her Dictaphones, tapes, camera lenses, rolls of film, notebooks, pens, press pass, ID, foreign currency, and a flask full of whatever she could get locally.

Bullen lay down while she palpated the bits of him that had been kicked. He winced, but the pain didn't go deep. He said, "I mentioned Seacourt to you; that's why you were there."

"Witch hazel," she said, and fetched it from the bathroom. "No it wasn't . . . well, not just that." She poured a little of the fluid onto his shoulder blades and massaged it into his ribs and the small of his back with the tips of her fingers. "You reminded me. I'd tried to get an interview with him once before, but got some underling. I guess he knew that what I'd write wouldn't be favorable. I wrote the article anyway; in fact I wrote three, all told. Today seemed like a good opportunity to report on the march and maybe shove a recorder under Seacourt's nose at the same time."

"Did you get close?"

"He left at about the same moment as the shit hit the fan."

He said, "Why do you think I found you? Anything could have happened. I might have been arrested, or involved in the fighting, or run a different way. But there I was, under that building when they caught up with you. What was that?"

"Luck."

He opened one eye and saw a packet of disposable syringes and a box of serum capsules; they were next to an envelope-sized pouch containing first-aid essentials: he calculated that she'd have five spare pockets on the fisherman's vest.

"When do you leave?"

"There's a problem," she said. "It should have been tomorrow, but the UN is considering whether or not to pull out. We have to wait for transport. Could be a week, perhaps more."

"You'll be here when I get back from France."

"I didn't know you were going."

"Roland owned some property there." He was improvising; he'd imagined that she would have left for Bosnia before he left for France. "My mother can't go, so I have to wind things up over there, put the house on the market, arrange to have the contents sold."

"Where?"

He guessed what was in her mind. "Near the Pyrenees; middle of nowhere."

"I was hoping you'd say Paris." A little laugh disguised her disappointment. "It's too far; I'm a working girl."

They watched the march on the early evening news, scanning the screen for their own faces. Anne had put a tape in the VCR in case they might want to replay some of the action. Most of the footage showed attacks on the police, or policemen throwing people into arrest vehicles. Bullen watched a sequence where a group of men was kicking another to the ground, and the soreness seemed to start up in his ribs.

Among all the people running, none was Anne.

Toward dawn he woke and went to find her.

She was sitting in an armchair, legs tucked up, drinking brandy and watching the videotape. She was crying silently, her face solemn, tears leaving a sheen on the plane of her cheek before beading on her jawline.

He held her, positioning his body to block her view of the screen.

"They touched me," she said, "but it wasn't that so much. It was what they said."

15

The rain was gray among gray houses. Bullen sat in his car on a street where all the color had leached out as if it had been underwater for a hundred years, one street in a drowned city. Building-site rubble looked like spillage from wrecks. Cartons eddied with the tide. Men like sharks went past him one by one.

His phone conversation with Seacourt had been a strangely guarded business. Bullen had called the *Godhead* office to say: "I looked for your name in the papers. I found it, but you were issuing denials."

"What did you expect to find?"

"I hoped you hadn't been arrested, or hurt in the fighting."

"That's thoughtful of you, but I couldn't have been since I wasn't there." A pause, then: "As you know."

Bullen had thought, He wonders whether someone's taping this. "I forgot." Seacourt had offered no response, so Bullen had filled the silence: "I wondered if we could meet again."

"Yes, I'm sure that would prove useful. If you come to the office tomorrow at eight o'clock someone will direct you from there." Bullen had been about to hang up when Seacourt had added, "And you?"

"I'm fine —"

"That's good."

"— though I hear people were hurt."

"Yes," Seacourt had said. "I heard the same."

Bullen waited until the street was empty of sharks, then got out of the car and found the street number he'd been given by See No Evil.

He went downstairs into a small basement area and rang the bell. Seacourt answered the door himself. He led the way down a corridor and into a room where two men held Bullen while Seacourt doubled his fist and drove it clumsily into Bullen's stomach. He didn't really know how to punch, but an amateur can get by on basic technique. He waited until Bullen had finished coughing, then hit him again in the same place.

They put Bullen in a chair. They didn't need to tie him because altogether they were six to one. For a brief while Bullen had to concentrate hard, because his breathing seemed to have lost its spontaneity; when he looked up, Seacourt threw a small leather wallet into his lap. Bullen opened it and saw Anne's face.

"She dropped it," Seacourt said.

"Who dropped what?"

Seacourt laughed as if he were genuinely delighted. "It's a press card, as you can see, in the name of Anne Warbeck."

"Who's she?"

Seacourt's laughter was just as bright. He stepped forward and cuffed Bullen lightly, finding range, then took his time and put some weight into the next blow. Bullen's head flew sideways; the slap made him bite his lip and he felt his mouth fill with blood. He leaned forward and spat a thick stream onto the rug: blue

93

spirals on grimy white, now with a damp ticking of red. Seacourt picked up a sheaf of photographs from a low table and went to stand alongside Bullen, showing them one by one, letting each fall to the floor in turn.

Bullen and Anne emerging from the cavern under the apartment buildings.

Bullen and Anne walking away from the wasteland, his arm around her shoulders.

Bullen and Anne retreating down a side street of shuttered houses.

A man stretched on the ground, almost indistinguishable from the rubble that surrounded him.

A man leaning against garbage sacks, his eyes giving back a hard, white reflection of the camera flash.

Bullen said, "She knows where I am; she knows who I'm with."

Seacourt moved to a chair that faced Bullen's and sat down with a sigh. He shook his head, and his jowls moved like turkey wattle. "It's not the fact that you hurt some of my people, Bullen, although I can't say it makes me happy. No, it's more that you obviously intended to hurt me. My organization. My campaign. We know about Anne Warbeck; she wrote a number of articles about Light. If I told you they weren't terribly sympathetic, I'd be understating the case." Seacourt gave a little chuckle; he seemed amused by his own coyness. "She wanted to interview me, but was rebuffed. She called me names anyway — evil, pathetic, dangerous, tawdry . . ." He laughed and looked at for approval the men surrounding him. They laughed, too. "She didn't seem able to decide whether

94

I was Satan or Coco the clown. But she did some damage. We had a few visits from the police — beyond the ordinary, that is. *Godhead* was seized and a private prosecution whipped up by some Jewish group. It was all rather costly and a very great nuisance. Now you're here. Her fifth column."

"She knows where I am," Bullen repeated, "she knows who I'm with. People at the paper know. The only thing you can do is let me go."

Bullen's remarks seemed to startle Seacourt. He said, "He might be wired."

Two men turned his lapels and the waistband of his trousers; they ran their hands into his groin and under his armpits. Seacourt waited until they'd finished, as if wanting to be certain of Bullen's full attention. He said, "I could let you go, yes. I could kill you." He looked at one of the men who had searched Bullen. The man was wearing a ring on every finger: a hand had gone between Bullen's legs to search for a mike and he'd felt them, like brass knuckles. "Nothing?" The man shook his head.

"How would you do that?" As he spoke, Bullen could see that Seacourt had an answer, that death was just outside the room waiting to be called.

"I'm not here. No one's here. I'm at a birthday party for Leonard's wife." He smiled at the man with the rings. "It's already been videotaped. All the clocks show the right time; all the guests tell the same tale. You'll die in a street near Whitechapel, doing some research for your article on the Nazi menace, mugged by an overenthusiastic black who's had a tab of ecstasy too many. We already know who he is."

95

"It's a good story," Bullen said. "I can see you take precautions."

"A shame you didn't possess the same foresight."

Bullen had assessed his chances and registered them as nil. The basement room was small and lit by a single bulb in a sixties balloon shade. The wallpaper was lilac with tiny repeated sprays of forget-me-nots. The air seemed heavy, as if the place had its own weather, and the press of bodies brewed a sour smell. Bullen felt as if he were the center of a crowd; the center of attention. He thought the room was just the kind of place people died in.

Seacourt said, "Forty years ago the Holocaust was everyone's problem. Now what? It's no longer such a problem to hate people. *Cleansing.* Do you like that word? I like it. You make a country clean, sluice out the shit. News today; a way of life tomorrow. You should have found something else to write about."

"I'm not a journalist," Bullen said. "I didn't know Anne Warbeck was going to be there. I couldn't care less about the men I hit; I hope they die — okay? But that was all chance. I came to see you because I'm Roland Cecil's nephew."

For a while Seacourt looked at Bullen without changing his expression, then he lowered his head and used the tips of his fingers to rub his eyes like a man wanting to soothe away a headache. He said, "Suddenly you're in more trouble than you were ten seconds ago."

Under the blue-and-white rug, in the trunk of a car, the weather was worse.

Bullen thought, They haven't killed me yet. *Yet* was hope and the end of hope. His head was light and he seemed to keep nudging the edge of consciousness, but couldn't tell whether fear was pushing him there or lack of air. He reasoned that the basement room must have been a place where they couldn't have held him for long.

The truth was that Bullen had told Anne nothing. Nothing about Cochrane or Shelley or that he was meeting Seacourt again. He wanted to involve her as little as possible.

The brakes went on and he hit the wall of the trunk and bounced back. When the man with the rings took the rug off, Bullen saw that the *Godhead* offices had a backyard entrance.

It was dark now, nine or ten o'clock. Anne wouldn't miss him. There was no routine of "your place, my place"; sometimes they wouldn't see each other for a couple of months — her absences, his disinclination.

He was on the floor in one corner of the windowless office with Fistful of Rings and Speak No Evil to keep him amused.

He remembered that the man with the rings was called Leonard. Stupid to believe that storing fragments of knowledge might be a means to salvation. Seacourt had been in and out. Now he was back.

"Roland wasn't killed for his beliefs," he said. "Did you think that? We're not powerful enough and neither was he." Seacourt was panting slightly as he spoke; they were two flights up and the building had no elevator. He dragged a chair over and sat down in

97

front of Bullen, his paunch heavy in his lap like a dead baby. "One day . . ." He smiled, looking forward to the time when he would be important enough to be killed. Bullen knew it wouldn't come soon enough.

"Nothing's happened. You hit me a couple of times. Let's forget that. What can I do? I left two men under a block of apartments, both in pretty bad shape. A trade-off."

"I wouldn't use them against you," Seacourt said. "I don't want anything to do with those men. Are you crazy?" He shifted slightly in his seat, but the paunch stayed put. "I'm talking to a few people about you. They're talking to other people. No one's made a decision yet, but I have to tell you the signs don't look good." He leaned across and patted Bullen on the shoulder like a doctor with bad news, then laughed at his own improvisation. "Not good."

"Why did Roland Cecil die," Bullen asked, "if not because he was a fascist?"

"Roland was a thinker, not a doer. A man of influence. A man of vision. Such men make enemies."

"That's not a reason."

"I know."

The cord that bound him went from his wrists to his ankles and was tied off around the leg of Seacourt's desk. Bullen reckoned it was about midnight. Seacourt had left.

Speak No Evil was listening to a Walkman, head turned to one side. All Bullen could see of her face was one charcoal eye and the corner of her mouth, magenta outlined in black. Leonard pulled the earphones off her head and said, "He can't move. If you want me, shout." The bathroom was on the other side of a small storeroom. Leonard pissing sounded like a horse on puddled ground.

Bullen said, "Tell me what you want and I guarantee you'll have it."

"You with a pole up your ass." The girl licked her teeth before smiling. "Don't bother with the guarantee, I've already got it."

He said the first thing that came into his head. "I can raise a lot of money."

"Of course you can. Who would offer less?" When Leonard returned, she said: "He wants to make me rich."

Leonard laughed. "Did you give him an answer?"

The girl stood up: good, long legs encased in thin black tights, a little bolero top, a thick torque necklace in Indian silver. She gave Bullen a little lopsided grin, very knowing, and suddenly she didn't look stupid anymore. She turned her back, jabbed her thumbs into the waistband of her tights, hooked them down over her ass, then bent over slightly and used her hands to give Bullen a sight of her asshole, furled tight, a little dark eyelet. She bent farther and looked at him through her legs. "Thanks but no thanks."

She walked over to Leonard with her tights still around her thighs and made some gesture with her hand that Bullen didn't see. "Want to show him what a good time looks like?"

Leonard laughed, but there wasn't a smile on his face. He said, "One thing at a time," a touch of treble in his voice, then looked away, avoiding her eyes.

The girl rolled her tights back to her waist and picked up the Walkman headphones. You could hear the tinny *shusss-shusss-shusss* of the backbeat like a thousand people laughing.

Seacourt didn't return, but he made a phone call in the middle of the night. Bullen woke at the noise, leaping violently and wrenching his arm sockets against the tether. The only light was from a lamp on the desk; it made a sharp chalky cone over Seacourt's clutter of office equipment. The rest of the room was brown and gray shadows.

Bullen listened for some clue in what Leonard was saying, but it was all "Yes," "No," "Okay," "Fine." The lamp gave a luster to the rugs; a tiny diamond flashed a beacon of white light.

Leonard hung up and went to the other side of the room. He sat with his hands between his knees for a moment, then lifted a liquor flask from the floor, uncapped it, and drank. The girl's hand came up from nowhere to get her share.

Bullen's fingers were throbbing. The effort of trying to stay awake sent him to sleep.

When he woke again, Leonard and the girl were fucking. Bullen could see them, darker shapes in the darkness, and the occasional paleness which was his flank or her thigh lifting. His mouth in the crook of her neck, snuffling and rooting. The curve of her breast. The boss of her shoulder moving as he dug at her. The line of her jaw as she threw her head back. The glint of an eyetooth.

She was making a high, whinnying sound, over and over, off-key music, until it hit a pitch that broke in her throat. Then silence; then the sound of her held breath going in little fragments.

Her shadow dissolved to darkness, but his kept moving for a while, *slap-slap-slap* as he worked alone. Bullen went back to sleep to the sound from her stereo headphones, distant laughter, an old joke.

Dawn was engines coming to life; a motorcycle starting up like a chainsaw. It was still midnight in the room.

Seacourt switched on all the lights. Leonard had gone. Speak No Evil came in with coffee, blurred makeup pushing her face out of focus. Seacourt was carrying a length of brass piping inside a wrapping of plastic. He showed it to Bullen, then put it on the desk.

He said, "You're a problem we don't know how to solve." Two of the men who'd been in the basement room arrived. Seacourt waved a hand. "Untie him."

Bullen's fingers were blue to the knuckle joint. When the cord came off, he shoved his hands between his thighs and fell forward, yelling with pain. Seacourt waited to be heard. Five minutes went by. Bullen stood up, then sat down on the desk, sending one of the phones clattering to the floor. He was sweating heavily and his arms hung straight down.

"No one seems to know anything about you except that you're Roland's nephew. No links with any pressure groups, political groups, bleeding hearts, or other pains in the ass. No one knows why you should be asking questions about his death. No one knows what might be the consequences of killing you. No one knows." Seacourt went to sit behind his desk: the chairman of the board giving his casting vote. "On balance it looks like a risk — killing you, I mean — and I'm sad about that, but personal pleasure has to be sacrificed to the common cause, yes?" He clasped his hands under his paunch like a sling. "So here's the deal. Go away and don't come back. If you try to use anything that's happened to you against us, we'll give that to the police." He loosed a hand to gesture at the length of piping. "There are a number of police officers who like us, like what we stand for." Seacourt's eyebrows went up, as if he were inviting comment. "That doesn't surprise you, does it? If you decide to make problems for us, we'll blitz you. One of the men you hit still doesn't recognize his mother."

Anne, Bullen thought. The man Anne hit. He said, "You stupid asshole, Seacourt. You think this is a crusade for me? I don't care if you want to goose-step through Parliament Square. Someone killed my mother's brother in a public way in a public place. I'm curious. I read his diaries — you're in them. You think I should have turned up and asked you about that? Guess what — I didn't think I'd get the truth. Just let me go, okay? You already told me you don't want to be connected with those men. The ones that got hurt."

"I don't know why Roland died." There was no fluency in the lie; Seacourt's gaze fluttered away, then back. Bullen could tell that Seacourt had been put at risk. Someone had said: "Your problem."

Seacourt walked around the desk, coming inside Bullen's range. It was safe enough; Bullen's hands were too hot and heavy for punching. "What are your contacts? Who's running you?" He peered at Bullen as if reading his eyes. "You don't look so innocent to me."

"Wrong," Bullen told him. "It's a family affair."

16

The gallery was triple glazed and had rubber baffles around the glass. It looked down onto an indoor shooting range where four men in blue coveralls were firing handguns at silhouette targets. Stuart Cochrane peeled back the top layer of a smoked-salmon sandwich and squeezed some lemon juice onto the fish. Nearby was a little thermos flask of Bloody Marys. He said, "I thought I'd come down and see for myself. Ten crates picked up at Tilbury Dock, all labeled Agricultural Machinery." He nodded down to the range: four men in ear protectors firing soundlessly. "They're just making sure that they really go bang — testing a few from each batch."

"What will you do with them?" Bullen asked.

Cochrane shrugged and his eyes flickered away for an instant. "Destroy them, I expect. Not my province. They came in from Italy, but probably originated in Canada. Someone has to sign a release order before they can pass from customs to us — in this case, it's me. I wanted to have a look at the bills of lading." He lifted a swatch of papers from the table in front of him and waved it like a fan. "Wonderful piece of fiction."

Shelley had picked Bullen up at a pub close by Vauxhall Cross. He'd said, "We're meeting Cochrane at a police gun range near Liverpool Street." He'd sighed: "Sorry, he likes hardware; he's taken a packed lunch." Bullen had pulled the car door closed with fingers that after two days were still hot and hard, as if he were carrying an infection. Shelley's tone had been sour. "Reminds me of the people who used to go to some vantage point or another to watch a battle — the men sitting on camp stools disputing tactics and body counts, the women with eau de cologne on their handkerchiefs and a damp patch between their legs."

Bullen had wondered why Shelley would bother to care. He'd said, "I expect it amuses him."

"He's not crossing London in the midday rush hour," Shelley had groused; and Bullen had seen it — a method of pulling rank — and had wondered how many such tiny humiliations Shelley faced in the course of a week.

Cochrane said, "I wanted the chance to talk to you before you left."

Bullen had agreed to make the trip to France, then pull out. He would have been happy to welsh on the deal, but now he wanted a favor from Cochrane and he guessed that keeping his side of the bargain was the price he'd have to pay.

"You're not there officially until you get to Paris in two days' time; Brittany's off the record." Cochrane added: "Also a waste of time."

"It's just a feeling," Bullen told him.

"Indulge yourself. In Paris you'll meet a man called Paul Lacroix. He's almost my French counterpart; not quite." Another little display of rank; Bullen caught Shelley's half smile. "As far as Lacroix is concerned you're official, but he doesn't really want you. Our stated reason for insisting is that a British MP has been murdered and no one seems to know who or why. They don't know about your connection to Roland Cecil; that could well work to your advantage."

"What makes you think I'll be good at this?" Bullen asked. "You train people for this kind of work."

"No" — Cochrane shook his head — "not really. It's all a matter of experience in certain areas. Other than that, it's just looking, listening, reporting back. . . . You've worked for us now and then; you've got a close connection with what's happened. Who better to send?"

Cochrane paused to watch one of the marksmen load a long-barreled pistol and take position — right hand on the gun, left hand cupping, elbows and knees slightly bent. The new target sprang around and the marksman's shoulders shrugged with each shot. The target's chest area disintegrated soundlessly.

"If anything occurs to you — if you see anything they haven't seen, hear anything they haven't heard — they'll expect you to share it with them, of course." He took a sip from the flask. "Don't."

Shelley said, "It wasn't someone working alone, the French must know that; perhaps they know more. Lacroix has been told to cooperate with you — with us — but he'll really consider that he's having you along for the ride and only for a limited time. He'll want to update you on the investigation, share a few leads with you, send you home. Go along with that and we'll see what happens."

"Stir things up a bit," Cochrane added, "if you get the chance."

The traffic had worsened. From the parking lot of the police station you could smell gasoline on the air and hear engines idling; nothing was on the move.

Shelley unlocked his car and got in. His mood hadn't improved. When Bullen leaned down by the driver's window and said, "I'll walk," Shelley nodded without looking up and swung the car toward the exit arch, driving fast as if to compensate in advance for the inch-by-inch trip back.

Bullen showed his clearance tag and found his way back to the range. The gallery was empty. As he looked down, Bullen heard the gunshots, audible now because Cochrane had left the doors to the range and to the gallery open. He went downstairs and took a pair of earmuffs from a pile in the outer room. They reduced the noise to a distant, angry rumble.

Cochrane put down the gun he'd just fired and took up position opposite the next target. The new weapon had a smooth, bulky sight canted over to one side of the barrel. When the outline target flapped around, Cochrane leveled the gun and Bullen saw a bright red dot appear on the dark surface; it switched to and fro as Cochrane amused himself — picking the spot, changing his mind, picking it again. He fired six times, shifting the aim dot to plant the bullets in groups of two — head, heart, gut — then took off his cans and laid the gun down. Without turning, he said: "I thought there must be something more."

The voice was thin and distant; it seemed to come from Bullen's own head. He pushed his ear protectors back and said, "Good shooting." Cochrane picked up the weapon he'd first used. "*This* was good shooting." The gun looked big and brutal, a chambered revolver in bright steel with a wooden stock. "Smith and Wesson Magna Classic, forty-four caliber. Shooters call it a six-gun. Seven-and-a-half-inch barrel and a kick that makes you feel you've punched a wall. But this" — Cochrane lifted the gun with the odd scope — "this doesn't leave so much to chance. It's really a target gun. Chambered for nine-millimeter Luger, locked breech, short recoil, self-loading. This scope is an Aimpoint Magdot 5000 — position the red dot, fire, you'll see the bullet hole replace the dot; no recoil to speak of, so you're back on target instantly. I should think these were on their way to someone who imports and sells to gun clubs — before they got diverted." He was holding a gun in either hand; now he weighed them as if judging their relative virtues. "One for the hard man, one for the cautious."

"Who was the buyer?" Bullen asked.

Cochrane shrugged. "Not a consignment for the professional, really. I expect they'd have found their way into various hands — just open-market merchandise."

"They won't be destroyed," Bullen said, "will they?"

Cochrane offered a wisp of a smile, a faint inclination of the head. "I expect we'll sell them on," he said, "with some sort of proviso that they don't go to the Irish."

"Is that possible?"

"No." Cochrane laid the guns down. "You want something you can't ask Paul Shelley for. Or don't want him to know about."

"Arthur Seacourt."

"Fat Nazi," Cochrane added, "encourages women and donkeys to embark on relationships that are bound to end in disappointment for both."

"He's suggested I stop asking questions about Roland, stop taking an interest in the diaries, stop looking for reasons for Roland's death . . . stop pretty much everything."

"Suggested?"

"Insisted."

Cochrane nodded. "Have a good time in France," he said. "I hope the weather stays fine."

17

In Saint-Malo a man and a bear were dancing together. The man wore a leather belt four inches wide and fitted with two steel half loops; the bear wore a leather collar with chains that ran to the man's belt. A group of three musicians stood slightly apart; like the bear trainer, they had dark, Gypsy features and wore a costume of full-sleeved peasant shirt and broadcloth breeches; their instruments were drum, fife, and pan-pipes.

Together, man and bear ambled and swayed to the measured thud of the drum. When the fife started up, the bear lifted its feet in a slow jig and pawed the air; it reared, showing patches of skin on either shoulder where the pelt had chafed away.

Bullen sat outside a café in the square and watched with the other tourists. He lifted a carafe of red wine and poured a glass for Jacques Nicolle, then one for himself.

It had taken him a day to get to Nicolle, but he already suspected that Cochrane had been right and that Brittany was a waste of time. Three people had died with Roland Cecil: the priest, the standard-bearer, and a man named Benoit Arnaut. Shelley had given Bullen the last name. Arnaut and the standard-bearer were Nazis and came from Paris; the priest was just doing his job.

Bullen had gone to the graveyard and followed the killer's escape route over the wall and up the hill to the small wood. When he'd looked down it had been clear to him that the killing must have been carefully set up. As you came clear of the tree line, the cemetery was half-hidden by the church and the killer's line of approach would have taken him into a natural dip in the ground: enough to conceal a short man for a further twenty yards. A row of yew trees inside the wall gave more cover — enough to take the gunman to within fifty feet of the burial party. If the distance between the birch trees and the last yew in the row was sixty yards, a man approaching the churchyard would only have to be fully visible for a quarter of the distance. You'd have needed to walk the terrain to know these things and make use of them.

Bullen guessed that the killer had made his own way to the birch grove, then waited for the procession to arrive. After his work was done, the helicopter had made the pickup. All that would have required planning and good timing.

Perhaps there was a virtue in being there, covering the ground, seeing it through the killer's eyes, running the videotape again in his head. Which deaths had been accidental and which deliberate was another matter, though you had to make it bad luck for the priest and the standard-bearer.

Bullen had stood in the place where his mother's brother had died and thought nothing much, except that some of the gravestones looked unnaturally clean.

Part of the background material supplied by Paul Shelley was a series of still photos taken from the video. Bullen had shown them around. Jacques Nicolle was the man who'd spat on the fallen flag.

The Gypsy and the bear made a promenade, then another, then took a bow. The chains were garish costume jewelry, something they'd picked out together.

Nicolle was a naturally thin man and age made him seem brittle, all dry-stick limbs and knobby cheekbones. He was smoking a hand-rolled cigarette and telling Bullen a story of terror that had been told many times before. It involved torture and the deaths of

110

innocent people fifty years ago when Nicolle had been twenty-eight.

"They killed everyone," he said, "everyone in my family. This was for harboring the enemy." The old man spoke softly, as if afraid of being overheard. "I had a wife, two children, a sister, mother and father, one grandfather; all dead." As if apologizing for his survival, he added: "I was an engineer. The Germans sent me to work for them in Lille. When I heard what had happened I thought I would find a Resistance group, fight with them, but I couldn't do that."

Bullen could see that Nicolle neither knew nor cared about the reasons for Roland's death. He'd gone to the churchyard with nothing on his mind but the memories of half a century ago. Bullen asked, "The Resistance — why not?"

"Nothing to fight for." Nicolle waited for Bullen to refill his glass, then half turned his back to watch the performance. The Gypsies were playing a folk tune; the bear and the bear trainer were going among the audience with a tambourine for a collecting box. "You say you knew one of the men who died."

"My mother's brother," Bullen said. "But his beliefs were his own."

Nicolle gave a little shrug and pinched his cigarette out with his fingers. "There's no need for an apology. It was a long time ago."

"What did you see?" Bullen asked.

"A man came down the hill — a small man, ugly; he jumped the wall. As soon as he was close enough, he opened fire."

"Close enough?"

111

"That he couldn't miss."

"Couldn't miss who?"

"The two older men. The priest and the boy with the flag, they were just in the line of fire."

"No doubt about who he wanted?"

"Oh, no. He knew them. They knew him."

"What?" Bullen had his glass halfway to his mouth. "How do you know?"

"Maybe not both of them. Maybe not the Englishman. But the Frenchman knew the man who killed him. I saw the gunman step up to the grave — he had his back to me; I was looking directly at the burial party. The Frenchman —"

"Arnaut," Bullen told him. "Benoit Arnaut."

Nicolle nodded. "I saw the newscast; I didn't remember the name. Arnaut saw the killer just before he opened fire. He and the Englishman were looking down into the grave — looking at the Nazi's coffin. The killer arrived and in the same moment, Arnaut felt fear. I thought he was going to speak — he made some gesture, some movement of the hand I think. But it was in his eyes; he knew the man, or else he knew what the man was there to do."

"You told this to the police?"

"No one asked me what I saw. Why should they? It's all on videotape."

"The police must have spoken to you."

"What do they want — to catch the gunman? To find out who planned the killings, perhaps? Either they will or they won't." Nicolle touched his glass, claiming the rest of the wine. Bullen poured. "They spoke to me, sure, but they didn't stop to listen." He sipped his wine: the last glass should take longer. "These men were Nazis and they are dead. That's enough for me."

A light rain had begun. Bullen had booked into a hotel near the Grande Porte. He saw the Gypsies sitting at a table under the canopy of a restaurant backing the city wall. They were eating *moules et frites,* their faces close to the plates. A white van had been squeezed into a parking place on a side road facing the restaurant — a windowless vehicle, the glass in the back doors painted black. It swayed and rocked, as if it were parked broadside to the wind.

The desk clerk handed Bullen his key and nodded at someone behind his shoulder. When Bullen turned, two men were standing close and at either side, boxing him in to the reception desk. One of them smiled at him — a horse-toothed, gappy smile that carried not a trace of humor — and held up an ID wallet. He said, "Bonjour, asshole." The men laughed. They walked Bullen out of the hotel, staying half a pace behind like dutiful wives.

Paul Lacroix was waiting in an unmarked police car parked twenty yards from the Gypsy's van. Lacroix was blond and had delicate features: high cheekbones and a narrow mouth; his brow jutted slightly, taking light from the eyes. When Bullen got into the backseat with him, Lacroix leaned forward a moment as if to register the other man's face more accurately. "No one told us you were in Brittany."

"Someone must have."

"I mean Shelley."

"I wanted to look around, go to the church, get a feel for things."

"Yes. No one told us."

"Does it matter?"

Lacroix's English was well learned; it lacked an accent of any sort. He said, "Of course it fucking matters."

The car moved off. Lacroix had turned away, half looking out of the window. Bullen kept his gaze on the womanish profile as if offering a challenge. "Shelley didn't know; he thinks I'm leaving for Paris today. I just wanted to see the place." He added, "I'm sorry if I upset you, but don't think you can talk to me like that because it's bound to make me angry."

They started over the barrage that spanned the Rance. There were blue and white sails on the water, heeling in a brisk westerly wind.

Lacroix said, "You spoke to someone."

"You've seen the video. The old guy who spat on the flag."

"Yes. You showed photographs at your hotel. We interviewed all the eyewitnesses."

"Did you?"

"The local police did it. There was nothing for us to learn from any of them."

"I know," said Bullen. "That's what I found."

They had been on the highway for twenty minutes when Lacroix said, "*Ne fait rien*. Forget it."

"Okay." Bullen put out a hand and they shook. Lacroix's fingers were slender; you could imagine

114

them tapering onto the shaft of a scalpel.

"He said nothing of interest, the man who spat —"

"Nicolle."

"Yes," said Lacroix, as if the name had just come back to him: "Nicolle."

"He said he was glad to have seen them killed."

"The war," Lacroix observed.

"Yes, the war."

"Two days ago some people went to a cemetery near Cahors and painted swastikas on all the Jewish graves. They wrote 'Yid shit.' But it is not just Jews and blacks. Everyone — every stranger, foreign workers, refugees."

"France for the French," Bullen observed.

Lacroix nodded. "You have this too I think."

"Everywhere. Everywhere in the world." Bullen thought of Anne and wondered if she'd left for the cross streets and snipers' alleys of Sarajevo. He suddenly felt unsafe, as if there might be more to lose than he could easily bear.

18

Paris was getting both rain and sun. The car took them through damp streets and into a cobbled square in Saint-Germain-de-Prés. Everything seemed to tremble slightly, glittering in a sudden, sharp light. Lacroix let Bullen out at his hotel then, on impulse it seemed, went with him into the lobby; it was small and dark and smelled of tobacco. Bullen had picked the place out of a tour book.

On a grassy patch at the center of the square, men were playing *boules*. Bullen's room looked onto a long, scabby terrace of back doors and shuttered windows. A triple-domed cage was hanging from a hook next to a set of blue shutters directly opposite his window, and a canary fluttered there like a soft, yellow flame.

Lacroix lay on Bullen's bed. "Nothing has happened since I last spoke to Shelley. I've been told to cooperate, but I don't know what you want, not really."

"We've got a dead Member of Parliament and no reason. I'm here for the reason."

"No one ever suggested a lone assassin theory." Lacroix sounded tetchy, as if Bullen had just challenged the notion. "We thought it might be someone acting alone — that's different. An individual, not a group. We always knew he had help. People saw the helicopter."

"That's a *lot* of help," Bullen observed.

"You can buy anything. Handgun, automatic rifle, fieldpiece, tank, helicopter. Buy or hire."

"That makes the pilot a patsy."

"Well . . ." Lacroix offered a lopsided grin that must have snared a hundred women. "Only if he had no idea what would happen."

"An accomplice, then."

"In the strict sense, yes. But not necessarily someone who was part of the plan — maybe just someone making a day's wage."

"What kind of someone?"

"The kind that run to small wars all around the globe. Rats climbing aboard a sinking ship."

"Who have you tried?" Bullen asked. "Where has it got to, your process of elimination?"

"Anti-Nazi groups, left-wing groups in general, Mossad and Sayeret Matkal separately because they might not be talking to one another. Also right-wing splinter groups in case there was some sort of a power struggle going on — though that's pretty unlikely at the moment; they're much keener on unity than disagreement. I think the idea is to form ranks of three and march on Poland."

"But you found nothing?"

"Nothing."

The rain had cleared completely. A low sun lit the back street; the canary rehearsed a few fluting notes, then began in earnest — a long, fluid song that ran between lines of sunlight on the wall of Bullen's room.

"The guy who was holding the flag —"

"Jean-Pierre Durant, aged twenty, convictions for auto theft, housebreaking, and assault, likes to organize the opposition when football fans arrive from other countries." Lacroix shook out a cigarette and lodged it in his mouth. "Do you mind if I smoke?"

Bullen opened the window wider, but allowed the shutter to swing back. "But no one would want to kill him — Durant?"

Lacroix let a thin plume of smoke drift to the ceiling. "No. At least not someone who goes to such complicated lengths. It was an attack on the event, of this I'm sure. A protest. The man who had died was known for his views. The attempt to dignify his death with ceremony was a provocation. The killings were planned and carried out by people who wanted to show that Nazism will not be allowed to gain a foothold in Europe again."

"But it has."

"They have no political power."

"Neither did Hitler, not at first."

"This is why the killings took place. Someone's saying, 'Never again.' "

Bullen thought Lacroix must have said all this before. A newscast, perhaps, or a report to his superiors. He wondered whether the man believed it. "Who?" he asked. "Who's saying, 'Never again'?"

"We are still looking."

"Arnaut. What about him?"

"A friend of the Englishman, Cecil. He had power in the FN. Generally speaking, he was responsible for liaison with groups from other countries. Otherwise respectable; a businessman who sat on the boards of several companies and had investments in many more. An ordinary member of the bourgeoisie."

"Apart from being a neo-Nazi, that is."

"All things are a matter of degree." Lacroix rolled off the bed, pushed the shutters back, and flicked his cigarette out into the street. "I'm sorry your MP was killed; he was in the wrong place at the wrong time." He thought for a moment about what he'd said. "Not sorry he was killed — sorry it has caused a fuss. So" —he peered across at the canary's cage, as if checking for the source of the noise — "that's all. I imagine you will want to be seen to do something before turning in a report to Paul Shelley. I'll get someone to give you a translation of what we've done — just a summary, you know. A bit of recent history about French nationalism, perhaps. And a conclusion that tells what everyone already knows — it was a political killing by some anti-Nazi faction, but we don't know who."

"What I'd really like," Bullen said, "is a list of the people you spoke to — especially where Arnaut was concerned."

Lacroix looked weary, a little sour, too. "You don't have to do any *detecting,* Bullen. We have detectives for that."

"Even so."

"Please don't be difficult. At the moment, this is a request."

Bullen said, "It's not difficult. There's nothing difficult about it. I'm trying to keep Shelley off my back."

"If I say no —"

"Don't say no," Bullen told him, "because I haven't allowed for that."

Lacroix seemed to be sizing Bullen up, looking at him straight on and holding the look, a boxer's stare. Finally he said, "I've been trying to work out why you're here."

"Paul Shelley," Bullen told him.

"Because there's something wrong, something detached, something angry."

Bullen opted for the truth. "I've been angry all my life," he said.

The river was a dark flow under the paler flow of

dusk — a vibrant band of aquamarine along the horizon — and the sky was full of birds.

Bullen found a brasserie close to the Place Saint-Sulpice. He ate soup followed by *moules et frites* and drank a carafe of red wine, remembering the Gypsies and the businesslike way they put their faces down to their plates to scoop in the food. He thought of the bear, dancing in chains.

Later, he took a bottle of brandy to his hotel room and sat in the dark, shutters half open, to watch a girl undress in the room opposite — treasure trove, he decided, the sort of fortune only to be found in a strange room in a foreign city. She went to and fro, unbuttoning, unzipping, untying, until she was naked; her body glowed in the shaded lamplight.

She took the canary in, standing framed in the window a moment and turning in half profile to reach the hook that held the cage; her breast and flank were doused in light from other windows; her waist looked a handspan, no more. She leaned out for the cage, her breasts drooping as if they should settle into a lover's palm.

Lacroix had lit another cigarette and gone to the door, the boxer's stare back in place. He'd asked, "Will you be trouble?"

"I don't think so," Bullen had told him. "Let's see."

"Hard man, are you?" Lacroix had wanted to know. "Tough guy. Wherever you go, ask me first, report back afterward. Except there's nothing to find. Everything's been done."

"Then why don't you have the answers?"

"Someone told me the British police have a one hundred percent clear-up rate. You can confirm that, I expect."

Bullen had raised a hand and waved him off with a flutter of fingers.

Lacroix had grinned. "Fucking *rosbif*," he'd said. "I never liked the English."

The girl put the canary down on a table. Lines of light ran on her shoulders like rain; her backbone was a deep furrow of darkness.

Bullen was drunk. He lay back on the bed, the still center of a turning world. He slept and the world continued its slow revolve, bringing people toward him through the dark.

Anne Warbeck was sitting at her desk in an open-plan office: thirty-five desks, thirty-five computer screens glowing, five people still working. Two guys had wheeled a TV and video up to a nearby desk and were scrolling through tapes of CNN news broadcasts for items that would fit a regular feature called "The World This Month." Anne was still waiting for her flight to Sarajevo. In the meantime, she was catching up on some research and the TV was a distraction: every so often a news item would catch her attention and she'd have to watch. She had considered moving to the far end of the room, but her desk was littered with books and notes and, anyway, she'd pretty much gone as far as she could go with ethnic cleansing and head counts. She was drawing up a map of enforced migrations, torched villages, concentration camps. She felt sick — some of it anger and disgust, though she recognized a makeweight of fear; within a week or so she would be back in Bosnia.

The men across the aisle switched the tape from fast forward to play. One of them said, "Did you see this?" and there was gunfire. Anne looked across. A woman in a white dress was dying. A young man was dying. An older man was pointing at the killer, then he died as well. Tables and white linen and fine glassware were set out under a clean blue sky.

Constance Bullen was dining by candlelight, as if the world had never turned at all, as if time could hang suspended like dawn mist among trees in the orchard. She had opened a can of corned beef, a can of red beans, a can of apricots in syrup, and a bottle of whiskey. The candles were fixed to the table by their own wax. They seemed to mesmerize her. She stared straight ahead while a little pile of beans toppled from her fork onto the front of her dress. That tiny accident seemed to startle her into remembrance. She ate greedily for a few minutes, taking forkfuls of beef and beans straight from the cans. She reached in among the apricots with her fingers and held the dripping fruit up to her mouth in readiness while she chewed. The other hand reached for the whiskey.

She swallowed, took a slug of whiskey, put the apricot into her mouth, swallowed again, drank whiskey again. Then she stopped as before, stalled on a thought.

She said, "Perhaps we could walk in the garden; the

122

air is so cool.'' Tracks of syrup ran up her bare arm as she raised it. She smiled a fond, reassuring smile. "The world cannot change, my dear, unless we would have it so." Candle flame sat in her eye like evidence of a vision; she didn't blink. "We must go back to our guests, but kiss me first."

The man watching her from outside the window was a technician; you could rely on him for a good job. He watched Constance and noticed her lips moving, though he couldn't hear what she said. He knew that Constance lived alone but decided to check the place out.

He walked to the back of the house and across the edge of the orchard, then over the lawn. Everything was so overgrown that all shape had been lost — trees thin and wasted, box hedges falling under their own weight, the terrace thick with wild grasses and botched with moss. He tried the handle and found that nothing was locked.

The house was bare: twelve bedrooms but only three with beds. The technician glanced into the room where Bullen had slept and into the room where Roland Cecil's blanket box had burned. All the lights were on. He noticed the soft drift of embers about the room and remembered holding Bullen's head to beat it on the ground — hard enough to stun, not hard enough to kill.

He went downstairs and stood just inside the dining room door. What he saw made him sick — the violent dyed yellow of Constance Bullen's hair, her face seamed with lines and caulked with makeup, her magenta lips. She was wearing a dark green satin ball gown, trimmed with black velvet, off the shoulder to show her wizened shoulders and the yellowish crepe of her cleavage.

At first, when he stepped into the room, she didn't notice him. She gouged some corned beef out of its can and speared a few beans. Then he went closer and she saw him; her mouth opened and a chewed gobbet of food fell out. She stood up and approached him, the rich material of her gown rustling as it brushed the floor.

She heard him say, "A moment to ourselves — why not?" and replied, "Perhaps we could walk in the garden; the air is so cool."

The technician hadn't spoken a word. He allowed her to slip her arm through his and together they walked through a drawing room into the long hallway. She looked to either side as they passed, admiring the pictures, the draperies, the vases filled with fresh flowers. He followed her gaze, seeing what was really there: bare walls, scabbed and filthy.

When they reached the terrace, she loosed her arm and ran into the orchard on light feet, her laugh floating back to him on the warm air. The technician watched her go, stumbling through the long grass and cawing like a mad crow. He went in among the trees and found her sitting on the rotting slats of a wooden bench.

She heard him say, "Nothing must change this — you or me or this house; every evening must be like this evening."

She smiled a fond, reassuring smile. "The world

cannot change, my dear, unless we would have it so."

The technician felt a little shudder in his backbone as the smile grew brighter on her ruined face. He took her arm and pulled her to her feet. Her body moved with his touch, rising to him, compliant. She heard him say, "I adore you, Connie."

He put his hands on her throat and she thought he might make love to her there, in the orchard, lifting her gown while she looked over his shoulder toward the drawing room and watched their friends going to and fro with drinks and coffee. The thought excited her and she took one of his hands in her own and moved it to her breast.

The technician pulled his fingers free and braced himself, splay-legged, pushing her slightly so that she went off balance: it gave him a better angle. When he began to throttle her, the smile was still on her face.

She was breathless; he made her breathless. She could see the trees and, above them, clouds moving across a three-quarter moon. She loved him so much that it hurt.

Something gave in her throat, like gristle pulling apart, and she retched a little gusher of vomit and blood. The technician let her fall and wiped his hands on the grass, then lifted her like a bride and carried her back into the house.

He propped her against the wall in the dining room and knelt down in front of her. He took out a thin-bladed gutting knife, using the candlelight to work by, and held her jaw tightly while he carved the shape of a swastika into her forehead.

19

A car collected Bullen at ten-thirty and took him to a café near the Luxembourg Gardens. The driver was a young woman. She'd handed Bullen a pocket file before opening the car door for him. He'd spoken a few words to her in French and she'd responded with even fewer in English.

Lacroix had a tall glass of tomato juice in front of him and a pitcherful on the side; nearby on the table was salt, Worcestershire sauce, and Tabasco. He said, "I was drinking last night — my wife left me."

Bullen opened his mouth, then closed it. He went to the counter and ordered a coffee. When he returned he asked, "Did you know?"

"That she would leave?" Lacroix shrugged. "She said she would. I didn't believe her. I was wrong. I've been wrong before, but I never minded quite so much."

The owner of the café came around the counter with a plate of fried eggs. "Eating is the only cure for a hangover, did you know that?" Lacroix tore a chunk of bread and pushed it into a yolk. He said, "I feel very ill. I feel like hell."

Bullen put the file down on the table and asked,

"You looked at all the business contacts?"

"Sure."

"All of them?"

Lacroix chewed for a moment and made a game attempt at swallowing. He got the yolk-soaked bread down on the third attempt and followed it with tomato juice. "Well, the police did that, of course. You know how it goes." Bullen shrugged as if he did know. "They pretend to cooperate with Security Services, but consider that we're secretive, arrogant, and given to invading their territory without bothering to tell them. All true, of course; however, it doesn't necessarily mean that they repay us by doing a bad job. They went through his company connections, his haulage business, his income-tax returns, his investments. Nothing strange. The usual tax evasion."

He drank off the tomato juice and refilled the glass. "Listen, Bullen, we're not looking for something of that sort — business matters or what have you. It doesn't fit. What could it be? I mean, someone wants to take over Arnaut's haulage company, Arnaut won't sell, so the guy helicopters a hit man to a funeral? Please!"

He finished the last of the eggs and wiped the plate with a chunk of bread.

"How do you feel now?" Bullen asked.

"I feel worse."

"Can I keep the file?"

"The file is for you. It's your gift to Paul Shelley — your reason for being here, your job well done. I hear that he has a new boss."

"Stuart Cochrane," Bullen confirmed, then responded to Lacroix's raised eyebrow: "Tough, devious, ambitious, difficult to know. Not really new — he and Shelley have worked together for years. Cochrane got the promotion."

Lacroix nodded. "Only the nice guys get on in life." He said, "There's nothing in the woodpile here, Bullen. My guess is the Israelis, okay? Other groups might seek publicity. If not the Israelis then a militant left-wing organization. It was bound to happen — the left moving against neo-Nazism; I'm surprised it should have taken so long."

"In the woodpile?" Bullen asked.

"An English idiom meaning something hidden, am I right?"

"No, not exactly."

"I'm a sick man. Make allowances. When will you return to London?"

"I think I'm supposed to do a little more than simply take a file home."

Lacroix sighed. "What? Do what? What is there to do? If it hasn't been done, then we're doing it. If we're not doing it, then it will be done eventually. I'll send you faxes. Here's another English idiom: fuck off. Did I get that one right?"

"Let me continue to look through the file. If there's something I want to check, someone I want to talk to, then I'll ask you. Wasn't that what you said?"

"There's nothing to look for; there's no one to see. I said that also."

"Then I won't be calling you, will I?" Bullen signaled for another coffee. He asked, "Why did she leave you?"

"I've been married for twelve years," Lacroix told him, "it could be anything."

There were two people in Arnaut's life who made Bullen curious: Charles Blanchot and Katherine Blair. The woman had been interviewed three times by the police, though she was simply described as a business acquaintance. The interview note didn't say much, but it was clear that they'd been asking her about Arnaut's movements on the evening before he traveled to Brittany. She'd said she didn't know and eventually the matter had been dropped. There was nothing concrete to make Bullen suspicious, but he was unsettled by the curtness of the final report and the fact that Katherine remained oddly anonymous. It read like a stopped tape.

Charles Blanchot owned a company which had recently taken Arnaut onto the board; that was one connection, but there was another. Among the entries in Roland Cecil's diaries there had been a mention of Blanchot.

Bullen was sitting in his hotel room leafing through the spiral notebook that held the abstract of the diaries. The canary was singing, but the room beyond was empty. In the manner of Roland's deliberately abbreviated record, the entry had simply said: PARIS/BLANCHOT/7:30. The date of the meeting was a month before Roland's death.

There were contact numbers for both people. Seeing the numbers was a prompt. Bullen lifted the phone and dialed and heard Anne answer on the fourth ring. He said, "How are you?" Then, as if the fact had just registered, "You're still there."

"I fly out sometime next week," she said. "What's happening?"

"Nothing. I'm in Marseilles. I thought I'd drive back, stop off in a few places, buy some wine." He was describing a holiday they'd once planned but never taken. "Before that, I have to arrange to sell Roland's place. You know France — everything closes for lunch."

"Maybe I'll see you before I go."

"Of course. It'll only take a day or so." There was something in her tone. He asked, "What's wrong?"

"Nothing," she said, then, "I'm scared. I don't want to go."

"Don't go." As soon as he'd spoken, he knew that he meant it. *Don't go, don't go!*

Anne sighed. "Don't say that, Tom. Listen, I'll see you soon."

How do I keep you safe? he thought. I can't. How do I love you properly when *being* loved is so difficult for me?

Charles Blanchot was in a meeting, so Bullen made an appointment for later that day. He said he was a business colleague of Roland Cecil's. Kathy Blair said that any friend of Benoit's stood a good chance of becoming a friend of hers and why didn't he come over?

She made coffee and heated some croissants and put a record on the turntable: a bluesy cover version of an Ella Fitzgerald classic. While she was heating milk for the coffee, she sang along in a husky voice, pitch-perfect.

Her apartment was in the Marais; Bullen's taxi driver had got lost in the narrow, twisting streets and finally let him out in Village Saint-Paul to find his own way. He sat by the window as she set out the coffee, the pastry, some sweet apple preserve. Her accent had the unmistakable soft flutter of somewhere below the Mason-Dixon line.

"Missouri," she said when he asked her. Then, answering an earlier question, "The night before Benoit was killed he was here; I told the police that. I also told them that he left at about ten o'clock. I guess they were wondering where he went next. Home would be my guess. Home to pack his jackboots." She laughed. "Home to pack his black shirt and his swastika armband."

"He lived alone?"

"Sure said he did. I never went there — he came here." A joke occurred to her: "Benoit came here; I never came here — well, not with Benoit."

"Why are you in Paris?" Bullen asked.

"You don't like Paris?" She wasn't asking for a response. "I arrived in this city just about a year ago. This was stopover number three. I'd already spent some time in Rome and Amsterdam. The plan was: fuck my way around Europe. Paris kinda appeals to me, so I'm staying a while. Stay anywhere and you get regular guys, you know? Benoit was a regular: twice a week, same time, same order."

"What was that?"

Kathy smiled; she looked a day over twenty-one. "Now, you've heard of client confidentiality, haven't you, honey?" She reached over and dabbed a crumb from the side of Bullen's mouth. "He liked me to put on black clothes and tie him up and whip him and sit on his face and suck his dick with my finger waaaaay up his ass." Her voice was mellifluous, the singsong of the South. "Now, if that made you hot I'd better tell you right now it's a basic thousand francs."

"Did he ever talk to you?"

"Sure. Last time I saw him, he said: 'Katherine, there are these guys out to kill me. Here's a letter that explains everything. If a guy called Tom Bullen arrives for breakfast one morning, give him the letter.' "

Bullen said, "Pretend I don't have a thousand francs to spend."

Kathy gave him more coffee. She was wearing a green silk robe with Chinese motifs in red; it was wrapped across her body in a way that revealed everything and nothing. When she laughed the laugh was deep, like her singing voice. "You know I'm foolin', honey. I couldn't take your money because there's nothin' to tell. The police got the same story."

"According to the report I read they didn't get any kind of a story." Bullen had told Kathy something close to the truth: he was a British copper asking about the death of a British Member of Parliament.

"Say that again — the report?"

"Your interview read: 'Yes, I knew him; no, I didn't see him; good-bye.' Until I actually met you . . ." He shrugged.

"You didn't know I was a hooker." She smiled. "How kind of them to be discreet."

"Them?" Bullen asked.

"Well, a nice guy called Paul Lacroix. You meet him yet?"

"Are you going to tell him we've spoken?"

"Matter to you?"

"Yes. Don't tell him."

"Okay, honey, I can help you out there."

Bullen had made up a list of names from the abstract of Roland Cecil's diaries and the report Lacroix had given him. He handed it to Kathy. "See any names you recognize?"

She looked down the list. "Hookers don't always know the names," she said, "just the regular guys. But I only see five a day and that's a maximum. Some of the stuff I do needs strength, you follow me? Working a bullwhip up some guy's asshole, that's sheer physical labor."

Bullen pointed to the name Charles Blanchot. "Know him?"

Kathy read it out loud. "No. Who's he?"

"Someone I have to see. A friend of Arnaut's."

"No," she said, "if I sat on this dick, I didn't know who was behind it."

The coffee was a good, rich blend and the croissants were made with butter. He finished his breakfast while Kathy made a few phone calls. She turned the record: now it was a folksy number about troubled times.

When Bullen left, Kathy was between calls. She smiled and said, "Good-bye, honey. If you had a good time, tell your friends."

"Is Lacroix a regular?" he asked.

"He likes afternoons."

"Anything special?"

"No, honey, he just wants to get laid. His wife can't do that for him anymore."

Bullen decided to leave that mystery alone. With one hand on the door, he said: "I understand that most people work their way around Europe by tending bar or waiting table, that sort of thing. . . ."

Kathy had dialed everything but the last digit. She said, "Yeah, sure. The difference is, I like this. For me, trick and treat are the same thing."

The last digit was a four; she held off until she heard Bullen's feet on the stairs. When Lacroix answered, she asked: "You know a guy called Tom Bullen?"

"He came to see you?"

"Just left."

"Asking about Arnaut."

"You got it."

"Did you tell him about me?"

"No, honey, why would I do that?"

"What did he say?"

"He asked me if I knew a guy called Blanchot. Charles Blanchot — right?"

"Do you?"

"Who knows? I don't think so. If I do, I don't know anything that matters."

"Kathy, I'm —" Lacroix's voice broke up; he was talking on a mobile phone and his car had just gone between high buildings in a narrow street.

Kathy knew he was saying, "I'm sorry you got involved in this." When his voice came back, she said: "Don't worry, honey. I'll see you later."

Bullen was there as a colleague of Arnaut's, someone who supplied contracts for goods to be trucked from northern France to other parts of Europe. He was making it up as he went along and considered he was doing a pretty good job. After a few minutes, Charles Blanchot said, "Who the hell are you, Bullen?"

"I need to find another hauler for —"

"Please." Blanchot lifted a hand to silence him. Short, meaty fingers, an arm that filled his shirtsleeve; Blanchot was solid and square, like an aging boxer. "What you know about haulage, my old mother knows about duck fucking. Why pretend?"

"Okay," Bullen asked, "who am I?"

"Police."

"No. I was doing business with Roland Cecil when he died."

"So you say."

They were speaking in French, Bullen understanding well, but having to fumble for words. "I wanted to find out if we were in competition."

"How would that be?"

"Shipping."

Blanchot laughed. "You don't know anything about shipping either."

"Of course not. I leave that to others. It's the merchandise that I'm interested in, not the means of transport."

Bullen was making it up with a little more confidence, now. Blanchot looked wary. He said, "I ship steel out of the Ukraine. You have an interest there?"

"My interests are the same as Roland's."

135

Blanchot rented a riverside office cheek by jowl with the grime and ugliness of Grenelle, but almost within sight of the Bois de Boulogne; the contrast told a story: rich man in a hard world. He went to the window and watched a row of barges being pushed upriver. Bullen waited.

"I can't talk to you now." Blanchot kept his back turned. "Not here; not about Roland Cecil."

"When?"

"Tonight if you like. There's a bar on the corner of this street. You'll see it. We could meet there at seven. Is seven all right?" Suddenly there was an eagerness about Blanchot. He said, "I have more appointments this afternoon — business to conduct. This evening would be better."

Bullen found the bar on his way back and went in. There was a swill of cigarette smoke and under it the thick fragrance of bad drains. A dozen men were taking an afternoon drink; they wore overalls and pea jackets and heavy boots.

Bullen went to the men's room, then wandered into the kitchen as if by mistake. He was checking for alternate ways out.

Stuart Cochrane's blond assistant came in with a tape and slipped it into a cassette player. They listened to a telephone conversation between Charles Blanchot and Arthur Seacourt.

At one point, Seacourt said: "It was decided that he's more dangerous dead than alive."

Blanchot sounded troubled. "That's becoming

questionable. What does he want?"

"We don't know. Roland was his mother's brother. Maybe he's telling the truth — he simply wants to know why Roland was killed."

"And maybe he's working for someone." There was a long pause. Blanchot said, "Hello?"

"Yes, that's what I think." Seacourt sounded as if he were talking to himself.

"What shall I do? When does he become riskier alive than dead?"

Seacourt said, "I'll get back to you."

"When?"

"As soon as I can."

"Listen," Blanchot said, "I'm out of this now. With Benoit and Roland dead — I'm out of it. Find another shipper."

"The deal's gone down," Seacourt told him, "we've lost it — we know that. But no one's out of it. We're just waiting for another contact, another deal. A couple of weeks; a month at the outside."

"Not with me," Blanchot said. "Not with me."

The blonde asked, "What about Seacourt? Which way will he jump?"

"Well, let's see . . ." Cochrane had the air of a man at a roulette table deciding whether to bet red or black. "If Seacourt decides to kill Bullen there will be reverberations; it's all a matter of how far they'll travel. If he doesn't, Bullen will go on causing reverberations of his own. That's happening already. On balance, he's more use to us dead than alive. But it's all a matter of degree."

"He said he'd quit after Paris."

"He needs a reason," Cochrane confirmed. "A reason for wanting to continue. We need that, too. He's a bear trap, but where's the bear?"

"If they decide to kill him and succeed . . . ?" The blonde was enjoying the speculation, now. If black was death, her money was on the red.

"I'll bet he can look after himself," Cochrane said. "I'd lay money on that."

"We still have the tap on Seacourt's phone — one way or another, we'll know what he tells Blanchot to do."

"Tell them to take a break, forget the phone tap."

"You don't want to know?"

"I like the element of chance in all this, don't you? I like" — Cochrane cupped his fist and made the motion of someone shaking dice — "I like the rattle of the bones." He threw his imaginary dice and watched them roll, then looked at the girl, smiling a broad, wolfish smile.

He put a finger on her mouth, a mime for silence, and said: "Nothing to Paul Shelley. Okay? This is outside the department. Nothing written."

"Sure."

He bit gently on the fullness of her lip. "Nothing at all."

"I'm a sick man," said Paul Lacroix. "Close to death, believe me." Kathy Blair laid him out like a corpse, mother naked, and fucked him back to life, then she gave him a brandy to keep his vital signs up and running.

"Tell me about the list." Lacroix drank, then turned onto his stomach, silently asking for a massage. Kathy sat astride him again.

"A list of names. He asked if I knew this guy Blanchot. I don't remember the others, honey. They were just names. . . ."

"And he told you he was going to see Blanchot?"

"That's what he said." She dug her fingers into the flesh around his shoulders, swaying on the small of his back like a rider. She could feel a little tickle of sensation growing and she shifted slightly to hit the spot.

"He didn't say why?"

"That's right. You know this guy — Blanchot?"

"Someone spoke to him after the killings; he's a business associate of Arnaut's."

"Why does Bullen think he's special?"

Good question, Lacroix thought. He'd put a couple of men on Blanchot's office as soon as Kathy had spoken to him. Bullen had been picked up going into the office, then again going into the bar; the same men were still there, watching the street. It was almost six-thirty and Blanchot hadn't left his office.

Lacroix glanced to where his clothes were folded on a chair. On top of the pile were his gun and a mobile phone. He felt Kathy's hips quicken as her fingers tracked up and down his spine.

"Just names on the list, nothing else?"

"Just names, honey."

Lacroix lay stock-still while she worked on him. He thought: Okay, he knows something I don't and I'm going to kick it out of the bastard, and Christ, I do hate the fucking English. When the phone rang, he put out an arm and found the chair was beyond his reach.

He lifted his back an inch, but Kathy sat tight. She said, "Don't move, honey, I'm getting off." He wasn't sure what she meant until he heard her yelp.

20

Kathy handed Lacroix the phone and drifted off toward the kitchen to look for a drink.

The LCD display told him to call the pager and the message told him that Bullen had returned and gone into the bar. He called the two guys on the stakeout and told them to stay close to Bullen — one in the bar, one in the car. By the time Lacroix arrived, Bullen had been joined by Blanchot. The observer in the bar went to the men's room and made a radio report: the marks were drinking and talking and must have been sharing a joke, because one of them was laughing.

It was Blanchot, laughing and shaking his head and saying, "What can you tell me about Roland's business? Nothing. What can you tell me about my business? Nothing. You're in the dark. Why go on?"

"I didn't tell you everything about Roland and myself." Bullen had decided on a lie that was almost the truth. "He was my uncle. When he died, I wanted to know why. Not so much who had killed him, but *why.*"

"Go on . . ."

"You say I don't know what Roland's business was, but I do — not the specific deals that were made or what they involved, but I know that Roland's part must have been to invest. It was all he understood. He never manufactured anything, or bought and sold; there was never a family business. All he knew about was how to make money multiply. Now, I don't know whether the man who killed him intended that he should die, or whether the real target was Benoit Arnaut and Roland simply happened to get in the way, but it seems clear that the gunman either wanted Arnaut or he wanted both of them." Bullen remembered Nicolle pinching out his cigarette and finishing the last of the wine: *It was in his eyes; he knew what the man was there to do.*

"My guess is he wanted both of them. But I don't think the killer was a Jew or a radical or anyone who cared about Nazism one way or the other. I think he was a professional. And if my guess is right, and Roland really was killed because of a deal rich enough to provoke that sort of action, then I want a piece of it. That's why I'm here."

"What's your offer?" Blanchot had decided to give Bullen his head.

"Money. Roland's money."

"Which you inherit?"

"Which my mother inherits; it's the same thing."

"Is it?"

"She's half-mad — very confused and there-

141

fore controllable."

"If I had sons," Blanchot observed, "I'd want them to be just like you." When Bullen didn't respond, he added: "There are some people I have to contact. I can't say yes or no."

"I understand."

"Why didn't you tell me this before?"

"I wanted to know what Roland was investing in. I thought that if you believed I was in the same business, you might tell me." He paused. "Will you tell me?"

"I ship steel out of the Ukraine," Blanchot said. "I thought I'd mentioned that."

They came out of the bar together. Bullen went in one direction Blanchot in the other. Lacroix's man emerged a few seconds later and got into the car. Lacroix said, "Follow Bullen," and the man got out again. The driver reached for the ignition key, but Lacroix said: "Give him a few minutes." He watched Blanchot unlock the street door of his office.

Lacroix's mobile phone rang. When he answered it his wife said, "Paul, I've been back to the apartment and taken my things. The camera and the CD player were mine, remember? I didn't want you to think you'd been burgled."

"A crazy Jew," Lacroix said, "that's what we need. A crazy, rich Jew whose mother died in Treblinka. A crazy, rich, vengeful Jew — rich enough to hire a mechanic and a helicopter, vengeful enough to dream of setting up an assassination, crazy enough to do it." He took a call from the guy following Bullen; they were going into the Metro, so there wouldn't be any reports for a while.

Lacroix sighed. "He's going back to his hotel to wait."

"Wait for what?" the driver asked.

"I don't know," Lacroix snapped. "I don't know anything."

The driver was just a driver; he didn't know much about the case. "Arnaut?" he asked. "Is this the Arnaut business? You think a Jew did it?"

Lacroix laughed despairingly. "Who knows?"

The driver wasn't really paying attention. "Bunch of bastards, the Jews," he said. "I've always thought so. Money grubbers. Grease my palm. Too much fuss made about the fucking Jews."

They sat and waited for Blanchot to emerge. After a while, Lacroix said: "I'm a Jew. My mother was a Jew."

A line of red crept along the driver's jawline and spread like the mark of a slap; he sat stiff-necked and silent behind the wheel. What Lacroix had said wasn't true, but it made him feel better.

"Here's the story: He admits to being Roland's nephew but kept quiet about it in the hope that I'd believe he was a business partner; he thought I might give something away — he wants to know what Roland was funding. That didn't work, so he's come clean: *I want a piece of the action.* I told him that I wasn't necessarily opposed to the idea, but there were people I had to speak to. He's gone back to his hotel to wait while I do that." Blanchot remembered something: "Also, he says he can lay hands on Roland's money."

"Kill him," Seacourt said.

21

The canary was singing. The girl had gone into the bedroom but removed only her coat. Now she was making a meal for her lover, who would arrive soon. He was the only man she had ever truly loved, and they'd met by chance in the Tuileries gardens — her hat had blown off and he'd chased it. By the time they had walked to the Place de la Concorde, they were in love. Their lives would be long and happy and ordinary.

She stood by the kitchen window, her head bent as she chopped vegetables. The story he'd invented about her made Bullen lonely.

Blanchot phoned and said, "It's not my decision — you know that. There are a couple of people you have to meet."

"Now — tonight?"

"I'll collect you in about ten minutes." As if to reassure, Blanchot added: "It's true that you can get the money?"

"It's true."

"Ten or fifteen minutes."

Bullen phoned the number Lacroix had left for him and was patched through to a diversion number for a mobile phone. He redialed, but the voice that answered wasn't that of Lacroix. He left a message — "Call me" — then dialed again.

Kathy said, "Honey, I don't know where he is. He just comes here and jumps on me and goes away." She laughed. "I don't have his home number."

Bullen tried to jog her memory. "Bars he goes to, places you've been to together — he's more than just a regular to you, isn't he? He looks after you."

"I look after him, honey. Listen, I don't know where he goes. Home to his wife, maybe? That's where most of them go."

"Okay." Bullen felt a lick of panic. "I thought he might have said something."

"He did. He said, 'Suck my dick or else I'll die.' "

The driver dialed the paging number on Lacroix's mobile phone and said, "He wants you to call him."

"Of course he does." They were parked in a side street within sight of Bullen's hotel. "A little knowledge can get you killed."

"Here we go," said the driver. Bullen had emerged from the hotel and was getting into Blanchot's car.

Lacroix said, "Don't lose them."

The traffic was heavy and reckless and the driver had to run a red light almost at once. For a while, Lacroix had his eyes fixed on Blanchot's brake lights as they lost ground then regained it, the driver trying to stay back without losing contact. After a while, he relaxed a little and knuckled his eyes. He said, "I think they're going back to Grenelle."

Five minutes later, the driver got boxed in at an intersection and lost them completely.

It was Blanchot's turn to lie. He told Bullen that a few questions needed to be asked, but they liked the idea of Roland's money. He apologized for the fact that precautions had to be taken, but was sure that Bullen understood; he tried a few phrases in English, laughing at his own ineptitude, and thought he sounded pretty convincing.

The area was factories and car repair shops and builders' yards and cheap housing rising skyward in grimy stacks. The sun had gone. There was no color in the sky, just a dim, watery light and clouds that seemed to be soaking up the last of the dusk. Blanchot led the way to a small warehouse and went to a side door. Bullen was watching him carefully; he wanted to believe that everything was going to be fine. Whoever Blanchot's friends were, their only requirement was money. Roland had been going to supply it, or maybe some of it. Now Bullen would be their new benefactor. He stepped inside the door and someone hit him full in the mouth. Blanchot closed the door. He helped get Bullen off the floor and onto a wooden chair, then he paced to and fro for a bit, looking worried. After a moment he stopped in front of the chair. "I said there would be some questions. Just answer them and you can go. We don't want to keep you and we don't want to know you, but we have to ask what you want and who you're working for."

The wall lights were clad in iron bands that sent shadows around the room. Standing upright, Blanchot

146

was in the limelight; bending, he was wearing a dusky half mask.

"This is stupid," Bullen said. "If you didn't believe me, why didn't you say so?"

"I believe you're Roland's nephew; I believe you can get the money. That's not it."

There were two men in the room besides Blanchot. One of them was holding a gun and looking at Bullen with an odd sort of intensity. The other stood still, arms folded, a man with a weight lifter's arms and torso; a little pigtail bristled from his neck.

Blanchot said, "It's easy. Tell us and go."

When Bullen didn't reply, the weight lifter unfolded his arms and walked behind the chair. He slipped something over Bullen's throat and held it —a necktie or a cloth belt. Bullen raised his hands, trying to get his thumbs under the garrote, and the man with the gun stepped closer, lodging the barrel over Bullen's left eye. He said, "No hands." When Bullen lowered them, the man slipped his gun into a pocket and took out some plastic handcuffs; he cuffed a wrist on one side, then took the strip under Bullen's knees and secured the other.

The weight lifter turned his hand through thirty degrees and Bullen stopped breathing.

Blanchot said, "Just tell us."

The weight lifter let slack into the garrote and looked at Blanchot. The air was like fire in Bullen's throat, like iced water in his lungs. He swallowed on the pain and said, "Ask me something; I don't know what to say."

"You made contact with a man called Arthur Seacourt. Seacourt's a friend of mine. He says you've been lying to me."

"No. I was lying to him."

"Why?"

"I was trying to get information without giving any away."

"What information?"

"The same I wanted from you — why was Roland killed? Is there a profit to be made?"

Blanchot shook his head. "You hurt some people. Seacourt's people."

"There was a reason; did he tell you what it was?"

"You told him you were a journalist; you're not. You told him you were sympathetic to his cause; you're not. You told him that you wanted to find out why Roland died, but you didn't give him the same story that you've given me." He leaned down, bringing his face close to Bullen's, scarfing himself in shadow. "Why not tell the truth and then you can go."

"Can I?"

Blanchot stalled on the answer. He and Bullen looked at one another, both a little startled, like friends who meet unexpectedly in a foreign country. The shadows fell away as Blanchot straightened; he turned his back. To the weight lifter, he said: "You'd better kill him."

The weight lifter turned his wrist over and Bullen felt a terrible thickness in his throat; he tried to stand, but his arms were locked under his knees. His tongue slid to the corner of his mouth and his lips fattened; things swam away from him in waves of sound, waves of color, waves of darkness.

Blanchot walked to the other end of the warehouse. He said, "Hurry. Do it quickly," his voice shaky and shrill. The gunman was watching, that same intensity on his face, his narrow features composed to straight lines.

Bullen was gargling and crowing. "For God's sake!" Blanchot yelled. He couldn't get out of earshot: the place wasn't big enough.

Lacroix got just about everything wrong except for the fact that Bullen didn't die.

It had taken ten minutes to find the car and that was complete luck. Now he came into the warehouse ahead of the two men with him, masking them, so that they couldn't get off a shot, although they drew fire from the gunman close to Bullen. Lacroix fired back and stepped sideways; one of his men grunted and went down onto one knee, his hands folded across his abdomen. The other emptied his gun, firing so fast that the shots made a single sound.

The weight lifter took a bullet in the side and another in the face; he dropped, but his hand still held the garrote. Bullen thought he heard his own neck break. He kicked out, hitting the ground with a heel and upturning his chair. The gunman stepped forward, looking for a target. Lacroix shot him four times, putting the slugs in a handspan group six inches below the man's throat; he fell on top of Bullen and the weight lifter.

After they got Bullen out of the sandwich he spent five minutes on his hands and knees, coughing like a dog. His hair was soaked with the gunman's blood; as he leaned forward it ran in crazy lines down his forehead.

Lacroix was thinking through the damage. His own man gut-shot, Blanchot's gunman dead, the weight lifter with a bullet lodged close to his heart and his nose shot away. He said, "Is this what you came for?"

Bullen had no voice. The hospital doctor had said, "Nothing's broken or damaged; bad bruising, trauma to the ligatures. If you get an infection take anti-biotics."

Lacroix asked, "Why did you talk to Blanchot? What made him interesting to you?"

Bullen shrugged. Lacroix had supplied him with a pad and pen. He wrote, *Associate of Arnaut.*

"That was all? You decided to check him out, so he decided to kill you? Good God, what did you say?"

Told him I was in the shipping business.

"He kills all his rivals? Listen, Bullen, I'm not having a good day, remember? It started with a hang-over; it's ending with a headache. I had a case of person or persons unknown and a file that was closing of its own accord. Now I've got one man dead, two men badly wounded, you half-strangled, and questions being asked that I can't answer. One of the questions is: who let this English bastard loose around Paris? Help me. Tell me why Blanchot wanted to kill you."

Bullen was wondering the same thing. He also wanted to know why Cochrane hadn't put Seacourt out of commission. He wrote: *Something I said that had to do with shipping.*

"What?"

Who knows? I'm guessing. I don't know anything about shipping.

"Mother of Christ," Lacroix said. He took Bullen by the arm and led him to the door.

In the car, Bullen wrote: *Where are we going?* and passed the pad over. Lacroix grabbed the pen from Bullen's hand and tossed it out of the window; the pad followed. He said, "Shut up."

The warehouse was a beacon, hissing with fierce, white halogen light. In the midst of grimy streets and darkened factories, it was all activity, all noise — police cars, radio talk back, men coming and going. Bullen's hair was still damp from washing and slicked back from his brow. There was a deep pain in his throat that analgesics had reduced to a hot throb.

He walked with Lacroix to the back of the warehouse, going between piles of crates until they reached the small side door that had been Blanchot's exit. Lacroix looked out. An alley led off into darkness. He pushed the door wider and the light showed the alley's mouth, a junction, a street beyond that. Against the sky were the outlines of tall buildings. The river was invisible.

He said, "We'll find him." Bullen could hear the lack of confidence.

The crates had been upturned and thrown around; they were all empty. When Bullen and Lacroix went back into the warehouse a small group of men were standing in a semicircle, all with their heads bowed like mourners at a graveside. One of them, a man wearing coveralls and a baseball cap, looked over his shoulder at Lacroix, then stepped out of the group, and Bullen could see the trapdoor thrown back and the solid square of blackness that lay beneath. Someone angled a lamp so that the walls became visible, and a flight of wooden stairs with a rope handrail.

Lacroix walked over and stood next to the man in coveralls. He asked, "What was on top of it?"

"Pallets. Under them, a tarpaulin. On top of the pallets, half a dozen crates holding machine parts."

"You mean it was hidden?"

"You can see the lines where the pallets stood. They might have been shifted from time to time, but they were always put back in the same spot. I'll send a couple of guys down."

"Who knows what we'll find." Lacroix was talking to Bullen. "Chests full of precious stones, statues inlaid with gold leaf and lapis lazuli, a three-headed dog, and then *Voilà,* the perfectly preserved body of the boy-king himself." The man in the coveralls must have spoken English because he stared at Lacroix a moment, then went back to stand by the edge of the trap. Lacroix followed him and took a lamp on a long cable from one of the men standing there. He asked, "Ready?" Bullen nodded and Lacroix went down the steps, one hand on the rope, the other holding the lamp aloft.

No Cerberus, no boy-king, no curse of the mummy's tomb, just twenty or more cases laid out along the far wall of the storage space. The room extended to about a third of the warehouse's total floor

152

area. Lacroix swung the light back and forth over the cases until Bullen took it from him and lit the wall close to the trap, illuminating the switches he'd expected to find. He pressed them all and a series of neon strips tacked to the ceiling joists flickered and hummed and came on one after the other. Close to the light switches was the running chain of a block and tackle.

The crates were labeled for Great Britain and Holland. Lacroix called out and the man in coveralls came down with a crowbar; he opened the cases one by one, exposing machine parts packed in grease and sandwiched between layers of heavy-duty cloth, Lacroix lifted them out. He asked Bullen, "What do you think we're going to find here? What's your bet?" He scooped the contents out onto the floor, cogs and pipes and ratchets, bright under their film of grease.

Lacroix stopped unloading the metal. He asked the guy in coveralls to get some of the other men. Bullen watched as they unpacked the machine parts. From the middle of each case they removed a cube of hashish about the size of a small suitcase and wrapped in plastic sheeting; the men stacked them eight long and three high, bringing the wall to eye level.

Lacroix said, "I'd like the chance to stand downwind when they burn it."

22

Lacroix was going from room to room in his apartment, Bullen following like someone being given a guided tour of an ancient monument. It was the evening of the day after they'd watched the hash wall being built in Blanchot's cellar and Bullen had a voice again — reedy, like the voice of someone who had smoked too many cigarettes.

"What we've got," Lacroix said, "is drug traffic. Pure and simple — is that correct?"

Bullen acknowledged the term. "Just that?" he asked. "Only that?"

Lacroix stopped dead in the half-empty living room — one chair, a small sofa, books collapsing on the shelves. "The bitch has even taken the TV." He went to the space where it had once stood and waved his arms through thin air as if to demonstrate the loss, then he crossed to a lone sideboard and looked inside. "Mother of Christ." He brought out a bottle of pastis. "Just this. Only this. No scotch, no cognac, no gin, no vodka . . . She knows I hate pastis; she knows that." He poured some into a glass and drank it off. "Fucking bitch." As an afterthought, he gave Bullen a drink before continuing to the kitchen. Without water, the liquor was powerful and sweet. Bullen sipped, leaving little milky threads where the moisture from his mouth had tainted the liquid. He topped up his glass from the kitchen tap and the pastis clouded to a dull yellow.

Lacroix was pulling open drawers with increasing savagery, yanking them out onto the floor. They were mostly empty. In the bedroom you could see pits in the carpet where the legs of the bed had once stood. Other dents spoke of wardrobe and dressing table. She had left a bedside table and a tallboy. A telephone sat in the middle of the room, its wire caught up in balls of dust. Lacroix hunkered down cross-legged and made three phone calls, yelling at Bullen between times as if Bullen had personally helped her to carry various items out to the moving van.

"No warning. Nothing. I left this morning, the place is intact. She's taken only the camera and the CD player. Okay. Now look — it's been ransacked!" One of the calls was to Kathy Blair, Bullen could tell from Lacroix's tone of voice and his responses.

After that, they checked the other rooms. She had taken what she wanted, taken the best. Bullen said, "Any trace of Blanchot?"

Lacroix glanced around, distractedly, as if Bullen's question were inappropriate in a moment of grief such as this. His wife had taken twelve years and the pick of their belongings. Three hundred kilos of hash and a gunfight were all in a day's work. As if he'd misheard, he said: "The man who was strangling you died on the operating table without ever having regained consciousness, so from him we will learn nothing. The other man will live" — he shrugged — "almost certainly . . ."

"I was talking about Blanchot."

"Yes, he's gone. I mean, we can't find him. His

office was clean — just business letters, business papers, nothing illegal.''

''You expect to find him, eventually?''

They were in a small workroom — swatches of material, carpet samples, color charts, catalogs for wall tiles and radiators and light fixtures — but it was bare of furniture. ''We *hope* to find him.''

''What did she do — your wife?''

''Interior designer.'' Lacroix indicated the catalogs and samples.

''These are old, not fashionable anymore. In this room there used to be a big drawing board, portfolios, two computers.'' Suddenly there was a note of nostalgia in his voice.

''And the thinking is that haulage and shipping and hashish and murder are two and two equals four? Not Mossad, not anti-Nazi groups.''

''What would you imagine?''

''Yes,'' Bullen said, ''I can see it makes sense. A cartel is organized — some people invest money, others provide trucks and ships. But you have to ask yourself how they got together — Arnaut and Roland Cecil, for example — how they knew about one another, what they had in common. And the answer is still that they were Nazis. You also have to ask yourself why they were killed.''

''They had rivals. Someone wanted their business.''

''I guess you're right,'' Bullen said. ''It must have been that. So it's a drugs case now?''

''That's how we'll treat it.'' He added, ''Whatever we find, Shelley will hear about. Okay?'' It meant: Go home; let's not hear from you again.

"And if it's drugs," Bullen said, "then Roland Cecil's role would have been to put up some of the money — for purchase, shipping, and so on."

"As part of a financing group — yes, of course."

Given what they'd found in the cellar it was the obvious explanation, but Bullen didn't believe it. Roland hadn't needed money; he was a man for causes. Arnaut and Blanchot, yes; haulage and shipping, yes. Perhaps there had been a deal, and perhaps Roland had been murdered because of it, but it wasn't just about a shipment of dope for the terminally stoned of London and Amsterdam.

"I ship steel out of the Ukraine," Blanchot had said. And hash as a sideline, perhaps, but Bullen remembered the news footage, the torches and drums, the flags, the black-and-red insignia.

They went back to the hallway, passing through rooms that held half of Paul Lacroix's life. He said, "All this is beginning to make me very sad."

"Perhaps she'll come back," Bullen suggested. "People often do."

"Not that. You. Everything is more complicated, now. The Drugs Squad is involved, I have a badly wounded man and two others who are dead, the press is inventing whatever they find most amusing. The air is thick with shit."

"I'm sorry," Bullen said. His voice sounded like a hasp going across metal.

"Cochrane has requested your return." Lacroix handed over a fax that could have been sent by anyone;

Bullen had never seen Cochrane's signature. "I'll drive you to your hotel to collect your things, then I'll put you on your plane. Okay?" It wasn't a question.

As they were leaving the apartment, Bullen thought to ask: "Why did you bring me here?" He had spent most of the day at his hotel, waiting for Lacroix to find an excuse for kicking him out of Paris. "We could have gone straight to the airport."

"I wondered whether she might be here. I wondered whether I might find a note explaining things. I should have waited; my apologies."

"What do you think will happen?"

"We'll find Blanchot, do a little plea bargaining, find out who's involved, who organized the killings in Brittany, who's been funding the —"

"I meant your wife."

"We have a good life; she'll come back."

"Bringing the furniture with her?"

Lacroix closed his own front door. He looked bleak. "I'm glad you're leaving Paris, Bullen. It's definitely time for you to go."

23

Warm autumn nights in west London mean busy roads and a racket in the side streets. There is a tang of nitrous oxide in the air, like the scent of a night flower that eats meat. Waiters bring food out to the crowded roadside tables. A film of dust collects on the surface of your wine.

Inside, the restaurant was cool and quiet: six tables were occupied. At one of them a man ate alone, reading a battered copy of a book called *Letters from a Dead Land*. It was propped up against the little silver boat that held oil and vinegar. The man was having lasagne and a green salad.

Close to the door — near enough to share the warm night without having to share the pollution — were four people who were just getting into their third bottle of wine. Hugh Macallun was pouring, filling the glasses of his guests first, then that of his wife, Susan, then his own. The guests were really there because of his wife — a school friend, Ruth Logan, and her husband, visiting London from Edinburgh.

Hugh didn't mind them; they were boring, but they could be ignored. He was letting his mind drift to a business matter that had been troubling him for a few days; it had to do with moving funds from one place to another without leaving any trace. Normally, he wouldn't have been in need of funds, but he was getting set to help finance something extraordinary.

The man dining alone was there to kill Hugh Macallun; in fact, he'd followed the Macalluns and their guests to the restaurant and could have done the job at any time, but once he'd waited for them to sit down and for the waiter to get out of the way, he'd begun to feel a little hungry and considered that some pasta and a salad would go down pretty well. He'd even allowed himself a single glass of the house wine.

Now he put the last forkful of lasagne in his mouth and mopped up his salad dressing with a chunk of bread, but continued to sit at his table, reading his book and glancing toward the window from time to time, as if a friend might still appear: late, apologetic, but welcome.

Macallun and those with him were ordering dessert. As the waiter passed back toward the kitchen, the killer waved an arm and asked for an espresso. He knew that he was savoring the moment; in fact, he knew that he had always intended to. Shooting Macallun in the first couple of minutes would have been a waste, like fuck and run. He liked to see the man behaving as if nothing would happen that night but a taxi home, a shower to get the grime off, a final brandy . . .

He watched Macallun smile at the woman opposite, make some reply, then slip away again into his own thoughts. He was sitting at right angles to Macallun and his wife, so he didn't miss the moment when Susan reached across, stirring the tablecloth, to slip a hand briefly between her husband's thighs. The gesture produced a jolt of pure pleasure in the killer. He thought: That's something else that won't happen tonight, my friend.

While Macallun was writing a check, the killer finished a certain passage in his book: *"How little resistance, my hand across her mouth as if to stifle any harsh word she might have had for me. . . . she died softly, as such creatures die, her face in the lamplight growing ever more distant. Later, I slept at her side like one who has found his heart's ease."*

He closed the book, put down enough cash to cover his meal, and dropped five pounds on top of that: he'd enjoyed the evening and wanted to show his appreciation by leaving a good tip.

The restaurant had filled up — only three tables left unoccupied — but that was fine, since the whole idea was that Macallun's death should be a public event, just like the others. He walked toward Macallun's table, which was the same thing as walking toward the door. In the same moment, Susan Macallun glanced toward her friend — she was about to suggest they have a final drink at home. She said, "Ruth, would you —," then stopped, transfixed. What she saw was a man advancing with a gun in his hand.

She stood up and extended her arm. It was an odd gesture, as if she were waving him off, or might persuade him to change his mind about what he intended to do. The killer gave a little hiss of annoyance: she was a distraction, also a warning to the others. Already, Ruth's husband was looking for the source of Susan's alarm and Macallun was turning in his seat.

The killer shot Susan Macallun twice in the chest, sending her back against the window of the restaurant like a slammed door. She struck and leapt forward, arms extended like a swimmer, leaving a great irregular star of red on the glass. She fell across her husband and the bullet that was meant for him struck her high in the shoulder.

It happened fast and slow, like a dream fragment. The killer let go a howl of rage and hauled Susan's body off by the hair. Macallun was getting to his feet. The gunman had to shoot him three times to make the kill; the last bullet hit Macallun in the throat, angling upward and lodging in his brain.

Ruth's husband was part of the dream fragment; he had no idea what he was doing, but as Macallun was taking the third bullet he rounded the table, arms extended like someone about to embrace a friend. He grabbed the killer, bearing him backward, and they danced together in a mad improvised jig.

The gunman wrestled and writhed but couldn't shake the man off. In the restaurant, people were rising, running, getting clear, ducking under tables. About twenty seconds had passed, though later people would say a minute, two minutes, three. . . . There was a shot, and Ruth's husband teetered backward, hit in the leg. He stumbled toward his wife, who was backed up against the restaurant window, breathless, about to pass out, then the leg wouldn't hold him and he fell among chairs and coffee cups and broken glass. The killer lined up and shot him square in the face with the last bullet in the clip.

He left behind a frozen moment. People sitting at tables outside the restaurant watched him go as if his departure were frames on a movie reel; things around him seemed brightly colored and bigger than they could have been in life.

Ruth had blacked out and come around again. She still couldn't get her breath. She was sitting in a chair at the table she'd shared with her husband and the Macalluns, one hand to her face, the other lying in a puddle of blood on the tabletop, fingers drumming like someone waiting for an overdue train. She looked at the three bodies on the restaurant floor and saw how people crouched by them, and turned them, but couldn't decide why that was happening. A voice spoke in her ear; the words were too distant for connection. Hands gripped her shoulders and she allowed herself to be raised and moved and put into a vehicle.

She said, "Are they all right?"

Much later, days later, someone told her they were dead. She said, "I know. I know that. But are they all right?"

She wasn't able to give a description of the killer, but lots of people had already done that. It was an accurate description. It fitted exactly a man who had broadsided a brand-new Buick on a crosstown street in Manhattan at just the time Hugh Macallun was being shot.

The man was happy to accept that the accident was his fault. He soothed the angry Buick owner: "I ran the light. I'm sorry. My mistake." People had gathered, a small circle of spectators. He said, "Listen — I ran the light; I admit it." He shrugged, his pale, liver-lipped, snub-nosed face shining with honesty.

24

When Bullen walked into his apartment, the first thing he saw was a note propped up on a bookshelf, a note explaining things, the sort of note Paul Lacroix had been searching for. *". . . when I asked you how much longer you thought the relationship had got?*

Was I the only one thinking about that? I can't believe I was. I never wanted much, but I wanted something. I suppose I hoped we could belong to each other in some sort of a way. . . . You don't know what I mean, do you? I'm sorry . . ."

Bullen poured himself a drink and sat down to reread Anne's message. I *do* know what you mean, he thought, but I don't know how to get it. I wish to God I did. He put the note in a drawer and freshened his drink, then went back to the drawer, took the note out, and threw it away. He lifted the phone and dialed his mother's number, then hung up after the second ring. He felt restless, as if he could sense the onset of some minor illness. He put the videotape of Roland's murder into the machine and ran it through. He was watching it for the third time when he realized that Anne was in the room with him. She said, "I came to get a few things . . . and leave my key."

"Did you want the TV?" he asked.

She was puzzled. "The TV?"

"It's a joke. I knew someone, his wife left him, she took the TV. It upset him; I couldn't quite understand why it should matter to him so much, but it did. She also took the bed."

"It's not my TV, it's not my bed, and I'm not your wife," Anne pointed out. "This isn't my apartment. There's the difference." Then she asked: "Are you all right?"

He shrugged. "Fine, yes," as if people left him often, as if he never minded; then he realized she meant his voice and he said, "A cold . . . it's nothing."

She put the key on the table. He couldn't look at her,

so he looked at the TV screen instead. He was running through his lines: *I find it tough to belong to things. I find it tough to have things belong to me. I don't save things: keepsakes, photos, documents. I haven't got the knack for ordinary living.* He didn't get a chance at it, because Anne said, "I've seen this before." Like him, she was looking at the TV.

"Sure. It was shown on all the news programs."

"No," she said, "not *this* before — not exactly this. I was in Bosnia — remember? Reporting the news, not watching it. But I've seen it in another version."

Bullen turned to her and stared. "Another version?"

"A different occasion." She was staring too, but at the screen. "A different country. But a man walks in like the angel of death and starts shooting." They both watched as the killer approached the graveside. "Not any man" — Anne picked up the TV remote control and pressed Pause, holding the image — "that man."

The room was a band of light in a dark tower block. Anne and Bullen sat at one end, screened by the dark blue half wall of her office space. She showed him the CNN report of the wedding in New England.

He said, "Can I have this?"

"It's news," Anne said, "and I work for a newspaper. No one has looked at the two events in tandem. It's the same man doing the killing. These people" — she nodded toward the bride as she died — "and Roland Cecil and Benoit Arnaut."

He wondered how much he ought to tell her — now that she was leaving him, now that she was becoming more important and more distant. No more than before, he realized. Her understanding was limited to his initial contact with Seacourt and their tangle with the men who had wanted to rape her. He realized that her decision to end things made him less easy to trust.

He said: "Give me some time on it."

Anne looked at him, her face solemn. "How long have we been seeing one another?"

"Two years."

"On and off," she reminded him. "Your terms, your pace. I wonder how much I know about you, Tom. I think I ought to know more." She switched the TV off and ejected the tape. "Okay, you're Roland Cecil's nephew, he dies in very public circumstances, you read his diaries. He's a fascist, his diaries mention Arthur Seacourt — but mention him in a cryptic and intriguing kind of way — so you decide to find out what that might mean. That's all okay, I suppose, except that you're acting a bit like some sort of policeman. But then why not? Maybe it's fun; you don't need a job and you don't live the sort of life that keeps most men happy. Now I show you a tape that suddenly makes things very complicated, very puzzling. Cecil's killer has killed other people — same man, same method — and no one has noticed this fact. Most people would take this tape to the police. What I would do is write the story, *then* take it to the police. You ask me to give you time on it."

"How long will you be in Bosnia?"

"A week."

"Until then."

"I can't do that. Do you really expect me to do that?"

"Anne, I don't know what this tape means. I'm not keeping secrets from you."

"About the tape — maybe, maybe not. Other secrets, though."

"What difference can it make? This is an old story. Tell it now, tell it in a week's time . . ."

"Jesus Christ, Tom . . ." Anne passed a hand over her eyes, then glanced at the blank TV screen, remembering the image of the bride who'd died on her wedding day. "I don't want to leave you, I don't want to go back to Bosnia, I don't want to be thinking the things I'm thinking."

"When you come back, come back to me." She stared at him, then laughed. He knew how bald it sounded, how tentative. He made things worse by adding, "There are things I ought to tell you that I can't tell you now."

"Ah . . . yes . . ." She dropped her head a moment, then looked at him directly: the look was enlightenment and disappointment and fear. "And you'll tell me when I get back?"

"Yes."

"And that's when I can write a story on the tape and that's when I'll hear the truth and it'll all make sense and when I come back I should come back to you — right?" There were tears at the brink of her eyes, rage or misery, and her mouth had gone lopsided. "That's the deal?"

"I'm not offering you a deal; don't think of it like that."

She reached across and took the tape out of the VCR, then tossed it into his lap. She said, "Fuck you," so softly that he read it on her lips but didn't hear it. He thought his next move was to get up and walk away, taking the tape with him, leaving her with the half-assed promise he'd made.

Instead, she got up and walked away from him.

A summer storm had turned the afternoon light a sulphurous yellow under blue-black clouds. People walking behind the glass walls of Vauxhall Cross had the cool luminosity of figures traversing a cave behind a waterfall.

Cochrane and Bullen emerged into the light and rode upward in the glassine elevator, the river behind them, two messengers from the underworld. Cochrane was holding the videotapes.

Bullen said, "What does it mean?"

"You're curious," Cochrane observed. "I'm certainly curious. Why not take it further — find out for yourself. Find out for us, too."

Bullen's voice still had a pebbly roughness about it. "I've come close to getting very badly hurt on two separate occasions," he said. "No one's paying me to do this."

"It's money?" Cochrane asked. "Well that's not a problem."

"An idiom," Bullen said. "It means I'm not in your debt."

"I see, not money. So what do you want?"

"A quieter life." When the elevator doors opened they stepped out. "Ask someone else."

Cochrane looked crestfallen. He said, "You've taken things this far . . . ," but he shrugged and shook

168

hands and walked away as if his mind were already on some other problem.

Bullen was leaving the building when Cochrane arrived with an afterthought: "I'm sorry about Seacourt."

"I'm sorry, too." Bullen was angry, but he intended to wait for an explanation. "He tried to have me killed. I thought you understood that he was a danger to me."

Cochrane nodded. "I'm really sorry," he said, and patted Bullen's arm, then walked past, taking the door first, heading for his car. The driver was holding the door open. Cochrane nodded at Bullen, a lifted hand, a diminishing smile.

He was drinking a vodka-tonic with a slice of lime. It was his sixth and he was slow in his movements; he had to think about what he was going to say. The telephone exaggerated the sluggishness, making him sound weary.

Anne said, "You're drunk."

"A little; not so it matters."

"Don't say anything you'll regret."

"What would that be?"

"Don't make any promises. Don't say anything about love or the past or the future."

"All right." He started to eat the lime. "I've been missing something."

"Please . . ."

"No, missing something about Roland, about the deaths, about the reasons for the deaths." He swal-

169

lowed and gave a tiny shudder at the green sharpness. "About why Roland died. If I know that, I know lots of things."

"What will you do?"

"Go back to Yorkshire."

"To your mother?"

"He used to visit her often; they were close. Maybe he talked to her about things that mattered. I don't know."

"Are you doing this for yourself?"

"For myself."

"Of course I don't believe that." A long pause drifted between them. Bullen poured himself a drink one-handed and lost track of the time. She said, "Tom . . . why did you call?"

"I'll be a day," he said, "away for just one day. I'll take you to the airport."

"I don't think that's a good idea."

"I'll take you to the airport and when you come back, come back to me."

They waited for each other to speak, but there was nothing to say that could make a change. Bullen drifted off to sleep with the phone still to his ear.

He was deep underground, in a part of the cave that was utterly silent — no movement of water, no earth sounds, no echo. He looked back, intending to remember the way in, but could see no opening or shaft; he looked forward and saw only a white wall of flowstone, fixed and viscous.

Images formed there, dim and imprecise, as if a screen lay behind the slow, white lava of the calcium.

They terrified him in the dream, though he forgot them on waking.

It was past dawn. His neck was sore because he'd slept sitting up. When he hung up the phone, it rang immediately. Anne's voice said, "I was worried."

"The phone was off the hook; I went to sleep."

She said, "If you're taking me to the airport, it's now. I've got a flight on Croatian Airlines to Zagreb, then on to Split, then I hitch a lift with the UN."

While they waited for her flight to be called, she showed him a map of the city. "The idea is to starve them out; also to take a daily toll with the bombardment and sniper fire. There's no electricity, little food, and you queue for water. Last winter people tore up the floorboards in their apartments and used them for fuel. There are farm boys up in the hills, drunk on Slivovic; it's like shooting hens in a barn."

He kissed her once, slipping a hand under her jacket to find her breast. He said, "It's not what you think."

"No? Then why did you want me to keep quiet about the tape?"

"When I see you next — I'll tell you then."

"Telling me might be the worst thing."

Cochrane looked at the image on the screen — a close-up from the New England wedding. You could see the killer plainly. You could see who he was killing.

Shelley asked, "When did you get this?"

"Bullen brought it in."

"Where is he?"

"Visiting his mother, I think he said." Cochrane yawned. "It's the same man."

Shelley nodded. "The man who killed Benoit Arnaut and Roland Cecil."

"Also the man who killed Hugh Macallun. But who is he?"

"Who does he work for — that's more the question."

"Yes, it is; I agree. Let's hope Bullen will provide the answer. He seems good at making a stir. We'll have to talk to someone in America. Preferably someone who owes us a favor."

"I think Bullen's gone as far as he intends to go."

"I know," Cochrane said. "He gave me the tape on the understanding that we leave him alone. A trade. He ought to know better than that."

"He's not easily pushed."

"In the wood," Cochrane said, "there's a cave; in the cave, there's a bear. You want to catch the bear, use a bear trap. Send someone into the wood to find the cave; then send him into the cave to find the bear."

"He said he wouldn't."

"I know what he said, I was there." Cochrane smiled. "For every bear trap, you first need bait. Dead meat will do it."

Several warm days and nights had made things worse.

She was a lumpy sack, chock-full of bad air. Her

172

skin had discolored to purples and greens; maggots foamed at the crook of her elbow, foamed in the fold of her chin. You could still see the shape that had been cut into her forehead, dull red with black blood tracks over her cheeks. Flies were knocking the window-panes, then returning to swarm.

Nothing must change; every evening must be like this.

Bullen saw how white had grown under the false gold in his mother's hair. He stood in the room and breathed the air, even though it carried the worst stench he'd ever smelled, the stench of his own mother's putrefaction.

No tradesmen, no friends, no anxious neighbors to wonder where she was. For the first time, he saw how she had lived her life these past years: ignoring people and ignored by them; isolated, half-awake, dreaming of the past. Roland had been her only contact, but not with the world — with shadows.

Bullen looked at his mother's corpse and wondered what the effort of hating her had cost him. He squatted down beside her as if some penance could be made simply by being there, by seeing what he saw, by breathing that air. Something stirred in a fold of her dress and he shuddered but held his ground.

"You mad old bitch," he said. "I remember you. All my childhood, all my life, I couldn't wring a drop of love out of you. I remember." He shifted in order to be able to look directly at her face: the crooked red legs of the swastika, the grape-dark eyes.

"Where are you?" he said. "Are you far under-ground, in the darkest part of the cave, in the depths?

Are you rotting in hell?"

Every word dry-eyed.

Cochrane's office was dappled with late-afternoon sunlight; a glass paperweight threw a rainbow across his desk. He asked, "Why are you telling me?"

"Can you do something?" Bullen wanted a drink but didn't want to ask.

Cochrane shrugged. He said, "Yes, of course. What could be easier? Heart attack, a quick cremation: standard stuff . . . Why do you think she was killed?" Bullen had spoken of the swastika adorning her forehead. "Something she knew about? Something she might have remembered?"

The lower band of the rainbow just clipped a report folder which held an account of Bullen's time in Paris.

"I don't know."

"It's connected though." Cochrane lifted the folder and let it fall. "It has to be connected."

"Of course."

A police sketch skated to Bullen's side of the desk. "That man killed someone in Chelsea last night," Cochrane said. "Several people, in fact, but most important a man named Hugh Macallun. Macallun owned a trucking business, mostly containers carrying white goods, radios, hi-fi systems. White goods?" Bullen shook his head. "Fridges, washing machines, stoves, dishwashers."

Bullen looked at the sketch without picking it up. "The same man."

"Yes. See any other similarity?"

"Shipping and trucking."

"Yes."

Bullen rubbed his eyes with his knuckled fists, as if he were thinking the matter through.

Cochrane asked, "Will you be there? At the funeral?"

"No, I won't be there."

"You told us that Paris would be the end for you."

"It's different now."

"Why is it different?"

Bullen looked up. "Someone murdered my mother; I thought I'd mentioned that to you."

"It's just . . ." Cochrane let the remark drift away, then retrieved it. "You don't seem to mind that much."

"I'll need some stuff."

"It's yours."

"I'll need all the press clippings and TV news reports on the killings."

"That's no problem."

Bullen sat in silence for a moment. Then he asked: "Do you know what I'm looking for?"

"No, of course not."

"What can you tell me?"

Cochrane shrugged. "I started with a dead MP; now I've got Nazis and drugs and Christ knows what. I'm asking for help." As if to underline the mystery, he said: "Lacroix tells me that Blanchot has gone to ground. They can't find him; they wonder whether he might be dead."

Bullen said, "I'll need some sort of ID — official status."

"Don't worry. We'll see to it that you have access to things."

"People."

"Yes, people . . ." Cochrane went to the window of his office and looked at the river traffic. He seemed edgy suddenly, as if matters were moving too far too fast. He asked, "Cremation's all right, then?"

Bullen said, "You'll need the signatures of two doctors."

"Sure," Cochrane said, "well, we can handle that." He strolled back to his desk. "Seacourt. You think Seacourt had anything to do with it?"

"Maybe."

Cochrane decided that Bullen was burying his grief. He thought, Dig as deep as you like, it's fertile ground. "Report to me," he said, "I'll keep Shelley informed."

The photograph showed her in a ball gown, but she was walking through the long grass of the orchard; you could see where the scalloped hem dragged in the morning dew. It had been her best memory; it was the only thing he'd brought away with him.

He said, "You think it's that easy? You think it's as simple as that?"

He was sitting on the tiny balcony that faced west from his apartment. It was close to midnight, but the city was lit for a fiesta; planes went over, one every thirty seconds, their navigation lights dancing.

"You think I can let you go? You think I can let someone take you away from me? There were still things to be said. I was waiting to hear you say them.

176

I've been waiting all my fucking life."

Voices drifted up from the street — laughter, a girl screaming for fun, someone calling a name. He hadn't eaten all day, so he'd made a sandwich and taken it out to the balcony with him, but it remained untouched. He was drinking, though.

His childhood came back to him in jagged images of loathing and desire. There was more than enough light to see the beautiful, golden-haired girl in the scalloped gown as she drifted between the trees. The disembodied arm, amputated by the photographer, would have been Roland's or his father's.

"Did I steal your youth? Did I make you ugly? No . . . you were just looking for someone to blame." Bullen took a long drink and felt the booze hit like a depth charge. "But look what you did to me. . . ."

Hour by hour the city closed down, the lights diminished, the voices faded. It wasn't the first time he'd cried in the dark.

25

Next day he worked.

The reports of the deaths in Brittany told him nothing new. He looked for a long time at the TV coverage of the Duval wedding and read the clippings. There were many eyewitnesses, but one name came clear: Sonia Bishop.

There had been many eyewitnesses to Hugh Macallun's death, too. They all said pretty much the same thing except Ruth Logan, who hadn't said anything.

Bullen lifted the phone and made a call to Cochrane; half an hour or so later, he arrived at the hospital where Ruth was receiving treatment. He spoke to a doctor called Trotman who spoke in metaphors.

"You won't find her here. She's in hiding."

"You're talking about trauma," Bullen said, "am I right?"

"Yes."

"I mean, she's here in the hospital?"

"You can talk to her; she can't talk back."

"Won't?"

"Can't."

Bullen had always feared the people who work around pain and death; it wasn't their courage, but their matter-of-factness that made dying real. He asked, "Have you tried?"

"Well, not really. A number of your colleagues had a go — against my better judgment. She's not damaged in any way that you can see."

"Something might have been said during the course of the evening. Macallun might have said something before he died — shouted a name, given some sign. Any version of what went on beyond 'man shoots people' could be helpful."

"I think 'man shoots husband' is the way she sees it — or tries not to see it." They were sitting in a tiny anteroom that served as Trotman's office. The paraphernalia of illness was everywhere. "The fact is," he said, "that questions aren't helping her, and they're not helping the police. She's tranquilized and she's

178

struggling hard to find a place inside her own head where what happened simply isn't true."

"Can I try?" Bullen asked.

Trotman slapped his desk and half turned in his chair, staring at a shelf of books as if something there might offer a remedy for cold-heartedness. "I've been told I can't prevent you," he said, "but I can insist on being there."

Bullen spent twenty minutes with Ruth Logan. He looked at her, but she never looked at him. He spoke a lot; she spoke twice: "Are they all right?" and "Ask someone to bring the car around." Bullen felt sick and helpless; he asked questions that she couldn't answer because her own life had become mysterious to her.

Trotman walked Bullen through a warren of corridors to the main entrance as if anxious to see him off the premises.

That night Bullen ran through the American footage and the press cuttings, trawling them for differences, for similarities, for anything that might tell him what to do next. He kept coming back to the girl.

Sonia Bishop's face in a newspaper photo, grainy halftones that made her seem solemn, as a witness should.

Her face on the TV coming into slow close-up as she described what she'd seen from the window.

Her face showing the stress of recollection — a tightness about the mouth, blue-gray eyes calling back the images of death.

26

A narrow face, not glamorous or traditionally pretty but handsome in the way of Renaissance women — long nose, high cheekbones, subtle shadows along the plane of either cheek. Her hair was straw blond and fell heavily to her shoulders. Sonia looked up and smiled as Bullen came to her table; he might have been a friend she hadn't seen for years. She had chosen a restaurant in Little Italy because she lived in the East Village and Bullen didn't know New York well enough to have an opinion.

They said their names to each other; Bullen showed her the fancy ID that Cochrane had given him. They ordered some food. Bullen drank a glass of mineral water straight off and gave himself a refill. "Jet lag," he explained.

Sonia said, "I'm intrigued, of course I am. I spoke to a man called Roscoe Tate about you. He said you were" — she looked for a term — "official."

"I'm not very official," Bullen said. "In fact, I've never been official in my life." As he spoke, he realized it sounded flirtatious.

"You know him — Tate?"

"I know who he is."

Before leaving, Bullen had contacted Cochrane and had been given a number to call. Roscoe Tate was a CIA operative who owed Stuart Cochrane a couple of favors. His voice on the phone had sounded both weary and wary. "It's okay to come here," he'd said. "It's okay to talk to Sonia Bishop — hell, in the first week after the killings the media did that nonstop. But you have no authority, no license to act independently, and you report to me. Just to me. I hope you can live with that. It's a police matter over here — no one killed a congressman or whatever; but you're SIS and that makes you my problem."

"No problem," Bullen had told him.

"That's limited cooperation from me, total cooperation from you. Probably sounds like a shit deal, but I'm just trying to make things plain to you." The good-humored tone had done nothing to disguise Tate's warning.

"I understand." Bullen had been sitting in his apartment, waiting for a cab to take him to the airport. He'd added: "Maybe we could meet up while I'm in New York."

"Maybe?" Tate had chuckled. "I'll be on your case, pal. I hear there are things you know that we don't. I can't tell you how nervous that makes me. We'll meet; forget maybe."

Sonia had ordered antipasti and spaghetti alle vóngole; she had the kind of figure that didn't carry weight — tall, slim hipped, narrow waisted. She said, "I've told everyone everything; you must have seen the TV and press coverage."

"I have, yes. The difference between you and all the other eyewitnesses is that you had time to watch. You weren't in the line of fire; your view of things

181

wasn't blurred by panic."

"You think so?"

"Fear, shock, astonishment — I don't know; but not panic. You saw what happened from beginning to end. You saw more than anyone else."

"I've told more than anyone else."

Bullen was looking for the kind of edge Jacques Nicolle had given him — the old man who'd spat on the flag. In that single gesture, Bullen had seen someone whose involvement in events had gone beyond a simple reaction to a horrifying moment, someone who might have seen what others had missed.

"How many times have you watched the video — who was it . . . ?"

"An outfit called Memories. They give you back the treasured day." Bullen was slightly startled by the remark until he picked up the trace of irony and realized that Sonia was quoting from an advertising brochure. She took a swallow of wine and started to eat as if to distract herself, then answered his question. "I guess I must have watched it fifty times."

"Ever see anything you couldn't explain?"

"Nope. Everything was as normal as weddings can be." She seemed to have a sudden recollection. "One thing — after the vows, some guy turned up with an automatic weapon and shot a number of people dead, then was airlifted out laughing fit to bust. That was a little out of the ordinary."

"You've told this story to a lot of people," Bullen said. "I accept that. I'm sorry."

"I'm not mad at you." She laughed, shaking her head, and her hair swung across her face. "I thought

182

the English were supposed to have a wry sense of humor.'' She seemed genuinely apologetic and Bullen liked her for it, liked her openness. As if to make amends, she said, ''There's something I can't see that bothers me — when I come to look at the video.''

"Can't see?"

"Well, I don't know if it's there and I can't see it, or whether it's not there and I think it ought to be, or whether it's something I'm seeing but can't recognize, or seeing but not understanding."

"You lost me."

"I lost myself. Each time I get through watching the tape, I realize that something's nagging at me, something wrong or something odd, but if I run the tape through again I can't find it."

"Describe it to me."

"I just did."

"No, describe it as a feeling, a smell, a taste; anything it's not."

Sonia wound spaghetti onto her fork, then let it lie in the bowl. Bullen had only wanted soup; he was still on English time. For the same reason, he felt a little drunk from the wine. He watched as Sonia tried to come up with a metaphor for something she couldn't remember. There was a delicate line of blond down on her jawline that ran back to a tiny, soft whorl just under her ear.

Finally, she said: "It's something out of kilter, like when you're alone in the house, you know you're alone, and your folks won't be back for a couple of hours, and you hear the cellar door close."

Bullen knew that she was describing something from her own childhood. He said, "Shouldn't be there; shouldn't be happening . . ."

"That's the closest I can come," she said.

"The sound of the cellar door closing." He saw the way she shivered, then turned the shiver into a shrug.

"But I can't see where it is."

Bullen decided that he was going to take a risk. He said, "There's something I want to show you. It'll have to be your place, because I don't have a VCR at my hotel."

Sonia poured the last of the wine, taking time to think. She asked, "Why does Chianti come in little raffia jackets?"

Bullen gave the question mature consideration. "Regular bottle, no raffia, twelve dollars; fat-assed bottle with raffia, eighteen fifty."

She acknowledged the invention with a likable, lopsided grin. "So you're a sort of cop, that right?"

"Well, I'm like Roscoe Tate, except there's more to it than that."

"More what? More how?"

"That's part of what I want to show you."

After they'd watched Bullen's news video twice, Sonia asked: "How did you find out?"

"A friend of mine, a journalist; I was playing the funeral tape and she'd seen a CNN roundup that included the Duval murders."

Bullen took the tape back to a place where Roland and Arnaut were at the graveside, the killer just in view. He said, "The man on the right was my mother's brother."

"Jesus Christ." She looked at Bullen as if he'd just confessed to the killings himself. "You're in deep, aren't you?" She used his own phrase, but said it with real feeling: "It's a family affair."

"It's a coincidence; they happen."

"Who knows about the other incident?"

Bullen handed her the police likeness. "Incidents. He shot three people in a London restaurant a few days ago. Everyone who ought to know knows. What we don't know is why."

"Or who," Sonia observed. She looked at the sketch, then back toward the screen where Bullen had put the tape on pause. The killer was confronting Arnaut and Roland; it was a moment in the sequence of events when both men were on the brink of death. "Who the hell are those guys? I mean, what's all this with the fancy dress; they look crazy."

"They're not crazy," Bullen said, "not in the sense you mean. It's a solid movement, all over Europe. They march, they burn the houses where foreign workers and refugees live, they attack those people in the streets, they attack blacks, they attack Jews. They fly flags and wear armbands and guess where you heard all this before."

"Who are they?"

"They're the same people they ever were."

"And he was your mother's brother."

"Well" —Bullen's turn to be wry — "I never liked him much."

"Did your mother like him?"

"There's something else," Bullen said, "and no one's mentioned it, so I guess no one's noticed it. According to the news reports, the Duval family died at about midday, is that right? The Friday."

"Noon, yes."

"So what happens is that the killer murders the Duvals, the helicopter flies him out, he catches a plane to Paris, travels to Brittany, kills Arnaut and Roland Cecil."

"You're saying the killings happened on the same day?" The time control on the freeze frame expired, switching the TV on automatically; two riders were coming in from the Badlands with a third man slung over his saddlebow. Sonia hit the Off button and went into her kitchen. "Can I get you something?" Bullen had been drinking vodka.

"Coffee," Bullen told her.

She brought a cup for herself and sat down to listen. He said, "Yes, the same day. New England, midday; Brittany, five o'clock in the afternoon. There's a five-hour time difference. Work it out." The guy had ten hours.

"Seem possible to you?"

"It's — what? — a six-hour flight?"

"Seven, seven and a half . . ."

"Three hours to spare. In that time he has to get to Kennedy, board a plane — let's assume a scheduled airline — get to Paris, from Paris get to a village in northern Brittany."

Sonia said, "They call you right up until the plane's going to taxi out. He wouldn't have been checking any baggage, would he?"

186

"No." Bullen laughed. "I bet he packed the Uzi in his walk-on luggage; I mean, who would have noticed?"

Sonia's apartment wasn't quite a loft, there were too many walls, but the large central area had three black iron pillars and a wood-block floor. She made a tour of the room, circling the three sofas that set the boundaries of the living area. The sofas were old and didn't match; they had cotton throws over the original fabric. A big country dresser stood against one wall, close to the entrance to the kitchen. She took their cups back into the kitchen and started to make fresh coffee. Bullen followed her in.

"Couldn't it be done?" she asked.

"Not without lots of help," Bullen said, "even then it's doubtful. The gun alone makes for a major problem."

"Okay, so he had help."

"Yes, well, that would certainly make things more mysterious."

"They're pretty mysterious already."

"Look at the pattern — look at what we're saying might have happened. A man kills several people in broad daylight at a society wedding in New England. A helicopter takes him out. The helicopter takes him directly to JFK airport, where he's booked on a plane leaving for Paris."

Sonia set the coffeepot on the stove. "Is there one at that time?"

"I haven't checked yet; I will. But suppose there is. Okay, he gets to Paris where there's a helicopter waiting. It flies him to the hill above the church with still enough time left for him to walk the ground and think about how he's going to handle things. Forget the time factor for a moment — what does the rest of it tell you?"

"Last evening," Sonia told him, "Ross Tate called me and asked if I'd be prepared to talk with you. I couldn't see what harm it could do; I couldn't see what good it might do, either. Now this." She spread her hands to take in the tape and Bullen's explanations and the puzzle they presented.

"I'm sorry." Bullen watched as Sonia shook her head and turned to attend to the coffee. Her hair flicked around her eyes; she was being mobbed by memories.

"I have dreams, you know? I dream about it all the time. I see his face, you understand? I see Caro Duval dying and her husband dying and her mother and father dying, and then I see his face as he rises up toward me in the helicopter."

Bullen thought she was going to say more, but she handed him his coffee and went past him into the loft space. When he joined her, she was crying; he sat down and waited until she stopped.

"I'm making things awkward for you."

"Awkward?" She laughed, cuffing the tears away. "I don't think so. I think that mad son of a bitch who killed Caro Duval has made things *awkward*." She paused as if the idea had never occurred to her before. "My life has changed. I guess I'm finding it difficult to adjust."

Bullen noticed that she was holding his jacket. He'd taken it off when they arrived in the apartment, and now she had picked it up and folded her arms over it, the collar resting in the crook of her neck. He couldn't decide whether she was seeking comfort or wanted him to leave.

He said, "I'd like to watch the Duval tape with you sometime." It was after 1 A.M. and he was in free-fall: no time zone, no sense of geography. His tone of voice was like a nudge in the ribs: *Let's do it now!*

"It's late, okay?" She sounded weary; her eyes flicked around the apartment, restless, trying to find a way to ask him to go.

"Sometime."

"Sure."

Bullen got up. He asked, "Where will I find a cab? I don't know the city."

Sonia handed him his jacket, the Roland Cecil videotape, and the briefcase he'd brought to the restaurant, then walked with him to the door.

She said, "Going uptown? You'll get one on Third Avenue. Don't walk into the Bowery."

She stood in the hallway as he started down the two flights of stairs to the street. She said, "It wasn't what I'd expected."

He turned after half a flight and asked, "Tomorrow — is that okay?" but she was closing the door.

New York was making its own heat. The night was soft and damp; sirens were distant, then close.

Bullen walked up Second for a way, then across to Third, where he flagged down a cab.

He rode uptown in a bare cage, sitting on torn leather and springs. Outside people moved quickly, heads down as if they were targets, as if dying were an easy option.

Sonia Bishop's scent lay on the collar of his jacket.

27

She called at ten-thirty and Bullen got out of the shower to answer the phone. It had rung twenty times or so, which let him know that she really wanted to talk to him.

"I don't know how to say this — how to make it make sense."

"Try."

"It's like a mild illness: I feel feverish. It's just lack of sleep, really. What I'm trying to say . . . I work in a design studio — a co-op, we've got an office uptown. This sounds left field, but it's not. I'm here now, I'm working on some costume designs for an Off-Broadway show. I've done a lot of this. I mean, I do it every day and it ought to feel normal, just a normal day's work, but I'm having trouble. There seems to be a world where this is possible — going to work, eating a meal, that sort of stuff — and a world where people get gunned down at weddings and funerals. I'm not sure which is the world I live in, which is normal for me — make any sense? I think this has been coming on for a long time — ever since I saw them die. I feel as if the dream has moved in."

"Why are you telling me this?"

"You're part of the dream." There was a long pause; Bullen tried to think of a way to let her escape. She said, "Look, this is just tiredness. It *is* tiredness; I feel woozy. I didn't sleep at all."

"Shall I pick you up at your office?"

"Okay, do that."

"I have someone to see first."

"Jesus," she said, "I didn't mean now. I've got a living to earn."

"What time?"

"Five-thirty." She gave him an address on Broadway. "I've been thinking. Early this morning, I got up and made some tea and thought about things. You're a spook, right? Roscoe Tate's a spook."

Bullen laughed. "If that's what you want me to be."

The other spook arrived at Bullen's hotel at midday and they sat in black leather armchairs in the lobby like passengers in transit.

"Stuart Cochrane tells me there are things you have to tell me."

Bullen said, "Sure." He handed over a photograph of Roland Cecil. "This is a British Member of Parliament who was murdered recently. It's possible he was killed by the man who shot the Duval family." He handed over the sketch of the man who'd shot Hugh Macallun. "We don't know why he killed Cecil and I gather your people don't know why he killed the Duvals — if he did, if it was the same man. I'm here to see if I can take things any further. Right now, I don't see any need to stir things up again or involve

191

any of the investigating agencies who were on the Duval case, but that's your decision. If I think it'll help me to talk to local law-enforcement officers at a later date, then I'll be asking you to introduce me — in fact, I'd like your advice on that. In the meantime, I'll report anything I find to you — but we're treating it with a certain amount of delicacy because Cecil was not only an MP, but also connected to British and European Nazi organizations."

Tate said, "That's everything?"

"That's everything."

Tate's expression said: I doubt that. He shifted in the armchair — a stocky frame, squarely set and muscled. He wore a light tweed jacket and a polo shirt like an off-duty jock. His cheeks had a dusting of freckles and his hair was cut college-boy style, with a side part, except it was a little overlong.

"It's noon," he observed, "do you ever drink this early in the day?"

They went through to the bar. Bullen asked for mineral water; Tate ordered a screwdriver. He said, "I've listened — I'll buy it for now, but I might be asking questions later. We can keep this unofficial; God knows, it's been done before — on both sides. Let's see what happens." The bartender put the tab down and Tate pushed it along to Bullen. "You're right about not stirring things up. I asked a few questions — no one has any answers. Grudge killing, mob killing, nothing fits. All they know is that it was carefully organized. It doesn't take much detecting to come up with that. They questioned all the guests, they dug into Kelly Duval's business affairs — nothing there that anyone could find."

Bullen had listened carefully to the newscasts. He said, "Duval was a millionaire, right?"

"Very new money," Tate confirmed, "the newest in New England. Started out in trucking in the late fifties, expanded into shipping and container haulage." He tried to read Bullen's expression. "There's a link?"

"There might be."

"I'll cheat for a while, but sometime someone ought to be telling our people this."

"Sure, well, you tell them," Bullen offered, "if you want to." He'd already guessed that Tate had decided to play a waiting game.

"What is it?" Tate asked. "What do you think it is? It's not grudge, it's not Mafia, it's not some crazy with a friend who flies helicopters."

"When I get close enough for a guess," Bullen said, "you'll be the first to hear."

"That had better be true. I'm taking a few risks, here; Cochrane knows that."

Bullen said, "Why was Kelly Duval carrying a gun at his daughter's wedding?"

"Yeah." Tate nodded. "That's in all the reports. No one knew. The best guesses were kidnap threat, death threat, extortion threat, or he felt underdressed without it. It didn't look like a kidnapping that fucked up, there's no evidence of any attempt at extortion, and so far as the police are concerned, no one had a reason to kill him."

"Nonetheless, he was carrying a gun."

"Listen," Tate said, "maybe she was pregnant and the groom had other plans."

Watching someone who doesn't know you're there makes a strange and strong intimacy.

Sonia was pulling a series of sketches from a portfolio and laying them like paving on the floor of her studio. She stood in profile to Bullen and looked down at them, shifting position slightly to see each at its best. She was wearing scuffed Cossack boots over blue jeans, an Indian beaded belt, and a T-shirt that read DON'T! Her long face was solemn as she scanned the designs, and when her hair fell forward, she hooked it behind her ears. When she hunkered down to one of the designs, he watched the movement of her breasts, full and rounded, a little out of proportion to her slim waist and hips.

He was looking through a porthole window cut at eye level into the door, and when he shifted his position slightly she lifted her head and saw him at once. They looked at each other through the round window as if struggling for recognition. After a moment she opened the door to him, formally, and invited him in.

The designs were for a theater play — clothes of the thirties. On their way downtown, Bullen asked about the play. "Girl meets boy," she said, "they fall in love, the world conspires against them, tragedy ensues. It's an old story; you might have heard it before."

"What's the play called?"

"Romeo and Juliet."

"I was fooled by the clothes," he told her. "Who are the stars?"

"A guy called Romeo and a girl called Juliet."

They rode in silence for a while, until she said, "I'm sorry. I guess I was hoping you might go away and leave me alone."

"I will if you like."

"No. I'll watch it with you one last time." After a moment, she added: "It's very Off Broadway; there are no stars . . . just actors, I'm afraid."

Bullen sat on one of the battered sofas while Sonia took the tape fast forward through scenes of domestic frenzy and caterers setting the silverware and cravats being tied and retied.

Bullen said, "I asked you how often you'd seen this tape; you said fifty times."

"Forty-seven, fifty-three, I don't know." She hit Stop and said, "What do you drink?"

"Anything. Vodka."

"Anything or vodka?"

"Vodka. What did you mean — the whole tape?"

"You mean the stuff I just wound past?"

"Yes."

"No, I don't watch that. I go from the moment the guy with the gun turned up. That's what they wanted me to watch; that's all there is to watch. All that matters."

She handed him a Stolichnaya over ice and the tonic bottle to make his own mix.

"Have you ever watched the tape right through?"

"Once. I watched it once. Once was enough. I couldn't handle it. There was Caro sitting with her hair in rollers getting a manicure at nine in the morning, Charley cutting himself shaving, Mrs. Duval herding

195

caterers and flower arrangers, the old man smoking a cigar and having Budweiser for breakfast. . . . In a few hours they'd all be dead." Sonia poured white wine into a big crystal glass; she brought it shakily to her lip, then lowered it without drinking. "I didn't want to see those faces again, or hear those voices. There's a moment when Caro first comes out in the wedding gown and her mother just cries."

"You remember it pretty well."

"Not really; there's two hours of it. The Memories people edit the tape before you get it, so they shoot lots of stuff. This is unedited."

"Let's watch it all," Bullen suggested. When she sighed, he added, "You're looking for a moment that unsettles you — the cellar door closing. Something you can't find. You think it's part of the section where the Duvals get killed — that's the section you keep rerunning. But maybe you don't find it simply because it isn't there."

Sonia sat next to him on the sofa for a moment, then got up and walked away; after a moment she returned bringing the rest of the wine, the vodka bottle, and a bowl of ice. While the tape was rewinding, she said: "I could pop some corn." The words snagged, and when he glanced at her she turned her head.

They watched the tape from end to end. It opened with Caroline Duval's sleeping face, first in a dim light, then in soft sunlight as her mother pulled back the drapes. A setup, Bullen realized; the girl was acting and the scene was called "The First Moment of Your Wedding Day." It ended just after the cameraman was hit: a wild kaleidoscope of lopsided people, tables tilting, chairs falling, then great cuts of sky and the tops of trees before the camera hit the ground and lined up on Caroline's face again, a gruesome parody of the wake-up shot. She was wide-eyed and stock-still, the blood flecks crowding her face like a rash.

Bullen asked, "Was it there?"

"Yes," Sonia said.

"What was it?"

"I don't know. I can find the feeling, but I can't find the moment."

They watched it again; it was close to eleven o'clock before they saw Caroline dead once more. Sonia said, "Enough, okay? Enough."

Bullen said, "Are you hungry? Do you want to get something to eat?"

"I don't care. I guess so." The tape went into automatic rewind and the noise seemed to make her edgy. She downed her drink, then collected her shoulder bag and keys and waited for him by the door.

They walked into Chinatown. Bullen noticed that the city felt warmer at night: an illusion, but he thought that maybe the streets seemed hotter as they grew more dangerous. Sonia walked alongside him but a few feet away, head down, keeping her own counsel.

They found somewhere to eat close to Mott Street. Sonia ordered crabmeat soup and chicken noodles and asked for a bottle of wine to be put on the table right away, but didn't have anything to say beyond that. After a while Bullen asked, "If you saw it, if it's there, the only way is to keep looking."

"Let me try to explain," she said. "I've never seen anything like that before. I've never been close to violence. I know I live in New York and you're supposed to see something terrible every day, but it really isn't that way. Most people most places are just normal; they lead normal lives." She glanced around, as if looking for confirmation from other diners. "I mean, what do you do? What do spooks do? Kill lots of people? Watch people being killed? I guess that's part of it, am I right? Well, it might be all in a day's work for you, but it fucked me over pretty badly. I've run that tape more times in my head than I've ever seen it on the screen. Yes, there's something there, something that's wrong, that nudges me, but it's like looking for a dime in a sewer."

Bullen said, "I'm not trying to upset you. I don't want to do that. The idea is to get closer to the reasons for their deaths."

"I said it this morning . . . I told you . . ." Sonia passed a hand across her face. Suddenly Bullen could see how close she was to tears. "Somehow, it's all pushing me, boxing me in. It's you — I thought I was through with it, then you appeared, you started pushing."

"It's stress."

Her head snapped up. "I know what it is, goddamn it!"

A waiter put her food on the table and she ducked her head to the bowl, eating as if she were famished.

He said, "I don't kill people. Death isn't a part of my daily routine; what made you think it might be?"

"I didn't mean you see it every day. I meant maybe

violence was more usual for you."

Bullen thought of the garrote on his windpipe. He remembered the terrible wrench backward as the weight lifter had fallen and the gunman had toppled onto him.

"It's not," he said, "it's not more usual for me."

They walked back to her apartment, both slightly drunk, and he steered her up the stairs, one hand on her elbow. She let him do it because she was suddenly too tired to protest.

He sat her on the sofa and played the tape again, saying: "Keep looking," and "Is it here, is it this?" He was drinking neat vodka, getting sharper as he got more drunk. "Have you seen it yet?" he asked.

Finally, he switched the tape off and left without speaking, as if he would be back before long.

He saw a taxi but let it go by. He passed a building that seemed to be shuttered, windows boarded up, though from inside came rap music loud enough to stun mice. He put his fingertips against one of the window boards and the vibration ran into his wrist.

He strolled through the Bowery as if he were fireproof.

On Third Avenue someone came out of the shadows, selling drugs or sex or both — it was a man or a woman or both. The someone fell into step with Bullen for a while and they walked together.

Bullen was drunk. He said, "Whatever it is you want, you won't find it until you stop looking."

He walked to the Upper East Side and prowled around like a lynx, then went back along Seventy-ninth Street and walked by the park railings, a man trailing his coat and waiting for something to happen.

There were sounds from the bushes that were either sex or death.

He walked all night; when dawn came he went back to his hotel and slept.

An hour and a half later, Sonia telephoned to say that she'd found the moment.

28

Proud parents of the bride, Kelly and Marion Duval, were in a production line of handshakes and kissed cheeks. They were standing by the top table while people passed in front of them, their real faces somewhere just below the merry eyes and taped-on smiles. A young woman arrived and kissed them both. A platinum blonde carrying too much weight; her arms above the sleeves of the evening gloves she was wearing were pudgy and pork-fat white. She seemed to be the last in line.

In the middle distance, you could just see the uninvited guest.

Caroline and her new husband, Charley Fleming, had been making a round of the tables, chatting and smiling, their real faces on display for all to see. Now they had returned to the top table. The fat woman approached them. She kissed Caroline and they exchanged a couple of words before the fat woman moved on.

The uninvited guest had arrived at the top table, his smile broader than anyone's.

Sonia rewound the tape to a set number and said, "Here she is again." It was a short sequence of guests arriving. The woman was on her own; she handed the keys of her car to the guy on parking duty and went through the rose-and-ribbon-trimmed arbor into the garden.

"It was family and close friends at the ceremony," Sonia said. "She's not in any of those shots." She wound the tape forward to the point where the woman spoke to Caroline Duval, then hit the Stop button.

"Who is she?" Bullen asked.

"Beth Parker."

"She's the mystery."

"She's it. I suppose I would have spotted her earlier, except for the fact that she used to be brunette and slim."

Sonia turned and went through to the kitchen; Bullen followed, propping himself against the doorjamb.

"So maybe she's someone else."

"No, that's Beth Parker. I found her when I wasn't looking, like you said."

She took toast from the toaster and picked up the coffeepot, then walked back toward the living area.

Her cotton robe opened to the thigh as she walked. "Butter's in the refrigerator," she told Bullen. There was still something jumpy about her, something uneasy and rushed about the domestic ritual of toast and coffee, but it seemed that finding Beth Parker had taken the edge off her distress. She loaded the breakfast things onto a low table close to the TV, then sat down on the sofa, catching the robe as it parted over her legs.

"She doesn't fit because she shouldn't be there. Watch." Sonia ran the tape. "I've played this section a few times. Let me tell you what happens — the way I see it."

She took a sip of coffee and a bite of toast, then started her narrative, talking around the mouthful.

"Here's Beth, saying hello to Kelly and Marion Duval. She kisses them. That's not so odd, since everyone kisses everyone at these things. Or it's not odd until you know something about the Parkers and the Duvals. Now, there's just a second of this, but watch their reaction, Kelly and Marion's. He looks at his wife and there's a puzzle on his face. Am I right? You wouldn't find it unless you looked hard or expected to see it, but doesn't he look surprised?"

Bullen took the video control from her and ran the fragment of tape again: the kisses, then the moment when Kelly Duval looked at his wife. There was something on his face; if it wasn't surprise it was exasperation. Maybe he'd simply kissed too many people. As Beth Parker passed out of frame, Duval leaned toward his wife as if to talk to her.

The camera picked up on Beth and Caro and Charley. The cameraman wasn't interested in Beth, of course; he'd panned around to find the newlyweds. For a moment it looked as if Beth might pass by without saying hello, then she paused. There was only a fraction of a moment to interpret Caroline Duval's expression. She seemed to take half a step backward, looking startled or pleased, the way people do when wanting to make a point of greeting someone. She spoke, but the camera's sound system wasn't good enough to pick up her words: she was too far away and the ambient noise was too great. Beth laughed and walked away, a considerate guest anxious not to take up too much of the bride's time. Caro and Charley moved on, reaching a point just behind Caro's parents when the shooting began. Kelly Duval was already on his feet and drawing a gun.

Sonia said, "Unless you look very closely, unless you know something's wrong, you don't see those expressions — it's just a moment or two of unedited footage, people coming and going, kissing, walking about. It's also the moment before the shooting starts, which is enough of a distraction on its own."

"How do you read them?" Bullen asked.

"Kelly is puzzled by the fact that Beth's there; Caro is puzzled and angry. I don't know what she's saying, but there's no smile when she says it."

Bullen took the tape back and froze it on the reverse moment when Beth Parker kissed Kelly Duval then seemed to back off. "Okay," he said, "now maybe you ought to tell me why she's the mystery."

"We were friends, Beth and Caro and me. We lived in the same town, went to the same school. But particularly Beth and Caro. Their families were friends; it was a closer thing because of that. A few years later it all stopped. Suddenly they weren't friends anymore; the families weren't friends either. Caro never spoke about it. It's all a bit hazy now, but I just remember that one day Beth Parker didn't come around. A little later, I discovered that it was something like a full-scale feud between the Duvals and the Parkers; I guessed that something really bad must have happened."

"When was this?"

"Would have been seventy-eight maybe seventy-seven."

"A wedding, Caroline getting married, a perfect opportunity for the families to patch things up."

"So where were the Parkers? Beth was the only member of the family there. And what about the reactions of Kelly and Caro? Caro and I weren't close friends anymore, but we kept in touch. We'd meet for a drink when she came to the city — I'd get the news. I last saw her a week or so before the wedding; she'd come to have a last fitting of her wedding gown. There was never any talk of the Duval family being reconciled with the Parker family." Sonia was peering at the screen, shaking her head sadly. "Jesus, no wonder I didn't recognize her. She must weigh two hundred pounds. Country singer's hair, earrings, cleavage, those ridiculous long gloves. Who in hell would wear evening gloves to a daytime wedding? She looks like the hooker from hell."

Behind Beth, the uninvited guest was poised on one foot, hand half raised, a smile blurring his face.

Bullen said, "Can you be late for work?"

"I guess so. Why?"

"I want someone else to see the tape. You don't have to be here . . ."

Sonia took a shower and dressed while Bullen made a phone call. When she came back into the living space he was asleep on the sofa; the TV had reverted to a news program. She picked up the plates and coffee cups and he woke at once.

"I'm sorry. I didn't go to bed."

"No kidding. What did you do?"

"I walked around the city until the sun came up."

She was staring at him. "No, that's okay," she said. "I once knew a guy who made a living eating razor blades and broken glass. Is he coming — whoever you called?"

"Yes," Bullen said, "on his way."

Arno Hoffmann said, "Roscoe Tate asked me to call."

After a clear three-second pause, Sonia said, "Sure. Sorry." She slipped the security chain and turned away, adding, "Come on up." Sonia had hesitated because Arno sounded like the composite electronic voice that tells you a number has been changed or rerouted — monotonal, the syllables separated equally.

He spoke again as he followed her into the apartment: "I imagine you asked me to come upstairs."

"Yes, I said —" She broke off. Arno's smile was nothing like his voice: it was full of warmth. Sonia said, "I'm sorry, I should have realized."

"Stone deaf," Arno said, still grinning. The words were two pebbles hitting bottom in a dry well.

He shook hands with Bullen. "You told Ross Tate you needed a lip-reader. I've worked with Ross from time to time — UN conferences mostly; I read seventeen languages." The grin returned to contradict the flat, mechanical voice. "All diplomats ever say — the day starts, 'No concessions'; the day ends, 'I'm out of here, let's get laid.' "

They sat on the sofa together. Sonia ran the moment when Caro Duval and Beth Parker met. Beth was in profile to the camera, Caro had turned in passing and was almost head-on. Arno laughed — a series of little, gruff yelps.

Sonia stopped the tape. On the turn, Bullen asked, "What did she say?"

"I can't read you," Arno said, "unless I can see your lips."

Bullen faced up to the man as if he were a mirror. "I asked you —"

"What she said. Yes. I could guess that much. Well, she said, 'What the fuck are you doing here?' "

Sonia went with him to the apartment door.

Arno said, "If you ever feel like a night out with a deaf man, give me a sign."

Bullen was putting coffee into a filter cone. He filled the kettle and switched it on. Sonia watched him making free with her kitchen until he shrugged and said, "Sorry, I guess you have to get to work."

"I work for me. So I give me shit if I'm late." She

rinsed their cups at the sink: little domestic moments, where had they come from? She was thinking about Arno's explanation and said so out loud: "Caro says, 'What the fuck are you doing here,' Beth laughs and walks away."

Bullen nodded. "It looks confrontational, doesn't it? It looks waspish and pleased, it speaks of motive, not chance. It's obvious that she's the specter at the feast. Which must mean that the next move is to talk to Beth Parker."

"I heard the way you said that."

"I know. And what's the answer?"

"It's a dream," Sonia said, "it's like something I recognize but can't quite make sense of. I ought to be designing costumes, I ought not to know you, I ought never to have met Ross Tate, I ought never to have seen people die at a wedding."

"It's your dream," Bullen said. "Just yours, not someone else's. Something happened that changed your life."

"I don't want it."

"It happened. So will you come with me to talk to Beth Parker? I can do it alone, but if you help everything will be a hell of a lot easier."

"Will it? Why?"

"Because if I have to approach her without you, I'll be Tom Bullen the spook, asking questions that she might not want to answer."

"Well, I recognize *him*." Sonia poured the coffee and took her cup to the other side of the room, as if Bullen might be contagious. "And if I come along?"

"I'll be able to lie."

When she left her studio that evening Bullen was sitting in the lobby of the building, reading an international flights timetable. They went to a bar along the block. Sonia said, "You're right, it's my dream; you didn't make it happen."

"What does that mean?"

"I'll come with you to see Beth."

"It'll probably add up to nothing at all; an afternoon spent with an old school friend."

"White wine," Sonia said to the waiter; then: "You don't think that; but I'll come anyway."

Bullen had put the timetable down on the bar; he nudged it. "I've been reading this, trying to plot a journey for the killer. The planes don't work — out of Kennedy, into Paris. Even if they did, the time allowable makes it virtually impossible."

"So the killings are impossible. Except we saw them happen."

"The only thing that makes sense is that he had a lot of help. Helicopter to Kennedy, that's the first piece of assistance. Then what? A private plane to De Gaulle, or there's an airport a few miles south of Dinard — which would put him maybe eight miles from Saint-Malo. But that's not just help, it's *official* help."

"Surely you'd know about that. Or Roscoe Tate would."

Bullen turned in his seat to face her. "Let me tell you something about myself. I'm a caver, that's my profession, or it used to be. It means that I spent a good deal of my life abseiling down into holes in the ground

208

that were very dark and seemed to go on forever. It probably seems a pretty pointless exercise to most people, but when there's more time I'll give you an insight into cavers' psychology. I used to mount expeditions — that means foreign travel and some of the countries we visited belonged to people who used to be known — rather romantically — as the enemy. I carried a few things, made a few drops, passed on information to a few people. It wasn't a big deal and I got paid. Not much of a spook, you might think."

"So why are you here?"

"I told you — Roland Cecil was my mother's brother."

"That's not the only reason."

Her look made him turn away, raising a hand to get the waiter's attention. "No, it's not. Something else happened."

"What?"

He shook his head, letting a silence grow between them.

They were about to leave when Sonia said, "Unless there are two." Bullen gave a little hop, as if he'd been stung. "You know," she continued, "unless the guy with the gun has a double or something."

29

When Kyle and Evan Bannick were born, their father was tripping and their mother was praying for death. The birth took place in a motor home in a trailer park south of Albuquerque. Grant Bannick called the paramedics from a pay phone and by the time they arrived there was nothing to do but deliver the children. Tina Bannick lay on a bed damp with her waters and got through the second stage of labor on curses and hatred. The curses were directed evenly at Grant, the paramedics, and the sons who seemed to be set to kill her.

The Bannicks had gone to New Mexico to search for a way of life, a way of truth, known only to the native Americans whose ancestors had built the pueblos — the way of the Hopi and the Navaho. Also because it was cheap.

Grant Bannick liked the alternative life-style of the sixties. Later, this free-life philosophy would move more in the direction of equalizing the nation's wealth by robbing gas stations and liquor stores, but in sixty-three love was all Grant needed.

There are good trips and there are bad, and the one Grant Bannick was having had tipped over into nightmare. Crouched on a brown plastic armchair, smoking Winstons with an uncontrollable hunger and too spaced to think of leaving, he watched as his wife bellowed in labor. The acid gave him eyes that could pierce flesh. Tina's vast belly grew translucent, until Grant could see his sons jostling and struggling to be born. Tina's body was a conduit, a vast food system — placenta, milk ducts, blood.

The eyes of the children burned back at him.

Kyle Bannick was born at 3 A.M. Tina screamed and

pushed and cursed while neighbors in trailers on either side jacked up the volume controls on their sound systems. Three minutes later, Evan was delivered into the blood fetched by his brother.

One of the paramedics had stretched a sheet over the chipped and torn sofa, and the boys lay side by side on it, silent now, as if deep in thought. Tina got up on her elbows. She said, "You worthless fuck." She stared at Grant and in each dark pupil there danced reflections of her children, each birth-battered head, each blood-streaked face the apple of her eye.

As the twins grew older, they realized that they could depend on their parents for nothing. They survived into childhood more by luck than intent. Grant and Tina drove the trailer from place to place living on welfare, casual work, and minor acts of theft. You couldn't call it a family. The twins didn't care that their parents ignored them: they had each other; they were absorbed in each other.

All twins have a special relationship; Kyle and Evan had something profound. They touched often: hands to faces, fingertips to eyes and lips. More than that, they looked at each other just as they had done as babies, when they would lie together, face-to-face, apparently absorbed in what they saw. Since they were identical, each was seeing himself.

The same wordless contact existed between them when they were older. There would come a moment when it seemed that each had called the other's name simultaneously, though no word had been spoken; and their heads would turn, their eyes meet. It would happen when Grant slapped Tina, or when he pushed her down onto the torn sofa, unzipping his jeans with his free hand. It would happen when they woke in the night to the sound of Tina wrecked on acid and moaning like a dog. It would happen when they played with other kids in some trailer park in Colorado, or Nebraska, or Utah, as Grant took them on a long circle to nowhere.

When the twins were seven, something else happened.

Grant was on the run from debts accumulated in five states. They had settled for a while in West Virginia. Kyle and Evan had found themselves in yet another school with another set of kids; it didn't trouble them. Other people only half-existed. Teachers found the twins quick to learn but oddly distant, as if their lives were being lived somewhere else.

It was a day when Grant was feeling bad — strung out and itchy inside his skin. He'd smoked some dope, but that hadn't helped much. He was hemmed in by his own life. He tried to look back to a time before Tina and the boys, but it was difficult to hold focus; he seemed to remember that things had been easier then, music festivals and warm nights and girls who liked to say yes. He was working as a pump attendant at a gas station five miles from the park, and the job was driving him crazy. The guy who owned the place was permanently ill-tempered, as if his life were boredom and broken promises. Grant hated the way people threw him tips; he hated the way his clothes bore the lingering smell of gasoline.

It was Sunday. Grant lay in bed thinking. When he'd finished thinking, he got up and took the bus into town, where he bought a Saturday night special and eighteen rounds from a pawnshop. Then he hitchhiked back to the trailer park, smoked a king-sized spliff, and got the motor home on the road. It was just after ten-thirty in the morning. The twins were playing a card game they'd invented for themselves, absorbed in number and color. Tina woke up when the vehicle bucked over the slowdown humps as they left the park. She said, "What's happening?"

"We're moving on," Grant told her. "It's been a year. I don't wanna see any more of West goddamn Virginia."

"Where are we going?"

"New York City," he told her, and she went back to sleep.

When he pulled in at the gas station, the owner was taking money from a customer. Grant waited until the guy had returned to his car before getting out of the cab of the motor home. As an afterthought, he called to the twins to go with him. Kyle and Evan looked at one another as if deciding whether to obey, but they left the card game and followed their father into the small, glass-fronted area behind the pumps. Grant was using them as decoys, a means of drawing attention; he knew the owner kept a pump-action shotgun on a magnet clamp under the counter.

The owner had seen him coming. He said, "I was expecting to see you here today, Grant. You sick?"

"These are my kids," Grant said, "the twins."

The owner regarded them, cocking his head to one

side. "Yeah? Jesus, they're kinda ugly, Grant, wouldn't you say?"

When he turned back, Grant was holding the gun and had stepped in close. He said, "You bitch a lot, you know that? I got real tired of you bitchin'."

The owner sat very still, like someone trying to be invisible when trouble starts; he spoke in a low voice. "Take what you want, Grant." He sprang the cash register and started pulling the money out, heaping it on the counter. "Here, I'm emptying it, okay? It's yours."

Grant shot him anyway. He shot him because the guy could identify him, but he also shot him because he wanted to know how it would feel. He held the gun out at arm's length, bringing it to within a few inches of the man's chest, and fired three rounds. The twins were staring at him. He laughed. He said, "Take some candy; take whatever you want."

Kyle and Evan looked at one another, then trawled the place for whatever took their eye. Finally Grant said, "We gotta go." He was conscious of cars passing on the road outside and jumpy in case one of them should pull over for a tank of gas. He reloaded the gun.

As they passed, Kyle looked down at the dead man. He asked, "What happened to him?"

"I shot him," Grant said. "I killed the son of a bitch."

Kyle said, "Let me," and held his hand out for the gun. Grant laughed and went to the door. Kyle and Evan stayed by the body. "Come on," Grant said, "for Christ's sake." He walked back and grabbed the twins by the arms to hustle them out the door, then he paused and looked at Kyle with sudden curiosity. The boy's face bore a strange intensity. He was looking at the owner's body as if it represented a great puzzle. Grant could feel Kyle trembling, a little electric pulse that traveled from his arm into Grant's fingers.

Grant handed over the gun and Kyle pointed it at the dead man. Nothing happened. Grant stepped forward and showed his son how to pull the trigger. He said, "Do it, for Christ's sake."

The recoil flung Kyle's arm into the air and he let go of the gun; it clattered against the plate glass. A new wound had appeared on the owner's body, a bullet hole in the cheek that was seeping blood. Grant found the gun and shoved the boys out the door. To Evan, he said: "Don't you go asking for your turn, there ain't no time." For some reason, the idea made him laugh — his sons standing in line to shoot a corpse.

He pulled out of the gas station, still laughing. The twins sat in the back, unloading from their pockets the things they'd stolen. Grant yelled at them over the head of their sleeping mother, offering an apology to Evan: "I'm sorry boy. If we'd had more time, you could have shot his ass off." His laughter turned to little whoops.

The twins looked at one another. Evan hadn't needed to shoot the man because Kyle had done it for them.

Tina slept the day away. They were crossing the state line into Pennsylvania when she finally woke.

She said, "I'm gonna start over in New York.

Things'll be different there."

Nothing was different. Grant sold the motor home and rented an apartment for them in Spanish Harlem. He robbed sixteen liquor stores at gunpoint before making the mistake of choosing a place the police had staked out. When they told him to throw down his gun he raised it and five policemen shot him until their weapons were empty.

You wouldn't say Tina was a mother to Kyle and Evan: she was around some of the time. Most people found the twins difficult to like. Their self-sufficiency was troubling, and they had ways about them that seemed close to being unbalanced. There were moments, for example, when the boys would look at one another and simply start to laugh, the laughter turning to little whoops before it cut out, abruptly, as if someone had pulled a switch. When this happened, they were remembering recent pleasures.

Kyle and Evan killed vagrants, but they didn't do it very often. Since the age of twelve they had killed two a year: one each. The first one they doused in gasoline and set afire. The second they stabbed. Stabbing was better — quieter and somehow more profound. You could get close; you could hear what happened; you could see.

The killings became ritualized. Only two a year — it was safe, but it was limiting, so they would choose the day well beforehand and count down to it as children count down to Christmas. On the day that preceded the killing day they would become almost ill with eagerness, their eyes fever bright.

216

Afterward they would find something to drink or something to smoke: there was always plenty in the apartment. They would sit in their room, getting outside themselves, and laugh a lot.

The twins were sixteen when they left home. Tina was asleep. They didn't bother to wake her; they simply left and never returned.

They stole a car from a parking lot in Brooklyn and drove to West Virginia. They went straight to the trailer park and found it was a superstore. The gas station was still operating, though it had grown in size: there were two cash registers and you pumped the gas yourself. There were three customers standing in line to pay, local people by the way they chatted and joked.

The twins waited until the customers had cleared the forecourt, then went in. They were both holding guns. The attendants sprang the registers, just as the owner had nine years before, and heaped the money on the counter. One of them said, "Hey, no problem." He laughed. "It's not our money, take my meaning?"

Kyle said, "It's your turn. You go first."

There are professions and vocations. Kyle and Evan would have killed people anyway; it was part of the way they thought about the world. The fact that there were people who would pay them to do it simply made living easier.

It was Kyle who killed the Duvals. Evan had killed Roland Cecil and the others in Brittany. Evan had killed Joe Chesnik while Kyle set up an alibi in Chicago. Kyle had killed Hugh Macallun in London;

it was Evan who organized a minor car crash on a Manhattan street.

The fact that neither of them had been apprehended had made the alibis unnecessary so far, but they liked to have the insurance in place. One in jail and the other free was an unthinkable terror.

Bullen hopped as if he'd been stung. "Two of them," Sonia said, "a double or something."

"Yes," he said. "I hadn't thought of it." When faced with the impossible, think laterally. People had died, someone had killed them. If it wasn't one man, it must have been two. "That's good spooking," Bullen told her. "You've just earned your spook's badge: second class."

She showed him a hint of a smile. "When do you want to go to New England?"

"As soon as possible."

"I should call Beth. Make some excuse for being there, fix a meeting, all that stuff. I guess the weekend would look better. Who do you want to be?"

"Sorry?"

"Long-lost British cousin, colleague, husband, lover . . ."

"You choose," Bullen said.

30

"This is Tom Bullen," Sonia told Beth Parker. "Tom's a colleague, over from England. He wanted to see a little of the New England countryside."

Beth smiled a lazy smile. She'd had only one drink, but it seemed to have gone to her head. She said, "That's nice. Isn't that nice, Frank?"

Both Bullen and Sonia looked toward Frank Parker as if his approval were what they were most seeking. Frank had driven Beth to the meeting. They were all having a drink in the bar at the Sheraton Inn, just half a mile from Lebanon Airport. Sonia and Bullen had driven up from New York; Frank and Beth had driven down the few miles from the Parker home just north of White River Junction. The bar was just a place to meet — Frank had nominated it.

It wasn't what Sonia had intended. She hadn't been able to speak to Beth, though she'd phoned several times. Frank had taken the final call. He'd said, "Well, she's not here right now Sonia, but you tell me when you plan to arrive and I'll fix things up; I'm sure she'd enjoy seeing you again."

Sonia remembered Frank from her girlhood — he was a couple of years younger, pushy and arrogant; there had been a pool party at the Duval house and Frank had turned up with a few friends to drink beer and nudge people into the water. Later he'd put a

219

hand on Sonia's breast and ducked the slap she'd thrown at him. Now he smiled as if he remembered that.

"New England's prettiest in the fall," he said; then, "You in the same line as Sonia, Tom? You a designer?" It sounded like, "You a faggot? You got anything infectious?"

"That's right." Bullen tried for a smile that said, "And I'll lick your face." He turned to Beth. "You know, I've seen you before."

In Frank's eyes, a touch of surprise quickly became concern. Beth looked at Bullen as if trying to pick him out from the crowd inside her head. "Yeah? I don't think so."

"Yes, on the video. Sonia showed me the video of Caroline Duval's wedding. I saw you then." Bullen wagged ice to and fro in his glass and shook his head, giving Beth time to make a mistake. "That was a terrible business."

Beth looked at Frank, as if for a prompt, then gave an awkward, high-pitched trill: almost laughter. Frank said, "Beth doesn't like to talk about that. I don't think you should have brought that up."

The lamps in the bar gave a soft light that emphasized other colors. Beth Parker's hair gleamed, her face was liverish. She said, "Caro Duval was my friend."

"She was mine, too." Sonia half raised a hand as if entering the bidding for Caro's affection. "So were you. I didn't know you were going to be there, Beth. Did you see me?"

Beth thought it through. "I guess we'd've bumped

into one another," she said, "if that guy hadn't started shooting."

"Did you have to talk to the police?" Sonia asked.

"Sure. They asked me what I saw. I saw what everyone saw, I guess."

Frank said, "Hey, now —"

"You were pretty close, weren't you?" Sonia pretended to think back. "You were standing by the top table when the gunfire began."

"Yeah . . ." Beth sniffed, then gave a little shiver. "I don't really remember anything, though. I was walking away, you know? I had my back to things."

"It's so good that you and Caro made up before she died. She never told me that you two had become friends again."

Frank said, "Okay, listen . . ."

"I had my back to the whole thing. I watched you on TV, Sonia. You were the star witness. I didn't see anything; I was walking away." Despite the even temperature in the place, Beth was sweating, the way all fat people sweat. Droplets had gathered like crumbs in the hairs at the corner of her mouth.

"Even when you see it," Sonia told her, "you don't see much. I didn't see you, but you were there. I saw you later on the video. But I remember the guy who did the shooting. Did you see him at all?"

Frank said, "She really doesn't like to talk about this stuff. Be a little understanding, okay?"

"I just heard the shooting. I saw people falling and got down on the floor." Beth looked jumpy; her gaze went from Sonia to Bullen, then back again, as if looking for confirmation of her own story. "She invited me for old times' sake, you know? We used to be real close."

"Yes," Sonia said. "I remember."

Frank rapped his glass on the table; he seemed about to get out of his seat.

"I don't feel good," Beth said. "Frank, I've started to feel ill."

"I asked you not to." Frank was already helping Beth to her feet. "She isn't in good health."

They all left the bar together. Frank put an arm around his sister and held her tight. Bullen said, "I hope you feel better soon. I hope we'll have the chance to meet again."

Frank and Beth walked toward their car, Beth clinging to her brother, leaning on him, her legs knocking each other as she walked. The breeze caught her silver hair and stood it up like spun sugar.

Sonia drove out toward Canaan, heading for the White Mountains. She said, "I grew up around here. Nothing ever happened — that's a safe life, wouldn't you say?"

"Nothing's safe." Bullen laughed at the way he said it — the oracle speaks. "I need to see her again."

"Did you get the feeling that Frank was there to keep tabs on her, make sure she stayed out of trouble?"

"I got that feeling, yes."

"And we were the trouble — potentially, anyway."

"That's how it seemed."

"What do you want to do?"

"I don't know. It wasn't easy to get in touch with Beth, was it?"

"I called a lot; someone else was always there to say she wasn't available and take a message."

"You know where she lives. What could be more ordinary — you're leaving and want to say good-bye. She was taken ill today — you're anxious to know how she is. Maybe Frank won't be there."

"Maybe he will." Sonia didn't speak again until they were driving through the National Forest — pines thick on the steep ridges, an occasional house like an outpost. "Tell me what you plan to do."

"I don't know." He was looking out the window, like any tourist being taken on the scenic route. "I think the idea is to shake things up a little."

They drove in a circle until the sky started to darken, then holed up in a motel. Sonia knocked at Bullen's door and found it open. He was ordering room service: they had agreed on seafood and salad and white wine. She took some miniature bottles out of his refrigerator. "You want the vodka?"

"You can have it."

She made a vodka-tonic for him, then opened a Michelob for herself and sat on the bed to drink it. "Tell me about yourself." It was a businesslike tone of voice — a challenge. "Tell me about the psychology of cavers."

"Easy to work out," he told her. "People descending into the dark to look for caverns older than time.

Think of caverns, think of Mother Earth, think of being in the dark, think of Doctor Freud."

"Easy as that?"

He smiled. "I'm not sure I know why. I started doing it out of curiosity and found myself with a full-grown obsession. Also I was good at it."

"What made you good?"

"I like being down there."

"Thomas Bullen," she spoke like someone reading a résumé. "Thirty-six —"

He said, "Thirty-eight."

"— private education, college, good background, a bit of a spook. Parents still living?"

"Both dead."

"You said Roland Cecil was your mother's brother."

"That's right."

"From the way you spoke, I imagined she was still alive."

"No, she's dead. She died a long time ago."

"When you were a child . . ."

"When I was a child."

"And that's why you go down into the dark looking for wombs."

"I don't think so," he said. "I never liked her and she never liked me. In fact, we hated one another. She hated me for having been born at all. I spoiled her figure."

"Was she a Nazi, like Uncle Roland?"

"She didn't have a uniform."

Later, when they were both a little drunk, she asked:

"Why did they all die? What do you think you're looking for?"

"Something that gets shipped. Freight."

Sonia laughed at him. "Now you're talking like a spook. Fuck it, Bullen, I'm up here with you helping out. Okay, sure, I'm involved anyway, but I'm making it possible for you to talk to Beth Parker and I'm giving my time, and I'm allowing you to push me back into all that shit that I really want to forget, you know? So why not loosen up and share your fucking theories with me — is that asking so goddamn much?"

All along, her tone of voice had been conversational; the only anger lay in her eyes.

He told her about Seacourt and he told her about what had happened in Paris. He told her everything.

She asked, "What is it, though? Shipping what?" The wine made her skip down the syllables in *shipping*.

"I don't know." She gave him a look and he shrugged. "It's the truth."

"But people are being killed for it."

"For it, because of it — yes, that's what I think."

"Drugs."

"Sure; why not? Listen, I don't know what it is, but I'll bet it's negotiable. I'll bet whatever it is turns into money at some point along the line."

The sky had been a fine, high blue all day; now the color had leached out, acre by acre, and a chill came into the room. Sonia said, "Why did she leave him? The policeman's wife. I can't remember his name."

"Lacroix."

"Why did she go?"

"He was seeing a whore on a regular basis; she found out."

"I thought French wives were tolerant of such things."

Bullen laughed. "French husbands say they are."

"This guy Blanchot. He was in shipping, like Kelly Duval, like the other man killed in London."

"Hugh Macallun. Yes, that's right."

"A lot of people have died," she said. "You almost died."

Bullen didn't respond, but he could feel her eyes on him, could feel the sudden weight of her curiosity.

"What did you feel when it looked like they were going to kill you?"

"There was this tremendous rush of adrenaline and I started to shake."

"When they shot the man who was strangling you — how did you feel then?"

"I was glad. He didn't die immediately, but I wanted him to die."

"Would you have wanted to kill him yourself? Would you have killed him?"

"That's something else."

"Is it yes or is it no?"

"It's I don't know."

"Do you think about it a lot — I mean, do you have to go back there?"

He told her everything; everything except how his mother had died.

They had eaten by the faint light from the window;

now it was almost gone. The room was shades of gray, pitch-black in the corners. Sonia emptied a brandy into her glass and let the tiny bottle drop onto the table. Her eyes were unfocused, and she had to concentrate on what she was saying.

"You're a spook, you're part of my bad dream, no one loves you."

"Did I say that?"

She laughed and rolled the brandy on her tongue. After a moment she got up, walked unsteadily to the bed, and lay down. "Is this your room or mine?" She was falling asleep.

"It doesn't matter."

"No one loves you," she said.

31

They were growing wheat and vegetables between the burned-out skyscrapers in Dobrinja.

Anne Warbeck had paid a cabdriver a hundred deutsche marks to take her into "Dobrinja Two," the only area where journalists were permitted to go. A sniper could look straight down the sights of his gun into the cross streets between the wrecks of buildings. The main street was known as Death Alley; the cabbie had shifted down a gear to get maximum acceleration and crossed it without expecting to make the other side.

Anne was given a guide, a young guy named Ivo,

who was really there to make sure no one said anything unwise to the press. She gave him a carton of cigarettes, chocolate, all the food she had on her, and a fistful of D-marks. He took them unsmilingly. When they'd finished their tour, he left her at the cab and walked away without a word.

Anne was staying at the Holiday Inn: a building of heartless design and appearance. Most people were agreed that it had been aesthetically improved by taking a few direct hits during the course of the war. The shelling had more or less stopped when the press moved in; everyone understood that it was a bad idea to kill people from the media en masse. The place had electricity and water only now and then, the elevators never worked, the food beggared belief. Compared to the lives of most people in Sarajevo, Anne was enjoying unparalleled luxury.

Anne had only one thing left to do before she thumbed a lift on a UN personnel carrier and started the trip home. She had spoken to the politicians and the soldiers and listened to the same tedious invective and nationalist cant from all of them. Now she wanted to talk to the ordinary people of Sarajevo. That was what she had been doing in Dobrinja. Next, she would go to the city's old quarter and talk to people there. It wasn't a healthy place to go.

Anne shrugged off her flak jacket and dropped her helmet on the bed. She started to read a few notes onto a Dictaphone, pausing to take the occasional sip from her flask. Her colleagues would have already gathered in the bar, and soon she would have to join them; not yet, though. Her first time in Sarajevo had depressed her, this time was worse. Anne had written Bullen a postcard—a self-conscious gesture since sending and receiving mail had been impossible for over a year. The message on the card was: "Wish you were here."

Now she sat at the chipped, plywood-and-veneer work area in her room and wrote a second postcard: *There ought to be a way for us to be together. Not your terms; not mine: just ours. Does that sound possible? I love you.*

Next morning, she got a ride aboard a UN convoy heading into the city center. They dropped her off close to Oslobodjenje Square and she walked past the burned-out ruins of what had once been the Evropa Hotel, its panels and doors and floors torn out for firewood during the previous winter; its windows smashed; its masonry pitted and broken by mortar fire. She was headed for the old town, and the snipers were looking straight down the cross streets.

That morning she had written Bullen a third card: *I don't care what it is you can't talk about, just help me out — talk about it eventually. I'll be home in a day; two if I'm unlucky.*

Half a dozen people were stalled behind the shell of a building opposite a burned-out furniture store, as if they were waiting for a signal. She joined them and they all crossed at the run.

The snipers shot two of them. An old man was running with his hand to his head just as Anne had described it to Bullen. He seemed to fly up into the air, as if some great hand had flipped him, then hit the

229

ground, legs and arms spread wide, a parachutist in free-fall.

Mortars started coming in. There was a dull, percussive thud, almost too big for hearing, that seemed to spread shock waves as if Anne were its epicenter. She felt a hammer blow to the head, then was rolling and bumping on the rubble in the road, then saw a great darkness coming at her fast, as smoke travels on the wind, then felt nothing and was nowhere.

Bullen was waking up in New England feeling the first blunt prod of a hangover at his temples.

He stayed prone for a few seconds as the bile rose and dipped in his throat; his door buzzer was blipping a little morse boogie. When he opened up, Sonia was standing there looking like a teetotaler on a mission to save, the tips of her hair still damp from the shower.

She said, "I spoke to Beth. I just got off the phone."

32

I kept calling and asking for her. I was getting a housekeeper, I think. Not one of the family, anyway. I said I'd keep trying, then hung up without leaving a message. Eventually Beth answered the phone."

"What did she say?"

"She said, 'Pick me up. You've got an hour.' "

"Means what?"

"I don't know. Do you?"

"Can we make it in an hour?"

"Fifty minutes." Sonia took a closer look at his face. "Gives you time to throw up."

Beth had told Sonia to go to Woodstock. They found her sitting in a red Spider convertible outside the Shire Apothecary. She said, "I'm not too good at driving these days; I'm a little shaky." Then, as if it were a related notion, "Can you get me on a plane?"

She took a slow, mazy path to Sonia's car. Bullen drove; Sonia installed herself in the back with Beth.

"Plane to where?" Sonia asked.

"New York. I have a friend there." Beth had taken a little velvet bag from her purse and was removing the things that would make her feel better — lipstick, blusher, mascara, eyeliner. She was dressed as if to meet someone; her brocaded blouse had thin red and black drawstrings at the wrist.

"You're on the run." Sonia held a vanity mirror for Beth as she flicked the mascara brush up under her lashes.

"Frank and Daddy had a meeting this morning. Two men arrived and they all went into the library. There are usually one or two hands around, but they were feeding the horses. Mostly there's someone with me."

"Who?"

"A housekeeper — supposed to be. She stays around me most of the time." Beth grimaced. "House-keeper — keeps me in the house."

"But not today . . ."

"She had to go to the supermarket; I said I was tired. I get tired a lot."

231

"How long before someone misses you?" Bullen asked.

Beth was dabbing blusher along the line of her cheekbones. She said, "Maybe another half hour. First they'll look in the back pasture, the woods, maybe. Can you get me on a plane?"

"Make a right here," Sonia told Bullen, "that'll take us down to the airport." To Beth, she said: "You can't go out, there's usually someone with you, Frank rides herd if you do go anywhere — what does all that mean?" Beth laid the bevel of a lipstick against her lower lip and dragged it across, rich red, the color of a bitten plum. The motion of the car meant that none of the makeup had gone on straight. Her eyes were overloaded and dark.

Sonia said, "Why wear long gloves to a daytime wedding?"

"To hide the tracks," Beth snapped back; she knew that Sonia already had the answer.

"What are you spending?"

Beth laughed. "I don't spend it, honey. Someone spends it for me."

"You know what I mean."

"I use it when I want to."

"When you have to." Sonia was trying to sound tough, but there was a shake in her voice.

Beth started to laugh. Her cheeks shook slightly. She said, "Are you here to save me, Sonia?" then held her hands up like one of the faithful at a revivalist meeting. A little crescent of sweat was spreading from under each of her arms toward the bright strips of brocade that decorated her blouse. She laughed louder. "I'm gonna wash myself in the blood of Jesus."

"I don't care what the hell you do," Sonia said. "You can mainline bat shit." She turned away to hide the pity in her eyes.

Beth improvised a tune — martial and fervent. "I'm gonna take a shower in the blood of Jesus, fill the tub with the blood of Jesus, wash my hair in the blood of Jesus . . ." Her laughter was sliding down the scale; she sounded like someone about to scream.

Bullen pulled the car over and cut the engine. He leaned over the seat and took Beth's purse, then found her gear and took it out: disposable syringe, heroin, things to cook it with, a loop of rubber tubing. He said, "We'll get you on a plane. Just listen and answer: that's all you have to do."

Beth said, "We might not have a lot of time." She was suddenly serious; her eyes were on the works in Bullen's hand.

"Why did your father fall out with Caroline Duval's father?" Bullen asked.

"When we were girls? Who the hell knows? Business. It's always business. I'll need that back."

Bullen was opening the self-sealing glassine pouch that held the heroin. "Why did you go to the wedding? Were you invited?"

"No. I didn't want to go. Frank drove me most of the way there in his car, then let me take it the final few miles. Two of the guys were shadowing us. They picked up Frank."

"Who wanted you to be there?"

"My father. Frank. They told me a couple of weeks

before the wedding. I thought they meant that Caro had invited me. I couldn't figure out why. Then they told me that I'd be gate-crashing — to just go along. Anyone can get into these things. You just have to be dressed right and look as if you belong.''

"People must have recognized you — local people.''

"I kept out of the way. One or two people looked surprised. Maybe they thought that this was a good time to bury old grudges. Why did you take that away from me?''

"What did you —''

"I'm going to need it back,'' Beth repeated. "We don't have too long. Let's go, okay? Why not start the car?''

"What did you have to do?'' Bullen was winding down the window on his side. "What instructions were you given?''

Beth said, "I'd sooner tell you the rest at the airport. And I need that back.''

"Don't ask,'' Bullen said, "because I don't want to disappoint you.'' He held the glassine pouch out of the window and tilted it slightly. A thin line of powder trickled from the corner and drifted away on the wind.

"Jesus Christ.'' Instead of going after Bullen's arm, Beth pressed back in her seat like a kid at a horror movie. "Jesus Christ . . .'' Her voice was a little moan, a little sob.

"Let's get you onto the plane,'' Bullen said. "Let's make sure no one stops you catching that plane.''

Beth turned to Sonia. She said, "I'm going to tell him. I just need my stuff back. That's first. That comes first.''

"Can't you give it to her?" Sonia laid a hand on his arm, to restrain or to plead.

Bullen gave the pouch a little shake. A thimbleful of powder shirred in the breeze and drifted past the window where Beth sat. She made a sound like a hurt cat, sudden and violent, and pressed against Sonia as if for protection.

"A guy was going to walk in from the paddock. They described him to me, they described what he'd be carrying. I had to watch for him. When I saw him, I had to go and talk to Mr. and Mrs. Duval and Caro. The idea was they'd be surprised to see me."

"So they wouldn't see the guy who was walking in from the paddock."

"That's right. Let me have it back now," Beth said. "Please? Okay — please? Did you want me to say please?"

Bullen kept the pouch outside the window, just holding it steady. The powder was piled up toward the open corner. He asked, "Did they tell you what would happen next?"

Sonia looked first at Bullen, then at Beth. It was an obvious question but it hadn't occurred to her. Beth's blouse was damp in the cleavage; she sat with her thighs parted.

Sonia said, "What's the answer, Beth?"

"Yes."

"You knew it would happen?"

"All they said —"

"You knew it would happen and you just let it?" Sonia shook her head; she stared at Beth. "My God, Caro died. She died on her wedding day."

"— there would be some shooting, that's all. I figured Mr. Duval . . . you know, I thought it was him."

"And still you didn't mind?"

"Give it back, okay?" Beth's attention was fixed on Bullen. Her remarks to Sonia had been made without turning her head. "Let me have it back now."

"Why would your father want to kill Kelly Duval?" Bullen asked.

"They're in the same business," Beth said. It sounded almost reasonable. "They were rivals. They always went after the same contracts. Sometimes my father would win, sometimes Mr. Duval. Maybe it happened once too often, I don't know. I don't know. Believe me that I don't know; please let me have that back." This time she put out a hand. "I'm going to need it soon. I have to get on a plane." She tried to make it sound like the real reason. "I'm a nervous flier."

"What did you have to do next?"

"Just . . . go up to Mr. and Mrs. Duval. Talk to them. Say hello. Talk to Caro if she was there. I've told you. Make them look at me."

"After that?"

Beth was watching his arm. "They didn't tell me."

Bullen grimaced. "Not even to get out of the line of fire?"

"I talked to the police. Everyone talked to the police. I told them that I didn't see anything because I was walking away. Someone pushed me down to the ground — I don't know who — and I could hear the gunshots, but I didn't know what was going on.

Then the shooting stopped. I heard the helicopter. Most of the time I had my eyes closed. When I got up, the helicopter was moving away — it was already above the roof. I didn't see the man and I didn't really see anyone die. I just saw them dead.''

Bullen thought that she must have told it exactly that way: word-perfect.

"What happened after that?''

"I drove Frank's car home.''

"What did Frank say to you? Or your father?''

Beth looked at Bullen as if she had suddenly realized who he was. "They didn't say anything. They just gave me my stuff back.''

At Lebanon Airport Sonia bought Beth a ticket to New York, La Guardia, at Business Express, while Beth bought herself a ticket to a happier place. She came out of the ladies' room with a gracious smile on her face, walking slowly, her eyes almost focused.

She said, "I have to make a phone call. My friend will meet me.'' She went away for ten minutes and returned with a little smug rosebud smile; she was carrying a doughnut and a cup of coffee. After she had taken the lipstick off with the doughnut she found the velvet bag in her purse and handed Sonia the mirror.

Beth was one of eight passengers. Bullen and Sonia sat with her until the flight was called ten minutes later, then watched her amble out to the little plane. Her silver hair had fallen out of its plait and was hanging like a sheep's tail.

"Her friend in the city,'' Sonia said. "I wonder who that is.''

237

"I think her friend in the city is probably her enemy."

"You mean whoever turned her on to heroin."

"It's just a guess." He caught Sonia's tone of voice and watched her as she watched Beth onto the plane. "How much do you care?"

"We used to be friends. All of us, really close. It doesn't please me to see her like that."

"She helped kill Caro."

Sonia didn't answer. As the plane taxied out, she said: "You know why she's going to him? The friend in New York?"

Bullen had seen it, too. "She's in love."

"Maybe he's in love with her."

"Maybe."

"No," Sonia said, "I guess not."

"Her father's pretty rich, isn't he?" Sonia nodded. "Yes," Bullen said, "well, here's another guess — maybe it's got something to do with that."

Bullen was unlocking the car when he felt the rush of movement beside him. He turned and Frank was standing so close that their heads almost knocked. Frank said, "Look down." When Bullen looked he saw that Frank was holding a gun, low but cocked up to point at Bullen's groin. In that position the weapon was barely visible. "Just turn and walk," Frank said.

Bullen looked across the roof of the car to where Sonia was holding hands with a man whose narrow good looks would have attracted any girl. He smiled at Bullen and nodded as if Sonia had just introduced him. He wasn't holding a gun, but then he didn't need to because he was holding Sonia.

They walked along the row of parked cars until they reached a Mercedes limo, its windows dark and reflecting the sky. Bullen saw a small plane cross the cloud image, angled up and climbing: Beth and her friend were already a little closer.

George Parker was a short man who had worked on his image: gray hair cut close to the skull, fifteen-hundred-dollar suit, handmade silk shirt, a fanatically close shave. The shirt collar was cut large to give the bull neck enough room. He shifted along the backseat of the limo to provide Bullen with some space. Frank got in behind Bullen; Sonia and Good-looking got into the front. There was a driver — a man of about forty wearing a plaid shirt and a Red Sox cap.

As soon as the door closed, Parker slapped Bullen hard in the mouth. He said, "Let's play it like this: don't go through any what? who? where? routines and I won't get any madder than that. Someone named Sonia called the house a dozen or more times this morning asking for Beth. She went out and she hasn't come back. Where is she?"

"Waiting for a plane to New York," Bullen told him. "You've got a few minutes."

The driver got out of the car and started toward the terminal building. Parker glanced across Bullen at Frank. "Go with him. You might have to haul her off the plane."

Frank said, "I should stay with you."

Parker reached over and tugged the gun from Frank's hand. "Christ on a crutch, do as I damn well say. I can handle this guy. You think I can't?"

Frank got out and slammed the door. Parker said, "That's fine, that's just the kind of answer I'm looking for. Let's try some more. Why did you want her?"

"She wanted us."

"Say what?"

"We met her a day ago: Sonia wanted to say hello. She asked Sonia to call her. I mean, she sounded as if there was some urgent reason to see us again."

"No," Parker said, "you're making a mess of things. She didn't say anything like that."

"How do you know?"

"Frank was there."

"Frank was buying some beers; that's when she said it."

"Frank didn't leave her side."

"He bought a round of beers. Shouldn't he have done that?"

Parker thought for a moment, then he brought his hand around fast and clubbed Bullen on the side of the head with the gun. "Try again," he said.

A gash had opened up along the line of Bullen's eyebrow and his vision fogged for a moment. Two blood beads chased down his cheek to the corner of his mouth. He'd heard Sonia scream and looked across to her, speaking softly: "Don't yell, it's dangerous."

"You're damn right," Parker said. "Okay, tell me again."

"Why don't you tell me what you want," Bullen countered, "or what you expect to hear. I don't know what the fuck to tell you. Frank was buying a round

240

of drinks. Beth asked Sonia to call her. She sounded upset and afraid. Sonia called, Beth told us to pick her up in Woodstock. Her car's still there. A red Spider? Okay, still there. She wanted us to bring her to the airport and we did. She's in there waiting for a flight to New York where — she says — she has a friend. I don't know why she was upset, or why she can't go out alone. It's not my business. What are you saying? I should have brought her back? You hit people in the fucking head with guns, Parker. Why would I bring her back to a son of a bitch like you?''

"Okay," Parker said, "we'll wait till Frank brings her out, then we'll go somewhere else and start again." Suddenly he seemed furiously angry. He put the gun against Bullen's temple and spoke to the man alongside Sonia, but without looking at him. "Smack her in the mouth. Hit her."

Good-looking held both Sonia's wrists with one hand and swung the other, casually, palm open but using the knuckles. The blow sounded meaty; there was no blood, but a red patch sprang up along her jaw and spread across her cheek.

"You like that?" Parker asked. Good-looking smiled shyly and put his hand out again, making Sonia flinch. He tidied her hair and brushed something from her shoulder. Parker laughed through his teeth, a long, wet hissing. It was clear that he was standing on the brink of fury, toes over the edge, teetering; Bullen wondered how much of the man's rage was fear. "You can have a lot more of that. More of that coming up for sure." To Bullen, he said: "Anything you can tell me is going to help. Anything at all."

Bullen smiled. "I can't think of a thing I'd want to say to a pint-sized asshole like you." He turned away as he spoke, inviting the blow, and Parker was too wired to do anything else. He swung the gun up, going for the face, and Bullen feinted sideways, crowding Parker to put him off balance and gathering the man's fist in midair — a two-handed catch.

Suddenly, Good-looking had a lopsided smile on his face and was breathing fast, little gasps like a thirsty dog. Bullen shifted position and jabbed Parker in the face with his elbow, finding the man's eye, but the gun didn't loosen. He tried again, lifting himself up from the seat to get his body behind the blow. There was a wet sound, like a soft explosion, and Parker said, *"Whooof!"* The gun came free. When Bullen turned, Parker had his face in his hands and blood was reaming the cracks between his fingers.

Sonia said, "Tom!"

Good-looking was trying to get over into the back of the car. He'd been shot when Bullen and Parker were wrestling for the gun: the bullet had gone through his upper chest and chattered around the windshield with a sound like a stick being run along railings. He was still breathing unnaturally fast; now he grabbed the seat back and tried to lever himself over. As Bullen watched, the man's face drained of color and his eyes rolled up to show the white; he fell back onto the front seat, going full-length, his head falling into Sonia's lap.

Bullen said, "The car keys are in the ignition, aren't they?" Sonia looked at him; she didn't move, she

242

didn't even push the man's head away; her mouth was open and she seemed not to be breathing at all. Bullen spoke softly: "Sonia, we have to get away from here right now — now — we don't have any time left, we're out of time because any minute Frank is going to open the car door, so please, just look and see whether the ignition keys are there, I think you'll see that they are."

She shuffled along the seat, sitting first on Good-looking's belly, then on his shins. She said, "They are."

"Start the car and drive away."

"He's bleeding a lot." She was looking along the seat. "We ought to do something."

"Start the car," Bullen told her, "and drive out of the parking lot. Then we'll decide what's what. But you have to do that now: start the car and drive. You have to do it before I've finished speaking to you, or else we're dead, okay? Either that or I'm going to have to shoot Frank and the driver and I don't want to have to do that, so what you have to do —"

She was reversing the limo out of the parking space. As she drove between the lines of cars, Bullen saw Frank and the driver coming toward them at a flat-out run. He said, "Go faster." When she didn't see the reason, he yelled at her and she turned her head. Frank was on a curve to intercept the limo as it arrived at the top of the row; the driver was running straight for them, coming down a line of cars, one hand slapping against them for balance and triggering alarms all down the row. Sonia gave a little yelp of fear and the car leapt forward. Her control was off and she sideswiped the rear end of a badly parked Chevrolet; it gave the driver enough time to reach them and close his fist on the door handle. In the same moment she whacked the limo into reverse to clear the Chevy, then went forward as soon as she had clearance. The driver lost his footing on the reverse, then was yanked along with the forward acceleration. He held on to the handle for a short while, his feet threshing as he tried to get up and run, but he was pulled sideways and his left leg snagged the rear wheels of another car, wrenching him off the limo.

Frank appeared between the cars at the top of the row when Sonia was still fifty feet away. Bullen was watching Parker, but turned at Sonia's yell. He said, "Drive at him, he'll move."

As if he'd heard, Frank started to run down the row. "Drive at him," Bullen shouted. He felt something wet on his face; Parker was scrambling onto his knees, trying to get upright, his hands running blood where he'd been holding his broken nose. He was going for the gun, his other hand clawing at Bullen's face. Bullen shoved him off and yelled at Sonia —now that Frank was just a few feet away she had stopped the car. She said, "What? What? *What?*" — panicky and shrill. Bullen reached over and pressed the central locking switch and Parker went forward with him, wrapping his arms around Bullen's chest.

Frank's face appeared at the window. Sonia was switching her head this way and that, like someone looking for a break in traffic: she didn't want to see Frank's face but he was a magnet — she couldn't look away for much longer. Bullen yelled: "He can't see in. He can't see us."

As if that made all the difference in the world, Sonia shifted into reverse and turned to look through the rear window. The limo bucked and started back down the row, Sonia steering a woozy line, hitting other cars, taking out a couple of brake lights, overcorrecting and clipping fenders on the other side.

Bullen beat at his back with crossed arms, like someone feeling the cold. The gun rapped Parker over the ear and the man fell back on the seat. Bullen sat down beside him and put the gun into the lip of fat on the side of Parker's neck. He said, "Sit still you bastard or I'll shoot your face off." Parker put his hand up to feel the new wound. His fingers and cuffs were solid red; so was the collar of his shirt. He leaned over as the adrenaline faded and the pain came back into his face. Bullen had to lean with him to keep the gun in position. Without looking up, Parker whispered: "You're a dead man. You don't know it, but you're dead already."

Sonia shimmied the limo out of the far end of the row, whipped the wheel over using the flat of her hand, and lined up the wrong way down the exit lane as Frank emerged running hard. Sonia felt his boot slam into the side panel of the door as she gunned the limo away. Bullen held the gun steady against Parker's neck and looked around. He said, "Drive faster."

Frank wasn't running after them anymore, he was clambering into a Toyota Land Cruiser that was parked on the end of the row the limo had been in. It hadn't occurred to Bullen that the men might have come in two vehicles, but suddenly he knew a little more about George Parker's style: for me the chauffeur-driven limo, the rest of you in the goddamn truck.

When Sonia got onto the interstate she said, "What now?" Her voice was small and shaky.

"First thing," Bullen said, "don't pass out. Second, do what I said and drive faster, because Frank came in his own vehicle and he's not a hell of a long way behind us and I'll bet he keeps a hunting rifle racked onto the door or something in the glove compartment."

"This guy's still bleeding," she said.

"Don't look at him, drive the fucking car. Where are you going?"

"Going? Holy Christ, I didn't pick a route. I'm just driving, just driving — I don't know where I'm —"

"It's okay," he said, "wherever it is, just go fast."

"He might die."

"In this situation, almost anyone might die. I don't want it to be you, I don't want it to be me." He turned to Parker. "Get on the floor, face down with your knees tucked up to your belly and your head turned away from me." When Parker was in position, Bullen shoved a foot against his rump and kept it there to detect any movement, then he turned and looked out of the back window. He said, "You're going to have to drive faster."

"How close is he?" Sonia asked.

"I can see him; that's too close."

She said, "I'm not a great driver. I mean, I'm just average, okay?"

246

"Sure," Bullen said, "that's fine. Frank'll be alongside pretty soon."

The car leapt and the Land Cruiser seemed to fall away. Bullen said, "Stay on the highway, try and put some distance between us and them." After they had driven in silence for a while, he asked: "You do know where you are?"

"On Interstate 91, about twelve miles from where Caro lived, fifteen from where I used to live, maybe eighteen from where Beth lives. Of course I know where I am, I grew up here."

"Get off the interstate when you can."

"Why?"

"I don't think Frank will expect us to do that."

"This man's going to die," Sonia said. The shake was back in her voice. "I don't see how he can still be bleeding."

Sonia cut into a network of back roads north of Hartford and drove aimlessly. There was no sign of the Land Cruiser. Next to the car phone in the back of the limo was a drinks cabinet. Bullen raked around among the mineral water and club soda until he found a bottle of brandy. He passed it to Sonia, but she shook her head; she was trying to get Good-looking out from under her, driving one-handed and struggling to fold his legs at the knee with the other. The man was lodged right on the edge of the seat, his head tilted back, his mouth slightly open, as if someone were about to give him the kiss of life. Bullen took a slug of the brandy and felt it hit like a depth charge.

Parker's voice was muffled. He said, "Let me have some of that."

"Shut up," Bullen told him. He took another drink and closed his eyes for a moment, letting the booze take him. He felt like a man on a parapet who has just looked down for the first time. He heard a rattle; Good-looking was wearing a snake-eye ring and it had just struck the dashboard as he fell off the seat.

The car threw a sudden, tight curve, tumbling Parker onto his side and sending a small splash of brandy over Bullen's knees.

When Bullen opened his eyes, Sonia was looking at the road again, holding a line, but her hands were shaking on the wheel. She said, "He's dead. I'm sitting next to a dead man."

Bullen capped the brandy and picked up the car phone. He had to check the number with a slip of paper in his wallet before he dialed. Roscoe Tate picked up his direct line after the fifth ring. Bullen said, "I'm in Vermont, having a little local difficulty."

"How difficult?"

"A man's dead."

There was a silence that could have broken stone. Tate said, "Who is he?"

"I'm in a limo with George Parker. He and some other men tried to pick us up at the airport. His daughter asked us to put her on a plane for New York and we obliged — he's upset about that; he thinks she's a little unstable. I gather that Mr. Parker has certain suspicions about us. At any rate, things became heated, Parker had a gun, someone got shot. One of the men he brought with him, he's the guy who died. He's in the limo with us."

Tate said, "What the Christly fuck are you talking about?"

"That's right," Bullen answered. "No, Frank isn't here, but he's in a vehicle not far behind us. My guess is that he's pretty angry. I think the idea was that they would take us for a little tour of the Vermont scenery, but it's happening the other way around."

"By 'us' you mean yourself and Sonia Bishop?"

"Sonia's a little shaken up, otherwise we're fine. The thing is, we might need some cover to get out of here."

"Can you tell me what in hell is going on?"

"No, I can't do that."

"You expect me to cover your ass, you've got a dead man there, I don't know who you're talking about, and you can't tell me because some guy I've never heard of is listening to what you're saying? Jesus!"

Bullen hoped that Parker wasn't catching any of Tate's ill-temper. He said, "That's right. That would be terrific." He waited while Tate measured caution against commitment.

"This Parker — is he a problem to you?"

"No, because I have his gun."

"Holy Jesus." Tate sounded like a man in pain. "Where are you — exactly?"

"Just come to the airport — Lebanon, New Hampshire. Bring some people with you."

"Are you crazy? No one knows about you, you don't exist, you're a favor Stuart Cochrane called in."

"That's okay. That'll be fine."

"You mean I can come alone?"

"Sure."

"When?"

"We'll be there as soon as we can. You do the same."

"What shall I bring?" Tate asked. "How about an armored personnel carrier and a howitzer?"

"Thanks. That sounds like a good idea." After Tate had hung up, Bullen kept the phone to his ear and went on talking, leaving pauses as if the conversation were still in progress. "No, we haven't talked about that. . . . Well, I think he might have guessed; he doesn't think I'm here to act as his daughter's travel agent. . . . You were right about that — one of her bad habits is a bad habit. . . ."

Sonia said, "Who are you talking to?" She sounded lousy — only just in control.

"Drive the car, Sonia. Don't worry, everything's going to be fine. I'm solving it. Drive the car." Bullen went on talking to the phone. "I haven't had a chance to offer him a deal, no, because George was pretty aggressive when we first met. . . . No he's not; he's on the floor of the limo with his ass in the air trying to stop a nosebleed. . . . I don't know whether he's in a mood to talk business or not. Given the circumstances, we might have to leave that for another time. . . ." Bullen had no idea whether he was saying anything effective. "No . . . just get to the airport, I've had enough of trees and fields." As an afterthought, he added: "Beth? Someone's meeting her plane. Someone with a sympathetic smile and a bag of smack . . . it's good to have a friend, don't you think?"

The car was bumping over rough ground. Sonia had pulled off the road. She said, "I can't do it. He's dead. He's in here with me and he's dead." She kicked the door open and ran across to the roadside trees, then walked a few paces in among them. Bullen watched as she put her hands on her hips and leaned forward as if she were throwing up.

Parker said, "What deal? You were talking about a deal." He got to his knees, cautiously, then onto the seat, leaning into the corner. His face was dark with dried blood that had gone to fissures and seams; his lower lip was caked.

"Why do you think I'm here?"

"Tell me."

Bullen gave a mental shrug: Let's try this. He said, "I work for someone who has interests in shipping and haulage — make sense?"

"Go on."

"There's always a deal breaker. It looks like Beth is going to be yours."

"Why is Sonia Bishop with you? She's nothing; just a local girl."

"She was at the wedding, remember? She saw the Duval family die. I asked for her help — said I wanted to meet Beth."

"Who does she think you are?"

"She thinks I'm someone with a lot of money to spend."

Parker looked out the window to where Sonia stood motionless inside the tree line, a look on his face that said, "Everyone's for sale." The look almost had a smile to go with it. He said, "You've been talking to Dexter."

"That's right." Bullen had faked his way into the bank; now he'd made a withdrawal. "That's right, Dexter."

"Look . . . why don't you tell me what you want. Then I can tell you to go to hell."

Bullen left a silence. He hoped it would seem portentous, but in truth he was trying to find a way of saying something and nothing. "You had a deal with Dexter. We're taking it over. You're a bad risk, now — Beth will talk to anyone about the Duval killings. We know where she is and we know who she's with. You don't. She's a loose cannon and Dexter knows that."

"It's the biggest thing in my life." Parker sounded passionate about his daughter, which puzzled Bullen until he realized the man meant the deal, whatever it was, with Dexter, whoever he was.

Bullen said, "I'll bet it is. But we want it."

"You can't have it," Parker told him. "How could you? You're a dead man."

"Dexter will take whoever presents the least risk."

"Jesus Christ, that bastard." Parker swatted at his own face, cuffing off some of the crust of blood. "I've been shipping for him, legal and crooked, for years. Now this comes along, and he's decided to take offers. Fuck him! This isn't a few goddamn crates of AK-47s on their way to a bunch of niggers with ambition."

A look came onto Bullen's face that said, "Guns. Of course, it's guns" —he couldn't keep it off. Parker read the look and gave a little yell of pure shock. He said, "Who are you? Who the hell are you?" his voice hoarse with worry.

Sonia opened the door of the car. She looked from Bullen to Parker and saw that something had happened.

"How do we get to the airport?" Bullen asked.

"Is that what we're going to do?"

"That's it."

"I can't get into the car. I'm sorry, I can't do it; don't ask me to."

Bullen said, "Give me your necktie." When Parker handed it over, Bullen used it to tie the man's hands to the inner door handle; then he got out of the car and checked the road for approaching cars before he opened the front passenger door. Nothing was moving anywhere. Bullen bent to his task. He thought: Where's Frank? He won't have stayed on the interstate for more than a mile or so. He'll know what we've done. Frank's got to be somewhere close, doubling back and forth along the narrow country roads. Frank's not far away.

Good-looking's narrow face seemed bruised under the skin, his tan fading to something pale and patchy, as if the pigment were going. When Bullen got his hands under the man's arms, he could see how everything was stained with his blood — shirt, pants, the seat of the car, the floor. He hauled him out and into the trees and dumped him like ballast. The man's boot heels had made twin tracks in the pine needles and

Bullen kicked to and fro, scuffing the lines, as if Good-looking might disappear along with them. He stood only just inside the leaf cover, but the silence seemed profound: no birdsong, no movement of wind among the leaves.

Bullen realized that the silence lay not in the wood, but in the man whose shoulders he had just dropped, and he remembered how his mother's body had lain propped against the wall in the house of his childhood, flyblown, going to rot, and embedded in just such a silence.

He thought, When I'm dead, that's what I'll hear.

As soon as he got back into the car, Parker said, "Who are you? You don't know Dexter."

Sonia climbed into the driver's seat, sitting as far left as she could. She was still shaky, but not so bad that she wanted to be in the back with Parker. As she pulled onto the road, Bullen asked: "Where are we now?"

"Outside North Pomfret," she said. "Five miles from where I used to live."

"Your house is around here?"

"Close by."

"But not your parents?"

"It's not my house anymore; not theirs. They live in Florida."

"You shouldn't have come here."

"You told me anywhere. You said somewhere I knew."

"Not here. It's the only place you shouldn't have come to."

Frank picked them up three miles down the road. Sonia made a right turn at a small-road intersection and he was there, waiting, like a traffic cop looking for a speeder. Sonia saw him in the instant that she passed him. She said, "Oh, Jesus Christ," and the limo seemed to pause a moment before picking up speed. Frank pulled out behind them, the Land Cruiser tilting as he came off rough ground. There was a faint squeal from the tires as Sonia took a bend too fast. She overcorrected, cursed, came back on-line.

The Land Cruiser gained ground on the bend but fell back when they hit the straightaway. When Bullen looked through the back window, he saw that Frank was using a car phone and wondered whether the people he was speaking to were ahead of them, waiting to bottle the limo up.

Parker smiled, breaking his blood mask. "You're a dead man, did I tell you that?" As if he thought that pressure might make Bullen forget himself he added: "Just who in hell are you?"

Sonia was heading out toward Bethel and Montpelier, throwing the big car around bends, getting the acceleration and braking all wrong; it was true that she wasn't much of a driver, Bullen was cursing himself for not having taken over. He said: "There's a danger that someone's up ahead of us. Frank's been using a car phone."

"That's great." Sonia's laugh was a little shout, a little howl. "What would you like me to do?" She hung the car into a bend, throwing Parker onto the floor. Bullen left him there to rock to and fro in the well of the car.

"Can we lose Frank? That would be a start — then we could try to double back. Where's the airport from here?"

Sonia sounded panicky. "I can't outrun him."

She put the right wheels into the rough ground at the roadside and the car hopped and lurched; when she corrected, the rear end shimmied dangerously. The Land Cruiser dropped off in the straightaway once more, but the straightaways were becoming shorter and the gradients steeper. Bullen knew that the limo wouldn't compete on rough tracks and steep hills. He said, "Just put some space between him and us. There may not be a lot of time."

Sonia gunned the car along two hundred feet of road, then went into the next curve without touching the brake and came out fast. She did the same on the next two straightaways, her shoulders up around her ears, her fingers wrapped around the steering wheel as if she wanted to tear it off the column. By the time she emerged from the third bend, only fear and anger were in control of the car; it was doing eighty and getting set to roll as soon as she got unlucky with a roadside boulder.

She took the fourth bend at eighty and upward, drifting across the road's natural camber to flick the opposite bank. Braking was the wrong thing to do and that's what she did. The car had everything you need to control a skid, so nothing too serious happened — they fishtailed a little, rode up the opposite bank, then clouted a roadside tree. The tree folded the limo's bodywork back under the wheel arch like a chock, trapping the wheel. Sonia was standing on the brake and cursing.

The car stopped broadside to the road and Bullen was through the door almost before it had stopped rocking. He went to the driver's door and yanked it open, then caught Sonia's arm and pulled her out. She ran because he was running and his hand was on her wrist like a clamp. Her legs stuttered as she tried to match his pace, running between maples and white pines, crossing a hundred feet of open ground. They came to a stiff slope and he released her so that she could go at it hands and toes.

At the top, she followed him into the trees again, but paused to look back. The road was invisible to her, but she heard a car door slam, clear on the clear air and loud enough to shake her heart.

Frank Parker untied his father and doused a handkerchief with water from one of the Evian bottles rolling loose in the drinks cabinet. He took the blood off with long strokes of the cloth as if he were shaving the older man. George sat in the road, his back propped against the limo's sill, and lifted his face to the light, eyes closed. After a minute, he said: "Give me a gun, Frank."

"Take the Land Cruiser home," Frank told him. "Can you drive?"

"I can drive. I can shoot, too, so give me a goddamn gun."

"I don't think so."

A second four-wheel-drive came around the corner — smaller and boxier than the Land Cruiser. When the driver saw the limo slewed across the road and Frank in attendance, he braked sharply, then pulled over and parked. Three men got out, each carrying a hunting rifle. They walked over and looked down as Frank continued to bathe his father's face and neck. One of them asked, "You okay Mr. Parker?"

"Give me a gun," Parker replied. "Give me your rifle."

The man looked at Frank, who shook his head: a scant movement.

"Take one of these vehicles and drive home, Dad. You're hurt, you ought to see someone."

"My nose is broke, that's all. I'll see someone. There's something I have to do first." Parker took the Evian bottle from his son and drank off the contents, then got up and walked to the Land Cruiser. On the driver's door was a clamp holding a bolt-action rifle. Parker flipped the brackets and pulled the gun free.

He said, "I pick up the tab for everyone here, and that gives me a right to say how this is going to be done." A light danced behind his eyes, accompanied by a blur of sound, and for a moment, Frank and the others disappeared. They came back like figures in a photograph, all fixed in position, their expressions intact. Parker stared as if he were seeing ghosts, then shook his head like a dog.

To Frank, he said: "If we wait a hell of a lot longer, they'll have too much of a start. I don't know who this guy is, but he says he knows Axel Dexter. I'm not sure. Either way, he paid Sonia Bishop to bring him up here, and he knows a hell of a lot more about my business than I know about his. I want to talk to him, then I

want to kill him. That's the way it's going to happen.''
He waved a hand at the men, then extended the gesture
to point at the limo. ''Get this off the road. I'm older
than you, so I'll be moving slower.''

Frank Parker followed his father into the trees. In
the same instant a wind pulsed through the leaves,
sending up a muted chatter: distant voices. Parker
turned a moment and slapped his son on the upper arm,
then laughed. ''I'm okay, Frank. I'm fine. You've seen
me take worse than this.''

What he couldn't hear was the way his voice clotted
in his throat, or the fact that it seemed to have a strange,
bass echo.

It was clear that Bullen was looking for something.
Sonia was glad that the pace had dropped off; he was
glancing all the time at the slope that lay above them.
They weren't above the tree line, but he was in hill
country and knew that the work of wind and rain
would have produced folds in the rock, shallow caves,
some small system that would provide cover.

Sonia said, ''Do we keep moving or what?''

''Our only real chance is to get back to the airport.''

''Who were you talking to — on the car phone?''

''Roscoe Tate.''

''What was all that shit about deals? Who's this guy
Dexter?''

''I was fishing. Dexter was what I reeled in. Up
there.'' She lifted her head as if she might find a man
silhouetted against the sky. What she saw was a fold
in the rock standing slightly bare against the foliage,
dark and domed, a shadow rolled into a shadow.

The path went below the cave by about a hundred feet, then turned back on itself, coming within twenty feet of the cave's lip. Bullen took a straight line to the cave without bothering to ask Sonia if that suited her. She started up the slope after him, then slipped and slithered until she managed to find a handhold among a cluster of saplings and get to her feet.

Bullen just kept hoofing upward. When he heard her fall he turned and said, "Walk backward if it's easier; don't forget to look over your shoulder."

If I'd looked over my shoulder, Sonia thought, I might have seen you coming.

The cave entrance was the shape of an inverted **V**, elongated and giving Bullen three times his head height. Its walls funneled steeply back over a distance of about twenty feet, at which point the roof suddenly dipped, coming down to a narrow space that allowed him to stand with his head bowed, or to sit in comfort. It wasn't much of a cave: barely more than a dent in the hillside. When his eyes became accustomed to the dark, he started looking around for faults and fissures in the rock. Sonia stood a few feet inside the entrance, unmoving.

"Do you think there's anything in here?" Her voice was lost in hollowness, the words running into each other.

Bullen had disappeared completely, a trick of the light; then he was back, dusting his hands and knees. "Like bears? Like snakes?"

"Like bears and snakes."

"No bears. Possibly snakes, though I don't think

any would be poisonous. It's a place to hide; the snakes will be hiding, too, so don't worry about them."

"If Frank sees the cave, he'll come in."

"We won't be here."

"How's that?"

"Come here."

He took her hand and led her to the deepest part of the cave, and she had to survive on trust because it was all that was left her.

The light was bad; she could see the planes of Bullen's cheeks and his hands reaching up. Part of the back wall of the little cavern was deeply fissured, three sides of a vertical tunnel that ran upward into the dark.

"A chimney," he said. "You go up like this."

Putting his back against one side, he lifted a foot and braced himself, then let the other foot join it. Tension between his legs and his torso kept him there. His arms were back against the rock, helping the pressure that supported him.

He seemed to walk up and disappear.

The chimney went on, becoming increasingly narrow, probably rising to an opening a hundred feet above. Just above the level of the cave's roof was a small rock platform, a shelf. Bullen had taken a few horizontal steps until he could hook his elbows over onto the flat surface, then heaved himself up and across to occupy the space.

Sonia heard his voice saying, "You try."

She was wearing sneakers and jeans and a tweed jacket, pretty well dressed for climbing, but it took her four goes even to find a horizontal balance. Each time she slipped back, she felt the sting of a graze on her back, through the tweed, through her shirt. Bullen said, "Lift your head up, move your whole body backward, and push with your feet."

"I can't look up into darkness. I don't know what's going to fall on my face."

"Either we get this right, or you stay up here. If it can't be done quickly, it had better be done only once." Sonia got her shoulders to the lip of the ledge and Bullen caught her under the arms. He said, "Keep the pressure on with your feet, or I'll be taking your weight. Keep walking." She went a couple more steps and he was able to haul her back onto the shelf. She sat with her head bowed for a moment.

She supposed it must be like going blind: complete blackness; she knew Bullen was there only because he was still holding one of her arms in case the disorientation caused her to lose her balance and topple into the shaft. After a short while, she could make out the smallest difference in the darkness where the chimney let into the cave. She could hear a faint rustling sound, which might have been the sound of wind in the trees funneling down from above. When she asked him, Bullen told her that's what it was.

"How do we get down?"

"We're only ten feet or so above the cave floor. Just turn around, lower yourself over the edge, go your length, then push out very slightly and drop. What are you, five seven?" She nodded. "Four-foot drop: bend your knees when you land." He went first — a sudden absence in the darkness — and she followed, getting it about right, except that she fell back against the chimney, taking another graze.

She said, "What did I hear when you jumped?"

"I took some bottles from Parker's bar. They're in my pockets."

"What?"

"Some water."

"What else?"

"Nothing else." After a moment, he said: "Some vodka."

"Okay," Sonia told him, "I'll drink that."

"Maybe later."

She said, "Give me the vodka and shut up."

When he handed it over she held it for five minutes, then took one small swallow and handed it back. Without looking at him she said, "I'm not an expert on situations like this — I mean, I'm not a *spook,* you know? — but I bet one of the first things to remember is don't get drunk."

They sat with their backs to the wall, watching the afternoon pass the entrance to the cave.

From time to time, they heard men's voices as they called to one another. Sonia thought she could tell Frank's voice from the rest, deep like his father's and full of suppressed anger. She and Bullen spoke in whispers, but the men hadn't come close enough to send them sky walking into the cavity above their heads.

One time, when the voices faded, Sonia asked: "Go now?" but Bullen shook his head.

"What are we waiting for?"

"Darkness. I don't know how many men, and I don't know what they're armed with, but I'd guess hunting rifles with scopes."

"They're going away."

"Maybe," he said. The voices came back, then faded again.

There was a touch of pink in the cut of sky they could see at the mouth of the cave; a touch of aqua-marine.

"Dark in two hours," she guessed, "or three."

Bullen handed her the vodka to pass the time. She smiled. "Just give me the water, Tom." When she spoke it, his name sounded infinitely strange.

She got up and walked to the cave's mouth. He let her go. With one hand against the wall, she leaned forward to breathe — someone coming up for air — and her hair fell over her face until the breeze lifted it back.

A voice sounded on the same breeze, very close, accompanied by the sound of a rock rolling down the slope. The man said, "I'll check this out."

"Want me to come?" Another voice.

"Okay, why not."

Sonia backed off, trying not to stumble or kick any loose stones. She covered the distance to the back of the cave without knowing whether the man stood behind her in the cave's mouth or whether he was still getting up the slope. When she reached the chimney, Bullen had gone.

She threw herself against the wall, slammed her feet against the rock, pressed back with her arms, and started the climb. Each time she gained height with her feet, she pushed up with her arms, then jammed her back against the rock in order to stay suspended. There was pain she was going to feel later; while she was climbing she knew only the headiness of panic.

A moment arrived when she knew she wasn't going to make it. Her back slipped several inches down the rock face and although she tried to compensate by maintaining pressure with her feet, she could tell that if she lost any more height she would fall backward down the shaft. It wasn't far to fall, but the noise would be enough. She was taking skin off the heels of her hands trying to lever her torso upward.

Bullen could hear her struggle, but couldn't see it. He sat sideways on the narrow ledge and leaned out into the darkness. She gasped as his hand touched her face, then looked up as he lifted her. She came up alongside him and he put his lips to her ear, his voice no more than a fluctuation of breath: "Breathe through your nose, breathe deeply and slowly. Don't make a sound."

Sonia closed her eyes and concentrated, letting her breath come and go in great soundless streams, trying to make the process slower and slower. She could hear the drum of her own heartbeat; it moved her chest and ached in her wrists.

The little moon of a flashlight beam flicked under the shaft and was gone, though Sonia could still see its glow, like a candle cupped in someone's hand. The man was scuffing rocks, making a lot of noise. The light went around one more time. Sonia wanted to draw her legs farther up onto the ledge — she couldn't know whether they would be visible if the man found the chimney and shone the beam directly upward — but Bullen's utter stillness beside her was like fetters.

A voice called: "What's in there?"

When the man in the cave replied, Sonia leapt. His voice was so close that he seemed to be talking directly to her: they were in the same phone booth, the same crawl space, the same bell jar. "Nothing. Bear shit and a few bones." He laughed at his own joke and the sound eddied in the narrow shaft. Then came a long silence.

He's gone, Sonia thought, or he's waiting: maybe he's smarter than he sounds. She knew that they couldn't move until they were sure, but couldn't imagine how that would become possible. Then she heard the man again, or thought she did — the sound that clothing makes, or a stealthy footfall, then realized it was the wind in the trees at the top of the shaft, a night wind coming in with the last of dusk and getting up strength. As she listened, the sound grew and changed; Sonia thought the leaves seemed like a distant echo of the man's laugh, but this time spiraling downward in the shaft, a whisper becoming a mutter becoming a rush.

Then she knew what it was.

One of the bats nicked her hair, another touched her cheek, and then they were all around, invisible but thick in the air, clogging it, passing in a tangled cloud inches from her eyes. If they had a smell, she could smell it; if they had a taste, it lay on the tip of her tongue.

Sonia gave a little shriek of revulsion and threw herself sideways, expecting to find Bullen there. Her arms met nothing but air and she tumbled off the shelf and into the chimney; she reached and grabbed, finding the shelf under her hands and managed to get a purchase on it as her legs swung around and hit the rock face. She hung there for a moment, then dropped, falling back against the rough surface but managing to keep her feet.

Bullen was returning from the mouth of the cave, surefooted. He'd heard her fall and knew where to find her. "Maybe we can go soon. It might be better to wait a bit longer."

Sonia took a step toward the entrance, and he laid a hand on her arm. She said, "There are bats in the cave."

"In the chimney; I know. They fly skyward — they'll be using the entrance to the chimney."

"Not all of them," she said.

He could hear the urgency in her voice. He sat down, pulling her with him, then took his jacket off and draped it over her head; next he put an arm around her and drew her in to his body.

She sat woodenly for a while, then fatigue started to take her. Bullen felt her relax, pull away slightly, relax again. After a few minutes the rhythm of her breathing changed and she seemed to go to sleep muscle by muscle, growing heavier against his side until her head rolled and he was forced to lie back against the wall of the cave to support her.

She said something in her sleep — one sharp syllable — and he put his fingers up to silence her, finding first her cheek in the darkness, then the soft dryness of her mouth.

Touching her, he thought of Anne.

The beam from Parker's flashlight passed over the pale slimness of a birch. He saw a woman standing naked, her arms extended above her head, her body painted in imitation of the delicate striation of birch bark; anyone could have missed her. He brought his gun up to fire, then paused, looking for the man. A gunshot would alert him, let him know that their method of hiding had been discovered.

Parker moved the flashlight beam slowly, going a full circle, and found the man in the final segment — stockier, darker, but standing like a tree and wearing the same body paint that the woman had used. Parker shipped the gun to his shoulder, holding flashlight and barrel with the same hand. The light wavered as he picked his spot and it mesmerized him for a moment.

He shook out of the dream and found himself standing upright in the middle of the wood, gun raised, just as he had dreamed it.

Christ, he thought, what in hell am I doing, throwing down on a goddamn tree?

Frank backtracked to see what had happened to his father. He said, "It's late. We've lost them. Jesus, we lost them hours ago."

"No." Parker shook his head, spinning off the last remnant of the dream. "No, they're here. This guy's smart. He knows that staying in the open is the worst thing to do. He'll have gone to ground somewhere."

"You're done in. Let one of the guys take you back

to the car. We'll keep looking.''

"I want to be there. I'm fine."

"Sure, okay. Take a breather then — okay?"

Parker nodded, pretending indifference, then turned away from his son and lodged a shoulder against the tree trunk he'd dreamed was Sonia. A bone fragment had been working its way through the skin just under the bridge of his nose, jabbing each time he took a step, and breathing through his mouth had given him a raw throat. His eyes ached and throbbed to his heartbeat. More than anything, though, he was tired to the back of his brain and most of the fatigue was from shock.

Frank got down onto his haunches and lit a cigarette, first shielding the flame, then cupping the coal in the palm of his hand to smoke. He sighed. "It's dark. I don't mind looking in the dark if that's what you want. It's stupid but I'll do it. Just take a break, okay?"

Parker shrugged like a man throwing off a coat. He said, "Okay, you look. I'll be here. If you find them, bring them back here to me." He sat down with his back to the bole of a tree. "Don't kill him. Don't even take the risk. I have to talk to him."

"What about her?"

"She's bought and paid for by this guy; he won't have told her shit. Kill her."

"We don't even know who the man is."

"We know who *she* is. Listen, kill the bitch, don't kill her — whatever makes you happy. Get the guy back to me in one piece."

Moonrise had thrown jagged light into the cave

mouth, splintered by branches and bushes, so that it seemed to be the reflection of some high, clear, domed window, its panes smashed, its uprights broken. Bullen could see the bats against the delicate pearl of the sky as they paid out from the cave like a thin hawser.

Sonia slept on his arm.

Something walked past the cave in the darkness, man or beast, something soft footed, something that liked the night.

Bullen hadn't heard any approach and there would never have been time to wake Sonia soundlessly and climb to the shelf; he sat tight, with George Parker's pistol in one hand, vodka in the other. Sometime earlier, he had shifted around to reach in his own pocket and find the bottle. Despite what he'd said to Sonia, he'd taken two drinks and it had been a mistake; it was why someone — something — had been able to get so close without alerting him. The moon made everything riskier. Bullen had decided that they would simply have to outwait their pursuers.

Frank Parker met the other men at a place they'd nominated as a rendezvous. They leaned their rifles against a tree and lit cigarettes. The moon gave them shadows that ran on the woodland floor and swarmed over the slender tree trunks: male shapes on female, dark and light. One of the men coughed and the sound rang on the air.

"We're chasing our asses." Frank looked in the direction of the spot, a mile back, where he'd left his father. "Dad's decided we can find them, but I know we can't. They could have hiked out of the county by now."

"Probably didn't," one man said. "Probably found somewhere to hole up. We'd've seen 'em on the loose."

"Yeah? So what difference? The point is, where are they now?"

"Yeah" — the man gave a shrug of laughter — "yeah, I ain't got no answer to that."

"Go home," Frank told them. "I'll talk to my father."

Another man said, "He pays the wages, Frank. He's right about that."

"I'll talk to him." There was a pause. "You want to go on looking?"

The first man said, "No." The others nodded agreement.

"Sure . . . I won't tell him you've gone." Frank let go a little *huff* of stored breath. "Listen, you do what the hell you like, whatever makes you feel easy. But I'm going to take him home now."

The men picked up their rifles and started downhill, dark shapes, dark shadows; moonlight spiking the trees.

George Parker could see how the trees seemed to move in the pale light: gaining an inch, standing still, gaining an inch. The bark was supple as skin.

He shook the vision off and wrapped his hand around the stock of the rifle. He thought he was rocking back and forth like a sad child, but it was the throb in his face, tugging him.

He saw the knot of the man's genitals, the rough vee of the woman's pubis where the trunk folded on itself. They stepped forward, gained an inch. He squeezed his eyes shut. When he opened them again, nothing had changed.

The woman's breasts were white; the man was broad chested but slim hipped. They only needed to get close to haul him up into those branches. They gained an inch, then another; their shadows shifted, going ahead of them. He could see their eyes burning through the bark. The man lifted his hand as if to take Parker's arm, as if to draw him up. It was obvious that his ruse was to pretend friendship. He said, "You're tired; you need rest."

Parker swung the rifle up and fired, then worked the bolt and fired again.

Frank said, ". . . tired; you need rest; it's time to . . ." The first bullet killed him, taking him right over the heart. He fell instantly. The second bullet clipped twigs from a tree.

Parker saw the dream evaporate. He knelt by the body and turned it over but already knew by the clothing whom he'd hit: there was more than enough moonlight to show him that.

The two shots seemed to be still echoing through the trees. Parker said, "Frank? Get up, boy; you ain't hurt."

He said, "Are you hurt?"

The three men turned to the sound of gunfire. They started to run back, going zigzag against the slope, arms pumping.

One said, "We shoulda stayed." The others just ran.

Bullen leaped at the sound and Sonia woke. She said, "What?"

"A gunshot," Bullen said. She heard it like a sudden recollection, part of her sleeping.

"What do we do?"

"Get up onto the shelf; get out of sight."

They were talking under their breath; Bullen led the way back to the chimney. Sonia glanced back continually, disturbed by the moonlight; she had gone to sleep in total darkness.

"It's so bright."

"We'll be fine up here. They cast shadows; we don't."

When they were on the shelf, she pulled her knees up to her chin and the coat over her head, as before.

"What does it mean? The shot?"

"Who knows?"

"I thought we were waiting for darkness."

"See the moon?"

"Did I tell you I'm frightened?"

"Did *I* tell *you?*"

"What will we do?"

"Wait them out. They can't stay here forever."

"Can we?"

"We have some water, some vodka." After a moment, he added: "We have each other."

He felt her move and wondered if it was laughter: just a little laughter, just a touch. They both needed it.

33

At first light, Bullen left her on the ledge and went out of the cave.

Sonia said, "Don't get killed." As he was going down, feet and shoulders into the chimney, she added: "Not yet."

The sky was pearl with shreds of pink; the light it shed was cool steel. Everything was still, apart from what was happening in the sky: great flocks of songbirds wheeling above the trees with a mechanical note like something churning.

He walked a hundred or so yards downhill and looked up, then came back to the cave and took cover. After five minutes, he walked uphill for the same distance and looked down.

He stood in the mouth of the cave and called, "You can come out. We're leaving."

Sonia made her last descent from the chimney, the rock scruffing her shoulder blades, and dropped onto the soles of her feet. She said, "Sure they've gone?"

"More or less."

"More, or less?"

"More."

She came to join him and looked down through a line of spruce to little pools of early sunlight on patches of flat ground. She said, "This is very strange."

"Why?"

"Because I grew up here. I know these woods, these hills — not well, but I know them. It's a hell of a way to come back."

"You didn't know them well enough to get us out of trouble. I found the cave."

He held her arm as they negotiated a slope covered in last year's leaves; they shuffled, then half ran, then galloped down, letting the pitch of the ground dictate their pace. As they slowed up she said, "I was never a Girl Scout." Her tone stayed light, but the little chatter in her voice was fear.

Bullen put an arm around her. He said, "Everything's going to be fine." For a moment, she almost believed him.

They got to the road at almost exactly the same spot that they'd left it. Sonia walked back to look at the tire marks the limo had made and the deep score in the tree she'd cannoned into. Someone must have knocked out the limo's front wing in order to free the wheel. While she was looking, Bullen flagged a pickup that was ambling toward them.

She ran over to join him when she saw the vehicle slowing down. Chicken coops were stacked in the back, four across, four down, and four high, roped on and held against the lugs on the side of the truck. Each coop held about five chickens. They jostled and turned and squawked, shoving their heads out between the slats. The driver was a woman of fifty or so. She asked,

"What the hell are you doing out here?"

"Our car broke down on one of the side roads last night," Bullen told her. "We've been walking around trying to find a house or a phone."

"Walking all night?" She beckoned to Sonia, who swung up into the cab; Bullen followed.

"No," Sonia told her, "we found some cover and slept for a while. We guessed someone would be along sometime."

The truck started forward, trailing a flotsam of straw and feathers. When Sonia looked through the rear window, she could see the chickens being whipped by the slipstream. The coops bristled with heads.

"Where are you making for?"

"The airport in Lebanon. We can arrange to have our car towed and get a plane."

"You from New York?"

"That's right."

"How'd you like a night in the backwoods?"

"It was okay. I wouldn't do it for a hobby."

The woman laughed. "Yeah, this isn't wild country at all; not really. You need to get right up into the mountains for that." She had a low mellifluous voice, cultured; not a farmer's wife. Someone on the run from the city, perhaps. "Break down or crash?" She was looking at the cut over Bullen's eyebrow, a little puffy, now, and dark with congealed blood.

Bullen replied. "We came off the road; my wife was driving too fast and we fishtailed a bend. But there's also something wrong with the car. It's not too badly beaten up, but it won't start."

"There was a good moon last night."

276

Bullen knew what she meant. "We could see," he said, "but we couldn't decide on a direction. It seemed safest to wait for a car to come along."

"I lived in New York for a few years," the woman said. "Worked in a bookstore in the Village."

"What made you come up here?"

"I like to kill chickens." The woman looked at Sonia's expression and laughed. "Listen, I'm kidding. I don't kill them," she said. "What, you think I get them out one by one and wring their necks? There are better than three hundred chickens back there."

"What happens?" asked Sonia.

"Some we shoot, some get a lethal injection." The woman's laughter grew louder; she'd told the joke before.

At the airport, they climbed out amid a little cloud of chaff and down. If Roscoe Tate hadn't actually been watching the road himself, then someone must have sent a radio message to him because he was striding through the parking lot toward them before the chicken lady had turned her truck around.

He looked more puzzled than angry. "From what you told me, I wouldn't have expected to be the only person waiting for you."

"No one's here?" Bullen asked.

"A few commuters. Ladies who shop." Bullen looked around at the parked cars. "We checked the vehicles," Tate told him. "No one." He turned to Sonia and picked up on the shadowy bruise where Good-looking had backhanded her. "Are you all right?"

"I don't think so. Not really."

"You didn't have to be here, you know that. You're under no obligation to help." Tate waved a hand in Bullen's direction. "What did he tell you?"

"He told me it might help to talk to a friend of mine called Beth Parker."

"Did it?"

"It helped get someone killed."

They were walking toward the airport building and Tate took Bullen's arm for a moment, casually, not quite friendly. "I want to talk to you about that. Not until you've talked to me, though."

They walked into the building and directly toward a departure gate. Bullen said, "We don't have tickets."

"Taken care of." Tate sounded eager to get them on the plane.

Sonia said, "Tom . . . ," her voice throaty, almost a cough. She spoke his name again, more sharply, and he heard the warning there. He turned left to see that George Parker had got up from a seat and was walking toward him from about thirty feet away, not hurrying, not strolling, just taking a direct line like a man with something to say.

Bullen patted Tate's arm reassuringly. "Wait here."

Tate looked for the reason and found Parker. He said, "Is this one of them?"

"Wait here."

As Bullen walked forward, Tate asked the question again, unbuttoning the jacket of his sports coat, his eyes everywhere.

"It's George Parker," Sonia told him. "It's Beth's father."

"See anyone else you recognize?"

"No one."

Sonia stared at Parker as people stare at a movie star found doing something ordinary: he seemed out of his element. He really belonged in a world of fear and violence.

The man's face had been cleaned up; he was wearing an expensive suit, a linen shirt, a discreet necktie. The fact that his nose was out of true and his upper lip was swollen made the clothes faintly incongruous. He looked like a corporate lawyer who had punched his way to the top.

Tate walked a tight semicircle so that Bullen wasn't masking Parker from him; he drew Sonia with him and she could see that he was looking for a clear field of fire. He looked back the way they had come, making eye contact with three men who had been following. The men deployed, one finding an angle of fire opposite Tate, the other two walking past to get behind Parker.

Sonia said, "It's okay — Tom's got Parker's gun."

Tate laughed soundlessly. "Tom's got *that* gun. You think it's the only one Parker owns?"

The two men met and stood close, facing one another, Parker a full head shorter. There was a strange intimacy about the way he had to lift his eyes to Bullen's, about the way Bullen hunched his shoulders, hands in pockets. Two friends sharing a secret. When they spoke, nothing was audible to Sonia or Tate.

"Frank is dead." Parker's busted nose meant that his voice slurred like a drunk's. He was speaking so softly that it was difficult to pick out the words.

"Why are you here like this — alone?" Bullen asked.

"I shot him because I thought he was you."

"You hoped to kill me and by mistake you killed your son. Are you here to blame me? Or do you want my sympathy?"

"He's dead because of you. Instead of you."

"I'm glad."

"I need a reason."

"Yes," Bullen said. "I can see how that's necessary."

"You don't know Axel Dexter."

"Sure I do. Dexter was planning to put some business your way. I want it. I came up here to find the best way of negotiating a takeover. Beth was part of the negotiation."

"No. Everything you know about Dexter came from me. I thought you knew about the deal, so I talked as if you did. You were just picking it up as you went along."

"What do you want me to be? I'll be that."

"Frank's dead. Beth's in New York." He made it sound like the same thing.

"You want to know who killed your son? Caroline Duval killed him. I'm here because of her."

Parker never took his eyes from Bullen's face. He had the half-crazed look of a visionary: fixed, fanatical. "Tell me it was your fault. Tell me you know it was, tell me you made it happen."

Bullen put out a hand — very slowly, so that he wouldn't be misinterpreted — and rested it on Parker's shoulder. To anyone watching, it would seem that he had made the gesture in order to console; in truth, he was preventing the man from walking away.

He said, "Frank is dead. That doesn't mean much to me. It means a lot to you. So you're grieving and I'm not. What's worse — what's going to make the whole business just *indelible* in your mind — is the fact that you killed him. It was your fault." Bullen leaned forward very slightly, as if he were worried that Parker might not hear him. "You killed your own son. Yesterday he was alive and today he's dead and you did it." Bullen patted Parker's shoulder like a fond friend. He said, "You look really tired, you know that? I wish I could tell you to get some sleep, but I guess that's impossible, now, isn't it?"

For a moment, Bullen had a brilliant and vivid flash of memory: his mother slumped against the wall, dead for days and putrefying, while he spoke to her.

He said, "I'll bet you never sleep again."

34

Sonia went from room to room in her apartment looking at things, touching things. It seemed extraordinary that nothing had changed. In the bedroom, she lay down and closed her eyes.

Roscoe Tate had been talking on the telephone for

the better part of twenty minutes. Finally he hung up and started to and fro across the living area like a puma in a cage. "I've got two dead men and a police department asking questions I don't want answered. What's your solution?" He'd raised his voice so that it would carry to Bullen, who was in the kitchen making coffee.

Bullen shrugged. "What was Parker's story?"

"They did it to each other — got into an argument, Frank shot the guy who was with you in the car, he shot Frank. Frank died outright, the other guy took some time."

Bullen handed Tate a cup of coffee. "Who's Axel Dexter?"

Tate shook his head at the question: he had something else to say. "Two things — one, this can't go on forever. I told Cochrane I'd cover for you and I have, but no one told me I was going to have bodies all over the goddamn place. Two, I can't help you long-distance and I can't get you out of a jam once you're in it."

"Who is he?"

"Parker mentioned him to you?"

"He thought I was trying to pull the rug out on a deal he'd set up with Dexter. Later he began to guess he'd made a mistake. The deal was for weapons."

Tate glanced sharply at Bullen. "Dexter's an arms dealer. That's about all I know. Someone else will know more."

"Where is he? Where does he operate from?"

"New Orleans."

Sonia was leaning against one of the pillars in the

282

living space. She said, "Maybe I could have a cup of coffee, if that's okay."

"What happens if I go down there?" Bullen asked.

"Who the hell knows? Here's an idea — why not go to the house, ask to see Dexter, say, 'Some people have been getting killed. Can you help me out?' That ought to catch his attention."

"Is there someone I can talk to, something I can see — background, whatever?"

"Someone, sure; and there'll be a file. I could get a printout to your hotel."

"Thanks."

"Don't do anything without consulting me," Tate said, "don't take a piss without calling in, okay?"

"I'm doing a job," Bullen said, "and I'm asking for your help. That's all it is."

"Sure." Tate nodded. "That's what Cochrane told me. And one thing leads to another, right?" He turned to Sonia as if he were seeing her for the first time. "You look tired," he said. "You look like someone who needs to sleep."

Sonia gave a sour little laugh. "I had a bad night."

Tate put his cup down and walked to the door. "You pick the wrong people to have fun with."

She had made something to eat because in theory they were both ravenous. The food lay on their plates. Bullen was drinking steadily without seeming to get drunk. After a moment, she said: "Just a job. That's what you said to Tate. You're a spook and you're doing what spooks do — am I right?"

"Yes, that's right." His tone of voice contradicted

the admission, which made her angry.

"It's a job. You get paid."

"Not really. They used to fund things I wanted to do — caves I wanted to see. It costs money."

"Okay, they bribe you."

"That's right," Bullen agreed. "Bribes."

"Tell me the truth," she said. "I don't understand you at all."

Bullen put down his glass. He knew he was drunk, but couldn't find any real evidence of the fact. Sonia had made bacon and eggs; the food was cold, now, but he suddenly discovered a booze hunger and began to eat swiftly, without pausing or looking up.

She went to the kitchen and back for coffee. Bullen held his cup out like a vagrant. "Other people died. Roland Cecil was just one of them."

"I saw the newscast."

"No," he said, "other people."

At a certain point there's a kind of airiness about being drunk. Your words come back to you from corners of the room, from high windows.

"In my childhood," Bullen said, "I once had a dream, and I might have kept dreaming it, night after night, or I might have remembered it and only thought that I'd dreamed it again, I'm not sure. In the dream my mother was kind to me."

He finished eating the cold food and put his knife and fork down in tidy alignment. He looked at her and his mouth twisted a moment, like the pucker a scald leaves.

"I grew up and went away, did this and that" —

mimicking Sonia's tone of voice — "became a part-time *spook*. No distraction, no amount of distance, no length of time ever made me hate her any less. I think it might have been that she simply didn't have the gift of kindness — but you can't tell that to a child. She was so self-absorbed, so completely caught up in her love affairs, the men she worshiped, the men she wanted to be adored by, that the little slipup, the by-blow in her life, couldn't have much chance of catching her attention. When I was young, I used to pray for her death. I saw myself at her graveside. She would have been repaid for her sins, you see, and I would be free to love her in death. When it actually happened it wasn't at all like that."

"She died some time ago," Sonia said, "isn't that right?"

"I started talking to people after Roland's murder — people he'd been involved with. Nazis, fascists, Jew haters, racists . . . I went to see my mother because she had some of Roland's papers. While I was there, someone got into the house and burned most of the documents."

Bullen felt as though he were scarcely breathing; his fingers were tingling and he wondered if he was going to faint.

"Later I went back — much later. They'd killed her. She was in the dining room, against the wall, and she'd been dead for a time. They'd carved a swastika into her forehead. Things were feeding off her."

Sonia was very still, waiting to hear whatever was next. Bullen seemed to have stopped speaking, though. He folded his arms, unfolded them, put his hands on his knees. They sat in silence until Sonia asked, "Who? Who'd killed her? Why had they killed her?"

"That's what I'm trying to find out, that's why I'm being such a diligent spook." He was smiling broadly at her. Sonia thought she'd never heard a voice so laden with pain.

Bullen got up and the booze hit him like a truck. He fell backward, grabbing at his chair and pulling it on top of himself. Sonia helped him to the sofa and swung his legs up, then brought a chair and kept watch for a while, in case he threw up.

She thought that sitting with him while he slept was like waiting for a bomb to start ticking again.

She brought him coffee and some acetaminophen when he woke. The light in the room was a soft yellow and she had drawn curtains against the city glare.

"I'll go in a minute." It wasn't as bad as it should have been — a tinny percussion behind the eyes, a thread of bile rising in the throat. He swallowed the pills and coffee like someone with a train to catch. He remembered everything he'd said.

Sonia had spent the time dozing and thinking. "I heard you talking to Ross Tate. What does that mean? Roland and the others were negotiating an arms deal — maybe through Dexter? They're after weapons?"

"They think of themselves as an army: the war is against Jews, blacks, liberals, refugees, foreign workers . . . *Ausländer*. Armies have guns, don't they? At

286

the moment, they're using gas bombs, knives, clubs, iron bars. . . . A few automatic rifles would bolster their street cred quite a bit.''

"Could it be more serious than that?''

"I don't know.''

"You're going to New Orleans?''

"It's the next thing to do: the way forward.''

"What about the way back?''

He shook his head. "I don't think so. Not now.''

"I can't be a part of that.''

"Jesus Christ . . .'' He stood up and put out a hand to steady himself, finding only air. Sonia took it and held him steady. "You think I was expecting you to come with me?''

"I don't think you were expecting anything. I'm involved. I can't make that any different. I've been involved since I saw Caro Duval die, and I'm a part of whatever's going to happen. It's just that my part has to stop here. I got scared. I sat in that little pitch-black space, that cave, and I knew that if nothing happened, if I didn't die, then I wouldn't be able to run those risks again.''

"It's okay,'' Bullen told her, "it's fine. Why are you saying this?''

"Because I feel I'm giving up on something; this is an apology.''

"To me?''

She thought about it. "You're right — to myself.''

Bullen made a move toward the door and Sonia realized she was still holding his hand. He smiled ruefully: "I can make it.''

She released him and watched him walk to the door,

but didn't go with him. Suddenly, she felt unsafe. "What do you think," she asked, "will I see you again?"

Bullen remembered Anne at the airport: she had turned to raise a hand before going through passport control and, in that moment, a sense of loss had hit him like the onset of an illness.

"Will I see you again?"

35

Bullen got out of the shower and walked through a tangled heap of clothing. The door buzzer was going with the kind of aggressive persistence that meant the caller had tried before. As he pulled on a robe, Bullen squinted through the security spy hole and saw Paul Shelley's face wrapped around the optic like a portrait in a fish-eye lens.

He opened the door but didn't step back. Shelley's response was to hold on to the file he was carrying, moving it from his hand to underneath his arm like a soldier's baton. He said, "I rang from the lobby, came up to your room and tried the buzzer, then went back to the lobby and rang again."

Bullen spread his arms to indicate the robe. "I was in the shower."

"Twenty-five minutes," Shelley informed him.

"I was in the shower for twenty-five minutes."

Bullen gave way, letting Shelley in. He went into

the bedroom and reappeared fully dressed. "Should I have expected to see you?" he asked.

Shelley dropped the file onto a coffee table. "Roscoe Tate wasn't at all sure he could manage to keep control of things. Some people died." Shelley offered the information as if Bullen might not know.

"Why are you in New York — in case an official voice is needed?"

"I'm here to help if I can."

"When did you arrive?"

"This morning," Shelley said, and Bullen heard the lie like a stone in a well.

"What do you want me to do?"

"You mean about Axel Dexter?"

"About him."

"Tell me what happened in New England." Bullen told it all. When he'd finished, Shelley nodded at the file. "Dexter's in there; as much as we know about him."

"Duval was killed because he went up against Parker, tried to muscle in. Are you saying Dexter was directly involved?"

"Duval died because he went up against Parker *and* Dexter — that's what we have to assume."

"Duval was a shipper, so let's assume he was trying to get Parker's slice of the deal — shipping, haulage, whatever. Where does Dexter come in?"

"The killings were orchestrated and financed by someone with a lot more clout than George Parker. He's rich, but he's local."

"Who's been briefing you?"

"Tate. We spoke soon after he left Sonia Bishop's flat. He told me what he knew — that it was weapons and that it was Dexter. Our speculations started there."

"Does Tate know about the Macallun killing?" Bullen asked.

"Yes." Shelley indicated the file. "You'll find a separate document in there; not concerning Dexter, but giving you some background on a man named Joseph Chesnik. He was murdered in the men's room at a Broadway theater about three weeks ago. Only a few people saw the killer — the guy who *might* have been the killer; he was leaving in a hurry just before the curtain went up for the second act."

"The same man who killed Duval and Roland and Macallun."

"We think so."

"Chesnik was a shipper?"

"No, a broker and relatively new to the business. I mean, he knew how to put a deal together, he'd been doing it all his life, but weapons were a recent development. He'd had the best training, though — he made a fortune as a sanctions buster. Anything that was forbidden, he could get it over a border; any regime that was outlawed, he could get them what they needed."

"Why didn't we hear about him before — about his death, I mean?"

"If we'd known that weapons dealing was the issue — that someone like Dexter was involved — I expect we would have."

"How soon before this goes official?"

"Ah, yes . . ." Shelley smiled, as if Bullen had just asked the only question that mattered. "Pretty soon, I should think. Ross Tate's preparing a file. Sooner or later, he'll have to show it to someone. It's there to cover his ass, but I suspect it's too small a file to do the job properly."

"Apart from which," Bullen suggested, "we're on their turf; there's also the possibility that at some point we might need backup." He thought, For "we" read "me."

Shelley steepled his fingers like the chairman of the board. "We want to know more before we ask for help, because asking for help is tantamount to handing it over, and we'd like to avoid that for as long as possible. The best scenario is that we don't have to say anything. We've got this far, let's keep going."

Bullen caught a whiff of something in the air, a faint smell of rot. "There's going to be a cover-up."

"When we know what's there to *be* covered up, I'll let you know." Shelley added crossed legs to the steepled fingers; he was becoming the elder states-man. "Look at the implications. Roland is among the murder victims of a guy who deals arms internation-ally. Roland is also a Nazi. We'd like to know what these things mean, how they connect. Roland's death has always been worrying; his political affiliations were worrying; a link between the two looks like potential dynamite. We'd like to have the answers before the CIA gets them. In fact, we'd like to have them before *anyone* gets them. Then we can decide what's best to do."

"Hidden voices," Bullen said, "hidden motives."

"We don't operate like Members of Parliament, you know that. No select committees, no accountability, no one pissing on about democracy and open societies."

"Tell me about Dexter."

"Some dealers operate on a small scale, some trade with governments and the armies of governments. Dexter's one of the biggest. He doesn't import weapons or warehouse them: he's a broker. He makes the contacts and fixes the deal between seller and buyer, then takes a fee. You want to see a tank demolish a building before you place an order? He'll get you a grandstand view. He deals with presidents and smugglers. A lot of what he does is legitimate, but a significant percentage isn't. A loose international axis of secret services was organized some time ago — the idea was to try to control the spread of arms, but Dexter doesn't like to be told what to do. He'll fix a deal between any two parties who want to buy and sell. Sometimes he'll even finance the deal himself, but not often, because the trick to being a successful entrepreneur is don't let your ass hang out."

Bullen listened carefully. He said, "You talk as if you know him."

"I know *about* him, I've read this file. One of the things I found out is that he's very well protected. We'd like to know more."

"Like what?"

"Like who's buying what and how much of it. Dexter talks to people who run countries. He talks to people who destroy countries. Now you see why we're worried about what your bloody uncle Roland might have been part of."

A couple of squad cars whooped and wailed their

way downtown, and Shelley got to his feet as if the noise had roused him. "What kind of weapons did Parker talk about?"

"He didn't. He was already beginning to wonder whether he'd said too much."

"I was sorry to hear about your mother."

Shelley's remark was so unexpected that for a moment Bullen could make no sense of it. A little silence rang in the room. He said, "What happened? Did something happen?"

"We're pretty sure that Arthur Seacourt was involved." Bullen couldn't judge whether Shelley was being arch, or whether he really believed that there might be evidence against Seacourt. "We won't be asking the police to make a case against him, of course, because the death certificate says she died of a heart attack . . . and in any case, we wouldn't want you involved in any of that. But there was a very useful incident during the big Nazi rally in the East End: a man was found under one of the tower blocks where the fighting started. He spent a few days in intensive care, then died. We think we'll have Seacourt for that."

"Cochrane asked you to tell me this?"

"Stuart wanted you to know, yes."

Bullen liked the irony of it — Seacourt going down for the death of a friend. Then he remembered that it was Anne who had hit the guy with her camera; Anne who had killed him. He thought that if she never found out, then he would never tell her. To Shelley, he said: "What would happen if I didn't go to New Orleans? If I chose not to?"

Shelley had been strolling around the room like a man looking for something to do. "If you chose not to . . ." he repeated. "Choosing's a matter of having alternatives, I suppose."

"That's right."

"What would they be?" Shelley asked.

It was a day for meetings. In a room at the Plaza, Cochrane poured himself a cognac and glanced at Tate, who shook his head. "No thanks, Stuart."

"You like being sober?" Cochrane asked.

"I guess that must be it."

"People have the strangest ambitions."

Tate poured a glass of club soda. "The one thing we haven't talked about," he said, "is percentages."

"Well, you can't have a *percentage,* Ross. No *percentages* for you." Cochrane made the word sound mildly offensive. "What you *can* have is a once-and-for-all payment."

"Like a divorce settlement."

"That's right . . ." Cochrane grinned so that Tate wanted to slap him. "And that will depend on the size of the deal. And we don't know what that is yet. We didn't know Dexter was involved until Bullen told us; we still don't know who Dexter's dealing with."

"Until Bullen tells us."

"Let's hope so."

"We still haven't talked money."

"It's not a question of how much, Ross. It's a question of when. When to make your move; when to negotiate." Cochrane laughed as if remembering some wonderful joke. "Christ, I didn't know this was going to turn into an opportunity to rob the bank. I'm playing it by ear, I'm winging it."

"So, you'll tap Dexter?"

"If that seems right. If that seems the most profitable way. But who knows? There might be someone beyond him, and someone beyond that man, and then beyond him, someone else. The further you go, the bigger the profit, I've found that's the general rule."

"You'd better pull this off, Stuart. You'd better make this work."

Cochrane smiled. "I'm glad it's weapons. I feel happier with weapons than with drugs. I feel happier with the people."

Cochrane woke when Shelley came in. Tate had gone. Shelley asked, "Do you want to know now, or shall I catch you in the morning?"

"Is he going?"

"Yes, he's going. He thinks he might need some help. So do I."

Cochrane grimaced when he heard the edginess in Shelley's tone. "Don't worry. We hide what has to be hidden, we erase what has to be erased, we report what needs to be known. What's new?"

A thought struck Shelley. "Parker," he said, "do you think he'll have phoned Dexter?"

"Who knows . . ." Cochrane was silent a moment; he nodded, as if the idea seemed more than possible. "I imagine he might have done that, yes."

"So he'll know about Bullen; he'll know about Sonia Bishop."

"So he will," Cochrane agreed. "So he will."

Bullen was talking to Sonia on the phone. Calling was the last thing he'd expected her to do.

"You're going, then?"

"Tomorrow," he told her.

"On your own . . ."

"Tate's my backup."

"He's going with you?"

"That's not the plan, no."

"What do you have to do?"

"Find a route to Dexter."

"How will you do that?"

"I'm working on it." He had been asleep; now he was talking to her in the dark. "Why did you call?"

"Because I'll never see you again."

"That sounds gloomy."

"No . . . People meet, people part." The line carried a silence between them. "I know everything about you. I know about what happened to your mother."

"That's not everything."

"I know you like the darkness underground."

"That's not everything."

On impulse she asked, "Are you in love with some-one?"

There are times when talking on the telephone is just like talking to yourself. Bullen said, "I am. She doesn't know it."

Don't get caught in the cross streets . . .

"What time's your flight?" Sonia asked. "I'll take you to the airport."

36

They sat in a hamburger place at JFK watching two of the staff eat.

He told her that Paul Shelley had come to his room —told her who Shelley was. It felt like insurance, but he couldn't have said why. He told her that Shelley wanted a cover-up, wanted to bury anything inconvenient.

"Like the truth," Sonia suggested.

"Especially that."

"Rolandgate," she suggested.

Bullen laughed. "The ones that get found out, they're the ones that have names. The nameless are buried too deep."

"We don't know a thing, do we? How the world's run, who runs it, what they do?"

"Not really. The British are very good at it. We love secrets. All the great families of England have terrible secrets; keeping them is how the ruling class rules."

"Not just the British — who killed Kennedy?"

"Everyone does it."

"Do you care?"

"How would it help?" he asked.

She went with him to the gate. When his flight was called they shook hands, then she laid a hand on his upper arm and moved closer, asking to be kissed, and they pressed cheeks.

He'd already checked a leather grip that held a few changes of clothes, razor, shaving gel, things like that. The heavy suitcase he'd brought from England was in the back of Sonia's car, a promise that could easily be broken.

Kyle Bannick watched her out of the airport building. Now that he knew she wasn't taking the flight with Bullen, he could relax.

He found a table and got out of his pocket the copy of *Letters from a Dead Land* he was reading before he killed Hugh Macallun. It wasn't his first copy of the book; the others had fallen to pieces with reading and rereading. He sipped his beer, enjoying it, eyes on the page. There was no hurry. He figured that Sonia would probably put in some time at the West Side studio before she went home to her apartment.

He read:

> *It is easy to kill strangers because they have no substance. No names, no history: a perfect match for "no future"* . . .
>
> *. . . The drawback is obvious: they can be easily forgotten. . . .*
>
> *To remember a kill, to value it, to leave it burning under your ribs and scalding your veins, the one you lay your hand on must seem human and full to you. If you cannot taste their loss in death, you cannot make yourself gain.*

A woman who had joined him at the table noticed

that the ugly little guy across from her must be reading a funny book. She saw the shake in his shoulders, heard a hiss from the corner of his mouth. Or maybe it was a sad book, because when she cast a glance at his pale snub-nosed face, she saw how the mottled lips were contorted, how the shadow-ringed eyes had gone to slits, and couldn't tell whether she was looking at glee or at sorrow.

37

Sonia closed her eyes and went shoulders-and-feet up into the darkness. She heard the rustle of the bats, a sound like whispers in an empty room. She felt better when she remembered that Bullen was beside her, but the disk of flashlight swaying under the chimney almost made her cry out. That was the worst moment in the cave.

She opened her eyes and saw the Bonnard print she'd had framed for the wall of her bedroom: a table laid for breakfast, a terrace wall beyond the window, trees, and a lawn beyond that.

She was cross-legged on the bed and what she was doing was a kind of therapy.

She closed her eyes again and felt the limo fishtail as she came out of the corner trying to correct the skid, trying to keep off the brake, and all the time Good-looking's legs were twisting under her as the motion of the car jolted his wound. His shirt was drenched with blood; the seat of the car was soggy with it. That was the worst moment in the car.

She opened her eyes and looked at the Bonnard print again, finding new things there. She had owned it for a few years, but was still learning from it. A woman stood alongside the table, facing the painter, empty-handed, doing nothing: either waiting to be joined or waiting to be dismissed. Sonia's bedroom looked the way it always looked and that was a reassurance in itself.

She closed her eyes and watched as Bullen pulled Good-looking's dead body out of the limo. She heard the click as his boot heels passed over the sill. She heard the telephone ringing. She opened her eyes and picked up the phone.

He said, "This is Kyle Bannick. Does that name mean anything to you?"

They had a conversation that went just as he'd hoped. Sonia said, "Kyle . . . ?"

"Bannick."

"No, it doesn't mean anything. Should it?"

"Charley's best man? Charley Fleming?"

"Oh . . ." Sonia was silent a moment and Kyle let the silence grow. She was conjuring up a mental picture of the man; she must have seen him going to and fro between the tables, but the uninvited guest had arrived before any speeches had been given. She thought she remembered someone tall with longish hair and a broad, Scandinavian face that she couldn't put any real features to. "Yes," she said, "Kyle, I remember."

"I came up from Iowa for the wedding — I'd moved there, you know, Barbara and me . . . you have to go where the company goes." He laughed like a trapped man.

"I know how it is," Sonia said. She tried to remember Barbara and thought she got a snapshot of dark, skinny, big smile, but maybe that was somebody else.

"I hope you won't mind my calling. We just met that one time, but I'm in New York on business and I've been meaning to contact you. I got your number from the wedding list Charley gave me. You know, to make sure everyone's invitation actually arrived. He asked me to take care of that."

"I don't mind, Kyle." Oh, Christ, she thought, I hope this isn't going to be: I'm in the city and all alone, will you have dinner with me and maybe we could screw later because my wife's in Iowa and will never know and our marriage is pretty much a formality and maybe I could call you next time I'm horny in New York.

He said, "You must have talked to the police, didn't you? After the killings?"

A little buzz of shock circled her skull: of course that's what he wants to talk about. What else? "Sure, I talked to the police."

"And you saw the sections of the tape that were shown on TV?"

"I saw the whole tape."

"Right, okay, listen, Charley was my best friend, you know? We go back a long way. I didn't know Caro too well, but I liked her a hell of a lot." Kyle was grinning as he spoke — making a terrific job of being

Joe Average, Kyle Harmless. "I wish I could have done more to help — help the police, you know — but I was so damn scared I couldn't remember much." Another silence, then a sigh. "I wish I could have done more to help Charley, that's the truth of it."

"To help Charley?"

"I saw this guy open fire. I was paralyzed. I was standing close, close to Charley and Caro. I did nothing." He gave a laugh. "I did nothing, then I got under a goddamn table."

So that's it, Sonia thought. You poor bastard. You poor, sorry son of a bitch. A guy walks into a wedding party and starts shooting and you think you could have done something. Should have done something. Your best friend's dead and you feel guilty. She said, "What could you have done, Kyle? Nothing. The guy had a gun; it all happened so fast."

"I feel bad about it. I've been feeling worse and worse. I try to talk to Barbara, but she doesn't want to do that — she wants to forget. She won't let me mention it."

"It's a common feeling, Kyle; I'm sure it's a common feeling." Who am I, Sonia thought, Dr. Bishop, a hundred and fifty bucks an hour for wedding-murder-related stress? She said, "I think the trauma affects different people different ways. Thinking you could have done something, saved someone — it's a means of burying grief, don't you think? The truly guilty person hasn't been punished, so you punish yourself."

"You think so?"

Sonia thought she heard a lift in the voice — the

rising, thinner, lighter tone that means someone's on the edge of tears. "Where are you, Kyle?"

"I'm at a pay phone in a hotel. I was just walking around, you know, trying to think. I shouldn't have called you. I'm sorry. I'll get off now. Thanks for giving me some of your time."

It was a perfect pitch. Sonia said, "Listen, Kyle, why not come over? I know how you feel. I have dreams myself — bad dreams."

She gave him the address but, of course, he already had it.

The door had two double locks, a throw bolt, a security chain, but no peephole. He said, "It's Kyle, Sonia," and she opened the door on the worst thing of all.

At first, she couldn't understand what had happened. The door had been a few inches open, then had come at her as if driven by a battering ram, striking her first on the elbow of her left arm, then her shoulder, then whacking the side of her head — enough to stun. She sat on the floor without knowing how she'd got there, a hand to her face, her mind turning circles.

The door closed and she looked up and saw Kyle Bannick.

All she said was, *"Ah!"* Her thoughts went away from her, a sudden vacuum, then flooded back, everything pin clear: his face as he approached the top table, his face as he killed them, his face as he stared at her from the helicopter, laughing, his face now, as he looked down and laughed that same laugh. All those

303

images floated before her, all those feelings went through her, but she said only, *"Ah!"*

"Kyle," he said, "Kyle Bannick. I was the best man." His laughter grew fizzier. "Didn't you think so? Didn't you think I was just the best man there?"

She lay facedown — which is what he had told her to do — while he roamed the apartment. She heard a faint *rip,* then a crash as a telephone hit the floor, and he returned to her carrying the phone wire.

"Hands behind," he said, and knelt to tie her wrists. While he was doing it he laid the gun on her ass: she could feel it, heavy on her cleft, a hint of violation. He threw a loop of the wire around her ankles and tied it off, then reclaimed the gun and turned her over. Her bonds weren't tight or painful; he'd tied her to make watching her easier, not because he expected she'd try to punch her way past him and out the door.

"Well" — he smiled a thick, red smile — "you're a sight for sore eyes. I remember you sitting in that window — damn! you looked so beautiful in your wedding finery." Sonia could hear the faint southern twang in his voice and wondered whether it was genuine. "You sure seemed surprised to see me, though."

When Sonia didn't respond, he sighed and let his head slump, looking away into the room; he seemed to have gone into a slight daze. Sonia looked at her feet, held close together by the phone wire, like shoes in a closet, like feet waiting for the music to start. What was happening to her was so stark, so overwhelming, that she experienced a moment of fantasy where it was too intense to be real. She half fainted and the dream grew stronger, making her feel that she could walk out of her own life and take up residency somewhere else. When she tested her arms and legs against the phone wire, the dream broke up and left her with Kyle.

She asked, "What are we waiting for?"

"We're waiting for the streets to clear a little, for people to go home from restaurants and movie theaters. We're waiting for the city to bed down," he said. "When things are quieter, we'll go then."

"Go where?"

Kyle gave her a fat, wet smile. "Je-*sus*. You are a very beautiful young woman. . . . I guess you've been told that before, though. I feel I know you a little bit already, after our meeting at the Duval wedding. I didn't get to communicate with too many of the guests, you know? I was too taken up with killing them." His laugh came, damp and bubbly. "But when I came up to rooftop level — hell, I couldn't believe it. There you were, sitting with your glass of champagne in your hand, wearing that pretty blue dress and looking straight at me as if butter wouldn't melt in your mouth." He put his head back to one side and smiled a fond smile, a man savoring one of his best memories. "I've thought about that moment a lot. What a great moment."

He fell silent again for what might have been five minutes, his head lolling very slightly, the smile fluttering on his lips like the reflection of a flame; he seemed to have stalled on an idea. His gaze — vacant, unfocused — made Sonia breathless.

"Yeah . . ." Kyle's voice was soft and fixed in

memory. "Yeah . . . that was one of the all-time great moments."

Paul Shelley's file on Axel Dexter had also contained Bullen's air ticket, hotel booking, an Amex card, and an envelope with two thousand dollars cash. Thomas Bullen, company man, had traveled business class on TWA. Now he stepped in out of the wet heat on St. Charles Avenue and presented his green card to the desk clerk. The hotel lobby was antiques and dark wood polished to a gleam. His room was silk wallpaper and chandeliers.

He got room service to bring a cold beer and a bottle of tonic to go with the vodka he'd picked up at the airport, then opened the file on Dexter to get his phone number. Among the few documents in there was a photograph, head and shoulders, pin clear despite the fact that it had been taken with a long lens. Dexter was looking away to the right, and he must have been speaking, because his mouth was part-open and his face had the animated look of someone who has just asked a question. Behind him you could see the porticos and pediments of a grand house, topped by a vast out-of-focus cloud of bougainvillea.

Dexter was dark and had a narrow face — almost triangular so pronounced were the hollows in his cheeks. It made Bullen think of the angularity of a snake's head, not least because the lips were slight and thin. There was something about the arrested motion of the snapshot — the way the camera had caught him — that showed the man's energy and authority.

The other details of the file were pretty much the

way Shelley had summarized them. Dexter wasn't a gun runner: the term was too cavalier. He'd equipped armies, he'd laid down the stockpiles for civil wars. In that sense, Axel Dexter had made history.

Other fragments of information had caught Bullen's attention: Dexter appeared to work by the rules. "Appeared to" was the crucial phrase, but he was clever enough to seem entirely legal. He had few permanent staff. Mostly he hired people when he needed them: that way no one became closely associated with Dexter, which meant that there was no chain to contain weak links; it also meant that people were never around long enough to know much about Dexter's business affairs or his work methods. The only person who seemed to have been on the payroll for more than six months or so was a man named Morgan Sorrell, who acted as Dexter's lawyer.

The other remark that caught Bullen's eye read: sexual proclivities — none known. It seemed a remarkable piece of information: *"none known,"* as if part of Dexter's common humanity had been missing at birth, or had later been surgically removed.

He dialed the number on the printout and got an answering machine, simple and economical, giving all the responsibility to the caller: leave a message stating your name and number and the date and time of your call. The East Coast voice was smooth and confident, the tone brisk. Bullen put it down to Morgan Sorrell.

He left his name and the number of the hotel, but didn't wait around. He thought it might show a little class to be having a drink at Lafitte's when Dexter called back.

Kyle said, "Okay, I'm going to bring the car around now, so I'd like you to take a nap."

Sonia had spent half an hour asking questions that Kyle had answered with silent laughter, then she'd grown sullen. She imagined he was going to kill her and couldn't decide why he hadn't already done that. They had sat for a while, unspeaking, until Kyle got up and put a Jimmy Guiffre album on the CD player. He'd seemed to be caught up in the music, though he would look toward her from time to time, and wet the blubber of his lower lip, and dart a smile like a secret lover in a public place. While the jazz had played, percussion and soft cadences, the night had grown up around them.

I'd like you to take a nap.

No one had said that to her since she was a little girl, and she couldn't imagine what he might mean, what he might expect of her, until she saw the white bulb of a gauze mask in his hand. He knelt beside her, all bedside manner, and placed the mask over her nose and mouth. She pulled her head to the side, then back again when he followed with the mask. Kyle waved his hand to and fro, looking to settle the mask, and she reacted by wagging her head in avoidance. He laughed and passed his hand over her face a few more times, just to show that he could keep doing that all night. When she persisted, his laughter stopped and he gave her a stern little slap across the cheek, where it would sting.

She yelped and started to cry without knowing she was going to. Kyle stroked the slap, gentling her, and lowered the mask over her mouth and nose. The rich, pungent smell of ether followed at once.

His voice was gentler than his hand. "Sonia, don't worry. Just breathe, Sonia, just a nap, just a nap, Sonia. Don't worry, now, don't you fret, don't cry, Sonia ... Sonia too beautiful to cry, Sonia too lovely to cry ... Sonia ..." She went to sleep with the sound of his voice in her ears, darkness curling in like waves on a midnight shore.

His hand was the hand that rocked her and her own name was the lullaby.

She woke to the sound of a door closing. The room was dark at first, then hazy light began to pick at the corners; it was consciousness returning. For a moment, she thought she was in bed and tried to roll over, then felt the line of cramp that ripped from her wrist to her elbow, and the pain made her remember. As the cramp faded, Sonia began to float back into sleep, the darkness eating into the gauzy light once more. She felt nauseous, as if she'd overeaten.

Kyle went into Sonia's bedroom and found a suitcase. He packed some clothes for her, taking care over the choices: these jeans to that shirt and sweater; this skirt to that jacket; some casual, some more dressy; a pair of shoes, a pair of sneakers, a pair of ankle boots with crossover laces. He selected her socks and panty hose; he picked out her underwear, letting each fragile, lacy item drift over his hands and back into the drawer so that he could pick it out again.

Sonia said, "My wrists . . ." She had been lying on them and hadn't the strength to turn over; a cramp started up again, flickering along her tendons like St. Elmo's fire. She tried to say more, but the words tangled on her tongue.

Kyle went out to the street and put the case into the car, then went back and untied Sonia. The ether was still fuddling her. She said, "Where is . . . where are now but . . ." and sighed and leaned against him as he supported her down the stairs. They looked like lovers who had overstayed their welcome at the party.

When she woke again, she was handcuffed to the car door and they were cruising the city. Kyle handed her a can of diet cola. "Drink this. You'll feel better."

"I got to . . . want . . ." She stopped and selected the words carefully. "I have a headache."

"Sure." He had the acetaminophen ready.

They were driving by the West Side piers, Kyle looking around as if expecting to meet someone. The dashboard clock read 2:40 A.M. The car slowed almost to a halt, then Kyle turned along Fifty-first Street and put on some speed, finally heading uptown on Eighth Avenue.

"What do you want?" It was a question that Sonia had tried out on Kyle fifty times at her apartment, before he put on the Jimmy Guiffre album.

"Right now? To show you something."

When they got to the Seventy-ninth Street transverse he started across the park, cruising, just cruising, like a small-town kid looking for fun on a Saturday night. Someone ran across in front of them, lit by the headlights for a second or two — fleet and furtive like a night creature, eyes glittering. Kyle slowed and looked toward the bushes where the man had disappeared, then seemed to have second thoughts, accelerating away with a little whinny from the tires.

They drove downtown on Fifth, Kyle with his elbow lodged against the door frame, peering out at the sleeping bodies on the parkside benches.

Sonia found she could speak without having to switch her brain to "word select," and the need to sleep wasn't so heavy on her. She asked, "What are we doing?"

Kyle's eyes switched from the road to the roadside, then back again. "Shopping," he said.

They drove a slow loop, right down Fifth Avenue then back uptown to Union Square.

"Shopping," Kyle said again. He made a jazzy little one-word song of it, *shop-bop,* and tapped his fingers on the steering wheel.

On Sixteenth Street he found what he was looking for. Outside a music studio, a man and woman were saying good-bye to a group of five or six guys — except the woman was standing a little way apart, refusing to be part of the group. They were all musicians: each of the men was carrying some kind of instrument case. The girl was empty-handed, so she was the singer unless she was the drummer. Her name was Jasmine, and it really was her name, and she'd been the only white girl on her block with a name like that. Jasmine had been having an affair with the sax player, Denver Redwing. Denver was born and bred in Brooklyn Heights, but he had the cheekbones to carry off the deception and native American was fashionable.

Jasmine thought that the affair was about over. Denver's little habits were beginning to pall — like the way he ignored her if they went for a beer with the guys; like the way he turned her this way and that when they were screwing. Worst of all, he had taken to jumping in all the windows whenever she was singing most sweetly, coming on strong with little staccato rills as if the sax were shoving her aside.

She walked a few paces farther while Denver and the guys continued to talk about the demo tape they'd just made. Kyle had seen her from some way off; now he pulled over while he was still fifty feet away from the group.

Jasmine waited, walked a few yards more, came back, waited again. Finally she said, "Denver, you comin' or what?"

Denver was laughing at some joke, but the smile slid away as he turned. "I'll be there."

"Because I'd like to go now." He turned again. "Right now — do you have a problem with that?" The anger was clear in her voice. A couple of the guys looked toward her, startled, then laughed and went back to the conversation.

Denver waved a hand at her. "I'm coming, Jasmine. I'm on my way. I'll be with you in a minute. Shut up, okay?"

"Denver, I'm —"

He walked a pace or two toward her, but he'd left his saxophone case close to the group, as if it were standing in for him. "You wanna go — go. Catch a cab, go, I'll see you later." He paused. "What in hell's the matter with you anyway?"

She opened her mouth to tell him, but then turned and walked away. Without looking around she said, "Son of a bitch." A little farther off she said, "Motherfucker."

Kyle let her make twenty yards then cruised past the group. One of the guys looked up to see if he was a cab, then dropped his head again. Denver was conducting the band, arms out and wagging up and down; he said something and everyone laughed.

Kyle tapped Sonia's knee as if he needed to get her attention. "We're going to take a long drive, you and me. A *long* drive — couple of days or so. Now, we're gonna be traveling by automobile because I figure that trying to make you behave yourself on an airplane or sit still on Amtrack might be a problem. I mean, you could just yell out, 'This guy's kidnapping me,' and there we are in a crowd and what in hell could I do about that, huh? That could be a problem for me. Driving, now, that's gonna be a lot easier. Just you and me in the car. Come nightfall, we'll make a stopover at some motel. Just you and me. But there'll be times when we'll be close to people — bound to be."

Jasmine was looking back over her shoulder, wanting a taxi to come along. It was almost 3 A.M. on Seventeenth Street and lower Park Avenue and she was right to feel frightened. Kyle passed her, still talking.

"So I want you to know that when I say to you — and there'll be times when I say this — do the right thing or I'll kill you" — he looked at her and saw the expected spasm of fear — "I want you to be certain that I will. That I'll kill you. I want you to believe me

313

and because you believe me, do what I tell you to do. You understand me? If you do the wrong thing, I'll kill you for sure."

Sonia nodded. After a minute she said, "Yes," and nodded again.

Kyle turned into a cross street and parked close to the junction. "Good," he said, "that's good. And here's how you'll know."

He got out of the car and locked it, then went back to the corner. Jasmine was about twenty feet away, too late to turn around or try to cross the street. She balked when she saw Kyle, then kept going because there was nothing else to do.

Don't be crazy, she thought, he's just a guy walking. I'm walking. Does every guy out late in Manhattan have to be a nut with a gun?

When she saw the gun, Jasmine slipped the strap of her shoulder bag down her arm and held the bag out to him. "Everything's in there — money, credit cards, everything."

"That's kind, but I don't want it."

"What do you want?"

"I want you."

Jasmine's eyes were everywhere: maybe Denver would appear, or one of the guys, or a passing squad car, and she could throw herself under its wheels and come out of this with nothing more serious than a broken back. She said, "Please don't hurt me."

She looked at his face and he was smiling to reassure her, a lick of spittle on his sausage lips. The smile scared her more than the gun. "I'm not going to. I want you to meet someone.''

"You want —"

"What's your name?''

"Jasmine.'' She was shaking and the word came out in three syllables: *J-as-mine.*

"Jasmine's pretty, a pretty name.'' That touch of the South in his voice.

He walked her around the corner, a hand on her arm, the gun up against her ribs, and they came to the car. Sonia's face was pale behind the glass, and solemn. Jasmine saw her and said, "What's this? What do you want me for?'' and her voice was like tinsel in the wind. When Kyle opened the door and Jasmine saw how Sonia was pulled forward by the handcuff, she almost fainted.

Kyle was holding her up with one hand. She stuttered the last couple of paces to the car and he released her so that she fell forward, throwing out both arms to break the fall. Her hands slapped against the bodywork of the car and she stayed on her knees because the alternative was to stand up and that was impossible now. Sonia's face was just a few feet away and looking directly at her. Jasmine asked, "What does he want?''

A garbage truck went by — Kyle, Sonia, and Jasmine all on the blind side. A couple of cars crossed the intersection, traveling fast up Park Avenue.

Jasmine was quaking so that she seemed to be in the grip of a monstrous fever: her hands shook, and her arms; her head nodded in a palsy of fear.

Kyle said, "This is what I wanted you to know.'' He caught Sonia's hair at the base of her neck and held her head still so that she could look neither right nor left, and shot Jasmine twice: through the throat and then, when she flipped back, through the chest.

He rounded the car and got in. As he drove away he told her, "Shut the door." Sonia was looking back to where Jasmine lay in the road; she saw the woman get up on one elbow, then fall back.

"She's still alive."

"She's dead. Maybe she hasn't found out yet." His voice was quiet and level. "Shut the door, Sonia, we have to go."

He was driving quickly now, circling west toward the Holland Tunnel. Sonia was crying without moving, without sobbing. "It's gonna be fine." Kyle gave a little chuckle. "I know it's gonna be fine. If you take a notion to run off, or yell out, or make some kind of a fool of yourself, just remember poor Jasmine and everything'll be fine."

Evan Bannick had eaten a terrific room service meal that evening; now he was watching TV and drinking a beer and having a good time at someone else's expense. Most people would have been asleep at that time in the morning but, like his twin, Evan didn't need much sleep. He thought he'd wait for the movie to end, drink another beer, then do what he'd come to do.

They were showing *The Alamo* and Evan was humming along to "The Green Leaves of Summer" when Kyle shot Jasmine. Like a delay on a transatlantic phone call, there was an echo of something before the moment carried to Evan. He looked away from the TV screen and toward the window, where the reflection in the glass was his own and Kyle's, too, as if his twin had appeared there to give him the news.

He said, "Something's happened," and paused for a while, holding his breath. "Nothing bad," he said, by which he meant, nothing bad for us. It was like the memory of a dream: you had to concentrate to retrieve the feeling. "Kyle," he whispered, "now just what in hell have you been doing?"

The tunnel was harsh with white light, and the car drifted as Kyle's hand jumped on the wheel. He pulled it back, smiling to himself.

Sonia saw the smile and closed her eyes. The skin on her face crawled, the skin on her neck.

Kyle thought, You know what that was, Evan? Know what it was? Guess. *Guess!* And it's your turn next.

Evan smiled and went to the window, watching his moony face advance on him, watching Kyle advance. He leaned forward until their pug faces were close, their breath misting the windowpane, a look in their eyes, a smile on their lips, their malice a perfect match.

Nose to nose, they whispered a fragment of song: *Remember my friend, it's never too late/Whether it's love or whether it's hate/Everything comes around that goes around/Do-do-be-do . . .*

Evan gave a soft-shoe shuffle and kissed the glass.

Bullen had taken a drink or two that night and the

phone rang twelve times before he came to and lifted it.

Evan said, "Thank you for contacting Mr. Axel Dexter; I'm returning your call on his behalf. Please go to the door of your room to receive our communication. Have a good day."

Bullen went to the door in darkness and opened it left-handed so that when it was wide he was standing inside the room with his back to the wall. Nothing happened. He looked out and saw a shoe box in the hallway. He brought the box into the room and closed the door, then, trapping the lid with both thumbs, shook vigorously. Something inside moved, though not of its own accord: no sounds of coiling and uncoiling, no angry hiss, no mechanical clicks and ratchetings.

Bullen put the box on a coffee table and loosened the lid until it was almost off, then stood holding a coat hanger at full length and flipped the lid onto the table.

Inside the box was a coffin; inside the coffin was a grave doll made of sacking and string. Under one arm the doll held a hibiscus flower, under the other a postcard.

Bullen lifted the doll out. She was very old; the rough stitching down her left side and across her abdomen had begun to unpick and little gray entrails of string stuffing drooped down. She wore a faded rust-colored cap shaped like a hood to cover her head and cheeks and the red velvet of her dress showed only in tufts. Her eyes were age-blackened scraps of pearl, and her mouth was sewn shut. Crumbs of earth still clung to her — the mold of the grave.

The postcard was a tourist's-eye view of Jackson Square. The message read: "Welcome to New Orleans. Stay by your phone." Bullen felt as though someone had transferred a touch, a light blow, just to get his attention. He noticed that dust from the doll had smudged his fingertips and he brought them to his nostrils, sniffing delicately the deep, sour smell of his own mortality.

It was four-thirty. Evan was back in the room at the west bank HoJo, where he'd been living for the past four months: he'd made the phone call from there. Now he made a second call to report that the package had been safely delivered, then lay on the bed fully clothed to drink a bottle of beer. The book on the coverlet, folded back midway through, was *Letters from a Dead Land.*
He read:

Tuesday, September 4. What delivers us? What dispenses mercy? What takes us out of the way of harm? Today I watched an eagle kill a snake. The great bird mantled its victim with its wings, one claw on the coils. The snake curled and uncurled, the thick length of its body thumping into the dust like a slow whip. This means that lofty things will prosper, things of fierceness and instinct. I made it my token. Much later I went out to kill, though nothing fell my way.

Evan slept, dreaming of the eagle and the snake.

319

Kyle and Sonia were on Interstate 78, west of Newark. She was woozy with ether fumes or panic or both; her chest had an iron band around it; her wrist a steel cuff.

Kyle thought of the passage about the eagle and the snake.

He glanced sideways a moment and saw their face twinned and solemn in the glass.

38

Bullen could have ordered a room service breakfast, but he went down to the restaurant for eggs, juice, and coffee. He could have sat on the elegant sofa in his room just an arm's reach away from the phone, but he went out into the damp, hazy day and walked where the tourists walk, then rode the St. Charles streetcar like a man waiting to be found.

No one found him.

When he got back to his hotel there was a message in his key compartment behind the desk. The desk clerk handed it over with a little bow and flashed a smile: "Yoh welcome. . . ." The envelope was sealed and only his room number was written on the front — clearly someone had delivered it. The paper bore just one line: "Stay by the phone or go home."

Bullen went to his room and sat by the window with a glass of vodka in his hand. The killer heat of high summer had given way to early October's humidity and damp, and the sky over the city was a dull pearl. The air was thick and seemed to lie in strata just above the streets.

He knew that Dexter was showing class by confining him. Bullen wondered whether the message meant: I wonder who you are. Sit still and shut up while I try to find out. It might mean: I hear you're trouble. Sit still while I draw a bead.

He sat still. He could see his own reflection in the blank TV screen across the room — *Figure in Hotel Room*, a sketchy portrait in tones of gray, pockets of gray light, gray dust from the grave doll.

They had stopped in Harrisburg, Pennsylvania — Sonia's first chance to die. Kyle had driven carefully and well under the limit, though not so slowly as to attract attention. They'd made the stop at seven-thirty. Uncuffed, Sonia had sat on a stool in a diner and watched Kyle eat a breakfast of scrambled eggs and muffins and drink three cups of coffee. She had juice. It rose and fell in her gut like mercury in a thermometer.

They had come off Interstate 81 a couple of hours later and found a small-town supermarket: she had pushed the cart while he'd tossed items in: cold cuts, cheese, hamburger buns, macaroni salad, fruit, mineral water, beer. They were just like any ordinary married couple — beauty and the beast. She'd looked at the faces of the people shopping and wondered how you made your expression say, "I've been kidnapped by a crazy man. This is him, right here. He killed a woman in New York City and he has a gun in the waistband of his pants under his coat. I don't know where he's taking me and I'm so scared I could faint." It seemed a complicated message for a mere expression, so she had just tried to make her face say, "Please help me." People had strolled past, transfixed by the need to buy.

Kyle drove for another three hours, coming off the highway again near Front Royal, Virginia, and covered ten miles of hill road before stopping. He waved an arm as if to share the view: a perfect place for a picnic.

Sonia shook her head to the food. Kyle cuffed her hand to the steering wheel while he ate; he cracked a beer and she shook her head to that.

"You need to eat, don't you? Don't you want something?"

"Just let me out and drive away. How about that?"

Kyle laughed. "Yeah . . . how about that?"

He got out and went to the back of the car. Sonia watched in the side mirror as he hunched and delved into his pants. A long arc of piss clattered out onto the roadside shoulder. When he got back into the car, she said: "I have to go."

"I know how you feel," he said, "but we're going to be together for some while yet."

She thought he'd misunderstood her until she saw the smile on his face. He waited her out, though, and in the end she had to say it to him, just as he wanted her to: "I have to go to the bathroom." The euphemism sounded ridiculous.

He uncuffed her and got out of the car, then walked around to join her. She said, "Get back into the goddamn car."

"I can't; I'm sorry."

"From the car you could see the top of my head."

"Maybe." Kyle shrugged. "I don't want to have to chase around the countryside after you. Lots of places to hide in this kind of landscape."

"I'm not planning to run anywhere."

"Okay." But he stood there.

"Turn away," she said, but he stood there.

Sonia wanted to cry. Why had he waited this long? she wondered. He could have done it to me in my apartment. She said, "Please don't hurt me. Just don't hurt me, okay?"

"Sonia. *Sonia* . . ." As before, his tone was low and musical. "I don't want to hurt you, I told you that. Didn't I? I thought I made a point of telling you that when I had to shoot Jasmine."

Sonia was wearing the jogging pants and sweatshirt she'd had on when Kyle had knocked at the door of her apartment. Now she turned her back and jammed her thumbs into the elastic waistband of the gray pants. Her arms were shaking, but there was nothing she could do — fear was making it worse. She hooked the pants down to her upper thighs, her panties too, and crouched quickly, tugging down the hem of her sweatshirt.

She puddled the ground under her and the stream she made ran back from her heels and wound through the roadside dust. When she was through, she pulled the pants up to cover most of her ass, then got up, dragged them the rest of the way, and turned to face Kyle, fearing his approach. He hadn't moved. The broad line of piss trickled to his toe cap, then doglegged and found a path between his feet.

He asked, "Feel better?"

They got into the car and drove back to the highway.

Evan Bannick took a cab to the garden district.

Axel Dexter's front door opened onto a vast hallway, a double staircase, statues and Persian rugs and carefully lit oil paintings. Heavy doors led to rooms which in turn led to further rooms, and rooms beyond those that extended all the way back to a room that was half-garden.

Someone had designed a perfect progression from dark wood panels to ceiling-high bookshelves, from bookshelves to brickwork, from bricks to pillars, from pillars to walls of glass that gave light to vines and hanging plants and blossoms dripping scent.

The pool was half in the house, half outside: you swam between marble columns in the room, then through a low glass arch out into the garden.

Dexter and Morgan Sorrell were sitting in cane rockers by a glass-topped table. A third chair faced them, as if they were interviewers waiting for an applicant. Dexter was sipping a bourbon and water that was nine-tenths water. Sorrell was buttoned into a dark suit like a corporation man taking a break from a convention; he was medium height and medium build, a man from an overused mold. The feature that

324

made you look twice was red hair, cut short and carrying two thin streaks of gray, close together, like fault lines.

Evan went to a small refrigerator close to the pool and took out a beer, looking over his shoulder at Dexter. "He's in the hotel whenever you want to speak to him."

"Who is he?" Dexter was asking the question of Sorrell.

"Who knows? He got to George Parker by way of the Bishop girl. His story was that he wants a piece of some deal or another." He looked pointedly at Dexter and raised an eyebrow.

Dexter said, "It's just a deal. A little bigger than most, that's all."

"Well, he fucked up George's life: that's the next thing that happened."

"I spoke to George," Dexter said. "He sounded terrible. We can't use him. Frank's dead and George killed him, poor bastard. And the girl . . ." Dexter waited for a reminder.

"Beth."

"Right, somewhere in New York with a habit and a loose mouth and some dipshit junkie hitting on her." He topped up his light amber drink with more water. "Any chance of getting to Beth?"

"We're trying."

"Try harder. Kill her. Kill them both." Dexter sighed, a man badly let down by chance. "Bullen said what to George — that he's a shipper?"

"George thought he was bullshitting."

"Meaning what? He's a government man?"

Sorrell shrugged. "It doesn't seem likely."

"We can check that — right?"

"We are checking. We're checking now. But we don't think so."

"Why not?"

"He came out of left field, no one's ever heard of the guy, he doesn't even seem to be too clear about what's going on — just that he wants in. He's a persistent bastard."

"When's the girl get here?" This to Evan, who brought his beer over and sat in the third chair.

"Kyle's bringing her down by car: only way to handle it. Kidnap on the move isn't easy. We're talking about better than thirteen hundred miles. They'll be here day after tomorrow, I guess, because Kyle can drive nine hours at a stretch if he needs to, but he won't be speeding and nine hours a day is a different thing than a nine-hour drive and he has to sleep. I reckon two nights on the road."

"We heard from him yet?"

"No need."

Dexter's narrow head swayed from side to side: reptilian, narrow eyed. "I told him to call in."

"Don't worry," Evan told him, "he'll call if you asked him to."

"Can we keep this sucker on ice for a while — this whoever he is, Bullen?"

"I don't know, Axel." Evan held up his hands: plump palms and ten raw sausages; his feet didn't reach the floor and he kept the rocker going with an obscene little thrust of the hips. "If I'd met the guy, I'd know more."

"We don't even know what he wants," Sorrell added.

"Whatever it is, he's come a long way to get it." Dexter sipped his watered bourbon. "There's a lot of difficult shit with this deal, a lot to set up. I don't need some asshole jerking me around. Maybe I ought to find out what he wants, what he thinks he can get."

"Also what he knows," Sorrell added.

"Yeah." Dexter had become suddenly agitated. He used a foot to start the rocker moving — just a tick — and he half closed his eyes in thought. He and Evan were rocking back at the same time, rocking forward, like creatures looking for an opportunity to strike at one another. Dexter said, "Call him. Set up a meeting."

"He'll ask for neutral ground."

"Yeah, I'm sure."

"How neutral do you want it to be?"

"If he's any damn good, he won't give me an edge, but you can try."

"I could kill him," Evan offered. "You want me to do that?"

Dexter turned his face away and gave a sigh. He stopped rocking. After a moment he looked at Evan head-on. "It's not a matter of whether he's dead, you understand? It's what he wants, what he knows, who he's told, where he's from. It might even be a case of what he can do for me. He wants a piece of the action? Maybe he deserves it; maybe he should have it. Maybe he's going to be *good news,* Evan. Think of that? It's why he's not dead already; it's why the girl's on the

327

way here — if it comes to negotiating, she's one of the things on offer."

Evan had stopped rocking. His stillness was the stillness of cold control.

"Go back to his hotel," Dexter instructed. "Stall him. Keep him there while I think about what's best to do. Remember he's seen your face."

"Kyle's face, too." He said it without a trace of a smile.

Morgan Sorrell gave a half laugh. "That's the same thing."

"Yes it is." Now the smile came, arriving in the same moment that Sorrell started to feel stupid. Evan hopped down from the rocker and left quickly, taking his beer with him.

Sorrell watched him out the door. "He makes my flesh crawl. They both do."

"They're killers. All killers are strange. The idea is to hire the best. The better they are, the stranger they come."

He held out his glass. Now that the ice had melted, the fluid was barely tinted with color. "Get me a proper drink." When Sorrell looked at him, he added: "Fuck doctors and fuck you, too."

Sorrell went to a table near the refrigerator and came back with a bourbon on the rocks. He said, "I know all there is to know about this deal except I don't know where the merchandise is going."

"You don't have to know everything, Morgan."

"Sure I do. I'm handling the Swiss accounts. Who's actually paying the money?"

"Sons of bitches."

"They're all sons of bitches, Axel. Don't fuck me around."

A silence came into the room, swift and cold as a snow wind. Dexter turned his head to one side, the same gesture he'd made when Evan suggested a quick kill, and sighed the same sigh. It seemed that he couldn't bear to look at people who disappointed him.

"Morgan . . ." Dexter's voice drifted off. The wooden ceiling fans gave long, feathery whispers like arrows in flight. "Morgan, don't ask me. Everyone knows a certain amount. Only I know everything. The money gets transferred, the merchandise gets shipped. Just make sure you get the numbers right. And the fucking timing."

Dexter pushed out of his chair with abrupt energy and left the room. Sorrell sat on, trying to keep his breathing even, giving a little, wry smile of apology — as if he were being watched, as if Dexter's chair, still rocking back and forth, marked his invisible presence.

For a long time, Morgan Sorrell had watched Dexter going to the limit. He knew that there would be a time to bail out, and his guess was that the time was soon. And maybe this deal was it.

Dexter had a bad heart. Sorrell thought that could be read two ways — ill-health or something evil at the center of things. The condition didn't detract from Dexter's power, nor did it seem to limit his energy; the man still put in fifteen-hour days when he needed to and made ten countries in four days in order to tie up a series deal.

Sorrell didn't like Dexter, but he liked the money

329

he paid. More of the same would make Sorrell's life a lot easier to live. He knew that the important thing was timing — in all things, timing. Don't go too soon, don't go for the wrong reason or on the wrong terms, don't go too late. Look for the moment . . .

Look for the moment, Sorrell thought, feel it, sense it, be sure you're right, then sell Axel Dexter to the highest bidder.

39

Mohawk Crossroad is where you find America Anonymous. Kyle drove off the highway and doubled back, ignoring Sonia's questions. Soon she would learn not to ask any.

When they came to the outskirts of a town, he said: "I'm going to give you a key, now. Unlock the cuff with it, then put both in my pocket. Think of Jasmine and do it right." He was driving right-handed, the gun in his left, deliberately visible.

Sonia didn't know where they were, but thought that Kyle must have spent time there because he obviously knew where he was going. Then she saw the Best Western and realized what had happened: Kyle had driven the whole route going north to New York. He knew how to pace himself and he'd looked for places to stop over — towns, motels — on the return journey south.

"I know where we're going," she said.

Kyle registered them as Mr. and Mrs. Bannick, as though he had nothing at all to hide and nothing to fear. Sonia sat in the car while he signed and got the keys. She was having a conversation with herself about the nature of risk.

"Lose? Lose what? You can't mean your life, because it's a fair bet you're going to lose that anyway. Just get out of the car and run. Scream your tonsils out and run."

"He'll kill me. Remember Jasmine?"

"Yes, I remember her. She's dead. She didn't run."

"All I'm saying is there might be a way out of this without getting myself shot in the back in the parking lot of a Best Western motel, *okay?* This guy isn't here to kill me, he's here to take me to New Orleans."

"So you're going in there with him, into the motel room."

"No . . . okay, I'll ask for separate rooms: I bet he'd go for that."

"And spend the night there with him."

"You think —"

"I think he's going to have a couple of drinks, turn on the TV, shove your underwear in your mouth, and fuck you flat. I think it's a sure thing."

Sonia opened the car door and Kyle slammed it closed as he passed and got behind the wheel. He said, "The difference between living and dying — your foot in the car, your foot on the ground."

Sonia was cold deep in her abdomen. She said, "I've been in the car for hours and goddamn hours and

I needed to stretch my legs. I'm getting cramps."

Kyle parked the car in front of their room and helped her out. "I understand," he said, "but listen —"

He closed the door of the room and turned her and slapped her hard, twice, high on the head where he wouldn't leave a bruise.

"—but listen: don't do anything without asking me. Then I can decide whether I believe you or not."

"I had leg cramps."

He smiled and stood very close to her. His body odor was sour and thin, like vinegar. "I don't believe you, Sonia, lovely Sonia, untruthful Sonia, Sonia my angel, my dear. But it doesn't matter." He smiled a broad, fat, pink-and-white smile. "No harm done."

At five-thirty Evan Bannick called Bullen's room again, using PA-speak because it amused the hell out of him that people should ever talk that way.

"We're interested in a meeting, Mr. Bullen. I haven't been advised yet of the time and venue, so we would be grateful if you could wait by your phone until we have better information on that."

"I can go elsewhere," Bullen snapped. "Tell Dexter he's not the only person moving weapons."

"I'm afraid I can't comment on that, but I'll certainly advise our people of your feelings in the matter."

"Do that. Tell them to hurry and tell them to make it neutral ground."

"Neutral," Evan repeated, seeming to hear the term for the first time. "Neutral ground. Yes, sir, I'll let them have your thoughts on that."

Kyle said, "Maybe you'd like to take a shower."

"Not right now." They were standing in the middle of the room like guests who haven't been asked to sit down yet.

"Uh-huh . . ." Kyle nodded and looked at her, waiting for the real answer.

"Maybe later."

He smiled patiently. "The reason I'm asking is I've been driving for a long time with just a couple of breaks. I'm really tired and I'm going to have to sleep. Here's how I'm going to do that: you'll have one hand cuffed to the bed and the other cuffed to me. So if you want a shower or take a leak or whatever it is, now's the time. There's no window in the bathroom, but I'll be sitting in the doorway to make sure you don't lock the door. You'll see the chair, but you won't see me. And I won't see you, if that's your problem; I'll be behind the door. Now you make your choice, but don't wake me up to tell me you've changed your mind."

He let her take a change of clothes from the case he'd packed, and she saw how careful he'd been in picking things out for her. When she turned on the shower, he brought a chair to the door and sat on it, obscured from her apart from his legs. She stripped quickly and stepped into the tub.

In that moment, the mirror above the sink caught her reflection and played it back to Kyle, her long legs, the way her back arched, the neat patch of blond hair in her groin, her breasts swinging free of her rib cage as she leaned forward to yank the shower curtain. Five minutes later, he watched her emerge, pearled with water. The mirror framed her, neck to thighs, her face unseen and unseeing. The image stayed for a moment. Her breasts trembled slightly, shedding water, and her skin was rosy from the heat. Then she went out of range to towel herself.

As she dressed, he glimpsed her now and then: shrugging into her bra, stepping into her jeans, emerging from a T-shirt.

She stood at the door, fully clothed, her face naked of makeup; Kyle caught a faint smell of soap, like almonds.

He handcuffed her as he'd said he would — one arm raised, the other alongside him — and slept almost as soon as he lay down. Sonia looked at the phone, at the door, at the curtained window, and put her chances at nil. Kyle slept without stirring. She looked for something to kill him with, as if that were possible, as if all it would take was nerve and a strong arm. His breath made a damp hiss as it snagged on his teeth.

His eyelids fluttered — butterfly kisses — and his fingers flicked, tapping the back of her hand above the steel bracelet. She realized that he was dreaming and the thought disturbed her, as if she might also sleep and find herself a part of his dream. After a moment he seemed to grow heavier as his sleep deepened.

Sonia turned her head to put him out of her sight and closed her eyes in despair. A moment later she, too, was asleep. Hands linked, heads drawn apart, they lay like statues on a tomb.

Bullen was writing a letter he'd never expected to send.

. . . I haven't done much to expect loyalty from you, or patience, or any measure of under-standing, so I suspect that "I love you" isn't enough — but maybe it's a start. You'll probably want to know: what's the deal here? The answer is: I'm trying to think of a fair trade. There probably isn't one — and I'm not used to giving things away, am I? Maybe it's time I started . . .

He went to the vodka bottle and back. Stalled in a hotel room, rash enough to get drunk, he was taking a risk he'd never expected to take. He tore up the letter and began again.

"Dear Anne . . ."

"Dearest Anne . . ."

Sonia woke and realized at once that she was un-cuffed. Kyle said, "Feels better, doesn't it?" as if the relief were something they could share. He had moved to the second bed and was propped up on one elbow, reading a tattered book. An open beer stood on the bedside table. There was a deadness about the air, a stillness that only comes with the small hours of the morning.

"Can I have a drink?"

Kyle gestured toward the fridge and she poured herself a brandy. He said, "Get back on the bed please, Sonia," and then, "Thank you," when she obeyed. There was something wanton about the way the bed rocked under her. She felt more at risk now than she had when he was lying alongside her.

"You're fine; you're safe with me." He might have

been reading her thoughts.

She drank off half the brandy and asked Kyle what he was reading, as if the rush of booze had immediately loosened her up and given courage. He smiled, recognizing the first moment of intimacy in the strange contract between hostage and captor.

"I've read this book to ruination several times. I buy a new copy when the one I've got falls apart." He held it up so that she could read the title, *Letters from a Dead Land*, then took the book with him to the fridge and pulled the cap off another bottle of beer. He settled on the foot of Sonia's bed, legs crossed, his back against the wall.

"This guy, the guy who wrote this . . . it's supposed to be a diary . . . he lives his life by signs, all his decisions depend on signs, on whatever he sees that's lucky or unlucky — you understand?"

Sonia had drawn her legs away as soon as he'd clambered on with her. Now she sat with her knees raised, arms clasped around her shins, trying to hold the position without trembling. "No," she said, "I don't."

"Omens," Kyle told her. "He looks for something to give him a lead, you know? A signal. Like this . . ." He flipped a few pages and began to read.

"Nothing as simple as a falling leaf or a flight of birds. Anyone could share such a moment. It must be something only I have witnessed — as if it might be meant only for me. Nor must I seek it out or try to invoke it. It must come unbidden, true chance. I'm a fortune seeker and luck is all

I can rely on. If you try to force your luck, it turns around.''

"What's he looking for?" Sonia drank the remaining brandy and went to get more — an excuse to change her position. Kyle watched her to the fridge and watched her back again.

" *'Today was golden, then pale, then dark, weather changes coming in over the horizon like color washes altering the sky, altering the land . . .'*

"He's by the sea, here," Kyle told her, "living in a beach house. It's too complicated to explain why."

Sonia nodded, accepting the mystery.

"He's alone. I mean, he's almost always alone anyway, but the other beach houses are closed up; the summer's over." Kyle's moon face was creased with delight, his mouth animated and gummy. "If he doesn't get a sign, if nothing happens, his life kinda goes on hold, do you see what I mean?"

Sonia didn't, but she nodded again.

"He can't do anything, just hole-up, usually takes to his bed, doesn't eat, doesn't do anything. Sleeps."

"Hibernates," Sonia offered.

Kyle stared at her, then smiled slowly. "You're right, Sonia, pretty Sonia, that's right, he hibernates." A page turned.

" *'A moment came when the sky was changing, gold again deepening to russet. A clear evening, now, after a day of cloud. A sea bird crossed the line of division and disappeared into the darker color, one moment there, the next moment gone.'* "

Kyle's brogue drew out the syllables: ". . . the laahn

uv diveesion . . . waahn moment they-uh . . . "

" 'As I watched, the bird had flown into oblivion —
deceived by a fault line in the sky. It was a gift quite
literally "plain and simple." The light was fading fast.
I got out of bed and dressed, released from my inertia.
It was all luck, nothing but luck. . . .' "

"How is he released?" Sonia asked. She wanted to
engage him, to conspire in liking the book.

"This man's a risk taker. He doesn't live his life like
ordinary folk. He waits for signs. No sign, no life: he
just stays in, might as well be dead — *hibernates*. All
the time, he's looking for something remarkable —
you understand me? — because life ought to be remarkable, because life ought to be risks, and he takes
the sign, like the disappearance of this bird, to mean
he can act. It gives him permission."

"He knows what he wants to do, but he can't do it
until some omen appears."

"That's right."

"And what is it he wants to do?"

"Kill people."

Bullen had written five drafts of his letter and
destroyed them all. He'd preserved a single sentence
and written it on a complimentary hotel postcard:
"Don't get caught in the cross streets." It meant: wait
for me.

He slept surrounded by torn-up pleas, excuses,
questions, promises.

In the instant of waking, Sonia had forgotten where
she was; a moment later she remembered and cried

338

out. Kyle put a finger to his lips.

"Sonia, too beautiful to cry . . ."

She put her head in her hands, hiding the tears, while he read to her.

". . . how little resistance, my hand across her mouth as if to stifle any harsh word she might have had for me. There was blood on my wrists and forearms. Her eyes were open like the eyes of a beast dragged down by predators, and she died softly, as such creatures die, her face in the lamplight growing ever more distant. . . ."

Fear exhausted her. When she woke again, he had cuffed her to the bed, both arms stretched above her head, and she could hear the sound of the shower. A thin halo of daylight glowed at the curtain.

He emerged naked, expecting her to be asleep, or perhaps he wanted her to see him. His body was muscled, but strangely smooth, and dead white like pork fat. She saw the thick droop of his cock and turned her head away, feigning sleep.

He said, "Time to get on the road, my Sonia, pretty Sonia."

40

The gun Bullen had taken from George Parker was a thirty-eight caliber short-barreled revolver. It wouldn't stick out of your pocket, but that didn't make it the perfect concealed weapon. He stood before the mirror and tried it in his coat pocket, then his pants pocket, and might as well have strapped on a Buntline Special, tied down below the knee. He shoved it into his waistband by the small of his back, then stood in profile. It seemed to him that his coat hung like a hunchback's, but it was the best he could do.

He wrote Anne's address on the postcard and gave it to the desk clerk for mailing on his way out, as if commitment were second nature after all.

Morgan Sorrell sat in a spread of shadow close to the door of the St. Louis Cathedral. A few tourists moved in huddles through the buttery light of candles. His gray suit and modest necktie looked dressy among the Bermuda shorts and polo shirts. Sorrell put a hand over his eyes for a moment and leaned forward as if in prayer; you might have taken him for a businessman in crisis, which was pretty near the truth.

People came to the cathedral as a congregation or as strangers, to pray, or to shoot a reel of film, but either way they usually came in groups. Bullen found a man sitting alone, dressed in the dark colors of a priest. Sorrell smiled at him. "Bullen," he said, "no surprise in this city to meet the walking dead."

Evan Bannick had been with Bullen since he left the hotel; now he stood close to the door of the cathedral and watched his mark sit down with just a hint of caution: a man with hemorrhoids or a gun tucked into his waistband at the back; either way, Evan thought, a pain in the ass. He stayed by the door like an usher.

Bullen said, "Your name's Sorrell."

"That's right."

"Why the filter system? We're on neutral ground, very public ground." Bullen smiled. "In fact we're on holy ground. What could happen?"

"It's a matter of making sure you're alone."

Sorrell's eyes lifted a moment and Bullen turned to follow the involuntary look. He saw a squat shadow against the light from the door; as he watched, it found more shadow, darkness bleeding into darkness.

Sorrell said, "Are you a company man?" There was something urgent about his tone; something hopeful.

"I've told you who I am and what I want. Well, I've told Dexter's answering machine."

"We know about George Parker."

Bullen felt a sudden rush of anxiety. If they knew about Parker, they probably knew about Sonia. All he said was, "Okay."

"Why was that necessary?"

"It wasn't. I wanted to talk a deal with George, but he wouldn't stop to listen."

"You messed his life up."

"George did that."

"You're not a player, Bullen. We've never heard of you."

"You've heard of me now. Everyone starts somewhere."

"If you're a company man, just tell me." Again the strange note of eagerness.

"A company man." Bullen repeated the phrase as if hearing it for the first time. "What company, Sorrell? Where's it based?"

"Langley, Virginia? Big sign out on the highway."

Bullen shook his head. "No," he said, "offices in Nassau and Liechtenstein, that any help to you?"

Sorrell gave a little sigh, as if he'd just heard the wrong answer to a simple question. Bullen thought: We're playing cat and mouse. This guy expects something — he has hopes of me. He let a silence fall between them, then said: "Am I here to talk to you? I don't think so."

"You talk to me *first*."

Axel Dexter was walking briskly toward the cathedral. Evan looked from the dim interior out into the pearly glare from a low, humid sky. Dexter seemed etched in black, a figure displacing his own body weight as he approached the door.

Bullen leaned toward Sorrell, lowering his voice slightly. "Tell me what you want. Then I'll tell you what I want. Maybe we can reach some agreement — without having to talk to another soul."

"I work for Axel Dexter," Sorrell said. "I only make deals on his behalf."

"I know that. I believe you. But a man has to make his own way in the world."

Bullen looked for a sign, and found it in Sorrell's eyes. The lawyer glanced furtively toward the door and back again, then looked at his own knees. His voice was a mutter, a hurried prayer. "What do you want?"

Bullen leaned toward Sorrell again: a brief pat on the arm, a moment of collusion. He said, "Dexter on a plate." A second later, someone sat on his blind side

342

and put a hand flat on his back.

Evan's voice was a little damp rush of sibilants. "Stay still, keep your hands in your lap." He lifted the flap of Bullen's jacket, found the butt of the .38, slipped the safety, and kept his hand on the gun. "Find a use for a second asshole, asshole?"

Sorrell sighed, as if Evan didn't know any better than to swear in church. "Just take it away from him; don't make a fuss."

Evan left the gun where it was; he curled his finger on the trigger and took up a quarter pull. "You do your job, Morgan, I'll do mine."

Dexter arrived one row back from the three of them. He leaned toward Bullen for a handshake — businessman's irony — then sat down and remained silent for a while, running his finger and thumb along the line of his jaw like someone feeling for the first signs of aging. The photograph Bullen had seen had made him healthier and more animated. In life, his face seemed all but lipless, the concave cheeks tight and dry.

Bullen couldn't hold out for another second: if a man has a gun tucked into the bevel of your ass, you need to know what he looks like. You need to know whether he's wearing a frown.

Evan smiled as Bullen looked over his shoulder. Bullen couldn't suppress a *"Yip!"* of surprise that chased echoes into the roof vault.

"See that?" Evan asked Dexter. "I'm famous. I'm a TV personality."

"Not in Louisiana," Dexter replied, "strictly limited appearances." He smiled winningly at Bullen. "Local people call this the Vieux Carré — this section of the city. Tourist maps call it the French Quarter; it's for people who know nothing about New Orleans, or for people who know everything. So, a perfect place for us to meet. Maybe you had better tell me why you decided to make George Parker's life so unhappy." Dexter spoke very slowly, very softly, a voice with the tiniest fragment of something European left behind.

"Self-inflicted," Bullen assured him. "George wouldn't stop to listen."

"He says you stole his daughter from him."

"No, I just set her free."

"A nice distinction." Dexter's laughter was silent but his shoulders rose and fell a couple of times. "No one seems to know who you are. There's a theory that you might be a member of some government agency or another — British SIS with connections in Washington, maybe?"

"No."

"And that your interest in my business affairs is altogether hostile."

"If George Parker had been prepared to talk to me, one businessman to another, a great deal of unhappiness could have been avoided. His son would be alive, his daughter would be safe in the family home, jacking up every hour on the hour."

"Am I going to hear a proposition?"

"I followed the deal down the line until I got to George Parker."

"Where did the line start?"

"I don't think I should tell you that."

Dexter sighed and rubbed his eyes like a man who'd

been up all night with the problem of Tom Bullen. "Tell me *something.*"

Bullen took a line from Morgan Sorrell: "Okay, the line didn't start in Langley, Virginia."

"I'm glad to hear that." Dexter's tone was a shade wry: *But I'd be happier to believe it.*

"I've had my money on the dubious side of legal more than a few times," Bullen said. "The weapons trade has loosened up a hell of a lot since they started chipping bits off the Berlin Wall. I'm always interested in growth markets, and I usually go to the people who know best."

"You're not a shipper?"

"An investor, like you."

"I don't need finance, Bullen. If you'd asked me, I'd've told you."

"I didn't know who to ask. I knew there was a deal."

"Where from?" Dexter persisted. "Who told you that?"

Bullen shook his head. "If you don't need me, I don't have to tell you." Bullen paused, then added: "Everyone needs finance. You can't buy the world."

"No. Can you?"

"I can buy more of it if I put my money together with someone else's."

"How much money?"

"How much do you need?"

"I don't."

"So why ask?"

"All right, Bullen, let me get this straight. You've heard on some grapevine that there's an arms deal going down. You decide you want to invest, so you

345

start looking for the broker. You find out from George Parker that it's me. Now we've met and I've told you that I don't need your help. Take your money somewhere else. I'm not the only person in the world who moves weapons."

"It can't be just any deal. People died. They died so publicly that someone was issuing a warning: stay away. I think it was you. I don't just want into a deal, I want into *this* deal."

"There are other things. Drugs, gold, pussy, spot-market oil, pornography —that's a really good market right now, so I hear. There are some snuff flicks coming up from south of the border that make you wonder who's left in the slums."

"I can do that, too," Bullen said, "thanks for the suggestion. But if you're financing this deal, I can help."

"It's not a matter of buying in the hope of selling, Bullen. I supply to order."

"Take more orders."

Dexter laughed. "You're pushing at a locked door."

Bullen shifted his position, slowly, letting Evan Bannick feel the intention, then the action. The gun barrel was slick with sweat; it nudged the fat of his buttock obscenely.

"I'm just trying to do business," Bullen observed, "by going to the best man in the business."

"Am I? You didn't know my name until George Parker shot his mouth off."

"I've talked to a few people since then."

"Who?"

Bullen shrugged. "I don't think I should give you

names. People I trust."

"I don't like the sound of that." Dexter's voice was slower and softer than ever. "I hate the sound of that."

The tourist groups were being rounded up as a congregation gathered. The priest came in to lay out the chalice, the ciborium, the host.

"People must have offered you partnerships before."

"If I need further investment, I know where to go for it. Most of the time I don't need it. I take it you've seen my friend before." Dexter glanced away as he spoke, as if to disguise the sudden backtrack. "The one with the gun against your sphincter."

"He was famous for fifteen minutes."

"So . . . and now you have seen him in my company. Now you know more than you should."

"I know as much or as little as I need to know. I've forgotten a great many things."

"Good. Forget me. Forget my friend. Forget this meeting. I thank you for your offer of help. Now we're going to leave the way we came."

Dexter left without looking back. Evan gave the gun a little shove, straightening Bullen's back. The sound of the hammer being cocked had its own double echo.

Even's laugh was a series of little hiccups. "I sure hope you don't have a hair trigger on that." The laugh grew. "A hair trigger across the ass."

Sorrell was the last to leave. He waited until Bullen had reached around and retrieved the gun, lifting it out finger and thumb, letting the hammer down, putting the safety on. Bullen and Sorrell seemed to breathe out

347

together, as if the experience had been divided between them.

"You'd better leave New Orleans," Sorrell advised. "There's nothing for you here, you can see that."

"What about you? What is there here for you?"

"Don't get tricky with me."

"Can you help me out?"

"How would I do that?"

"What will it take?" Bullen asked. "How much to finance this business of Dexter's?"

"I don't know. If I did, I wouldn't tell you."

"Sure you do. Of course you do." Bullen was still holding the gun — in plain view of the saints and martyrs, cherubim and seraphim. "Let me in." His voice was a whisper. "Let me get into the deal."

"Go on talking this way and you're dead, I guarantee it."

"Let me in — we'll cut Dexter out."

Sorrell laughed, sending broken syllables into the shadows, then getting them back. "I'll tell him you said this. He'll be amused."

"Don't tell him, just do it."

Sorrell got up. "You crazy bastard," he said, "is this the way you always do business?"

"Do you want to be rich? You will be."

"I work for Axel Dexter. For *Dexter,* understand? Why are you still talking to me?"

"Why are you still listening? And you won't have to worry about Dexter, because —"

"Good-bye, Bullen."

The priest raised his arms to the congregation. He struck the bell.

"— because he'll be too busy talking to someone in Langley, Virginia."

Sorrell joined the godless as they walked in file toward the door. He looked back at Bullen, his eyes wide.

Kyle didn't stop until he'd driven them clear out of Tennessee and down into Alabama. When they pulled up for gas, Sonia decided it was time to leave. They walked together to pay the cashier, then walked back, like a couple too devoted to be out of each other's company for a minute. Sonia was slightly woozy from tension and disturbed sleep, not quite in her right mind.

She thought: *So long, it's been good to know ya!* A smile came to her lips and she turned her head to hide it as he helped her back into the car. The handcuffs were in the door pocket. *These foolish things remind me of you. . . .*

Kyle drove from the gas pumps to the rest rooms and cafeteria. He said, "Do I have to remind you of Jasmine? Surely I don't have to do that."

"No."

"See, we could have bought ourselves a little picnic, like before, and found some pretty spot to eat it, but I'm just happier being on the road. How about you?"

"Sure."

She realized he was talking as though they were making joint decisions, as though they were planning the trip together. She thought they must be around five hundred miles from New Orleans, maybe a little more.

Kyle seemed nerveless behind the wheel, an automaton. He could drive six-hour stretches without shifting his position. It seemed he was planning to arrive that day: sometime during midevening, even if they made another stop or two.

He sat with her while she freshened her makeup, pleased that she should care about the way she looked, pleased that their relationship should encompass a moment so ordinary, and so crucial. He thought back to the previous evening when her reflection had suddenly filled the mirror, the rounded fullness of her breasts, the contour of her belly sloping to the patch of hair darker than the hair of her head. As she stroked lipstick on, he saw that nakedness and felt a leap of feeling that emerged as an exclamation, "Ah!", and he hid it with a cough, then got quickly out of the car.

Sonia used her lipstick to write *HELP* on a tissue, which she tucked into the sleeve of her shirt. She was loading her makeup back into her purse when Kyle opened the passenger door, smiling and attentive. A little swell of dizziness struck her when she climbed out.

It's a long road, baby, and I gotta travel on alone. . . . She smiled again and this time Kyle caught it; he smiled back as if to say: You're welcome.

She tottered slightly as they crossed the parking lot and Kyle stepped closer to steady her. Once his hand was on her arm, he wanted never to let go.

Sonia felt his warmth as an electric shock fizzing along her nerve endings, and he moved his fingers on her flesh like someone playing an instrument. He held her as they went to the restaurant section, held her as they were shown to a table, held her as she settled into her chair. She thought he might stand behind her as she ate, helping to steer her fork. A girl in gingham and a T-shirt that read BARNEY'S RIBS brought them ice water and left a couple of menus.

"You know why he kills people?" Kyle asked, as if their conversation had never been interrupted.

"Why?"

"It makes him more alive. Not makes him *feel* more alive. *Makes* him more alive. You know why he looks for a sign?"

"Why?"

"It's a magical thing. It's a thing of terror and grandness." Kyle flushed; what he was saying seemed to be making him breathless. "You understand that?"

"Ritual," she said, and his eyes glowed when he looked at her. Sonia sipped water to take the dryness off her lips. She asked, "What about you? Are the signs good?"

For a moment, Kyle said nothing. He stared at her solemnly. Then he laughed, a wet hiss exploding through his teeth. "Sonia, pretty Sonia, lovely Sonia, don't you worry, don't you fret, nothing's gonna harm you."

The waitress returned and Sonia held her menu in her lap. "Hamburger, medium, no fries, side order of coleslaw." She folded the card and handed it back. Kyle ordered and surrendered his menu, then changed his mind and asked to look again. The waitress sighed and deleted his order from her pad; Kyle reached out and took the menu from her. He opened it, letting the tissue fall into his hand, and read for a short while.

Finally, he said, "Steak sandwich and a beer."

He was looking at Sonia and he went on looking at her, his face solemn, his fingers shredding the tissue like someone fingering worry beads. When the food came he watched her eat, leaving his own meal untouched on the plate.

She said, "You blame me for trying?"

He didn't speak; in fact, he seemed depressed, his face drooping with melancholy, his eyes damp. Sonia ate in silence for a while, then gave up. She said, "What do you want me to say — I'm sorry?"

Kyle paid the check and they walked back toward the car, Sonia slightly ahead. When they got close, Kyle stooped slightly to pick his spot and punched her hard and fast in the kidney, dropping her to one knee.

She said, "Oh, Christ," and slid a yard, taking a bad graze from the asphalt. Kyle picked her up without breaking his stride, his fingers pinching her bicep, unlocked the car, and shoved her in. As he walked to his door, he saw two guys sitting on the tailgate of a pickup drinking beer. They were just four vehicles away. One of them said, "That ain't no way to treat a lady."

Kyle stood by the door of his car, smiling. "She ain't no lady," he told them.

Forty minutes later, he picked up the interstate going southwest.

"This is tough." Kyle glanced across at her, his face solemn. "We're almost there."

"Why is it tough?"

"I feel we're just starting out, you know? I feel

we're just at the beginning of things."

Dexter was hooked up to two telephones, shoulders hunched; a third, lying on his desk, was on hold. He said, "Shut up," to one line and listened on the other, then reversed the priority. Finally he hung up both phones and took the call waiting on the third. This time he was more respectful. "I'm obliged," he said.

Evan Bannick and Morgan Sorrell were on the other side of Dexter's desk. Dexter started to play with a baseball, flipping it from one hand to the other, twisting his fingers to make it spin against the run of the seam. "Well," he said, "no one knows who the fuck this guy is. We'd better kill him."

Sorrell asked, "Why not wait till the girl gets here — draw him in, find out what he really knows, what he really wants?"

Dexter shook his head. "I think he's dangerous. The longer he's alive, the more dangerous he becomes. Same goes for the girl."

"Kill her too?" Evan asked.

Dexter looked at Sorrell but nodded toward Evan. "Kid in a candy store." To Evan he said, "Sure . . . I could be talking to your brother about that if he'd taken the trouble to call in. Do we know where they are? Do we know what's happening? Do we know when they're likely to arrive?"

"Maybe they'll be here tonight," Sorrell said. "Depends how he's pacing it."

"Maybe, yeah, maybe." Dexter gave an angry shrug.

"Why not wait till then, Axel?"

Dexter ignored him. He turned to Evan. "What? You think they're in trouble or something?"

"No, I don't think that. Kyle would check in if something happened."

"Unless he was dead."

"If he died, I'd know."

"Then what the fuck's he doing?"

"He'll have a reason." Evan spoke quietly to reassure. In truth, he couldn't think why Kyle hadn't made a progress report, though he had a weird sense of urgency like hunger, and wondered if that was coming from Kyle.

"Make it a clean kill," Dexter said.

Evan smiled. "Don't worry."

"In and out, no trace."

"You sell guns, Axel, I use them."

Kyle drove south through Mississippi while Sonia slept. The restlessness that was troubling Evan was affecting him, too; he registered it as little adrenaline bursts, part of a fight-or-flight syndrome. You couldn't call it a warning — just a bad feeling.

Sonia was sleeping with her face turned toward him, mouth slightly open, a drift of hair falling across her cheek. Kyle could see what it meant — that she hadn't turned her back on him to sleep: she was apologizing; she was saying: I'm sorry I tried to run out on you. I suppose I got scared. I can see there's no reason for that. I feel as you feel — we're just at the beginning; there are things to be learned, there are secrets to be shared.

Kyle put out a hand and brushed the hair away from

her face. The patch of down at the point of her jaw sent a shock of emotion through him like a sudden, sharp wind among leaves.

He said, "I've never told anyone about the book before. I'm glad it was you, because you understand. You said 'ritual' — you could see that the sign is a kind of ritual for him. That's important."

The thunderheads were rolling on south with the look of bad news made visible.

"I don't know what I'm going to do. The deal is I deliver you to Axel Dexter and he makes the decisions, but what happens if the decision he makes is a bad one — bad for you, bad for me? He wants you as bait, you know that? Had you guessed? He figures that you and this guy Bullen must be close, so you're some kind of insurance, because whoever Bullen is, he scares Dexter — he's already derailed the train once."

A flurry of raindrops silvered the windshield; Sonia stirred and the screen of hair drifted down.

"Something's happening to Evan, I can feel that. I should've called and now he's angry. Something else, though . . . something . . ." Kyle paused, trying to gain a true sense of it. "Something that makes his blood hot."

He drove in silence for ten minutes, hitting the tail end of a rainstorm, then emerging into shaky sunlight.

He said, "I know what it is."

When Sonia woke, they were crossing the border on Pearl River.

Kyle said, "Sonia, pretty Sonia . . ."

She wiped her face with her free hand. "How much longer?" she asked.

He didn't want to answer. "How do you feel?"

"My back aches. There's no skin on my knee."

"I'm sorry. I'm sorry it happened." After a moment, he asked, "Know what the sign was?"

"Sign?"

"Like in the book — he has to see a sign."

She realized he was talking about Jasmine. He waited, glancing at her from time to time to see whether she was coming up with an answer. "Okay," she said, "what?"

"You. You were the sign."

Evan Bannick walked the length of the hotel corridor, passing Bullen's room, then walked back. It was the dead hour between eight and nine in the evening; everyone was somewhere, no one was coming or going.

There were two ways of doing it. Enter the room and find Bullen there and kill him; enter the room and find it empty and wait. He listened and heard nothing. Checking from the street he had seen that the light was on in the room, and although that meant nothing, he would assume that Bullen was in there. Then he knew for sure — a sound like a door closing, or maybe a window. He imagined Bullen going around the room collecting his things, emptying drawers into a suitcase.

Evan walked that stretch of corridor one more time, looked around the corner, walked back, and opened

Bullen's door with a maid's passkey that had cost him a hundred dollars. Gun up, he entered the room and closed the door.

A woman was on all fours across the bed, head down, ass up, naked as the day. The man kneeling up behind her saw Evan at once and slammed still like a train hitting the buffers. The woman said, "Jesus, don't stop, don't —" then caught the fear in his silence and looked up. She made a tiny noise, like something defenseless dying.

The man said, "Everything's there." He looked toward an antique bureau by the window. On it lay a billfold and a credit card wallet.

"Yeah," Evan said, "that's what I came for." He shook his head, as if to clear it, more puzzled than angry. He knew Bullen hadn't checked out. He'd made a phone call to the hotel from a "business colleague" to confirm it.

He walked to the bureau and picked up what was there. The man said, "Don't hurt us."

The idea hadn't occurred to Evan until that moment. He looked at them up on the bed like a blue movie on freeze frame. The man was slim, just carrying a slight paunch. The woman was fleshy, her big rump hoisted toward her partner, her breasts lying on her forearms like a bolster.

There's a lot of potential here, Evan thought. So many things to do. He laughed, making the woman tremble and cry out. No time, though; business before pleasure.

They had decided he was a burglar, so that was what Evan had to be.

He went over to the woman and crouched down to look into her eyes. "I don't believe I've heard from you, honey. Surely you've got something to say."

"In my purse." At the back of her eyes, almost too deep for seeing, was a lifetime of nightmares — the reflection of Evan Bannick's face. *"Please. In my purse."*

Evan savored the moment a little longer, drinking from her eyes, then walked away and emptied out the purse, taking her wallet. To the man, he said: "Fuck her. Just keep fucking her."

The man could see bad things coming. He said, "I can't."

"Just stick it to her, will you? I can't stay here all night." The man moved back, then sat down on the bed. "No? Well, okay," said Evan, "find something to tie her with."

Bad things, bad things coming: it was all over the man's face. He shook his head until Evan raised the gun and pointed it at his belly. He went to a suitcase that lay open on the floor and removed some neckties, some panty hose, the cord of a robe. He tied the woman's hands behind her back, then her legs, then joined the two tethers, pulling her legs up toward her hands. Evan smiled. The man was trying to find a position where she'd be impossible to fuck.

Evan said, "Now you." He made the man lie down on the floor and tied his hands and feet to the bed legs; finally he found some handkerchiefs in the case and pushed some into first the man's mouth, then the woman's.

He rolled the woman onto her back and knelt up beside her. His voice was the ghost of a whisper, just for her, his lips brushing her ear. "Now whenever you feel horny, whenever you're getting it on, whenever you've got your legs wide and your eyes closed, honey, I want you to think of me." He let the gun barrel rest for a brief moment between her breasts. "Think of me, think of me, think of me."

Before they reached Lake Pontchartrain, Kyle swung west toward Baton Rouge. Sonia had been watching the highway signs for the last fifty miles; now she turned and gazed at him until the look nudged him into speech.

"Sonia too lovely to leave."

Bullen had simply left the first hotel and checked into another — smaller, quieter, safer. The room had a ceiling fan and a big mirror in a gold frame, the glass tarnished to a cool pewter. Morgan Sorrell went to and fro. His reflection was dull and indistinct, but the anxiety clouding his face was plain to see. Bullen was sitting in a brocade armchair, motionless, as Sorrell brushed back and forth.

"When will they get here?"

Sorrell shrugged. "Today, in theory. Tonight."

"What happens?"

"First she was going to be insurance. Dexter didn't know who you were, what you wanted, who you knew. . . . All he knew was you'd caused some trouble and might cause more. She was there in case he needed a lever. Now he's decided to kill you.

That makes her of no use.''

"How come you're not sure exactly when they'll arrive?"

"She's with Kyle Bannick. The guy who had a gun in your ass today? — his brother. Kyle should have checked in from time to time. He hasn't."

Bullen felt as if he were falling: a slow swoop into space. He caught his breath. *Brother . . . his brother.* He closed his eyes for a moment and saw Roland Cecil falling, saw Caro Duval falling, saw the little plug-ugly face behind the gun — the same face behind both guns. He looked at Sorrell and laughed. "Twins. They're identical twins?"

Sorrell nodded. "Twins, that's right." His thoughts were elsewhere.

"What is the other one called?"

"What?"

"The other twin; the one in the cathedral."

"Evan."

"He was supposed to kill me?"

"I took a chance, you know? I had to call you from Dexter's house."

"I'll remember the debt."

Bullen went to the window. The night was lights and music and velvety heat, but he felt a thin chill that sank to his bones: not the ceiling fan, not the air-conditioning. *I should be dead. And Sonia is some-where — who knows where? — with a man who likes to kill.* He imagined her fear, her desperation, and a fierce energy possessed him — a mix of panic and anger — as if he might sprint out into the night and keep running until he found them and made her safe.

Sorrell's image rolled through the mirror and back, a small shark in a grimy cage. "Let's talk a deal," he said.

Bullen knew that all he could do was wait. After a moment he said, "I'm listening."

"You wanted a piece of Dexter's action. I want it all. Those are my cards on the table."

"Can you handle it?"

"Everything's in position, all the contacts are good, the client list is second to none. It's like inheriting a Mercedes instead of trying to build one yourself."

"Would it work for you?"

"I know where the bodies are buried — and some are buried pretty deep. I know the people who've been lining their own pockets and the people who haven't paid their dues. I'm the bookkeeper, Bullen. I know pretty much everything there is to know."

"What makes Dexter vulnerable?"

"This deal: the one he's setting up, the one people have died for. A lot of Dexter's business is legal, or close to legal; this isn't."

"Tell me."

"No, you tell me. What happens to Dexter?"

"Give me something to hang him with, I'll guarantee he hangs."

Sorrell stopped pacing and his gunmetal image blended with the reflection of lamplight. He was utterly still, seeming to make a final decision about what to say, what to risk.

"Dexter had Kelly Duval killed. He had the others killed, too — Arnaut, Cecil, Chesnik, Macallun."

"Why?"

Sorrell looked amused. "You don't know, do you?" It was plain that Bullen's ignorance reassured him. "You really are a Company man — the CIA is about five years out of date."

"I can guess — those other people wanted the deal."

"More or less. Arnaut and Cecil were raising funds in Europe. They'd had a couple of meetings with Dexter's principal contact and were planning more. They had already got Kelly Duval's agreement that he'd ship and truck the merchandise. Macallun was one of their backers, but was also another means of shifting merchandise — he owned a trucking business. He stood to make money on the investment and the haulage. Dexter didn't want any opposition, so he simply put Kyle and Evan on the case."

"Chesnik?"

"Organizing a separate funding here in the States: a cartel, like with Europe. It was turning into an auction. Dexter didn't want that. Until Cecil and Chesnik got interested, the whole thing had been under wraps. His contact was setting up a dream deal — the deal of a lifetime — and things had gone pretty far between them. But that didn't stop the guy listening to other voices, you know? Other offers."

"Which guy? I mean what's his name?"

Sorrell paused again. He was like a man taking his first free-fall. Step one was warning Bullen that Dexter planned to kill him: that was getting into the plane. Step two was giving the name Bullen had asked for: that was strapping on the parachute.

He said, "Viktor Petrenko."

362

"Russian. Living here?"

Sorrell shook his head. "Moscow."

Bullen was allowing Sorrell to take his time. "What kind of a deal are we talking about?" he asked. "What's the buy price?"

"Ninety million dollars."

The tarnished mirror seemed almost to efface the two men, reducing them to dark silver silhouettes.

Bullen could hear the pulse rustling in his wrist vein. He asked, "What does ninety million buy?"

Step three — as if Sorrell had gone to an open hatchway and looked down, feeling the tug of the slipstream. He moved away from the mirror and went toward the window, his dim reflection diminishing further, like the image of a man falling through dull skies, his parachute yet to open.

"It buys three first-generation nuclear devices. Three nuclear bombs."

41

Bullen had an image of silos out on the bayou, ICBMs bristling up alongside loblolly pines, of juggernaut trailers hauling support cranes along the Jefferson Highway.

"What's Dexter's role — broker?"

"Broker, yes. Even he couldn't finance that kind of a deal."

"Who's the customer?"

"No one you'd recognize. He's a front man for a front man's front man. Use your imagination: Saddam, Qaddafi . . . there aren't too many places to go."

"Does Dexter know — I mean the real destination for the bombs?"

"He knows. He also knows there's ninety million on deposit to make the payment."

"Is there?"

Sorrell nodded. "In Zurich; no problem."

"Dexter's piece of the pie?"

"A commission: ten percent of the buy price."

"Jesus!"

"Plus expenses," Sorrell observed.

"Why doesn't the front man do the deal himself?"

"You don't understand, Bullen. The world's been waiting for this since the USSR went down the tube. There's a dumb theory that the Russian nuclear stockpile is on offer at cut-rate prices. That's not so. Whatever the location, stockpiles are under the aegis of the KGB: closely guarded. There's as much chance of sneaking a nuclear device out under the wire as meeting Hitler in heaven. Saddam — or whoever — can't do the deal because the world's watching. The front man can't do the deal for the same reason. In this particular case, Dexter's deputizing for the front man. Why? Because he's a dealer. He's expected to meet people with weapons for sale."

"He's shipping the bombs in among other weapons?"

"No. We're being smarter than that."

"Roland Cecil, Chesnik, Duval — they were threatening to undercut Dexter?"

"Duval was nothing — just a rival shipper. But he was helping facilitate the deal for Chesnik just by earmarking ships and land vehicles, so he had to go. Chesnik was raising the money from investors all over."

"Mafia?"

"I don't think so. Oil money, steel money, respectable money. It was an investment. Arms dealing's a respectable business."

"Roland Cecil?"

"Less of a problem, but dangerous all the same. He and Arnaut raised a million here, a million there. Who knows whether they'd have been ready in time? The deal took about five million to finance: that money came back as overhead — above the commission. But you have to lay it out in order to set things up. We knew they'd lined up a shipper. We didn't know who, or I guess he'd have been dead."

Charles Blanchot, Bullen thought. He remembered the crates of machine parts disguising hash in the cellar beneath Blanchot's warehouse: a taster, just an hors d'oeuvre. And nine million dollars in commission to go to the neo-Nazi effort throughout Europe, he thought; they could have funded a lot of candidates for parliaments in Germany, France, Belgium, Austria, Great Britain . . .

Sorrell lit a cigarette; the flare of the match made a soft yellow nimbus in the mirror.

"Tell me the deal," Bullen said.

"I'll give you everything you need to put Dexter

away in return for total immunity. No plea bargaining, no limited sentence — *total* immunity. Also, I don't have to testify."

"I can't give you that guarantee."

"Then it's no deal."

"I mean *I* can't give it. I didn't say you can't get it. There are people I have to talk to."

"There have to be safeguards."

"I understand."

"I'm a lawyer — I know about these things."

"I'm sure."

"After Dexter's arrested, I get left alone. You stop the deal for the nuclear devices. I pick up where Dexter left off — conventional trade only. You can arrest him on some technicality."

"Give me one."

"How about income-tax evasion? There's an amusing precedent for that. Also, it's easy to prove in this case."

"How?"

"I'll give you a list of undisclosed earnings — bribes mostly. More than five million dollars over the course of twelve years or so. That should keep him busy for a while."

"What about the ninety million dollars already on deposit in Zurich?"

Sorrell smiled. "I want Dexter's business; I want Dexter out of the way. At the same time, I have to look clean. How you got to Dexter is nothing to do with me, right? If you make me testify, I'll do everything I can to protect him. As for the deposit, I'll need that customer again. You get the bombs and the front man;

the ninety million goes back."

"All of it?"

"All except the ten million Dexter squirreled away in a numbered account."

"Did he?"

"He must have," Sorrell said, "because it's not there now." He laughed. "What a son of a bitch."

"What would he tell the buyer?"

"Not the buyer," Sorrell explained. "The salesman. So far as the buyer's concerned, the price hasn't changed. Dexter would have been planning to bargain the salesman out of ten million at the last minute."

"Confident," Bullen observed.

Sorrell shook his head. "Nerveless."

"Okay, there are two conditions," Bullen said, "no room for negotiation. One, you tell me how to contact the man Dexter's dealing with in Russia — Petrenko. It's information that's no use to me except that if you fuck me over, I can make him run for cover before Dexter can be accused of anything. That's my insurance. Second condition: nothing happens until Sonia Bishop is either safe or dead. If she's dead, it makes no difference, but part of Dexter getting busted has to be that Kyle and Evan Bannick get busted right alongside him. They're wild cards." Bullen hesitated a moment. "Unless there are others . . ."

"Other bodyguards, you mean? More like them?" When Bullen nodded, Sorrell said: "No. Dexter hired them on a free-lance basis. They're on board for this job. He takes a bodyguard on if he's going to dangerous territory, or he'll hire muscle when it's needed. Not on the payroll, though. Like I told you — arms dealing's respectable.''

"Okay. So I want Sonia safe if she's alive. Think of a way.''

"Well . . . Dexter wants you dead. She's supposed to be the bait. Play it like that — like it was supposed to be played. Let him contact you and tell you he's holding her; let him draw you in.''

"And then?''

"I'm the tactician here, Bullen; you control the fucking troops. Do what you want. Shoot them all shitless — it'd suit me. No trial, no hassle, no Dexter.''

"Three nuclear bombs,'' Bullen said. "It didn't trouble you?''

"I didn't invent them. Who am I — Oppenheimer? I didn't manufacture them and I wasn't intending to drop them. The plan was to redistribute them. Why not?'' He laughed. "It's not going to happen now. Maybe not this year. It'll happen next year or the year after that.''

Sorrell went to a table that stood in front of the mirror; on the table was a bottle of bourbon. When he bent to pick it up and pour, his cropped red hair with its double stripe of white showed like an animal's pelt, vivid and feral; when he straightened up, his corporation lawyer facade was in place once more: dark suit, blue shirt, narrow tie.

"How much does she mean to you? Sonia Bishop.''

"Why do you ask?''

"It's a complication. I was wondering whether I could buy you off.''

"How would that work?''

"It's easier if you just go ahead and bust Dexter and

the hell with what happens to her. I mean, it's safer for me, and there's less risk of things going wrong." Sorrell loomed up in the dark mirror like a figure from the underworld.

Bullen sat still. He said, "No, I can't do that. Sorry."

Sorrell finished his drink. He said, "Don't let it fuck things up. And I need to see some legal documentation — immunity papers."

"I can get it for you," Bullen said. "After the girl's free."

"Or dead," Sorrell reminded him.

Kyle came out of the motel bathroom with a glass of warm water and a fistful of tissue. He said, "Take your pants off and get up on the bed."

"I can do it," Sonia told him. "I can handle it."

"Take them off."

She did it. Kyle sat on the bed and began to soften the crust of blood that covered her kneecap. "There's likely to be some dirt in this, maybe some grit. It has to be cleaned right."

He worked softly, trying to keep her from pain. She asked, "Where are we, Kyle? Why have we come here?" It was the first time she had used his name.

"You know why."

"It's easy —" She was frightened and didn't know how best to handle him. At the same time, she felt things she couldn't explain: complicity, gratitude that she was still alive, a desire to please. She felt bound up in the experience and strangely close to him.

"It's easy . . . just let me go." With great daring, she added: "Say you had to kill me."

"Here's the problem," Kyle said. He spoke without looking up from his task. He'd lifted her knee slightly to bathe it, and the warm water had freshened fifty tiny wounds, sending runnels of thinned blood along her thigh. She smeared them with the flat of her hand, then wiped her palm on the bedcover. His fingers cupped the back of her knee.

"Here's the problem — I don't feel we've reached an end of it yet. Like we were still on the journey."

"What do you want?"

"I don't know," he said.

When he emptied the glass and threw away the tissue, he found himself confronting his image in the bathroom mirror. His image and Evan's, too.

"You haven't called and you haven't arrived and you're not in trouble, so it must be the girl."

"I'm on my way."

"Don't lie to me, Kyle. Bring her on back."

"Sure, that's what I'm doing."

"Listen, Kyle, listen to me. If you want to fuck her, do that. Fuck her all ways from Sunday. Fuck her till she goes deaf and blind. Fuck her so she has to walk on crutches, but do it and then bring her back here."

"It isn't that."

"Sure it is."

"Okay, it is; but it's more."

"What more? How more?"

"I don't know yet. It's too soon to know. That's the goddamn problem."

"The problem is you're there and I'm here and Dexter's shitting rocks."

Kyle's eyes were burning; he could feel the anger as if he owned it. He could whisper his own words and whisper Evan's too.

"Give me tonight."

"No, bring her in now."

"Evan, I'm asking for tonight."

Kyle's eyes were dark, now; the flesh of his face was shaking.

"You know how much money there is in this for us?"

"I know."

"Bring her in."

"Tomorrow morning."

"This has never happened between us before."

"I know."

"Why is it happening now?"

"I don't know."

"Bring her in, Kyle. Put everything back the way it was."

Kyle went through into the room. Sonia was tethered at the wrist. He hadn't given her pants back. She watched him go to the phone and dial. He hung up without speaking.

Axel Dexter put down the phone. He said, "Very few people have this number. What do you think?"

Evan Bannick was sitting in one of the cane rockers and drinking a beer. With Bullen away clear, Dexter was edgy; Evan had been rehearsing possibilities with him. The worst of these was that Bullen was a government man; the best that he was a buccaneer with more cash than style.

"You think that was Kyle?"

"Who knows." Evan could have whispered his own words, and whispered Kyle's, too.

"Tomorrow morning."

She lay like a woman of stone while he read out loud: *Letters from a Dead Land.* She had closed her eyes because he was sitting so close, alongside her, like a visitor to a sickbed.

> *"It is easy to kill strangers, because they have no substance. No names, no history: a perfect match for 'no future.' If you do not know who loves them, whom they love in return, what pain they have endured or what joy, then it is impossible to make them matter.*
>
> *"The drawback is obvious: they can be easily forgotten. The experience is trivial. It is like reading a newspaper account which tells how three hundred people died in an air crash.*
>
> *"To remember a kill, to value it, to leave it burning under your ribs and scalding your veins, the one you lay your hand on must seem human and full to you. If you cannot taste their loss in death, you cannot yourself make gain."*

Kyle paused. "This was his first kill; his first sign. And he loved her, you see that? He loved her before he killed her and he still loved her afterward."

"Yes," said the stone woman. "I see that. Yes."

Kyle watched Sonia's reflection as she stood naked, hair slicked back, droplets of water drizzling from her shoulders to the soft hang of her breasts. She lifted a foot against the side of the bath to dry her legs, like anyone you love, like anyone you watch in stolen moments.

She was too frightened to do anything but behave normally.

Kyle sat close by as she pretended to sleep.

He moved a ribbon of hair from her cheek, he kissed her temple, kissed her neck. He loosened the belt of her bathrobe because she had made it too tight, much too tight. He stroked her to make her calm.

His breath was so sour it left the smell of scorch wherever it touched.

Sonia too lovely to leave. . . .

Sonia lay in the darkness, cuffed by one wrist to the bed, by the other to Kyle. He slept easily, dreamlessly. A line came back to her from the book: "*. . . she died softly, as such creatures die, her face in the lamplight growing ever more distant. Later I slept at her side like one who has found his heart's ease.*"

Axel Dexter took pills to thin his blood and pills to regulate his blood pressure, and on nights when he couldn't sleep, he drank a spoonful of bourbon in half a pint of water.

Evan Bannick sat with him like a night nurse.

"We're talking to another shipper," Dexter said.

"You'd be surprised how many of those guys are prepared to kid themselves. It's freight to them — just freight, once the container's been closed."

"No thought of using George Parker?" Evan asked.

"George is a basket case."

The phone rang and Evan picked it up, looking at his watch as he did so. It was close to 3 A.M. He listened a moment, then put the receiver down on Dexter's desk. "It's Bullen."

Dexter's narrow head flicked around and his tongue dabbed at his lips. He lifted the phone slowly, as if certain of bad news.

"I thought you were leaving, Bullen. Wasn't that the deal?"

"I didn't make any deals. That's why I'm calling. I'm still in the city — but I thought it would be sensible to move around. I want some of what you've got, Dexter. Cut me out, and I can fuck this deal for you."

"How?"

"Tie you in with Bannick."

"It's not as easy as you think."

"Maybe . . ." Bullen wondered what a jury would make of it — a TV news clip of one man killing people but, in court, two men, indistinguishable from each other. Also in court, independent witnesses to swear that a man who looked just like that was nowhere near the killing. Each man says he's guilty. Or else they say they're innocent. Or maybe they take the fifth amendment. Now what?

"I can do a lot. I can still finger Bannick as the killer; I can still link him to you. Or I can simply —"

"That doesn't let you into the deal. That puts you

374

in a court of law as star witness; it leaves you explaining to the police how you came to know me at all."

"— or I can simply travel with you until we both arrive at the same place."

Dexter laughed. "How in hell would you do that?"

"I'll call again tomorrow," Bullen told him. "Let's talk then. I'm not asking for much. A small investment opportunity. Say —"

"The deal's financed already."

"— say five million. Just to buy into the market, so I can go back for more."

Something was troubling Dexter. He hauled the conversation back. "How?" he asked. "Just how would you plan to travel with me?"

"Buy a ticket to Moscow."

Dexter stared into the swimming pool. Points of light from the chandeliers trembled in the water like planets too distant to be believed in.

"He knows about Moscow."

Evan shook his head. "How could he?"

"He knows your name."

Bullen put in a call to Roscoe Tate.

"I might need some help down here," he said.

"I already covered your ass once." Tate sounded alert, like a man used to being woken in the middle of the night. "I'm not sure how much I can do. In fact, I don't think I can do anything."

"You could come yourself." Bullen gave Tate the name of his hotel.

"Maybe. I'll have to think it through. One thing's

sure — I can't come down to New Orleans with Eliot Ness and the Untouchables, so don't get your back to the wall."

"It's there already."

"Jesus Christ . . ." Tate sounded wider awake than ever. "Just don't kill anyone, okay?"

"I could use some help."

"Don't count on me. I'll be there if I can. But let me tell you something — I'm not at risk here, you are. And that's the way it's gonna stay."

Bullen hung up and dialed again. Stuart Cochrane picked up the only line on his desk without an intercept and heard Bullen say, "Axel Dexter is brokering the ninety-million-dollar sale of three first-generation nuclear weapons."

The thin tinnitus on the line was the sound of two men listening to one another.

"Where from?" Cochrane asked. "Who's buying? Who's the salesman?"

Bullen thought there were two ways of getting Sonia out of trouble — the first was not to mention Sonia. She could easily become makeweight in an exchange game. The second was to dangle a little bait of his own. He said, "I don't know. I'm talking to someone inside Dexter's organization. I'm making promises I can't keep, but he doesn't know that and, in any case, he badly wants them to be true. This is someone who wants Dexter in jail, or dead. I'm getting the information piecemeal in return for promising to do that."

"Who? Who are you talking to?"

"Judas."

Cochrane sighed. "What is it you want me to do?"

"I need a little help down here. There are problems. I've spoken to Roscoe Tate. He's not sure he can oblige."

"Tell me about the problems."

"I need to nail Dexter. Then Judas believes me and I get the name of the salesman."

"I'll talk to Tate."

"Thanks. Tell him to hurry."

"Don't get killed."

"Okay," Bullen said.

"Judas gives you the name when Dexter's out of the game?" The anxiety in Cochrane's voice was plain to hear.

"When he's sure Dexter can't bite back — right. He also wants guarantees of immunity. Unless he's clean and free, we get zero."

"Promise him anything," Cochrane said. "Don't lose him, you understand?"

"I can hear you."

"What does he think we plan to do?"

"Expose the nuclear deal — stop it happening. He knows he can't keep it up and running. He wants the business — including the goodwill. That means the customer gets his money back if we fuck the deal."

"Stay close to him," Cochrane said. "Don't let anything happen to him."

"Sure," Bullen said, "that's why I'm asking for help — make sense?" He hung up.

Cochrane called back within twenty minutes to say that Roscoe Tate was catching a plane from Newark at 7:05 — the first available flight. He'd be landing at

Moisant Field just after 9:30.

From an open window, lines of jazz and lines of dawn light in the city sky. The mirror was cloudy pearl.

Bullen tried to sleep but all he could see was Sonia's face: the long nose and high cheekbones of a Renaissance aristocrat, the slim body, the way her hips ticked as she walked. He remembered how fear had come off her like musk as they'd sat on the ledge and watched the wafer of torchlight skip around the walls of the cave. A smell had come off Evan Bannick, too. In the cathedral, the sour scent of death like something burning.

He closed his eyes, then opened them at once. He couldn't escape the nightmare whether he slept or not.

Sonia the captive, Sonia the hostage to fortune. . . . She dressed swiftly, half turned from him but taking no special care to keep from his eyes. Already she had developed the prisoner's collusion with the guard: a bitter intimacy.

Kyle watched her like a man hounded by loss.

"What are you going to do?" she asked.

"Let you go."

"Free?"

"No, not free. Let you go from me. Leave you."

"What will happen to me?"

"Dexter decides that."

"Don't you care?"

He took her to the car, one hand on her arm, the other inside his coat pocket. "Remember Jasmine," he said, as if nothing had happened between them.

Out on the highway, he made her put on the cuff.

The weather seemed to have tracked them all the way: dark skies building darker cloud.

Outside the car, the air was shipping in like freight.

Kyle put on the radio and found a crooner singing an old song.

"... *Whether it's love or whether it's hate/Everything comes around that goes around/Do-do-be-do* ..."

"Don't you care?" she asked again. She knew he was trying not to. He looked at her and shrugged; there was a smile on his face, but the smile was set in stone.

42

Roscoe Tate said, "It's just me, me alone, me and no one else. I'm not a fucking army, so let's keep this simple."

"All we have to do," Bullen told him, "is make an exchange. They've got Sonia."

"What have we got?"

"Nothing just yet. But that's going to change. First off, go and see Morgan Sorrell. Tell him he's going to get so much immunity that he'll find it difficult to catch a cold. He's a loose cannon and I don't want him to change his mind about what's good for him. We

need his silence now and his information later."
Bullen was holding the hotel's complimentary city
guide. He asked, "How well do you know New Orleans?"

"Voodoo, graves above ground, Cajun music, jam-
balaya, and gumbo," Tate said. "Second highest
homicide rate in the country, street crime's a way of
life, the police take shit from no one." He took a
breakfast-time beer from the fridge. "Just a tourist's
view of the place, you understand."

"Local restaurants?"

"On your own."

Bullen consulted the guide and found a place that
was said to be famous for its food but more famous
for its prices. "Here," he said to Tate, "make two
reservations: one for two people, another just for
yourself. I'll get there at twelve-thirty; you get there
ten minutes before that. Okay?"

"Who are you having lunch with?"

"Axel Dexter."

"But he doesn't know that yet?"

"He'll be there. I'm too important in his life to be
ignored."

Bullen ran through a couple of game plans with
Tate: if that happens do this; if this happens do that.
Tate said, "Let's try not to kill anybody, all right?"

Sonia sat between Kyle and Evan Bannick on a
Regency sofa in the largest drawing room of Dexter's
mansion. The room was cool and dim. She was feeling
slightly ill — the sort of muzzy disorientation that
comes after a migraine. She had come close to fainting

when she'd seen Evan; as her senses had begun to close down, though, a voice had been saying: "Twins, they're twins, of course, that's it." She had seen Bullen and herself sitting on bar stools; she was saying ". . . unless the guy with the gun has a double or something."

As her knees started to fold, Kyle had caught her. Evan had stepped forward as if he were about to land a blow. They made an odd tableau — the brothers standing close, Sonia drooping between them, Kyle holding Sonia, Evan holding Kyle with his gaze. Now they sat on either side of Sonia, silent and sullen.

Dexter came into the room like a man in a hurry. He said, "I think we've flushed this son of a bitch out."

"He wants the girl?" Evan asked.

"He says he does. He's found a very public place for a meet. He'll say he wants to trade. He gets her back, then he goes away and we never hear from him again."

Evan laughed. "Is he crazy? Why believe him?"

"I don't. Listen" — he nodded at Sonia — "she's bait, not trade. Bullen's not going anywhere, with her or without her. He's gonna die right here in Louisiana." To Kyle, he said: "Take her out of the city. I don't want any bodies found, any questions asked."

Sonia heard him talking about her death as if it were punched into the morning-review program on his personal organizer. He brought a map over to the sofa and unfolded it so that Kyle could follow his directions; as he spread it, a couple of folds cascaded over Sonia's lap.

He pretends I'm not here, she thought, so that killing

me doesn't matter.

Kyle was looking at the map. "The bayou?" he said. "Have you looked out your window?"

"It's nothing," Dexter told him. "There's a hurricane blowing itself out in the gulf. We'll likely see one of the rainstorms that travel along with it. This is a dirt road —" He brought Kyle's attention back to the map. "There's a house at the end of it, right by a dock. You're looking at a ninety-minute drive, no more."

"I've been out there," Kyle said. "Evan and I took a fishing skiff out from there."

"Yes?" Dexter shrugged, a man too busy to remember all the favors he handed out to his staff. "So you know where it is." He refolded the map, but kept his eyes on Kyle; narrow eyes in a narrow, hard-boned face. "Just keep her close, and kill her when the time comes. You know when that is?"

"When's that?" Kyle asked.

"When Bullen dies. When you know he's dead. As soon as you see him fall, you can kill her. Okay?"

Kyle nodded and Dexter handed him the map: "Take it anyway." As he left the room, he added: "Just shoot her fucking brains out, okay?"

Evan got up and went to sit in a chair so that he could look at Kyle as he spoke to him. "What happened?"

"Nothing happened."

"Don't bullshit me."

"You worried about Dexter?"

Evan laughed. "He pays us, that's all. You were supposed to check in."

"I couldn't find a quarter."

"Kyle, I want to ask you something. We went out one night — would have been three years ago, I guess — we went down to one of the West Side piers, and there was this old woman — you remember her? She was —"

"I remember," Kyle said, "so what are you — ?"

"— she was pushing a shopping cart that had come from some store in Chinatown, bags and papers in it, and she was all done up against the cold, layers of clothes and gloves with no fingers and a wool hat. You remember what we did to her?"

Sonia felt the kind of chill people get when they know they're about to be attacked.

"Yes," Kyle said.

"Remember who kicked her legs out from under her?"

"No."

"Remember who spilled the gas on her?"

"No."

"Remember who put the flame to her?"

"No."

"Neither do I. We both did everything. You couldn't separate us in that, couldn't tell us apart."

"Nothing's changed."

"Okay."

"Your turn, my turn; nothing's changed."

Sonia thought, I might as well be dead already.

Kyle looked at Evan; Evan was looking at Sonia. Kyle said, "Don't think about that."

"Go bring the car around," Evan said. When he and Sonia were alone, he slapped her lightly on the face,

383

then harder, then harder still. A tooth dug her lip and she felt a dribble of blood go from the corner of her mouth.

He put his hand on her breast and held it hard, until she cried out. He pushed her back on the sofa and punched her between the legs. "He get a piece of your candy, bitch?" She turned her head away, but he grabbed her jaw, digging his fingers in, dragging her face out of shape. He put his mouth close to hers and she could smell Kyle's smell: hot, like something charred.

He put his tongue in her mouth and licked her teeth. "Well . . ." — his voice was a whisper — "you're just meat. You understand me? Meat, just meat, dead meat."

On his way to Morgan Sorrell's law office, Ross Tate had remembered the conversation he'd had at four o'clock that morning. He'd asked, "What are we talking about, here?" It was the fourth time he'd put the question.

"As much as you can spend," Cochrane said.

"Come on, Stuart. Don't fuck with me; let's hear a figure."

"The deal is for ninety million."

"Where's the money?"

"Zurich."

"How in hell do we get hold of it?"

"This guy Sorrell — he's going to tell us."

"Tell us?"

"Tell Bullen. He knows he can't go ahead with the sale; he's all set to take some off the top, but he knows

384

that the price of giving us Dexter is that he loses the deal. What he gains is everything else Dexter's got.''

"How?"

"He's the lawyer, the bookkeeper. He can pick up where Dexter leaves off. So far as he's concerned, the international community" — Cochrane had laughed at the notion — "is going to jail Dexter, close down the source, and leave the money where it is — until someone withdraws the deposit on the grounds that the deal's gone down.''

"Can you see it through, Stuart? Are you sure of that?"

Cochrane had laughed. "The closer I get to ninety million, the more confident I feel."

"Who are they selling to?" Tate had sounded really edgy. It was the third time he'd called, each time looking for reassurances.

Cochrane had wondered whether the question had anything to do with moral scruple; the notion had worried him. "Ross, almost no one knows about this deal. Almost no one in the world. Some people did, but Dexter had them killed. Now, all we have to do is move in on the deal. Everything's falling into place. But I need Bullen to be my ears and eyes, so please get down there and prevent him from being killed, okay?"

"What's the plan, Stuart — let the sale go through and hijack the broker's fee? Three fucking nuclear weapons for Christ's sake? We know where they'd be going, don't we?"

"All I'm doing," Cochrane had told him, "is getting within sniffing distance of a lot of money. If we have to let the bombs go — so what? I'm prepared to take the risk."

"Doesn't sound to me like you're taking too many risks, Stuart. I'm taking them; Bullen's taking them."

"You take yours now," Cochrane had told him, "I'll take mine in Moscow."

In truth, talking to Morgan Sorrell didn't seem much of a risk.

Lawyers, Tate thought. I've shit lawyers.

Sorrell listened to Tate's assurances, nodding his head like someone counting sheep through a gate. He said, "I need it lead lined, Mr. Tate. Nothing gets said, nothing official happens until I see the documentation guaranteeing me unconditional immunity."

"We're talking about three nuclear devices, here," said Tate. "I can get you the attorney general swearing a deposition in front of the heavenly host and a blood-brother pact with the president."

"Good. Get it."

"When Bullen says so."

"If Dexter's got the girl, she's as good as dead. Want my opinion? — dead."

"You told Bullen this?"

"I didn't want to disappoint him. Dexter'll want them both dead."

"He won't get what he wants."

"Sure, okay. Listen" — Sorrell smiled — "I'll deal with whoever's left standing."

Kyle crossed the Mississippi and came off the bridge heading west, driving into dark weather. Sonia was beside him, one wrist cuffed to the door handle.

Kyle said, "Just like old times. Isn't it just like old times, lovely Sonia?"

He started to laugh and he couldn't stop. He laughed until the breath stuck in his throat. The car weaved from side to side, raising a chorus of horns.

He laughed until he cried.

The house was a couple of hundred yards from the bank of a bayou: double fronted, two stories, a veranda that went all the way around. It faced a stand of live oak at the end of a big, rough, grass patch that ended in a small jetty. A little way off, a long line of cypress hung with Spanish moss showed where the swamp bayou curved away from the house.

Kyle parked the car out of sight and led Sonia across the grass. They walked to the jetty and looked out over the water toward a channel that was clogged with water hyacinths. Cypress knees — wild, outgrowing roots — crowded through the carpet of green. There was a stillness that couldn't be accounted for and the air was like flock.

A sudden fury in the water almost at their feet made them both look down. A snake had taken a frog. The water showed slow ripples where the violence was being absorbed. The snake slid on the surface, the frog in its mouth still making slow, spasmodic thrusts with its long back legs, as though reflex could carry it to safety; then it thrashed suddenly, ugly in its death throes, and the snake flicked like a whip, traveling toward the far bank.

They went to the house and Kyle found the key

hidden inside a gutter pipe. He used the handcuff to fix Sonia to a cane rocking chair, then made some coffee. They both knew what it had meant, the snake killing the frog, but it was Sonia who gave it a name.

"It was a sign, wasn't it?"

"Yes," Kyle agreed. "It was a sign."

Dexter ordered Perrier, then veal with a green salad: a bloodless meal.

He said, "It's a different kind of deal now, isn't it? You'd better tell me what's on offer from your side. Sonia's in good health, by the way. She's anxious to see you."

Bullen smiled at the stagy afterthought. "It's a shame," he said, "I'll have to find another way in. I would have preferred to work with the best."

"It's a growth market, that's for sure."

"Another good thing — it's more or less legal much of the time."

"Yeah," Dexter agreed. "Drugs can be a hassle, but people don't mind about weapons, you know? Governments don't mind. Guns are for war; we've always had war." He smiled. "You're making a good choice, I can't deny that."

Bullen smiled back. They were playing a game called friendship — it involves thinking one thing while saying another, and it's a game that only enemies can play.

Dexter sliced his veal, then sliced it again and left it alone. His fingers tapped a little jazz rhythm on the side of his plate.

"Wars," he said, "everyone wanting to outgun the

next guy — literally, outgun. Hell, I wish I were a young man again." He pointed a finger at Bullen. "Get a globe and dab on a spot of kerosene for every war zone, then light the fuel — that fire goes right around the world. There's a deal on every street corner. Jesus, this is the time to be doing it. You'll have a hell of a time."

Bullen agreed: "That's what I intend to do."

The game had changed from friendship to families; you pretended loyalties and a common aim, but spent your time in secret plots, just like any family.

Dexter lifted a forkful of salad. As if it barely mattered, he asked: "How did you know about Moscow? How did you know Evan Bannick's name?"

"How do I know Viktor Petrenko is planning to sell you three first-generation nuclear devices?" Bullen said. "Ask yourself that."

A viscous line of salad dressing ran down the shaft of Dexter's fork, over his palm, and was soaked up by his shirt cuff. After a moment, he put the fork down and used his napkin to clean his hand and wrist, dabbing fussily. "Well . . ." His smile was a smudge. "You'd better let me hear the rest."

"I'm Roland Cecil's nephew. He's dead, but the syndicate he was setting up is alive and hungry."

Dexter sighed. "I don't need this shit. Listen: the money's in place, the buyer, too."

"Ever heard the term *counterbid?*"

"Too late, for Christ's sake."

"Is it? Then give me a piece, and the counterbid's a dead issue."

"A piece, what piece, piece of what, you asshole?"

"Three bombs? You buy two, I buy one."

"You're dead, Bullen. She's dead and you're dead."

Now they were playing enemies.

"Or I'll just muscle in anyway. Warn Petrenko, put a scare into him, talk to someone at Langley about the real nature of the consignment."

"The European bid wasn't that far advanced. You couldn't outbid me, you couldn't change the play."

"Fine. In that case I'll screw the deal."

"I'm expected to deliver three items."

"Deliver two. I'm being generous. And Sonia Bishop is returned to me unharmed." Bullen put down his credit card and caught the eye of the waiter. "Unless you want dessert," he asked, "or maybe coffee?"

Dexter lowered his head; he swayed slightly to and fro, like some creature crowding the bars of its pen, then got to his feet and walked away without looking back.

A moment later, Roscoe Tate passed Bullen's table.

Dexter and Tate got into Dexter's car at the same time. Evan Bannick had time only to make a half turn in his seat: enough to be able to see Tate's gun.

Dexter said, "Who in hell are you?"

"Friend of the family," Tate told him; to Evan, he said: "Head for the street. First, let me have your gun. If you turn around, I'll shoot you."

Evan handed the weapon over his shoulder. Dexter said, "I don't have a fucking gun."

"I know." Tate grazed Evan's ear with the gun barrel. "Now drive."

Bullen was waiting as they came out of the parking lot. He got in alongside Tate and passed Dexter a little roundel of gold foil with a crest on it. "They give you a mint chocolate after the meal — helps clear bad tastes from the mouth. I certainly needed mine."

"What is this, Bullen?"

"You've got Sonia Bishop, I've got Axel Dexter. It's an exchange."

"What — you're saying you'd kill me?"

"Why not?"

"I don't believe that."

"Well, listen, I've already made a start — you're my prisoner, I have a gun, I've got a lot to gain — also I don't like you. All the prerequisites are in place." He cuffed Dexter's shoulder to let the man feel his anger. "Now, where's Sonia? How do you get in touch with them?"

"In touch?"

"Don't fuck around," Bullen told him. Dexter dialed a number on the car phone. "Be careful what you say," Bullen added.

Dexter told Kyle what had happened, then handed the phone to Bullen. Kyle said, "Is my brother there?"

"When we get to where you are," Bullen said, "bring Sonia into the open. Don't be carrying a gun. I'll tell you what to do then."

"Is my brother there?"

"He's here."

"What's his position in this?"

"His position is that he's driving the car."

When they reached the house on the bayou, the cloud had closed in, dark gray carrying a liverish yellow undertone, and the air was so damp it seemed to swaddle them. A flicker of sheet lightning lit the sky just beyond the horizon.

Dexter and Evan got out of the car and stood in front of it; Bullen and Tate took up position directly behind, giving themselves human cover from the line of fire. They waited for a couple of minutes, then Bullen shouted Kyle's name. A wind came up, sending a rattle of loose twigs along the veranda, then the weather fell silent and still.

"Give me the car phone," Bullen said. Dexter passed it back and told him the number. Bullen dialed. The sudden stillness was like a curtain drawn on birdcall and the cries of animals: the sound of the phone ringing in the house was plain to everyone. Bullen let it ring for a full minute, then switched it off. He said, "He doesn't think I'll shoot you, but I will."

Dexter called for Kyle, but no one came. Bullen gave the phone to Tate, then started toward the side of the house, watching the windows, watching the door. He said: "If I don't come back, shoot them."

Tate was thinking: ninety million. The buy price is ninety million. It made him feel better.

Evan called, "Kyle . . . *Kyle!*" Tate took a step forward and kicked him in the small of the back — anxiety transmuted to aggression. He said, "Shut up. It's too late for that."

In the same moment, the phone rang. Bullen backtracked fast and took it from Tate. He heard Kyle say,

"I'm going to have to kill her. There's nothing left to do."

"If you do that, I'll shoot Dexter and your brother. Just let her go. Bring her outside and let her go."

"Maybe we'll all have to die," Kyle said, "maybe that's the answer."

"Give it to me." Evan held out a hand without looking back. Bullen handed the phone over, but stood close so that Kyle's voice was audible to him. "What's the problem, Kyle?" Evan's voice was low, an intimate murmur. "Why can't you bring her out?"

"Her mouth's been cut, Evan. Someone hit her. Was that you?"

Evan spoke slowly, as if to a child: "I'm standing out here with a gun alongside my head. So is Axel. Now the only way out of this seems to be that you bring the girl out and we make some kind of a deal." A fast flurry of rain swept the area in front of the house, stirring a small stand of live oaks growing between the house and the water. The sky was bruise yellow, bruise black, and seemed to belly down slightly in the middle. The wind carried scraps of debris and feathers of Spanish moss; it rattled the shutters on the house.

"You don't understand; see, I came down —"

"I understand, Kyle, sure I do, but listen, I'll bet she thinks —"

"— came down all the way from New York City and it started out just a drive, you know, somewhere I had to get to, some merchandise I had to deliver, but then something started that didn't get finished. I used to read her the book, and we hadn't gotten to the end of it, Evan. We were talking to each other, you know, and it all depended on it being just me and her, it's a bond, you understand that, don't you? You can't say what it is, but it's her smell when she's sleeping and the pain I had to give her to make her understand me, and the times we ate together and the music we played on the tape deck." His voice grew lighter as he began to cry. "It was there, *it was there,* but now you're telling me to let her go again, *again,* and I think I'd better kill her, I think that's best."

"— I'll bet she thinks you're an ugly runt with a face like a pig; I bet she hates you."

"I think that's best," Kyle said, and switched off the phone.

Now the weather had finally turned. Rain was traveling up the bayou in twisting squalls and the wind was thumping at the backs of the men who stood out in the open. Bullen had started out being able to hear Kyle's voice over the phone, but then the noise of the wind had drowned much of it.

Evan said, "He's going to kill her. Let me go in to him."

"How would that help me," Bullen asked, "the two of you together in there?"

"You got my gun, you've got Axel, what you won't have is the woman unless you let me go. I'm the only person he'll let go in there. I'll bring her out, don't worry."

"It isn't quite the simple exchange you think," Dexter said to Evan. "He knows about Moscow and he knows what the deal is."

Evan looked at Bullen and nodded slowly. "You're one dangerous motherfucker." To Dexter, he said: "We've still got to get out of this alive. Maybe there's a way to negotiate the deal."

"Fuck that," Dexter said.

"Maybe you'll just have to, Axel."

Tate said, "Someone's got to do something. There's one hell of a big wind traveling up these waterways."

"You stay here with them," Bullen said. "I'll go."

"Look," Evan told him. At an upper window of the house they could see Kyle looking out at them, a dim silhouette. "He hasn't quite made up his mind to kill her, but he'll do it if he sees you moving on the house."

"How can you be sure?"

"Talk to me," Evan said, "it's just the same as talking to him." They were having to shout to be heard over the wind. "You think I care if she lives or dies? Think I care if you do? The only way out of this is you get the woman back — am I right?"

"You're right."

"Then let me go and get her for you." Evan started to back off.

When Bullen made no move to stop him, he increased his backward pace, then turned and made for the house.

Sonia was sitting in a far corner of the upstairs room, uncuffed now, her arms linked around her knees, hugging herself in fear. She was past crying.

Evan's look was an open razor. He went to stand alongside his brother and together they gazed out at the figures on the grass.

Kyle said, "If there had been more time . . ."

"You're fooling yourself. She's not worth killing and she's not worth dying for. Let her go out to him."

"You hit her, Evan? Was that you?"

"Yes," Sonia said, "he hit me. He did other things . . ."

"Shut up, bitch."

Kyle brought a hand to his brother's neck. "Don't say that. Don't talk to her like you know her."

The rain had stopped and the wind was falling off.

Bullen's eyes were fixed on the upstairs window of the wooden house where the two figures stood, one with his hand resting on the other's shoulder, brothers in arms. He said, "I've made a mistake."

"Give it some time," Tate advised.

"I'm out of time."

A terrible silence was spreading from the center of things. The sound of thunder came up from the south.

Kyle's fingers were tight on Evan's neck. He said, "I love you, but you have to understand, I can't let her go and I can't keep her. What does that leave?"

"I can feel things breaking up." Evan's voice was tight. "It's time to go. Hand her over. We can be in New York by this evening."

"You think it's easy, you think —"

"Don't go away from me, Kyle."

"— you think it's like killing anyone, just *anyone?*"

There came a sound — shrill, eerie, frantic — that seemed to flow along the watercourse and flood the open spaces. It was all the birds of the swamp calling at once, their cries feverish and distraught.

A wind poured into the clearing and shook the live oaks from root to crown. A pair of heron went over, arrowing down the airstream, and a litter of debris was whipped upward and thrown against the house, breaking a window. As if heeding a warning, Evan and Kyle stepped back, then disappeared. The rain started again, slow but heavy.

Dexter said, "It's going to hit us; it isn't played out like they said it would be."

Bullen turned to Tate. "Put Dexter in the car, get in with him. With any luck, they'll assume that we've all taken shelter."

He ran forward against the rain.

Sonia looked from one man to the other. Evan was saying, "We can't stay here and we can't walk out if she's dead. Think it through." She remembered a time when he'd called her *"meat, just meat, dead meat."* Now he needed her life to trade with.

They stood close, their heads bent, and Sonia thought it was like watching a man talk to himself in the mirror. They were wearing the same cotton suit, a cream weave, over T-shirts. One man wanting her alive, the other needing her dead, and unless she watched closely it wasn't possible to say who was who.

Kyle said, "I saw a snake kill a frog — just a couple of hours ago, when we arrived. It was waiting for us — the moment was waiting for us."

"It's just a book, Kyle."

The room was growing noisy, like a ship's cabin far out to sea. Kyle took out the gun. He said, "I think it's best."

Bullen's footsteps were nothing more than wind-borne litter against the glass, or the bang of shutters. He came into the room and a man turned to him, arm out, yelling. Bullen fired three times and the man backpedaled, his shout still on the air: "Jesus, don't —" He was falling and walking and grabbing at his chest where the bullets had taken him at close range.

Kyle was behind his brother, also going backward, driven by the force of Evan's movement across the room. Both arms were out, as if he were pleading. He fell as Evan fell, arms there to catch, body there to break his brother's fall. The impact knocked him to his knees and his gun clattered across the floor. Bullen swooped on it and turned fast, but there was no need.

Kyle knelt close to the wall, his hands under his brother's arms. Evan's body slipped sideways, falling into Kyle's lap, his legs trailing on the floor, his head lolling on Kyle's shoulder. They were an arm's reach from Sonia. She got up like someone trying not to disturb the dust and walked to where Bullen stood.

He said, "Which one have I killed?"

43

Kyle looked around the room as if he expected someone to step forward and change everything. When he found Sonia he stared a minute, then looked down at Evan's dead body, searching for a connection. He opened his mouth to speak and closed it on silence.

After a moment he got into a crouch, supporting his brother across his thighs, then straightened, his arms around Evan's back and under the crook of his knees. He seemed puzzled, not knowing what to do next. Bullen kept a gun trained on him; standing close, Sonia could feel the tremble of tension in Bullen's arm. Finally, Kyle walked to the door and down the stairs.

The storm had deafened Tate and Dexter to the shots. All they could hear was the bellow of the wind and the sound of things hitting the car as it rocked on its springs. Tate looked through the rain-beaded window and saw Kyle as he came out of the front door, Evan in his arms. He said, "Oh, holy shit," and Dexter looked around for the cause, finding it at once.

Tate said, "Out of the car. *Get out of the fucking car!*"

They emerged into a wild funnel of wind and blinding rain. The whole swamp was airborne: great streamers of Spanish moss, small branches, birds being flung down the sky like rags. Dexter fell over and crawled a few yards before he could manage to stand up. When he looked toward the house again, Kyle had disappeared.

Tate and Dexter ran for the house, Tate staying slightly behind, as if it mattered any longer who had the gun. He waited while Dexter used both hands on the door, pulling against the wind. Inside, the house echoed like a beaten drum.

Bullen and Sonia were standing at the top of the stairs. Bullen still had the gun in his hand, but his arm was around Sonia because she had suddenly found the strength to cry.

Tate prodded Dexter up the stairs, both men dripping water from sodden clothes, and shoved him into the room where Evan had been shot. There were ragged lines of blood on the floor, and you could see where Kyle had put up a hand for support when he lifted his brother, because high on the wall were three red handprints.

Tate said, "What the fuck now?"

Kyle stood by his car and howled into the wind, Evan still in his arms, rain and birds and detritus from the storm whirling past him in a great cloud.

He stumbled around the car and opened the passenger door, taking care not to let Evan's body slip. His lips were moving, but the words were torn off by the wind.

He settled Evan in the seat and removed his jacket, spreading it on his brother to hide the wounds and the blood. He got in and started the car.

"We'll go home," he said.

The car bucked up the dirt road, whipped by debris and torn branches. Kyle drove almost blind, catching a glimpse of the road now and then, gunning the engine against the weather.

"We'll be fine," he said, "just fine, just fine, we'll be *fine*."

They crouched in the corners of the room to wait out the storm, no one under the window, no one opposite the window — you could see the glass flexing, just on the edge of fracture.

Dexter said, "I wish I'd never seen your goddamn face. If I ever get the chance to kill you, I will."

There was a muted explosion — the sound of windows breaking elsewhere in the house — and a fusillade of roof shingles clattered onto the veranda. Bullen got up and risked a look through the glass; he saw that the grass area between the bayou and the house had disappeared; the car was up to its wheel tops in water. The wind was driving waves across the bayou, raising white tufts.

"How long does this kind of thing usually last?" he asked.

"It's just the edge brushing us," Dexter told him. "If it was the hurricane itself, we'd be sky-high along with the house. A few minutes, a few hours."

"So we sit it out?"

"No," Dexter replied, "we all swim back to Lafitte's for a beer."

Sonia slept for a couple of minutes, then woke and

stared at the splashes of blood staining her jeans. She put a finger down and it came away sticky.

She was about to say, "Can't we go? Can't we get out of here?" when the window bellied in an inch too far and shattered with a bang. She screamed and folded herself against Bullen's side as glass slivers filled the air.

The weather roared into the room.

The water was no more than three inches below the veranda. A few creatures of the swamp had found refuge there: a family of raccoons, three muskrats, about fifty bullfrogs, and two cottonmouth snakes. They were motionless, all ignoring one another.

Every window in the house had gone and most of the roof shingles. Rain barreled in, washing Evan's blood from the floor and walls, washing away Kyle's handprints. Sonia leaned against Bullen, her eyes closed, her mind inventing terrors that had almost happened.

The wind backed off over the next three hours; the rain went from brutal to merely threatening. Then the storm seemed to drain away toward the horizon, drawing wind and rain with it, leaving a sky that looked flayed — tinfoil and ice blue and patches of pearl where the sun beat against thin layers of cloud.

Bullen went to the window. The world outside was wrecked — trees down, branches strewn everywhere, bird and animal corpses bobbing slowly in the water past the upturned car.

"We're going to have to walk to a road," he said.

"How long will that take us?"

Dexter shrugged. "Depends what's in our way. Two hours, maybe."

They went down to the screen door that opened onto the veranda. The water was falling away as you watched, a brown flood becoming a thin silt and patches of grass showing through.

"We could get the car back on its wheels," Tate said. "Maybe it'll start — over on its side that way, most of the hood was out of the water."

"We'll try," Bullen said. "I doubt it."

Dexter looked at Bullen, the narrowed lids showing just a glitter. "Are you going to kill me?"

"Why ask that?"

"Because it's going to be one of us."

"You say."

"I say."

"No." Bullen turned away from the look, unimpressed. "I'm not going to kill you. Not here and now, anyway. If you come after me, I might have to. A better idea is that you take me up on my offer."

"Fine," Dexter said, "then if I'm not going to die, let's go. Let's go now." He stepped through onto the veranda and immediately stooped, like a man trying to free his foot from a snag. When he straightened up, a cottonmouth was hanging from his wrist like a quirt, the broad, brown bands and black-patched underside clear to see. It fell and Dexter hopped away, banging into the wall alongside the door. His shout was an inhuman thing — deep and wrenched. He stayed with his back to the wall for a few seconds, then opened the door and stepped back into the house, a half smile on his face, almost a look of embarrassment. "It hit me in the leg," he said. "I did the worst thing — reflex thing — I put my hand down." He sat heavily on the board floor, the smile fixed on his face, then got onto all fours and threw up, his shoulders hunched like a dog's.

Kyle had driven through the hurricane's rim like a man looking for death. It hadn't come. Now he was out on the highway, northeast of the city, where the storm was a fading hint of yellow falling away at his back.

Evan's body had rocked and lurched as the car had hit potholes on the dirt road. Kyle wasn't able to bear the lifelessness of it, the terrible inertia; after a while he'd stopped the car and put Evan in the trunk.

"We'll be fine," he said to the aching space beside him.

His teeth were chattering slightly and a little foam of spittle lay on his underlip. He went on talking to Evan as he drove north, an amputee coming around from the bomb blast, not feeling the loss, not in pain, not afraid, still going forward on the torn-off limb.

Bullen and Tate were taking turns to support Dexter.

The dirt road was littered with obstructions: swathes of leaf, bushes, an entire tupelo gum torn up and dropped, its roots still thick with soil, birds still hopping among its branches. They looked closely for alligators and snakes. At every turn, Bullen expected to see Kyle's car crushed under a tree trunk. Their own car was a storm victim. Tate had spent fifteen minutes trying to start it, but the engine was full of silt.

Bullen asked, "What do you know about the snake?" It was his turn with Dexter. The man's legs were in motion, but his torso was asleep.

Tate answered. "Cottonmouth. Poisonous all right, but I don't know how poisonous." He thought back to army basic training. "A lot of snake bites aren't lethal if you get to an antidote serum in time."

"In time?"

"Yeah, I don't know. But I think it's hours, not minutes."

"So you're going to make it," Bullen said to Dexter.

"Thanks for letting me know." He sounded slightly drunk.

They came to a log that had floated onto the road and got caught up in a buttonbush. Sonia stepped over it, then turned to support Bullen as he supported Dexter. The air was heavy again, almost a summertime humidity, and her face glistened with sweat.

She and Bullen had spoken to each other only once during the time they'd been waiting out the storm. Sonia had woken with his arm around her, his body angled to keep off the worst of the drench. He had put his mouth close to her ear and she'd heard his voice under the wind: "I'm sorry."

Sonia had nodded. After a moment she'd said, "It's not your fault. I went to a wedding. I saw what I saw." Bullen hadn't been able to hear what she'd said, but he'd seen that it was sadness in her eyes, not anger.

Bullen handed his burden over. Dexter hooked up to Tate, leaning sideways so that he had to push with his legs to get purchase on the mud. He said, "It was a bad bite." Again the words seemed to slide around his mouth. "My heart's not good."

Tate said, "No, listen, it takes days — snake bite takes days . . ."

Sonia helped Bullen haul the crown of a small willow off the road. "Kyle was going to kill me," she said. "In fact, he was *always* going to kill me. He was very close to it. You did the right thing."

"I did the wrong thing," Bullen told her, "I did it at the right time."

Tate said, "Hey!"

Dexter's feet had tangled. He was sliding down Tate's side because he couldn't support his own body weight any longer. His hands grabbed Tate's neck, his shoulder, his arm. Bullen went over and helped lower him to the ground; he could see that the narrow face was colorless and a thin layer of grime seemed to lie beneath the skin like smoke-stain in the wax of a candle. Dexter's eyes, far back in his skull, were yellow and metallic, taking light but giving none back.

"It's too soon," Tate said. "There's no reason for him to die."

"His heart, maybe?"

"Maybe. I don't think so."

Bullen lifted Dexter's wrist where the snake had hung. It was massively swollen and discolored. You could see the bite, two little purplish tears. "The snake hit the vein." He lifted the arm further, showing the wound to Tate. "The venom went straight into a vein." Dexter's feet started moving, a treadle motion digging lines in the mud, and his head nodded re-flexively.

"He's dying." Tate sighed and sat on his haunches, forearms draped across his thighs.

"Can we do anything?" Sonia stood back a little, as if death itself might be infectious.

"Leave him's one thing; stay and watch him die's another. I don't mind."

The sound of something tearing was Dexter's breath in his throat. He grew still, just his bitten hand fluttered in the mud, *pit-pat, pitter-pat.* . . . He spoke in a voice that seemed to stutter in black bile.

"Who in hell sent you to me?"

Kyle made a stop in a rest area and went to sleep so fast that it was like fainting.

In his dream, he and Evan were children. They were fishing in a dead calm, the water of the lake so still that it reflected the slope of the boat, the fishing poles, the boys' faces peering over the side.

Evan said, "It's your turn. From now on, it will always be your turn."

"I need a sign."

Evan reeled in and a sleek shape hauled up out of the water. Kyle looked and saw Sonia, her hair stream-ing, water pouring from the slopes of her breasts, just as she'd looked when she'd stepped out of the shower.

Her face was raised to the sun by the hook in her lip.

There was a moment when Dexter could see cuts of blue in the cloud break, then he saw the sky darken

407

again, except that the darkness lay in him, lay over his face like a pall.

When he died, his muscles went into spasm, then locked: legs, arms, neck, his torso arching like a bow. You could almost hear the ligaments snap. Tate pounded on his chest for a minute or more, but there was never a flicker of response; it was like hitting a statue.

They left him as they had agreed they would. His death told its own story: the storm, the battered house, the upturned car, a man who had made it just so far up the dirt road with cottonmouth venom working through a vein to get directly to his heart.

Sonia walked quickly, plowing through mud and leaves. She asked, "Is there anything to stop us from just going — going away from here?"

"No," Bullen told her. "There's someone we have to see, then we can go."

"I don't know what's happening. You found out what the deal was?"

"I did, yes."

"Was I part of it? Why did they want me?"

"Bait."

She thought this through for a moment. "To trap you. That's why he didn't kill me?"

"Kyle?"

"Yes."

"Did he want to?"

"Oh, yes."

"Why?"

"Because he couldn't keep me."

Tate was walking a few paces back. Bullen and

Sonia spoke without looking at one another.

"Did he hurt you?"

She knew what he meant. "What is it?" she asked.

"What?"

"The deal."

Tate said, "For Christ's sake don't —"

"It's to broker a deal for three nuclear weapons coming out of Russia."

"— tell her."

Sonia stopped walking. "Are you going to stop that from happening?"

"Yes, we are."

"How?"

Bullen jabbed a thumb over his shoulder. "Ask the CIA. The second move is to contact the guy who's selling them."

"One guy?"

"I shouldn't think so, no. But I only have one name."

"What's the first move?"

"See a man called Morgan Sorrell. He's got something we need."

They walked for fifty minutes more before coming in sight of a road. The traffic was moving slowly, cut down to one lane by storm blockage.

Sonia said, "It's going to take me years . . ."

"Just lie low," Bullen told her. "Pick up where you left off, live an uneventful life."

"Sure," she said, "I'll do that, what could be easier? I see his face everywhere I look."

44

Sorrell met them at his office after dark. He opened the street door and led them to his room, past the strange lifelessness of silent phones and shrouded computers. He walked quickly, swaying slightly like a deckhand. Bullen could smell whiskey in the air.

The room was lit by green shaded lamps that shed a glow on the walls. They might have been underwater. Sorrell's eyes were hidden in shadow but his smile was as broad as the Mississippi River.

"Snake bite?" he said. "Jesus, a *snake bite?*"

"How about a drink," Tate asked, "if we're here to seal an agreement?"

Sorrell poured for them and the whiskey glowed in the lamplight, gold against green. "You need information," he said, "I need certain documentation."

"You've got your immunity," Tate said.

"That's good. I need to see it."

Tate sighed. "You know we can't do that. What? Something signed in front of a notary and sealed in wax over a red ribbon?"

Sorrell looked at Bullen, then back at Tate. "That's the deal."

"No — here's the deal. Give us what we need and you're free and clear: my guarantee. Fuck me around and you won't be going home tonight. There's no trial, no reason for you to give evidence. We don't want any of this made public. We just have to trust one another."

"I need it in writing: airtight."

"Can't happen."

"Unless I give you Petrenko, he's free to make the sale somewhere else."

"Maybe. Or maybe we can find him ourselves."

Sorrell sipped his drink. "I'll be running a legitimate operation," he said, "more or less. Don't come looking for me in the future." After a moment, he added: "This conversation never took place."

"I'm happy for you," Tate said. "You can asset strip his business, take on his client list, move into the biggest antebellum mansion New Orleans has to offer — buy your dreams. Let's have another drink." He poured it himself, topping up Sorrell's glass.

Bullen hadn't touched his. He asked, "Who was the customer for the bombs?"

Sorrell shook his head. "Dexter knew. Petrenko knows. What's your guess? Somewhere in the Middle East, right?"

"North Korea," Tate cut in, "Pakistan, Brazil, Argentina, Algeria —"

"Yeah . . . more likely some towel head."

"— Iran, Iraq, Libya, Syria, Egypt —"

"Wherever . . . they're not going to arrive," Bullen observed. "Just give us what we need to get to Petrenko and block the sale."

On a piece of plain paper, Sorrell wrote a telephone number and handed it to Bullen. "This is the number of a room in the Hotel President. In Russia, every hotel room has its own line — I mean, you don't get a

411

switchboard operator and ask for the room number, or give the name of the guest, you just dial the number for that room and get straight through. Dial this on a Tuesday or a Thursday at nine A.M. Moscow time and Petrenko answers. Okay? So do it next Tuesday. But call at nine-thirty. I'll have spoken to him. I'll tell him that Dexter's dead of a heart attack and that someone else is going to complete the sale.''

"He knows you?''

"Yes, he knows me; we haven't met, but we've put in a lot of telephone hours. I guess he'll be a little edgy about the fact that Dexter's out of things, but there's no reason why he should disbelieve me.''

"How was Dexter going to complete the sale?'' Bullen asked.

"It's a simple jigsaw. Dexter's already seen the merchandise. If you want to make it look good, you could ask to see it, too, but the bombs have been inspected by experts.''

"When?''

"Dexter took someone with him — someone appointed by the purchaser. They saw the devices and talked to Petrenko about shipping.''

"Where? Where did they go to see the bombs?''

"Ask Petrenko. Want my guess? The Ukraine. Lot of conflicting messages coming out of that part of the world. No one's really sure about their stockpile: the KGB claims to be, but I doubt it.''

"What about haulage? I mean, Dexter was going to import the weapons to the States?''

"Sure. The world is waiting for this one, Bullen. From what I can see of the European operation, they had the same idea. Make it a roundabout route: bring the bombs to America, or France, or Spain, or whatever was the first port of call. Then, if you're happy, you truck them on to a place where you can either hold them for a while, or keep them traveling if there are no problems. You put them aboard ship again, this time with different papers and a different description, bounce them off a couple more ports, truck and reload each time — make sure that they disappear, then disappear again, then disappear a few more times before they actually arrive at their destination."

"Out of sight, out of mind," Tate observed.

"Remember Operation Babylon?" Sorrell asked. "The Brits were selling Saddam a supergun. Did they ship it straight into the gulf? No — via Chile." Sorrell took a gulp of his whiskey. "Dexter was still setting up the trucking here — now that George Parker isn't in the game. Still, you don't have to worry about that. Petrenko doesn't know that the bombs aren't going anywhere." Beneath the phone number, he wrote a series of numbers and letters. "You'll need this."

"A bank code," Bullen guessed.

"No, half a bank code. Petrenko has the other half. That's why I called it a simple jigsaw. Put these two together and you've got access to part of the money — first payment. Or, rather, Petrenko has. You get the bombs, he gets the other piece of the bank code. The account on this number contains half the sell price. When the merchandise reaches home, Petrenko gets another half a number." Sorrell wrote it on the paper and put a bracketed two alongside. "He has a matching half number."

Sorrell turned the paper around and pushed it across the desk. Tate looked at it. Bullen picked it up and folded it into his shirt pocket. He asked, "What about Dexter's share?"

"A third account. Dexter already stashed half of it — the commencement fee. Which is now my fee." Sorrell affected an expression of mock glumness. "I'm reconciled to never seeing the second half."

"Bad breaks," Tate said.

"Make it look good," Sorrell said. "Whoever makes contact with Petrenko on my say-so can't be involved in seizing the bombs."

"Don't worry." Tate wagged his head reassuringly. "No one'll link you to it. We'll collar the bombs at the port, or on the road. When does Petrenko get his part of the code?"

"When the bombs are on board ship and the ship's out of territorial waters."

"He'll never get to use it."

"Who will it be?" Sorrell wanted to know.

"Who will what be?"

"The man who approaches Petrenko — the man I've got to vouch for. I'll have to give him an identity, you know? Some kind of status."

Bullen had already put the question to himself and supplied the answer. He remembered the moment underground on the day when Paul Shelley had arrived at his cottage — remembered the narrow tunnel, the dogleg that had trapped him, the unending, stifling blackness. He remembered that there was only one way out and that was to keep going.

He felt himself edging forward into the dark once

more. "Me," he said, "it'll be me."

After they left, Morgan Sorrell booted up a computer in his office and started to scroll through the names: people in high places, people in government. He scrolled through lists of places, contacts, suppliers, routes; he scrolled through accounts, columns of figures.

Finally he scrolled through orders of the past, orders of the future, the names that would change his life: Uzi, Kalashnikov, Heckler and Koch, Steyr, Ruger, Remington, Smith and Wesson, Sidewinder, Piranha, Walleye, Bullpup, Exocet, Grail, Sagger, Gecko, Sego, Swingfire, Hades, Entac, Peacekeeper.

They sounded like a great chorus, a hymn, swelling to a crescendo. He got up and walked around the office, going nowhere, seeing nothing, breathing elation like air.

Kyle had bought a tarpaulin in one town, a shovel in another, a flashlight in a third. Miles from any town, now, he drove ten miles along a mountain road, then cut the lights at a dirt driveway and sat for ten minutes contemplating what he was about to do. It seemed an impossible thing.

He lifted Evan out of the trunk, drawing his brother's arm across his chest, then stooping to take the weight on his shoulders and back, tossing the body gently to and fro to get it balanced. He draped the tarp on top of Evan, held the flashlight in his left hand, the shovel in his right, and made a hundred yards into the wood before he had to stop, leaning against a tree and listening to the knock of his heart. The wood was full of sounds, owl hoots, the bark of a fox, predators' footfalls sifting the undergrowth. "We'll be fine," Kyle muttered. "We'll be okay, okay, we'll be just fine." He straightened and carried Evan another fifty yards, then set the body down and dug a grave.

He dug deep and put the tarpaulin into the pit, then got into the grave and hauled his brother's body down. The corpse rolled over, arms flung out as if for an embrace, and Kyle fell under its weight, going full-length. He lay still, as if not sure of what his next move should be. The earth smelled rich and loamy; he lay next to his dead twin, neat and snug, and stared up from the grave at the dark treetops stirring in the night wind.

He said, "What do you want me to do?"

For a long time he lay unmoving; then he kissed his brother and eased him off, and climbed out of the grave. By torchlight he shoveled the earth back, working quickly to cover Evan's legs and torso, then stopped and looked at the face, his own face, his own dead face in a grave. He remembered that people used to hold a mirror above the face of the newly dead, looking for a blush of breath on the glass, just in case. Evan's face in the mirror was Kyle's face too — the living eye to eye, lip to lip with the dead.

Kyle knelt down and took a handful of soil, then held out his hand to let the soil slip gently down; he was shaking like a man with a violent fever; little by little, handful by handful, he watched his own likeness disappear from the world. He asked, "What do you want me to do?"

After a while he had to use the spade again. He put the earth back, trod the mound flat, then raked brush over, and pine needles. He walked back to the car and sat there, unmoving, waiting for an answer.

Evan said, "Kill her." Kyle heard it plain, as if his brother sat alongside him, his clothes heavy and damp with grave soil. "Kill her."

45

In a room in the Hotel President a man with three nuclear weapons to sell lifted the phone and listened. After a short while, he said: "I know, Mr. Bullen, I have been expecting to hear from you." His voice sounded unremarkable: the voice of someone ready to barter twenty Hiroshimas.

"Tell me what to do," Bullen said.

"Is simple. Come to this hotel where there will be reservation in your name. There are certain informations you must bring. You have these?"

"Yes."

"Good. Then there is no problem."

"I shall need to see the merchandise."

Stuart Cochrane was ambling back and forth tapping his lip with a finger like a philosopher arguing a point. When "merchandise" was mentioned he stopped and looked directly at Bullen, as if he could hear the silence on the line.

"That has been taken care of, Mr. Bullen. Morgan Sorrell knows this."

"I know it, too. But it was Dexter who made the inspection, not me."

"Are you nuclear expert?"

"I just want to see them; it'll make me feel better."

The silence drew out until it gathered a harsh sigh. "It will be possible."

"Good."

"Who are you, Mr. Bullen, that you should be in authority here?"

Bullen repeated what he'd been told to say by Sorrell. "I'm the senior partner in Dexter's holding company. I'm where some of his funding comes from on a deal of any size. Now Axel's dead, I'm running things."

"Not Sorrell?"

"Sure, Sorrell, but he's an administrator. I have a major investment to protect."

"Not on this deal."

"There are other deals, Mr. Petrenko. We're an international company. We take a percentage on our investment, we don't think too much about individual sales."

"But you're thinking about this one."

"It's exceptional."

"You're right, it is." Petrenko's English was clear, but heavily accented. "I am sorry Dexter is dead. It is good to deal with people you know and like."

"You'll get to know me, Mr. Petrenko."

"Will I like you?"

"Is it necessary?"

Petrenko laughed, a pleasant musical sound for the room to absorb. "No, Mr. Bullen. Is not necessary. Can you arrive on Thursday?"

"I can."

"You are English, Mr. Bullen."

"But America is a land of opportunity."

Petrenko laughed. "Any taxi driver will take you to the hotel."

"What time can I expect to see you?"

"I will get message to you, Mr. Bullen." A slight pause. "Have you been in Moscow before?"

"No."

"You will like it. Moscow is just like Western city now. Mugging, prostitute, McDonald's. Once I was poor man with job. Now I am rich man with no job — I am *bisnizman*. I like progress, Mr. Bullen." He put the phone down on his own laughter.

Cochrane turned off the wiretap and played the conversation back. "Ex-KGB," he said.

"You know him?"

"Don't have to. They're the ones in control, so they're the ones making sales. Until now it was stolen conventional weaponry and a lot of promises, but the Russians have always had a cavalier attitude toward nuclear matters. They've dumped eighteen reactors in the Kara Sea, some of them with their fuel rods still in place. Chernobyl is still killing people: the whole area's fizzing with radioactivity; they just lie about it." He laughed. "So do we, of course, but we're better at it."

"How will this Petrenko have got hold of the bombs in the first place?"

Cochrane smiled silkily. "Bloody good question. Ask him — we'd like to know."

"Tell me what's going to happen."

They were in Cochrane's suite at the Plaza. Bullen wondered whether the SIS kept it on permanent reserve; it would certainly have suited their aristocratic life-styles — Cochrane's especially. At Vauxhall Cross there were czars and bureaucrats.

Roscoe Tate and Paul Shelley, both bureaucrats of a sort, sat in armchairs on the far side of the room and said nothing.

"Make contact," Cochrane instructed. "Insist on seeing the weapons — we need to know where they're stored. Find out about the shipping methods: where and when. Arrange to hand over the code that releases the first half of the money when the cargo's afloat — although things will never get that far. Try to find out who else is involved. Even better should you be able to get some information on the European consortium. If they were hoping to fund local Nazi groups to the tune of nine million, then that's serious political penetration. We ought to know who they are and just how serious they hope to get." He spread his hands, a man grateful for small mercies. "But once we've located the weapons and got as much information from Petrenko as he'll freely give, then we'll snap the bastard up."

"You'll be there?"

"Well" — Cochrane gave a little laugh — "not single-handed."

"If Petrenko finds something wrong with what I'm telling him?"

"We'll be close by, Tom." Bullen's Christian name sat on Cochrane's tongue like a fleck of tobacco. "If things look bad for you, we'll lift him: don't worry."

Bullen took a taxi down to the East Village. He paid the driver and stepped out almost directly onto a woman sitting with her back propped against the street door to Sonia's apartment. Her legs were spread in a rigid V and the skirt of a filthy greatcoat was thrown back to show a flabby thigh marbled brown and red. Her hair was thick, falling on her shoulders, a dirty yellow tangled with gray. She held a bottle of Thunderbird wine, the neck just below her lip, and her eyes were as far away as happy days.

Bullen pressed the doorbell and said his name when Sonia answered. He pushed the door open, making the woman shift, but he didn't go in.

The woman raised her head and the effort cost her. "Whatcha lookin'?"

"I thought you were my mother," he told her.

"Yeah?" She nodded as if admitting the likelihood. "Gimme fi' dollar."

"What's your name?"

"Wha' say?"

"Tell me your name."

The woman's head sank forward on her chest and she thought for a moment; her lip touched the neck of the bottle and reminded her, so she took a long drink. Bullen pulled some money from his pocket and handed it over, then stepped past her.

"Beth," she said. "Used to be Elizabeth."

"I'm okay," Sonia said as soon as she let him in. "I'm okay on my own."

"I can go."

"I didn't mean that: I didn't mean don't come here."

"What then?"

"I've been walking around the apartment, I went out to get some food, I came back, I put some music on the stereo, I was fine. I'm okay on my own — it's a discovery: I'm telling you about it."

"Good." He nodded.

Sonia spoke brightly; her eyes were bright. She led the way to the kitchen and asked Bullen to open a bottle of wine. He started to search drawers for the corkscrew. The music was still playing — a cello piece, dark and low and melancholy, as if Sonia's genuine mood were circling the room, disturbing the air.

She started to wash some lettuce. "It's just a tuna salad," she apologized, though she hadn't asked Bullen to eat with her, and he hadn't said he would. "What in hell are you looking for?"

"Corkscrew," he explained.

She pointed to a drawer and went on talking. "Tell me what you're going to do."

"Make a trip to Moscow."

"You don't have to — isn't that right?"

"Someone has to."

"What will happen?"

Over dinner, Bullen told her about Petrenko and

how Moscow hotel rooms have their own phone lines. Sonia was drinking quickly; halfway through the meal, Bullen had to open a second bottle.

He told her about Morgan Sorrell and Stuart Cochrane. He told her pretty much everything there was to tell.

They stacked the dishes together in perfect pretense, talking together just like people who are easy with one another, people who have nothing special to say. When he went to stand by the door, ready to say good night, Sonia joined him and raised her face for a kiss. Bullen put a hand on her shoulder and stooped to her upturned face.

His touch was the jolt of power in a circuit. Sonia swarmed over him, lips on his lips, her hands washing his face, her body pushing against him so that he went back against the door. He could feel energy crackling in her nerve endings, gathering like electricity that has to discharge.

She released him and stood back, eyes wide.

Roscoe Tate was leaving. He said, "I've done about all I can do."

"I owe you." Cochrane smiled.

"You do. Don't forget the exact amount."

"The bank codes?" Cochrane asked.

Tate wrote them on a piece of hotel notepaper and handed it to Cochrane. "Once seen, never forgotten." In Morgan Sorrell's office he had memorized them in the time it would take to read them aloud.

Paul Shelley waited a count of ten after the door

closed. He walked to a sideboard and uncapped a bottle of Jack Daniel's, giving himself half and half with plain water until the glass was almost full.

"And me," Cochrane said.

Shelley sipped, then drank more deeply; he didn't pour for Cochrane. "I've covered for you, Stuart. I shall continue to cover for you — only because it's my ass, too. That aside, I'm going back."

Cochrane stared at him, as if noticing some disfigurement for the first time. "We've taken a little off the top before. The difference here is that we're going to be seriously rich. There's no danger, Paul. The salesman can't complain and neither can the buyer. What are they going to do — raise the issue at the Security Council? It's a fortune to nothing at all: even if we don't win, we can't lose."

"The difference here," Shelley told him, "is that we're running the risk of passing three tactical warheads to countries that are still ten years away from developing their own — countries that are run by sociopaths. That's the fucking difference."

Cochrane shook his head and smiled: a friend arguing patiently. "You know what they say, Paul. It's not the gun, it's the person who uses it."

"I know they say that. It's bullshit."

"Well, you must do what you like."

"People will ask questions."

"Not many. I'll be in Moscow in three days. I've already let it be known at Vauxhall Cross. I don't think you'll have to tell too many lies for me."

"What are you doing — officially?"

"*Officially*" — Cochrane gave the word great sardonic emphasis — "I'm looking for some fucking KGB man who's boasting about having some bombs for sale. I'm using an off-the-books operative called Tom Bullen as a bear trap. It's all much as advertised, you see." Cochrane gave a good-natured laugh. "I don't think I stand much chance of finding the man; I think I'll probably decide that he doesn't exist."

"What do you plan to do with the bombs?" Shelley asked.

"When I find out who the buyer is, I'll make some arrangements. Until they're delivered, it's only half the money. Petrenko will have to deal with me once he knows who I am. I'm sure he'll be happy to come to some sort of agreement."

"And Bullen?"

"I'll send him home. He can go into hibernation for a long time."

Shelley went to the door. He said, "I'll get a plane home in the morning."

"Okay, Paul." Cochrane's smile was cheery and his tone was light; he was carrying a vast weight of anger.

As an afterthought, Shelley asked: "Why didn't you tell him about Anne Warbeck?"

Cochrane had turned away. He took a drink before saying, "Who?"

Sonia had lit candles, which made Bullen remember another life.

The glow made her skin dusky. Shadows puddled in hollows below her breasts, on her belly, down to the deeper darkness of her groin.

He kissed her, stroking her legs open, and she

grasped his arms and hoisted him up. He couldn't tell whether her strength derived from passion or from fear.

Their shadows piled into one another, becoming one thing, then becoming two as he held himself on straight arms to look down at her. Her eyes were closed and he wondered what she could see.

She put him on his back and straddled him. She dashed herself against him again and again like waves on a rock.

She yelped and gulped air, sitting down hard on him to keep the sensation going, then fell into his arms like a lover.

Too late, Bullen thought, and came inside her without moving, a gentle, dying pulse.

Smoke climbed the little thermals over each candle. Sonia had taken a spliff out of her bedside cabinet and was smoking it without Bullen's help.

"He had a book, he seemed obsessed by it. *Letters from a Dead Land*. A man killed people, but first he had to witness a sign."

"What kind?"

"Anything. Well, something remarkable. The signs energized him; without them he slept all the time, as if his life was wasting."

"He saw a sign, then he killed . . ."

"No, it wasn't like that. If there was a sign, he *could* kill, but didn't have to. It liberated him to kill, gave him permission. I think he did that — I think they both did." She wouldn't use their names.

Bullen said, "How do you know?"

426

"They talked about killing a bag lady. They torched her." Sonia kept a lungful of smoke down for a count of five. "I don't know how I'm alive. I don't know how I'll ever find my life again."

She slept in the diminishing light, the candles burning down, darkness taking over in corners. Bullen lay beside her dealing images from the day like a gypsy's pack of cards.

Beth . . . Used to be Elizabeth.

Her hair — tawdry yellow and gray — was the hair of his mother's head, still growing in death, the dull color pushing the bright color out.

46

In a fourth town, Kyle had bought some clothes and a bag to put them in. In a fifth town, he bought some food and some booze. As well as seeking out these items he was looking for the place he'd promised to take Evan to — he was looking for home.

He slept a night in the car on a hill road south of Knoxville, Tennessee, having driven hard all day. Next morning he traveled through Kentucky and crossed the state line into West Virginia. He knew the trailer park no longer existed, but he found another that leased homes like a motel. He put down his credit card for a minimum one-week stay and moved into a two-bed mobile home that stood in a row of fifty others, just off a path bordered with tubs of flowers. The brochure told him about the on-site stores and conveniences. The whole place was bright and had a sense of community about it. Kyle noticed none of this. He moved in and holed up.

In his pocketbook, Kyle carried a photograph of himself and Evan as children. The boys were sitting together on the scabbed sofa in some motor home; you could see the lower half of a bottle of Jack Daniel's on a table to the left. They stared at the camera, mute and giving nothing back, a double portrait, two faces, the same face. Kyle removed the photo and set it in a little alcove by a fitted mirror and sat before it — a necromancer before the shrine.

Evan's voice scrolled the glass: "I am the sign you seek."

"I know," said Kyle.

The next night, Kyle picked up a girl in a bar. She told him her name was Amanda but that people called her Buzz. When he asked her why she laughed and flicked a snake-tongue at him: "Don't I give you a buzz, honey?" She was forty, but her hair and makeup said twenty-five. She wore a crossover top under a silk jacket and a skirt that cut her thighs.

Buzz thought that Kyle was one hell of an ugly son of a bitch, but then most men were. They had a couple of drinks and set a price, then Kyle left and waited in the car; Buzz joined him a few minutes later. She said, "Thanks, honey. I don't like to walk out with the johns, you know? I pay the barman, but I don't like to put it in his face — he's got a job to do." She climbed into the car and said, "Are you out of town?"

"Not to speak of."

"I need a lift back to my car."

"Sure, that's fine."

Buzz put a hand on his thigh and ran it up into his crotch, a little down payment. Her hair was cut spiky and was dyed jet black; you could see a tiny fan of wrinkles beside her eyes that bunched when she laughed.

On the way to the trailer park she asked him about himself and he told her things that were soothing in their ordinariness: wife, two kids, steady job as a salesman, using the trailer park to make a little money on the side during his selling trip. He could pocket the difference between hotel expenses and what it cost at the park. Buzz laughed at the suburban daring. Kyle was talking without listening, but he noticed the laugh; it meant she was relaxed.

On either side of Kyle's mobile home people were watching TV: a Babel of voices and gunshots and sirens. He led the way to the bedroom area and found a country music station, then asked Buzz if she'd like a drink.

"Scotch, honey . . ." She was already taking her clothes off while he poured the drinks; plenty more time to work the bars tonight if she sipped while she fucked. The music was loud. The singer was a woman with a voice like molasses.

She put her clothes on a stool in front of a recessed mirror in a little vanity unit, then turned, naked, smiling still, as Kyle came toward her with the drinks. She said, "Okay, honey, if you like what you see, let's see what you like."

Kyle gave her the drink, then walked behind her as if to set his glass down by the bed. He took a short length of metal tubing out of his pocket and swung it at Buzz's head, taking her low on the skull just above the neck. Buzz wasn't sure what had happened. She felt the first pain of the blow, then, immediately, a numbness that seemed to go straight from her head to the backs of her knees. She stepped sideways, her legs folding, and muttered something unintelligible. She heard a low drone, like distant machinery; then the noise stopped and she was unconscious.

She woke to the sight of herself in the mirror. She could barely move, because she had been tied to a small chair with electrical cord, her arms pointing straight down and bound underneath the seat, her legs fixed at calf and ankle, a single strand of cord around her throat pulling her head back and her body upright, then tied off on the back rail. She could hardly breathe because a cloth had been pushed into her mouth and her lips taped shut. But she could see, foggily at first, then a little better, then with the bright clarity terror brings.

Her own face in the mirror, then the knife, and above, Kyle's face, eyes glittering with purpose.

Kyle said, "I'm killing her, Evan: see? I'm killing her." He started to work on her. "Look, look at this."

Buzz's head was heaving and tossing as she tried to get air through her nose. Her fear was so great that only the pain was keeping her conscious.

"I'm killing her, Evan. Look, look, watch me killing her."

Kyle wrapped his arms around her, holding the knife with both hands. He said, "Evan watch Evan watch me Evan killing her killing her now Evan *watch watch watch*." He felt his hands soak and heard the roar of blood in Buzz's stopped-up throat. He fell to his knees, then onto all fours, panting like a hound.

After a moment, he got up and stood behind the chair again. Buzz's head was hanging from the cord.

"Whose turn is it now, Evan?" he asked.

Evan's voice was a low whisper that only Kyle could hear. "Yours, Kyle. It will always be your turn from now on."

Bullen and Sonia spent the time together: they had two days. Sonia wanted to do all sorts of normal things: a concert at Carnegie Hall, a movie, Sunday morning in Central Park and, afterward dim sum in Chinatown . . . It wasn't possible to pretend. They stayed in the apartment and talked about themselves.

They went shopping for food and he bought the ingredients for a Caesar salad. While he was making it, she gave him a look and he walked to her and set her wineglass aside and cupped her head in his hands to kiss her mouth. They went to bed and he made her cry out with a sound of weeping, a sound of pleasure.

Bullen walked to the bed, naked, carrying two glasses and a piece of paper he'd taken from his pocket. Sonia liked the way his hips were lean and his chest deep from hauling himself up by his arms.

He told her about his life underground, about being trapped in the dark. She thought he was offering her a metaphor.

He leaned over and ignited the piece of paper in a candle flame, then let it drift, blazing, into Sonia's ashtray.

"What was that? Numbers?"

"Bank codes."

"You don't need them anymore?"

"That's the theory."

Because he was leaning across her to crumble the ash, she nipped his upper arm with her teeth.

She held the back of his neck while she kissed his mouth.

Her body seemed to flow under his hands.

Sonia was damp from him, damp between her legs, her breasts damp, her hair damp with sweat.

She said, "Who is there — in London?"

Bullen spoke Anne's name and immediately her image came to mind, strong and sharp; he could see her smile of disapproval.

"Why don't you call her?"

"There's too much to say."

"I'll bet you're right," Sonia observed, "there's *always* too much to say."

Bullen put his vodka down carefully on the bedside table and rolled over. He kissed Sonia's breasts and asked her if she liked that.

"I like it."

He kissed her belly and the inside of her knee.

"I like that, too."

He pressed her thighs apart and went on kissing her. "And that," she said, and then she couldn't speak.

Kyle stood in the shower for a long time. He felt depressed. It hadn't gone well. He didn't feel the same way about killing Buzz as he had when Evan and he had prowled the New York City streets together. Evan was displeased, he knew that. He could see that Buzz wasn't right: as a victim, she had no power to appease.

It would have to be Sonia.

"Will I see you again?"

"I'll come back through New York."

"You don't have to."

"Sure, but I will."

"A lot of the time I think nothing will be normal ever again —normal like normal memories, a normal future."

"No, it won't. But time will pass."

"Sometimes I'm afraid to go to sleep. He's there waiting for me."

"That's all over."

"Is it —"

"Yes, of course."

"— because where is he, where did he go, will he come back? Do you understand?"

"I understand. But I don't think he'll come near you. He was doing a job. The job's over."

They were seeing the night out, lying in bed, far from sleep, the detritus of a meal surrounding them, wine bottles, glasses, a spliff smoldering in the ashtray on Sonia's side of the bed.

"His face . . . when I close my eyes."

"He'll fade."

They both knew he was lying; they both knew it was all that he could do.

"Will you? Will you fade, Tom?"

There were words on the tips of their tongues that were scalding, but couldn't be spat out.

"I wish," he said, "I had met you in another world."

She covered his body with hers, cool and damp, a faint smell of dope as if it were leaking in her sweat, a fall of hair stroking his cheeks and covering his eyes.

All she wanted to do was leave her imprint, like a leaf on stone.

A
BANQUET
IN
RUSSIA

47

Bullen emerged into the arrivals hall at Sheremet'yevo 2, where half a million people were scrambling over one another, screaming, embracing, weeping, offering taxi services, picking pockets, and waving placards bearing the names of strangers.

No one knew his name. He negotiated with a taxi driver — asked for a king's ransom, Bullen offered a pittance and they agreed on ten dollars. He thought that Moscow had learned some bad habits recently. There was a smell in the air, thick and slightly putrid, as if someone had distilled "market economy" and bottled it as a perfume, but had added a touch too much corruption.

The taxi driver offered him gambling, dope, and whores in a rattle of broken English. Bullen faked deafness and the driver settled down to curse the traffic on the M-10.

The Hotel President was a monstrous red brick folly surrounded by iron railings: once a party hotel where visiting dignitaries stayed, it now specialized in conferences. In the vast entrance lobby, ethnic groups shuffled this way and that while conference organizers yelled and waved clipboards and handed out plastic ID tags. Petrenko had reserved Bullen a suite on the seventh floor. He dumped his bag and gazed from the window across to the onion domes of the Kremlin, then he looked at the telephone.

"I'm here," he said, "where are you?"

The hum of the old-fashioned radiator sounded just like a broken connection.

When Stuart Cochrane arrived on the next plane, Charlie Roper was waiting to take him straight to the VIP lounge. Roper was head of SIS operations in Moscow, which was a little like being a thief in an empty orchard. Cochrane would sooner have avoided Roper's company, but there was no way to do that. They collected Cochrane's baggage on the far side of customs clearance and went straight to a car with CD plates and smoked glass, Roper's chauffeur muscling a way through the crowd.

Roper was all eagerness and irreverence. "It's like the fucking Klondike," he said. "The whole country's up for sale. The crime rate makes Miami look peaceful. Ten years ago we had a police state — try being a criminal in a police state. Now the *mafiozniki* run things, along with ex-KGB men, muggers, opportunists, local gangs — and some members of the government. We reckon that about twelve billion dollars of gold bullion was shipped out of the country during the time Gorbachev was in office — God knows where it went."

They had hit traffic on the Leningradskij Prospekt. Other drivers were staring at the car as if the dark glass might suddenly clarify and show them a secret.

"Kidnap's popular," Roper observed. "Drugs, prostitutes, the usual — though there are more exotic ways of thieving; caviar poaching's big business at the moment." Roper laughed. "When I last heard, Moscow's anti-Mafia squad had one typewriter, one Lada, no fuel. Meanwhile, we're getting gunfights in restaurants, car bombs, assassinations. Who's your man?" He asked the question as if Cochrane were flicking through mug shots.

"I'm not sure there is a man. This is what the police call 'acting on information received.' I've got a contact number. We'll see if anyone answers the phone."

Roper seemed faintly aggrieved. "I could have done that for you."

"But suppose someone *does* answer?" Cochrane asked, which made Roper blink, then look away and hold his silence. As if to compensate him, Cochrane said: "Thanks for finding me somewhere."

"It's in the Arbat: nice area. Old houses, alleyways, Moscow as it once was. Not too many muggers. We used the house a lot in the old days." Cochrane could have sworn he'd heard "good old days." "This guy claims to have a bomb for sale, does he?"

"Claims to have three."

"Go to any big hotel. Sit in the lobby for an hour or so. What do you see? *Bisnizmeni*. What are they doing? Buying and selling. What's for sale? Anything. I've heard rumors about nuclear weapons before" — Roper shook his head — "not possible."

"This is a strong rumor."

"A wrong rumor."

"I'll bet you're right," Cochrane said. "I don't even expect to find the man in question. He'll be a figment of somebody's imagination —" he spread his hands

439

in exasperation — "but I have to look."

"Ten thousand of the bastards," Roper muttered.

"What?"

"Ten thousand warheads, bombs, devices of one sort or another. That's how many are stockpiled here. The country's in chaos, nationalist movements springing up every hour, people want to sell, others want to buy, corruption's a way of life." He smiled willingly at Cochrane. "I expect it's all a matter of time."

The nighttime streets were busy and seemed full of risk. Bullen waited until after eleven o'clock for the phone to ring. His suite was depressingly opulent: rich wall hangings, gilt furniture, molded covings, a teardrop chandelier. If Bullen coughed or sprang the lock on his suitcase, the echo seemed to run from one end of the room to the other. An enormous gold mirror, swarming with cherubim, covered most of one wall and forced Bullen to watch himself as he went to and fro in the room.

The elevator was antique double doors under steel mesh and dragged down at half the pace of the slowest guest using the stairs. Bullen walked through the lobby. Even at this time, the big leather sofas were occupied by men doing *bisniz*. A slow drizzle had started, turning silver corkscrews in the lights beyond the door.

During a brief tour of the city, you could see the burned-out upper floors of the White House, the burned-out floors of the mayor's office, the burned-out floors of the Ostankino TV station. You could see lines for a Big Mac off Gorky Street; you could see

440

nine-year-old hookers in Red Square. Bullen smelled something in the air that made him heady. It was dope and hysteria. Everyone was going to a party.

Bullen's party was being held in a building that had once been a cinema. From the street it was all lights. The music was loud enough to stun mice. The doorman wore leather and studs. A tattoo on his upper arm showed a likeness of Hitler. Bullen couldn't read the smudged blue inscription that said, KILL JEWS & SAVE MOTHER RUSSIA. The man put a hand on Bullen's chest and asked a question.

Bullen held up a twenty-dollar bill: "Enough?" The man laughed and took the money.

The cinema had a stage but no seats. What the band lacked in talent, they made up in energy: even the drummer covered a lot of ground. People were dancing, or were drunk, or stoned — soldiers, punks, Hell's Angels, kids in torn denim and leopard-skin vests. *Mafiozniki* in shell suits and Adidas sneakers danced slowly on the fringe of things. They had brought girls who were still wearing their furs, as if they might be naked under the fox or the mink.

In the half dark, high above the action, there was a large cage in which five girls stripped one another, put on one another's clothes, stripped one another again. A strobe rig had been positioned so that you saw cuts of flesh like a fast-forward total recall of sin.

He stayed for an hour, wrapped by unrelenting noise. At one side of the space below the stage was a group of kids all dancing together, heads down, arms waving wildly. They wore rags of denim and black scarves, tattoos and black lipstick.

Bullen saw that Moscow was lawless and lost; it seemed the perfect place to find someone ready to sell a million deaths. As he left, he looked again at the kids in black. They seemed to be dancing at the very edge of the world.

He walked back to his hotel through the quickening rain and no one approached him because he looked dangerous.

The desk clerk handed him an envelope with his name on the front. The message simply made a date for dinner the next evening and was signed Viktor Petrenko.

48

Cochrane called at nine the next morning. "Any contact?" he wanted to know.

"Tonight. An invitation to dinner."

"Take a long spoon. Report back as soon as you're free." Cochrane gave the telephone number and address of the house in Arbat. "This is where I'll be when you need me. Remember — you have to see the merchandise."

"What difference does it make?"

"Where there's three there might be five, ten, fifteen."

"Is there backup?" Bullen asked.

"Of course."

"I haven't seen any."

"If you'd seen them," Cochrane chided, "they wouldn't be much fucking use, would they?"

"This city is insane," Bullen observed, as if he and Cochrane were the first to set foot. "This city is on the brink of disintegration."

"Russia is on the brink. That's why they're unloading their resources."

"The people here are desperate; it's the party before the world's end."

The restaurant at the Hotel President was quiet and still. Five tables were occupied out of a possible sixty. In all of that vast room with its lush carpeting, its cascade chandeliers, its wall drapes and sconces and sprays of dying flowers, only five tables; but still the service was glacially slow. Waiters appeared empty-handed and — even more mysterious — went away again.

At the far end of the room, separated from the other customers by a sea of linen and silver and glassware, Viktor Petrenko sat alone. Three tables removed were two men who could have been either psychopaths enjoying a night off or Petrenko's bodyguards. They were splitting a bottle of vodka and smoking incessantly.

Bullen sat down opposite Petrenko, which meant that he had his back to the bodyguards. He looked over his shoulder, then back at Petrenko, who smiled.

"Why don't they join us?"

Petrenko's smile lengthened; he broke into a

chuckle. "They are not hungry. Also they have their own matters to discuss."

"Yes? What?"

"Football or boxing or fucking or money. It is no good to look in there." Bullen had picked up the menu, which was about the size and thickness of a photograph album.

"They might not be hungry. I am."

"Yes, but nothing is good in there. Also nothing is available." There was a bottle of wine on the table, uncorked but still full. Petrenko poured a glass for Bullen, then, as if it were an afterthought, another for himself. He handed Bullen a slip of paper with a series of figures on it. "If you need to contact me," he said, "leave a message at this number. This is precaution only; more usual is I will contact you."

On the far side of the room, a waiter appeared with a tray and took it to a table occupied by two couples. He set the dishes before each diner, not bothering to ask who had ordered what. A thin steam rose from the food. The diners looked at it but didn't make a move.

"They are having soup made from cabbage," Petrenko said. He gave a couple of hard coughs that were really laughter. Petrenko wasn't the plug-ugly image of a party boss, but he wasn't pretty, either. His face bore a long furrow, dark and pitted, that ran from the corner of his mouth and along the jawline, then rose to a point just below his earlobe. It was a burn or a knife wound. His hair was thin, a soft brown, and developed a natural forelock that fell to the left. His eyes were hard and brilliant, like glass struck by light.

"I was sorry to hear about Axel Dexter." Petrenko

444

looked solemn for a second. "I hope it was quick."

"Dropped like a stone."

Petrenko laughed. "You don't feel it necessary to show sadness — a token?"

"He was business. This is business." He saw recognition flash in Petrenko's eyes, and suddenly, Bullen understood the awful rightness of what he'd said. He wasn't going to have to act this one out; he wasn't going to have to search for a role or worry about whether he sounded sincere. Just saying it, "This is business," made him feel how it was all possible. *Eto bisniz.*

"Can I know your given name, Mr. Bullen?"

"Thomas. Tom."

"And I may call you Tom?" Bullen lifted a hand to give permission. "Tom, there is one thing I must ask you. Is this: do you have bank codes?"

"Yes."

"Please tell me first one."

"I think I would be stupid to do that."

"Tell me something to help my belief."

The codes were in three parts. Bullen recited the first part of the first code: three letters, four figures.

Petrenko smiled happily. "Thank you. It makes me feel so very good. Is this your first visit to Moscow, Tom?"

Now they were friends. They had the whole evening before them and there was no need to talk of *bisniz* for a while. Bullen conceded that, yes, it was his first visit.

"Things have changed." Petrenko laughed and looked up at the ceiling and clapped his hands lightly to applaud the differences. "Oh, yes, how things have changed." He made a frame of his hands like someone offering a proposition. " 'There is a specter haunting Europe.' You have heard these words? You know where they come from?"

"The Communist Manifesto."

"Correct. Let me tell you what is now the specter. It is Russian free enterprise. You think crime in West is bad? You think Triads and Mafia and Yardies so bad?" He smiled and the dark scar along his jaw grew deeper. "Nothing. *Nothing!* Here is another quote: 'We will bury you.' "

"Khrushchev."

"It is irony that politicians could only threaten this. Remember neutron bomb? This was never built, but theory was to kill people and leave property intact, leave wealth intact. How clumsy, this concept. How better to overwhelm in other ways. We will bury you with heroin, with crack, with whores. After all those years of threats and world in danger and Cuba and Star Wars . . . Is simple. Greed will do it."

"You speak like a true patriot," Bullen told him.

Petrenko laughed loudly. "I will be far away," he said, "somewhere else, somewhere quiet. The *mafiozniki* must work hard, must control borderlands by China and Afghanistan, protect poppy fields, set up heroin factories, make international connection, all the time kill to keep respect" — he waved his fingers and blew on them — "not for me, I thank you."

"Three bombs," Bullen said, "one deal."

"One deal, then comes easy life."

"Where will you go to?"

"England, maybe. America. Tell me about England."

They chatted like people with all the time in the world. The bodyguards drank their vodka in shots, each throwing his head back with the tiny glass welded to his lips; they smoked hard, leaving their Marlboro packs open on the table in case they forgot. From time to time, Petrenko glanced toward the door that led to the kitchen, as if he were expecting something.

After fifteen minutes, two of the other tables emptied. A short while after that, the final group drifted away — three men, dressed in identical brown suits; they looked as if the restaurant of the Hotel President had saddened them.

"When will I be able —" Bullen began, but Petrenko was looking off to his left, toward the kitchen door again, and he raised a hand to silence Bullen.

A waiter was emerging, pushing a trolley; behind him another; behind him, a third. They came in a little train across the deserted restaurant, dark suited and dour. When they reached the table, each set about his allotted task. A bottle of champagne was opened; glasses were filled, and the bottle set in an ice bucket. Then, one by one, the dishes were unloaded from the trolleys.

There were so many dishes that the idea of which should come first didn't arise. Another table was pulled up to hold the weight of food. As each dish was unloaded, a waiter muttered its name and Petrenko smiled and nodded, offering Bullen a translation.

"Smoked salmon, well you know this, caviar — is

447

Beluga, here is maybe eight ounces, soused herring, this you eat with the green pickle, soup is borscht but is with Indian spice, blini here with sour cream, or you can put caviar in, okay. Oysters, well you can tell, and here mushrooms in oil and garlic, now quail's eggs, scallops . . ." His eyes went from the food, as it was placed on the table, to Bullen as he watched. A waiter brought another table and the count went on.

"Duck," Petrenko advised, "with wine sauce, now pheasant with pickle cabbage, now chicken in casserole with wine, now this is beefsteak, has been flash fried in butter, now lamb done in oven, done very slow . . ."

He glanced at the waiters all the time, making sure not to miss their descriptions, then back to Bullen.

". . . this now shish kebab, this is small tart with leek and onion, now salmon comes inside pastry, and this — don't know what this fish is called in English — is *paltus* — this is potato with cream *dauphinois,* now *escalope* of veal, has bacon inside, now vegetable with glaze, these you know, and spinach and now salads: this is red cabbage with, I can't think — *ukrup* — yes, dill, here is rice salad, green bean salad, now eggs are poached here and here eggs in omelette . . ."

He stopped for a moment and smiled at Bullen, but another trolley had arrived and the loading went on.

"This is baklava, pastry and honey, very sweet, this is apple tart French way, this is pecan pie, lime pie, this is pears in brandy, coffee ice cream . . . now peaches in white wine, chocolate mousse, strawberries in cage, is made of spun sugar, now lemon soufflé, cherry tart . . ."

He sighed as the dishes began to peter out. A waiter put a platter of twenty cheeses on the table; another poured more champagne; a third cracked a napkin like a whip and set it on Petrenko's lap, then did the same for Bullen. The linen was heavy and embossed with the crest of the czars.

The waiters departed and the bodyguards fell deeper into their routine of vodka and nicotine. Petrenko took a fork and sampled an artichoke heart; he took a morsel of duck. He said, "We go tomorrow." Now it was *bisniz*.

"Go where?"

Petrenko gave a little moue; it meant: you know better than that.

The sheer weight of food had caused Bullen's appetite to fade. In a country where anything is a luxury, conspicuous waste is a powerful way of showing class. He cut a leg of pheasant, as much as he could eat, and asked: "If you can't tell me where, maybe you can tell me how."

"In old USSR, all nuclear weapons were under control of three organizations. KGB controlled actual warheads; military controlled means of delivery: missiles, planes, cannon; Politburo controlled detonators."

"Which were you?"

"Guess."

Bullen didn't need to, but in any case he said, "KGB." Petrenko shrugged. "So there is one other man who was once in Politburo and then one who is in military even now. These are my partners."

"They get a cut."

"Sure." Petrenko raised one shoulder — an extravagant, slow shrug. "A 'cut' . . . good word. Not as much as me perhaps."

"Why not?"

"They need money; they must accept me as their leader."

Bullen wondered why those men needed money and how hard Petrenko had worked to put them into debt.

"Also," Petrenko observed tartly, "I set up deal. Without me, these men are nothing."

"The man who is in the army runs a base where nuclear weapons are stored," Bullen guessed.

"No, not quite. He used to do this: it was a while ago."

"You mean, the bombs were stolen a while ago. . . ."

"Of course. I am no longer in KGB; I cannot account for weapons, now. Also, second man is no longer member of Politburo" — Petrenko laughed — "no surprise."

"When was the device stolen?"

"Seven years."

Bullen tried to picture someone toting a nuclear weapon from place to place. "So where was it taken?"

"Taken nowhere," Petrenko said. "It was kept in different area of warehouse is all. The important thing — it was accounted for." Bullen shook his head. "Look, I am bank teller, okay? You have one million dollars in my bank. I steal hundred thousand dollars, but all I do is transfer them to different account in same bank, okay? Do you say, 'Where is missing hundred thousand?' No. You don't know it is gone."

"Until I come to spend it," Bullen observed.

"But spend it means take bomb and blow something up with it. This did not happen. Now it never will." When Bullen laughed, Petrenko corrected himself. "Okay, you know what I mean. *Someone* might blow up *someone,* but nobody will point finger at me — this theft is history, now, like USSR."

Bullen felt it was time to play buyer to Petrenko's salesman. "How will you ship?"

"You have haulage set up?"

"All set up. I asked about the shipping."

"K-class Greek heavy-lift vessel. This ship carries gear of over sixty tons; no need for shore gear — it can lift all cargo."

"Where will you store the bombs?"

"Project cargo — stuff that cannot go below decks. In this case, refinery storage tanks. The bombs will be inside. Special welded compartments have been made."

"Then you're shipping from the Ukraine."

For a moment, Bullen thought he'd managed to be too clever. Petrenko's annoyance showed itself in a flush that spread on his cheek, making darker and deeper the flaw along his jawline. He spread caviar on a blini and parceled it up. "Okay," he agreed, "Ukraine."

"What time tomorrow?"

"Morning. We collect you." Petrenko ate the blini and looked away toward the door; suddenly, he seemed to have more pressing things to do. He wiped his mouth on his napkin and threw it among the dishes,

451

where it began to soak up syrup from the peaches in white wine.

"Will we be gone long?" Bullen asked.

"Not long. There is not much to see."

Petrenko reached into the inside pocket of his jacket and produced a gun. Bullen felt a rush of adrenaline that fizzed in his pulses and made his head sing. He wondered whether he'd made some involuntary sound, because Petrenko looked at him sharply, then cleared a small space among the plates and laid the gun down.

"This is nine-millimeter Makarov automatic pistol. Nice gun; I have many. If you must go for walks in Moscow," he said, "take this one with you. I have heard English idiom — dead loss. I am not sure of its true meaning, but if someone kills you, then to me you are dead loss."

Bullen picked the gun up and turned it over in his hands, then set it down again. He thought he heard a brief laugh from one of the bodyguards, but when he glanced over they seemed to be smoking in their sleep.

Petrenko got up from the table. "I will see you tomorrow, Tom. Quite early. Be ready at eight, please."

"Okay."

The uneaten food lay between them, enough for twenty, enough for fifty. Petrenko's largesse meant power, it meant wealth; too much for one man, or else not nearly enough.

The bodyguards went first. Petrenko shook hands, then followed them. When Bullen picked up the gun, its barrel struck against a plate, making a loud *clank* in the stillness, but Petrenko didn't look back. After a while, waiters came and loaded the dishes back onto trolleys.

They left Moscow for Sheremet'yevo airport in a Mercedes 600. The tape deck was playing songs from Broadway shows. One bodyguard was at the wheel, the other rode shotgun; Petrenko and Bullen sat in the back and stretched their legs while Petrenko told Bullen how to run cigarettes on the black market, cut opium paste with cough syrup, smuggle caviar, control the market in foodstuffs, and fake an antique icon.

From the class divisions of the Mercedes to a single class on the plane: they all sat on ripped and stained upholstery and listened to a loop tape of folk songs rasping through battered loudspeakers.

Everyone smoked all the time. They smoked during the taxi out to the runway, they smoked during takeoff, they redoubled their efforts as the No Smoking light went off. When the pilot came on the intercom to give flight arrival times, he had the slightly muffled tones of a man speaking with a cigarette in his mouth.

Bullen and Petrenko were faces in a fog. The plane gathered speed, then angled abruptly upward, shaking its nuts and bolts.

That morning Bullen had called Cochrane at the house in Arbat and started by asking whether it was safe to speak.

"Phone taps? That was then. Now we've brought them mirrors and beads and blankets cunningly infected with the virus of commerce. Where's the merchandise?''

"Somewhere in the Ukraine. I don't know where.''

"What's your guess?''

"My guess is that I'll be flown to Kiev and taken to wherever the bombs are being stored, then brought back to Moscow and the sale finalized. If I don't come back, it means I'm a bad guesser.''

"Other players?''

"A military man, also an ex-Politburo man. You were right about Petrenko — he was KGB.''

"Why the other two?''

Bullen told him, then added, "I wouldn't be surprised to learn that Petrenko had a hold over them: in the past, if not now.''

"I expect they'll be happy to take their share.''

"I expect they'll be happy to see it,'' Bullen said, "but who cares?''

"Okay. Call me as soon as you can.''

"Am I getting company on this trip?''

"You're flying solo, I'm afraid. Safer on Aeroflot.''

From Kiev airport they traveled in a Zil limo. Petrenko handed out heat-sealed ID cards, each with a photograph. Bullen's was a replica of his passport shot. He looked up from it and Petrenko was smiling broadly: See? First I give you a banquet, now I turn you into a member of the Congress of People's Deputies.

"Where are we going?'' Bullen asked.

"AY-270/4/D.''

"Thanks.''

"It is military base; they don't have names and theory is they don't have locations. However, this one is called Zoltyje Vody, because this place is nearest."

"Did Axel Dexter come here?"

"He came, yes. With him came expert. They were both happy."

"I don't have an expert."

"Who needs two? Listen, I will show you something; when we get there, I will show."

Bullen clipped on his ID card. "Who are they?" He meant the bodyguards.

"Men from Alex."

"Who?"

"Not 'who' — is name of security firm, mostly ex-KGB."

"Bodyguards," said Bullen. "No fake ID. They're being themselves."

"Sure. Every person has bodyguard now." As if Bullen hadn't noticed, he said, "I have two. It is expected," then spread his hands for emphasis. "Free enterprise — understand?"

The landscape reminded Bullen of the Somerset flatlands: grass, pines, the occasional stand of broad-leafed trees; the ground rose from time to time, but the slopes never grew to a full hill. He remembered walking with Anne, west of Glastonbury, a day of watery sunshine and wind and sudden squalls of rain. They had found shelter in a bird blind and made love there, gently, standing up, her back braced against the lath and leaf wall. The hide had creaked and shifted and her sudden yell at the end was wilder than any bird cry.

Bullen guessed that she would have received his postcard by now. He hoped that she knew what it meant. He hoped that she was prepared to take the risk.

"You are thinking," Petrenko assured him, "of how you will spend your commission."

"You're right; I was thinking of that."

The Zil slid past three or four miles of chain-link fence topped with razor wire; above that were four heavy-duty metal cables with voltage signs attached.

They reached a double gate and went through the first on their security IDs. Between gates was a guard hut, painted gray. The driver-bodyguard stopped the car but left the engine running. After a minute or so, a man stepped out of the hut; his gray uniform seemed a camouflage against the drabness of the building. He hitched the leather strap of a machine pistol around so that the weapon was out of the way, then walked across to the car. He was carrying a great bulb of paunch under his uniform jacket, but his face seemed thin and drawn, gray pouches drooping under his eyes. What looked like a small battered attaché case was tucked under one arm.

"This man is Dimitri," Petrenko informed Bullen, then laughed at a joke he hadn't yet told. "He is sergeant with income of a colonel."

Dimitri opened the back door of the Zil, put the case on the floor, and swung onto one of the drop seats. He said, *"Mnye ostanyetsya polchasa, potom ya pashal."*

"Nyet problem." Petrenko translated for Bullen. "We have half an hour: more time than we need."

The car was driving along an outer road that seemed

to ring the base. In the middle distance were administration buildings, barracks, a cluster of aerials, one spinning slowly like a summer weathercock.

"We won't be challenged?" Bullen asked.

"This man says who comes and goes. There is no one to ask questions now we are inside. People have their own jobs to do."

The base must have covered two square miles. Bullen could see nothing moving. The sky was clear and frosty and empty of birds. After half a mile, the Zil turned along a slightly narrower road that terminated in a large warehouse building, with an armed guard standing in front of each of its double doors. This time the bodyguard cut the engine. Petrenko looked at Dimitri, but Dimitri didn't move.

"Shto-to nye to?" There was a faint weariness in Petrenko's voice, as if he'd been expecting all along to hit a problem.

"Mnye nushnim eshcho tisyacha dollarov."

Petrenko sighed and looked away, staring out the window as if the weather had suddenly changed for the worse. Bullen had understood one word. "He wants money?"

"He wants more money." Petrenko kept his face averted. He made an offer. *"Pyatsto."*

"Syemsto pyatdyesyat."

"Nyet, pyatsto, mnye nadoelo."

Bullen heard the ice in Petrenko's voice. He asked, "Do we have a problem?"

Petrenko shook his head. "In new Russia, everything is deal, everything is negotiation. He wants one thousand dollars, he will take five hundred."

A long silence developed. Petrenko stretched out his legs and closed his eyes. *"Pyatsto, Dimitri . . ."*

They all sat like statues, Bullen looking at Dimitri, Dimitri looking at Petrenko, Petrenko looking out the window. It was Dimitri who broke the tableau; he got out of the car and walked to the double doors of the warehouse, his back hunched in angry defeat. Petrenko smiled lazily. He took out a two-inch fold of bills fastened by a money clip, peeled five off the top, and put them into his breast pocket. As he and Bullen climbed out, the armed guards were rolling back the doors.

Petrenko led the way as if he were on home ground. Dimitri huffed up to get his five hundred, then fell back to count it. The doors rumbled shut and Bullen saw how the warehouse resembled a vast cavern, cool and dim, with windows high on either side like bore-holes. He remembered caves he'd explored where a perfectly normal tunnel would open out into a gigantic vault that reached all the way to the surface, the space dizzying, the rockfalls like dark stairwells.

This cavern, this vastness, bore racks that went from the floor high into the dome of the roof. Everywhere Bullen looked, he saw boxes of weapons, small arms mostly, but also rack upon rack of shells, belts of ammunition, stacks of bulletproof vests, component parts for tanks and armored vehicles.

Petrenko pointed to a rafter-high rack of oblong crates. "Kalashnikov," he said, "better than M-16, better than Uzi or Israeli weapon, Galil. Axel Dexter sell lots of these, I bet." He pointed to another rack. "Over here is Abakan, machine gun that Americans think can't be made. Pretty much no recoil. Is secret, understand? You should be interested in this some other time."

They were walking alongside howitzers and bazooka shells, assault rifles and handguns — all left out of their packing like toys abandoned by children.

"Horses for courses," Petrenko said, "isn't this what you might say? Means right combination, yes?" Bullen nodded. "One time, Russia didn't always give good value. Good idea to keep war going but not to win — for economic reasons, for political reasons, too. Good example: We give to Arabs tanks that are not much good in desert. Israelis have much better tanks. So, we have income, we have continuing war against Zionist imperialism, but we do not have embarrassing victory." He laughed at the wiliness of it all. "Politicians are worst of all, Tom, do you think this?"

"I think this."

"Not Vietnam," Petrenko corrected himself, "good weapons in Vietnam. We wanted victory in Vietnam."

"And now?" Bullen asked.

"Now there are no politics, Tom, no ideology. Just make money — that's all. Now everything is top quality." He stopped and threw out an arm, rather like a warm-up man bringing on the star of the show.

It was just a crate among crates.

Dimitri opened the lid and peeled back a preformed

molding about a foot thick. He stood back to show Bullen what he'd come for: three blunt, steel casings that looked like shells, except that the housing section made a broad flange two-thirds of the way down. They were seated in a heavy, gray flock like wine bottles packed for travel.

Petrenko pointed to the packing material. "This is material to deflect infrared detector — is aluminum strip covered in plastic — many sheets, each separated by silk mesh. They just lie here, among these other" — he waved a hand, trying to summon up the right term — "other items. Mostly shells for 205-millimeter cannon. These can be fired in same way. This is why Operation Babylon — to make gun that has range of many miles."

A rhythmic ticking started up like a jazzy metronome. Dimitri had opened the attaché case and was assembling a Geiger counter. When he waved the sensor over the crate, the tick rose to a crackle; closer still it became a high-pitched howl.

"This is what I promised to show you," Petrenko said as Dimitri wafted the machine back and forth. "Radioactive, okay? Here are our babies, Tom."

Petrenko laughed. Dimitri looked at him, trying to read the joke. He made the Geiger counter swoop down, then up again, making music with the ratchety whine. He joined the laughter. Petrenko stepped back and raised his arms to the ceiling, taking in the stacked weapons, cased and oiled, as if to say, *All for sale, all available.*

"You see, Tom? You see?"

Bullen followed his gaze up to the neon strips, the

gray glow at the windows, the metal racks packed with rifles, rockets, mortars, shells, grenades, missile launchers, howitzers, machine guns, row upon row, column after column, reaching from the recesses of the roof to the concrete floor.

Outside the sun topped a cloud, sending a rod of light down into the stacks, and the glare blinded them for a moment. Bullen watched as the brilliance shrank back to leave images crowding the edges of his vision. It seemed to him that he was looking at dark repeating shapes, the same rifle, same shell, same bomb making a pattern around the vertical line of light, as if it were a glass kaleidoscope. The light fell through swarming dust, through stale air, and seemed to distill, at the very heart of the enormous room, a whorl of smoke.

Bullen stared. The smoke was a face forming, its features coming together piece by piece, a tiny homunculus that grew as he watched. And the face was every evil, every slaughtered child, every lost hope, every jot of pain, the death of laughter. He looked at the face as it rose toward him and rushed from the room out into the world.

A voice spoke. He turned to find Dimitri and Petrenko cut in negative against a blue-white backdrop.

"You see, Tom?"

"How does he propose to move them?" Cochrane asked.

The house in the Arbat was on four floors and had ornate balconies set in old stone. Double glass doors opened from a pastel blue drawing room onto a garden of white and black birch, stripped of their leaves now, and slender as dancers. As Bullen watched, a few flakes of snow rocked slowly down out of a clear blue sky.

"The sergeant simply loads up a jeep and drives them out of there."

"Of course," Cochrane observed, "why not? You saw them?"

"I saw them."

"Three . . ."

"Yes, there were three."

"You have a contact number for Petrenko? I mean apart from the phone number at the hotel?"

Bullen handed over the paper Petrenko had given him. "Call and leave a message."

Cochrane put the paper under an ashtray, close at hand, as if he meant to lift the phone as soon as Bullen left.

"Should I make the call?" Bullen asked.

Cochrane had rehearsed it. "We've got long-lens photos of him — pretty handy ones — he's been followed to three addresses, now we have this contact number — I don't think there's going to be a problem. Most important, we know where the bombs are and we know about Dimitri. A contact in the military — we know that — and someone who used to be in the Politburo. It's time to give him to his own security people. The idea is to be discreet, Tom. The last thing we want is an international scandal about some towel-head country laying hands on part of the Russian nuclear arsenal."

"Yesterday I saw the bombs," Bullen said. "This

morning I'm supposed to call him to set up the exchange."

"What did he suggest?"

"He suggested a trip to Switzerland."

"Makes sense. Avoids all possibilities of sleight of hand. You authorize the transfer and he sees it go straight into his account. He gives the go-ahead to ship the bombs, and you go through the same routine when they get to their destination — right?"

"That's how it works," Bullen agreed.

Cochrane smiled winningly. "You can go home. Want to go home?"

49

Viktor Petrenko passed the double doors carrying a glass of scotch in his hand. He'd been hearing how the rest of his life was going to go.

The bodyguards had stayed with Petrenko during the first few minutes of his conversation with Cochrane. Now they were waiting in the car. They wondered who this second Brit was and why Petrenko had looked as if he wanted the man dead.

Cochrane had phoned almost as soon as Bullen had left. He'd started by simply outlining the whole deal, as if Petrenko had known nothing about it. He'd mentioned Dexter and Morgan Sorrell and ninety million dollars. He'd mentioned Zoltyje Vody and he mentioned Dimitri. A silence had developed that could have grown leaves.

"Why do you tell me these things?"

"Please . . ." Cochrane had chuckled. "Let's not bother with that kind of talk."

"What do you want?"

"What do you think I want?"

"I think you want money."

"You're right."

"This is very dangerous thing you are doing."

"I'm in no danger at all. On the other hand, you've got a problem; there's no mistake about that."

"We shall meet."

"You're right, we shall." Cochrane had given him the address.

"Tom Bullen," Petrenko had said. "Very clever. How did Axel Dexter die?"

"Not what you think. A snake bit him."

"Same snake now in Moscow."

Cochrane was sitting in an armchair. His hair, with its dusting of gray, was lit on one side by the morning sun and he was gazing out at the garden trees apparently lost in thought. When Petrenko passed on his third circuit of the room, Cochrane said, "I can see that you're angry, so perhaps I ought to say that I've made extensive notes, which are in a diplomatic bag and on the way home to a man called Paul Shelley. Shelley works with me; I'm sure you see what I mean. I'm also making a phone call, each morning and night, to a second man called Roscoe Tate; if he fails to hear from me, the deal's

464

blown and you're fucked. Understand that?"

"I understand fucked," Petrenko said. "I understand very well." He laughed loudly and without a trace of mirth. "KGB and MI6, what a collaboration; together we fuck the world." He swallowed his whiskey and pointed with the glass. "Cochrane, if ever I can kill you I will kill you. Is promise."

"Good." Cochrane smiled in a businesslike way. "Here's what we'll do. We will split the first half of the money, you and I. I'll be telling my people that we're shipping as planned in order to make sure we nail all the contacts both here and in the country of destination. What I won't tell them is that we'll be shipping shit — a fake cargo — that way they won't worry about the bombs disappearing en route. The vessel can be bounced around several ports until it's theoretically camouflaged. When it gets to its destination, there'll be a large international fuss, but we'll be prepared for that. The cargo will be innocuous and there'll be egg on a few faces, but there will also have been some satisfactory arrests. You understand what — "

"Egg on face, yes. So — fake cargo. Go on."

"The real bombs will have gone straight to the gulf, no other ports of call. They'll get there far ahead of the fake cargo. When it's delivered, we get the rest of the money and split it as before. By the time questions are asked about the locations of the real bombs, we'll be long gone." Cochrane laughed. "I imagine that the customer will find it very amusing to be in receipt of the bombs and also be able to act out injured pride when NATO grabs the second ship. More than happy

465

to make a few token sacrifices if the international community needs some. The hunt then starts for the real bombs. But you've disappeared and I'm in the dark — fooled, like the rest of them."

"So where am I after you make your first report? What do you tell — that I'm in jail?"

"No. You've been turned, recruited to put the finger on other illegal arms deals in the former USSR, infiltrate the Mafia . . ."

A long frruitwood buffet stood against one wall, decorated with street-market icons, painted eggs, a rosewood bowl filled with dried rose petals, a group of crystal decanters. Petrenko gave himself another scotch. He said, "Good plan. Wonderful plan. We should go into business together, I think."

"We have," Cochrane reminded him.

"Yes, sure, but this is not by my choice. However, I like your style, yes? And there are many more possibilities; red mercury, for example."

Cochrane gave a half smile that faded, as if Petrenko's remark had taken a moment to get through, then he asked, "Red mercury?"

"Red mercury 20/20 is highly compressed, highly fissionable substance. With this material, critical mass of bomb is very small. You could build nuclear weapon size of cigarette pack. After all, such bomb is very simple device."

Cochrane said, "Yes, I remember red mercury 20/20. I also remember your sales pitch."

"Yes," Petrenko agreed.

"Tell me if I've got this right. The PLO paid someone three million dollars for two pounds of the substance. Others followed suit. In fact, a *lot* of red mercury 20/20 was found — and sold. For a lot of money."

"Yes."

"About the same time, two couriers were stopped crossing the Finnish border with eight ounces each in body belts. The stuff was highly radioactive and the couriers had wrecked their livers carrying it that way. They died."

"Yes."

"But despite the risks, the deaths, the PLO's three million dollars and other millions from other sources, red mercury 20/20 was discovered to be nothing but common or garden mercury with red dye added, together with a fistful of strontium 90."

"Common or garden," Petrenko said. "I have not heard this before. But, yes, you have it right."

The two men looked at one another. Petrenko was grinning as he witnessed the slow dissolve in Cochrane's eyes. Cochrane opened his mouth to speak, then closed it on silence. Petrenko's expression said: *Yes, you've got it right. You wish you hadn't, but you have.*

A laugh circled the room that seemed to belong to no one. Cochrane spoke softly, as if he wanted to hear neither question nor answer. "You're telling me that the bombs are fakes."

"Yes. They are fake. You speak of shipping shit to fool SIS. We would be shipping shit anyway."

Cochrane remained silent for a full minute. He was twisting the loose flesh on his cheek, trying to defeat pain with pain. When he stood up, Petrenko backed off a pace.

"What was the idea? Not to ship the bombs at all?"

Petrenko shrugged. "We would have shipped — Axel Dexter would have wanted to see the cargo in transit. When it arrive, no second payment, just many angry people."

"Dexter didn't know?"

"Of course not. It would be the end for him; he would never have found business with anyone again."

"He went to Zoltyje Vody with an expert; the bombs were checked."

"He went to Zoltyje Vody with scientist, paid by me — a man highly recommended by members of Faculty of Sciences, also paid by me. Any of ten physicists would have done it; they fought to get the job."

"How did you choose your man?"

"He was Jew" — Petrenko smiled — "of course."

"No one from the Politburo, no one from the military?"

"From military, Dimitri only. Also a few guards Dimitri must bribe. But other people must be paid. Man who built bombs, for one."

"What are they?"

"They are casings that look like nuclear bombs — authentic; they have strontium 90 inside. Is all."

Cochrane walked toward the decanters as Petrenko was making a slow circuit of the room. They met by the double glass doors, not knowing which side to pass on, and went through a little dance of avoidance. When Cochrane had given himself a drink, he said: "I'm amused."

"What is to happen?" asked Petrenko.

"Everything happens the way you intended it should happen," Cochrane told him. "I'll settle for half the money . . . well, not half, no. Half of the first half."

The second scotch had brought a dab of color to Petrenko's face; the scar was a dark welt across the flush. For the first time, anxiety turned to anger. He banged his glass down on the buffet. "You will settle, you bastard . . . you tell me *you* will settle. It was two years — the making of this deceit. I must pay people, bribe people, get contacts, pick who is good to deal with, who is safe. You think Axel Dexter walked into Hotel President, saw me, said, 'You look like good man to make deal with, got some nuclear bombs?' You think that? Now you tell me, 'Half or I fuck this deal.' You bastard."

"You're right," Cochrane agreed, "you're absolutely right. It's half or I fuck your deal." He seemed in a better humor. "A sting," he said. "Jesus Christ, a sting."

The sun had left just a few lacy scallops of snow at the edge of the lawn. Cochrane said, "Let's go for a walk."

The bodyguards ambled through Pyatnitski Market, ten steps behind. Petrenko had brought his whiskey with him and was sipping from the glass as he walked. The market stalls were littered with debris, mainly military supplies: Red Army wristwatches, hats, medals, bulletproof vests. Petrenko picked up a vest and tossed it to Cochrane. Strands of gold webbing had escaped from the seam; there were several heavy indentations in the fabric. "There are six weights. This is Elephant. It will stop machine-gun bullet." He seemed to be in good humor now; a pragmatist, Cochrane thought. "Probably Rutskoi came to this market when he planned coup. Look hard, you find maybe a couple T-72 tanks."

Cochrane thought he'd give the man his head.

They walked alongside Gorky Park. The railings were hung with paintings that were breathtakingly bad. Vendors offered pecking-chicken toys, Yeltsin dolls, brand-new icons. Petrenko offered the same arrangement he'd mentioned to Bullen. "We each have code, yes? Neither can risk handing it over without guarantees. Yours is you can spoil the deal — if I cheat, no one wins."

"That's right." Cochrane was looking at a Siberian sunset: violent skies over wind-whipped tundra. The painting flapped in the light breeze that was blowing across the park.

"And if you cheat, I can shop you."

The idiom seemed to amuse Cochrane. "Yes, you can shop me."

"Best way is go to Swiss bank and make our transfer there. We move money from the main account to new accounts; it is done simultaneously, we see money move simultaneously."

"Sounds fine," Cochrane said. "I like that."

They sat in the Hard Rock Café, in the center of the park, and drank imported beer under posters of Alice

Cooper and the young Bob Dylan.

"Tom Bullen . . ." Petrenko shook his head. "You have good man there." A sudden thought struck him. "Bullen — he has bank codes also."

Petrenko's English was heavily accented and not helped by the whiskey. His remark wasn't a question, but Cochrane heard it that way. "No," he said, "he was the bear trap: you're the bear. Bullen knows nothing. He's on his way home."

They walked back through the park, heading for the river, and made a date to steal forty-five million dollars. Cochrane said, "Remember, Shelley will have my letter, and I check with Tate night and morning."

"What would I do — cut my own throat?"

"I just don't want you talking out of turn."

Empty seats on the Ferris wheel turned against a sheer blue sky.

"Is just like the English," Petrenko said, "taking turns to speak."

Bullen took the boat trip from the pier by Borodinskij Bridge. He kept his eyes closed most of the way because even though there was little heat in it, he wanted to turn his face to the sun.

He bought a postcard and put Anne's address on it. A while later, he added: "Believe me (this time)."

Later still he signed it.

Traveling light wasn't the issue — just to travel was Bullen's goal, to travel with the hope of rest at the journey's end. He had bought himself a fur hat in a street market and was trying it for size when Petrenko walked into the room.

The bodyguards were standing by the door; one of them was carrying a gun. Bullen looked this way and that, as though a door might appear in the wall, or a trap open up beneath his feet.

"Let me tell you why I am here." Petrenko sat on the bed, then swung his legs up and leaned against the gold-tasseled bolster at the bedhead. "I am here because a man I spoke to today made some mistakes. His name is Stuart Cochrane, a friend of yours. I think he believes that you are no longer in Moscow — here is first mistake."

"You met Cochrane," Bullen repeated. *"Met Cochrane?"* He saw that Petrenko was smiling.

"He said to me, 'Bullen is bear trap; you are bear.' "

Bullen nodded slowly. He wiped a hand across his face. "Yes," he said, "yes, of course."

Outside, there was sunshine in the western sky and a light snowfall in the streets. The flakes danced and drifted in front of the window. Bullen walked over to watch them, his face so close to the glass that a little patch of his own breath grew there, filling and fading like a pulse. *Of course, how could I miss it? Of course, how could I be so fucking stupid?*

"What's the deal?" he asked.

"Deal is I give him half the money."

"Half the commission?"

Petrenko shook his head. "Bombs you saw were

472

fakes, Tom. Sorry: everywhere is deception. There is a term for this in magic making." He made a motion with his hand of someone concealing something, then revealing nothing.

"Sleight of hand."

"Exactly. It is how we must make our way in life. Bombs were fakes. Cochrane thought he could do deal for half of all the money. Now he realizes he must settle for half of half."

"What happens when the buyer loses both the bombs and the money?"

"Yes," Petrenko agreed, "this will be unpleasant surprise. As for what happens — I do not know. I will be somewhere else."

Bullen looked over his shoulder at the bodyguard with the gun. "Have you come here to kill me? What's the point?"

"The truth is I was angry with you, Tom. You fooled me; you led Cochrane to me. But killing is not practical solution. I said Cochrane made mistakes. First was thinking you had left Moscow. Second was he told me you did not have bank codes. But I think you do. You gave me first part of code when we had dinner. So, I am here to ask for the rest. In return for the codes, I will give you one million dollars. Perhaps you don't believe this. Really, it doesn't matter whether you believe or not, because if you refuse to give me codes, I will kill you. It is easy, you see. If I get codes from you, I can dispense with Cochrane." He paused. "Dispense — is correct?"

"Depends what you mean."

"I think I mean dispense. You get a million dollars,

I get the rest, you live. Otherwise, if you choose to die, I can simply go back to deal with Cochrane. Half of half is still a lot of money, but here is principle involved."

Bullen turned back to the window and rested his forehead against the pane. "The bombs were fake." Each word left a patch of pearl on the glass.

"So what do you think, Tom?"

"I think you're a con artist."

"What?"

"Confidence trickster; someone who tells clever lies to get —"

"Ah, yes, I see. I hadn't heard it called 'artist' before. I like that."

Bullen walked to a tall, walnut-veneer wardrobe and took out his jacket. From the pocket, he took out the gun that Petrenko had given him, then dropped the jacket on the floor. He was standing so that Petrenko was in a direct line of fire between Bullen and the bodyguard.

"This would have been my thought also," Petrenko said, "but sadly, gun does not work. Giving this to you was a gesture to inspire confidence, not — I'm sorry — to display trust."

The bodyguard's gun was also a Makarov. Petrenko glanced around and the man stepped forward, putting out his free hand. Bullen held the gun up and pulled the trigger a few times. The man didn't blink. Bullen opened his fist, letting the weapon swing from his finger by the trigger guard, and the bodyguard removed it.

"You must ask yourself another question,"

Petrenko advised. "Do you owe Stuart Cochrane any favors?"

"Tell me what you suggest."

"Give codes to me. Tonight, you stay here with these men. As soon as the banks open for business tomorrow, I can check combinations you have given me. If correct, all's fine."

Bullen tore the front page from the room service menu and wrote the letter-number combinations on the back.

Petrenko looked at them for a long time. "I hope these are good," he said.

Bullen laughed. "No, they're fake, just like your fucking bombs."

"If Cochrane is true, or if you are true — whichever way I shall be leaving Moscow tomorrow night. Now there are things I must do."

"Why bother to pay me," Bullen suggested, "why not kill me anyway?"

Petrenko shook his head in wonderment. "Tom . . . It is less trouble to give you a million dollars."

The bodyguards drank vodka and smoked and took turns watching television. One of them had locked the door and kept the key, the other had shown Bullen his gun before putting it into a pocket — one way of offering a warning. Bullen sat in an armchair by the window watching pale lozenges of streetlights dance against his own reflection. The man with the gun had made a nest of pillows and was lounging on the bed.

There was an access hatch masked by a small sofa on the side of the room opposite the bathroom.

Bullen wondered whether he'd have the chance to get close to Cochrane — just for a while, just for long enough. He hoped so. The bodyguard watching TV grunted with laughter. He was sitting about three feet from the screen, a shot glass of vodka nipped delicately between thumb and forefinger.

The hatch was about two feet wide by three feet high, covered with the same pattern as the wallpaper and bordered by an ornate frame. The decorator's idea had been to hide it as much as possible: the frame in turn matched rectangles of fancy paneling on the walls. It opened onto the heating system; you could see the duct going straight up the wall, a long obtruding channel, and disappearing through the ceiling.

The bodyguards had sent for room service at eight o'clock. At ten-thirty it arrived. One of them took Bullen into the bathroom and put a gun to his head, while the other took delivery of the food. They had also called for a fresh bottle of vodka. Bullen couldn't understand how they stayed on their feet, but their speech was clear and their actions deliberate. They shared the food with him: shish kebab and green beans, black bread, ham, vegetable pickle, goat's cheese.

He tried not to look toward the access hatch.

They took turns sleeping. Each time Bullen woke, a different man was watching him.

There were noises in the hotel: a door slamming, a woman calling someone's name, the clang of the elevator door.

Hot pipes ticking behind the access hatch.

Dawn was a clean, hard light that broke the city down into silhouettes. By midmorning all the lines had softened. Petrenko phoned and spoke to Bullen.

"It is a two-hour delay. Soon I will know. Soon everything will be fine?" Bullen heard the question mark.

"Sure, things will be fine."

"How do you like the idea of being rich?"

"How do you like it?"

"You sound unhappy, Tom."

"There are two men here with guns. For all I know, they're waiting for a phone call from you telling them to kill me."

"I already said it — you are more trouble dead."

Bullen put the phone down. He thought, No one is more trouble dead.

The bodyguards had a little conference and one of them left. The man with the gun stayed. Bullen wondered why the first man had gone, then realized that neither of them had smoked for half an hour; it must have seemed like a lifetime. The gunman put the door key in his pocket and sat so that he could watch both Bullen and the television. After five minutes he went into the bathroom, leaving the door open.

Bullen waited until he heard the man pissing, then crossed the room, took his jacket from the floor, and put it on. He moved the sofa another twelve inches into the room, giving himself space to open the hatch. It swung out on hinges. The duct housed eight copper pipes, each about an inch in diameter, four going left to a set of radiators under the window, four toward another set close to the bed. Bullen backed into the space, head and shoulders first, then drew himself up. He could stand in the space but not turn around. The pipes were singing with heat; he could feel the scorch on the back of his head.

He got his heel onto the lower frame of the hatch and pulled back sharply, closing it with a small thud, then he waited, listening.

An exclamation, silence, the door of the wardrobe opening and closing, silence, the curtains being pulled back, silence, the bed being lifted aside, silence.

Bullen could interpret everything but the silences. When the door of the room opened, he waited for a count of three, then started to chimney up the heating duct. He was working on the assumption that the man would at least walk to the end of the corridor, since the only explanation for Bullen's magical disappearance was that he'd left by the door — that he had a duplicate key or had somehow picked the lock.

There was only one way to chimney the duct: Bullen had to brace himself against the wall, make height with his feet, then reach overhead and haul himself up by grabbing the pipes. He did this three times, then stopped, feet and shoulders rammed against the duct, head bowed, face creased with pain. He thought he might have another thirty seconds before the body-guard came back into the room; maybe a minute. Anyone would hear the noise.

He caterpillared three more times, his mouth wide open in a silent scream, then wedged himself again. It was completely dark in the shaft. Bullen put up a hand hoping to touch the trapdoor of the inspection hatch in the room above, but found nothing. He realized that if the trapdoor was missing, he might go past the hatch and start climbing the shaft in the upstairs room — except that his hands were so burned that he'd never make it. Every time he stopped, the heat from the pipes was cutting through his clothing.

He chimneyed another three feet, almost unable to keep a grip on the pipes, then did it again while his nerve endings screamed at him to stop. The second time, his head struck the trapdoor and lifted it.

There was a line of light around the edge of the access hatch. He listened and there was nothing to hear: no one walking, no one talking, no one sounding alarmed. Bullen hit the hatch with the heel of his hand and pushed with his feet, like a swimmer shoving off from the side of the pool — an action that brought him head and shoulders into the room. He shuffled along with his elbows and lay still for a moment, then sat up.

He was looking at the face of a man so profoundly asleep that he seemed to be on the brink of coma. He had a pudgy face and a mop of curly hair dampened by sweat; his features looked crushed by the weight of sleep that lay on him.

Bullen got to his feet and backed off a couple of paces, glancing toward the door, looking for signs that the man might register, somewhere fathoms deep, another presence in the room. Then he noticed two things. The first was that a bottle of vodka lay on the floor by the bed; it was two-thirds empty. The second was the telephone. The man was sprawled naked on the bed, only half-covered by the quilt. His arm was trailing to the floor, and the telephone was still in his hand.

Bullen could see that a whole drama lay in the booze and that still-clutched phone; act two would open with a late awakening and a vicious hangover. He went to the bathroom and ran cold water onto his hands for a few minutes. The chill took the redness out and a little of the pain, but Bullen knew he was going to suffer later; even now, he couldn't make a fist.

When he emerged, the man was lying exactly as before. Bullen noticed a smell in the room that he hadn't detected in those first few moments: a mare's tail of perfume.

He stood in the corridor on the eighth floor, punching the elevator button. Before the clock indicator had swung to three, the footsteps on the stair were clearly audible — two sets, overlapping and coming fast. The first man must have reappeared with the cigarettes, then helped the gunman search the room again before they took to the stairs. Maybe they'd found the access hatch and looked up to see the trapdoor knocked out on the floor above.

Bullen ran to the elbow of the corridor and looked into a dead end. He went quickly down the row of doors, shoving each in turn, getting ready to walk in and demand to know why whoever he found there was in the room he'd reserved: maybe that would provide enough time for the bodyguards to pass by. None of the doors yielded. He was about to start back when he saw the fire exit, a narrow, black door with a lock bar across it. He hit the bar with the heel of his hand and the door sprang open. On the other side stone stairs went both up and down from a small landing. The stairs turned on themselves four times in the course of each floor, and the stairwell was narrow with black, waist-high railings on the drop side.

The logical route was down, so Bullen went up, making two turns of the stair then crouching with his back to the wall. He tried to second-guess the body-guards: they would check every open door, check the rooms the maids were cleaning, check the public rooms, the barber shop . . . On each floor sat a woman whose job it was to make sure that people had their keys, that they made no noise, and to report any problems. In the days of the Cold War, she would have also been eyes and ears for the party. They would check with those women. They wouldn't think it important to check the lobby or the restaurant because if he'd reached the ground floor, he'd've left the hotel.

They would definitely check the fire-escape exits.

Although Bullen tended to think of one of the body-guards as "the gunman," he knew it was likely that they both carried guns. He hoped they had a technique for searching that involved splitting up: one to check the public rooms and talk to the floor woman, perhaps; the other to make a few landings of the exit stair-well. The last thing he needed was two-to-one on a stone stair and his hands so scalded he couldn't make a fist.

There was a scrape and a faint *whoosh* as the exit door was shouldered open. Bullen realized it had been too much to hope that the released lock bar would go unnoticed. He moved farther into the angle of the wall and looked down through the railings. He could see his pursuer from the chest down, and from the clothes he recognized the gunman. Bullen went three steps up the next flight, taking himself out of view.

The door closed, whispering on the stone. The gunman stood still for a few seconds, then stepped back and peered up the stairwell. Bullen was listening hard, trying to make actions out of tiny sounds, out of exhaled breath. Trying to read thoughts. The gunman went downstairs, moving fast and going on his toes, leaving a repetitive pattern in the air. Bullen thought the man would go three floors, no more; he'd assume that if Bullen had more than three flights start, he must be away clear.

Bullen walked down one flight and positioned himself at the turn of the stair above the exit door. He was in plain sight, but was gambling that the gunman would return in a hurry, head down, covering a couple of stairs with each step maybe, and thinking ahead from the stairwell to the next move.

He came in just that way, except that he was making three steps with each bound, hauling himself up on the rail as he climbed. He'd extended a hand to the door when Bullen hit him, coming from behind, using the rail and the wall to brace his torso as his legs swung out in a great downward leap. His feet caught the gunman in the small of the back just below the ribs, and he smashed forward into the door, then continued to fall with Bullen on top of him, his face whacking first the door, then the stone surface of the landing. In most men, the shock would have been enough to immobilize. The gunman hunched his back, already

482

trying to get onto his hands and knees, his body set to turn the moment that he found his balance.

Bullen scrambled to one side as the gunman made an arch of his body, supporting himself on the flat of one hand while the other went to the pocket of his coat.

Two paces back to find equilibrium, then a single pace forward — Bullen went up on his toes and kicked like a football player. His foot landing was a depth charge in the gunman's torso. A rib broke, his heart faltered, then picked up shakily; his elbow slipped, dropping his face onto the stone. He turned his head and a strange, creased smile, like crumpled paper, came to his lips. His hand was still delving in his pocket.

Bullen stepped in and landed a second kick flat on the site of the first. The gunman was instantly still, his body arched, his head turned toward Bullen. He laughed, or seemed to laugh. After a moment, the sound dissolved into a sudden, violent sneeze and a gargle of phlegm. He had the gun in his hand, now, and was trying to lift it. Bullen placed the third kick flush on the same spot. The man put the gun down, almost delicately, and brought his hand around to his chest, the movement very slow and very careful. He raised himself a couple of inches with his other arm, then gave a little whinny and gobbed up a mouthful of bright red frothy blood. Bullen stood still. All he could see of the man's eyes were white crescents dabbed by fluttering lashes. The fluttering stopped and the man gave a great shudder, then settled into his own weight on the floor.

Bullen went down the stairwell at a gallop, stowing

the gun inside the waistband of his pants at the back. He hit the street running, holding up his hand for a cab, looking left and right for the other man.

50

He walked through the Arbat like a man on *bisniz,* hands swinging purposefully. He wanted the cold air on his burns.

The safe house had an alley to either side where people could pass each other but not stop to talk without blocking the way. The alley became a wall, the wall a chest-high wooden fence. Bullen hoisted himself over into the garden where the black-and-white birches made a screen. Two women passed by with baskets of vegetables. They watched him drop into the garden, then walked on.

He went back along the fence, then by the wall, until he was at right angles to the double doors. He crossed and risked a look. The room was empty. He was set to break a pane of glass and reach through to the lock when he realized that the doors opened inward; they swung back on broken hinges. He took out the gun, then stepped into the room.

There was a glass with a swallow of scotch in it, an empty plate, a jacket thrown over a chair. When Bullen listened at the door, he could hear faint sounds of the street. In the corridor, there were rooms to either side, stairs leading up, stairs leading down. He checked the rooms and found only stillness, shutters drawn, furniture gathering silences.

He went downstairs, as if he had known all along that whatever he found here he would find underground. The staircase took him straight into a basement room, windowless, the glow of lamps, the sight of Stuart Cochrane sitting quietly alongside the body of Viktor Petrenko.

Bullen stopped at the bottom of the staircase. Cochrane cleared his throat, a dark, fruity sound.

"I knew why he was here as soon as he walked in the door. You gave him the codes."

"Yes."

"This must have been an ops room" — Cochrane made a little circle with one hand — "when the place was in use as a safe house." The hand was holding a Walther automatic, which seemed to draw Cochrane's attention as if he were noticing it for the first time. He slipped it into his pocket, then looked at Bullen and shrugged. "He's dead."

Petrenko had fallen straight back, like someone who has lost his footing on ice. He was gazing at the ceiling, startlement and fear still on his face, and the grouping of the bullets in his chest was textbook shooting. The long ellipse of blood that had spread on the wood-block floor was beginning to gel.

Cochrane was sitting on a radio-operator's chair, swivel-backed and running on castors, which rolled him a little way across the floor when he shifted his position. He winced, and Bullen saw that he was wounded in the thigh, sitting in the sop of his own blood, his hand not resting in his lap, as Bullen had thought, but pressing the artery high in the crook of his groin.

Bullen followed the line of Petrenko's outstretched arm and saw a gun under a desk on the far side of the room.

"He's dead," Cochrane said again.

"You shot the bear."

Cochrane laughed, his mouth open wide, his shoulders shaking. "I shot the bear," he said, "I shot the fucking bear." His laughter stopped abruptly. "Ninety million dollars in a locked room in Zurich and I've got half the key." He swayed slightly in the chair, falling forward, then checking the motion; his voice was gravelly. "How could I have known? Ninety million . . . It was all guess and go; it was all look and see." He might have been talking to himself. "I knew there would be some pickings, especially when I heard about Axel Dexter, but it was just a matter of set the bear trap and wait for the bear. Ninety million . . . I've managed to turn a profit before — a shipment of arms sold on, a shipment of drugs, bearer bonds, gold transfers, a little here and a little there, something skimmed off the top, a gift for services rendered — but ninety million . . ." Cochrane rolled the chair in the opposite direction in order to change his position again. Bullen saw how the material of his trousers peeled soddenly away when he raised himself up.

"I was thinking," Cochrane said, "before you got here — thinking that perhaps I was too greedy. But it can't be that, can it? The amount doesn't matter — five million, ten million, fifty million, ninety. You just keep counting, but nothing really changes." Suddenly, he looked down at Petrenko and held a long, fierce gaze, as if the codes that lay inside that lifeless head could be read in the clouded eyes or lifted from the parted lips.

"I was the bear trap," Bullen said, "he was the bear."

"As things turned out, he was."

"I was involved because Roland Cecil was my uncle. I was involved because I'd done a few jobs for you."

Cochrane said, "I was under pressure. An MP had been murdered in public. Later on, I could see the potential." He looked again at Petrenko's body. "You fool," he said, "you fool," meaning himself, or Petrenko, or both.

"Who killed her?" Bullen asked.

"Does it matter?"

Bullen stared at Cochrane. He nodded his head for a moment, as if words simply wouldn't do it; then he said, "Oh, yes. It matters. It matters more than you could possibly know." A silence fell between them; they might have been strangers on a train. Finally, Bullen said, "They cut a swastika into her forehead."

"Does it matter?"

Bullen was sitting on the third from the bottom stair. He put his elbows on his knees and leaned forward, staring at the floor, then he covered his face with his hands. "Tell me" — his voice was muffled — "how you knew what would happen next."

487

"If you had loved her, you'd have mourned, but you hated her, so you were working off guilt. Someone had done what you secretly wanted; it must have been unbearable. How could you stop? It was a debt."

Bullen didn't look up. Speaking into the darkness behind his hands, he said: "Wrong. You got it wrong. While she was alive, there was always hope — just a little, just a scrap. When she died, there was no way back — no way back for me." His voice dropped. "I felt robbed, yes. But not of her death. I was robbed of the last chance for her love."

Cochrane was busy with his pain; he heard the words only as a broken rhythm. He said, "We can do a deal, can't we, Tom?"

"Was it you?" Bullen asked. "You ordered her death?" After a moment, he said: "Of course it was you. Who else would it have been?"

"We can do a deal . . ." Cochrane was having trouble holding up the flow of blood, fingers dug in, shoulders hunched to the task. Bullen took out the bodyguard's gun and looked at it, a thought suddenly occurring to him.

"I don't know which gun this is."

"What?" Cochrane shook his head, seeming impatient with Bullen's confusion.

"Petrenko gave me a gun. It didn't work; it wasn't supposed to. Two of Petrenko's men were guarding me. One of them took the gun away from me. Later, I took this gun away from him. I don't know whether this is my gun or his gun — do you see?"

"Yes, I see."

Bullen got up and walked over to stand behind

Cochrane, who gave a little shove with his good leg, sculling the chair past Petrenko's body to the far wall. Bullen walked with him. He said, "What on earth have you got to live for?"

Cochrane gave a little cry and pushed away from the wall. The chair turned a circle and knocked against a desk, upturning a lamp. Cochrane yelled with pain and bent forward, his teeth clenched. Bullen positioned himself behind Cochrane again. "No money," he said, "no bombs. And here you sit in an underground room in an SIS safe house in Moscow, a dead man on the floor and you losing blood fast. . . ."

"Call someone. Call Charlie Roper, I can — "

"I don't know Charlie Roper."

" — I can box my way out of this."

"That's right," Bullen said. "I believe that. I believe you could."

Cochrane pushed off from the desk, tracking across the polished wood until the wheel checked against Petrenko's outflung arm. He made an attempt to get his hand into the pocket where he'd put the gun and his fingers curled with cramp. Blood drizzled from his trouser cuff. Bullen stood behind him as before and put the gun barrel to the back of Cochrane's neck. His scorched hands made the weapon difficult to grip.

"I don't know if this is going to work." Bullen sounded almost apologetic.

Cochrane spun in the chair, taking both hands away from his thigh to spread them wide in supplication. Bullen held the gun stiff-armed and lined up on Cochrane's forehead. "This might not work," he said. "Who knows? You might not die."

He pulled the trigger and the room seemed to balloon with silence. Echoes crashed around the walls waiting to be heard. He sat back down on the third step of the stairs and after a moment the underground room delivered the noises to him: Cochrane's plea, the gunshot, the chair trundling backward and hitting the far wall.

Bullen closed his eyes. When he opened them, Cochrane's dead face was giving him a canny look, eyes wide with knowledge.

While she was alive, there was always hope. Just a little, just a scrap.

Bullen wept. He wondered who he was crying for.

51

Kyle Bannick was dreaming, and in the dream his brother watched him from the niche by the mirror. Buzz sat nearby, much plumper than in life, blowflies busy around her mouth and eyes.

Evan said, "You think this is enough?"

Kyle dreamed that Sonia appeared at the door. She spread her hands as if she were offering something. Offering herself.

She came out of the shower, beads of water running like pearls on her breasts, and when Kyle lifted his hand to show her what he was carrying, she smiled at the knife.

She sat in the chair, foursquare to the mirror. Her face, Kyle's face, Evan's face. She had fifty different names for pain.

52

They were in a bar on the West Side, Roscoe Tate and Tom Bullen, sitting in a booth and having a farewell drink, old friends who might never meet again. They spoke softly.

"Here's my insurance," Bullen was saying, "a close friend in England who has a terrific reputation as an investigative journalist. I've sent her what you might term a press pack. If I get back alive, and stay that way, she'll never open it."

"You're crazy," Tate said. "You believe I want to kill anybody?"

"No, but you might think it was necessary. Sonia Bishop is covered by the same insurance."

"Go away," Tate pleaded. "Leave me the fuck alone and no one says anything to anyone." He swallowed his drink and signaled for another. "Talk to Paul Shelley when you get back."

"What happened?"

Tate shook his head. "Stuart Cochrane was killed by intruders — probably an attempted abduction. Holding businessmen for ransom is pretty fashionable there right now, and that's what Cochrane was: an English businessman. Cochrane resisted and they killed him. Later, one of his attackers was shot by the police."

"What has Shelley said?"

"Nothing. I told you — that's what everyone's saying." He asked a question of his own: "Where's the money?"

"How much of the action did you have?" Bullen wanted to know.

"Who cares? I've got fuck nothing now."

"It's in whichever numbered account Petrenko nominated. I imagine it'll stay there forever."

"Jesus . . ." Tate shook his head. "You have to give it to Cochrane for nerve. He came close."

"He's dead," Bullen observed, "how close is that?"

On Broadway, Sonia stepped out of the street door of the design studio and started to walk the three blocks to the bar where she'd arranged to meet Bullen. She was feeling light-headed, a little shaky on her feet, because she and Bullen had been awake all night. He'd called her from the airport, then taken a cab to her apartment. When he'd arrived at her door, she had put her arms around him and found it was like holding a ghost.

Early that morning — four o'clock, maybe five — she had said, "What will you do?"

"Go home," he'd replied. "What will you do?"

"Go away."

Go home . . . Bullen no longer knew what that

492

meant; nor could he guess that it was Anne Warbeck moving restlessly from room to room, unable to settle, or walking the streets late at night like a refugee. Her hair had begun to grow back, but you could still see a long stripe of shadow on her skull, a dent in the bone like a fault line. She had come close to death twice during the operation to dig out the shrapnel: the surgeon had worked at speed on a conveyer-belt system of the near-dead under dim lighting and with shells falling in the streets all around. Anne was still healing, although there were times when she thought that might never truly happen. She had dreams now that were worse than memories. She would cry without warning, grow fiercely angry without warning.

Often, her anger was with Bullen. His postcards were jammed between the glass and the gilt frame of a large mirror in her apartment like the spokes of a mandala. Anne stood in front of it and saw how thin her face had become, how dark her eyes. She plucked one of the cards and turned it over to read again what he'd written.

Do you mean a word of it? she wondered. Who knows. I doubt it. And even if you do, things have changed. I've changed. Life's short, Bullen. Sometimes it's a lot shorter than we think. Can you change?

Anne slipped the postcard back into the frame, half masking her own face. I don't think so. I don't think it's going to be easy. I'm not sure we even have a chance.

Kyle wondered where Sonia was heading and whom she might meet. He started after her; he was wearing a long raincoat that concealed the machine pistol slung at his back.

His drive had brought him to the city early that afternoon. He'd gone to his apartment and collected the gun, then to Sonia's apartment, guessing she wouldn't be there; but he had known where to find her and how to be patient.

Sonia too lovely to leave . . .

He could hear Evan's voice above the city noise.

Tate said, "Don't worry; I've paid my dues to a dead man."

"What did you owe?" Bullen asked, but Tate shook his head.

"Would I tell you?" He finished his drink and got up, then paused as if he half expected that Bullen might extend a hand. "All Petrenko was doing," he said, "was selling the future. Today it was a lie, but tomorrow —"

"I know." Bullen picked up his drink and turned away, waiting for Tate to leave.

"— tomorrow, it'll be true."

Three people on the street, all within fifty feet of one another. Sonia was approaching the bar; she didn't see Tate as he started downtown. Tate was looking around for a cab.

Kyle only had eyes for Sonia and wouldn't have recognized Tate anyway. He paused for a brief while after Sonia entered the bar, giving her time to find her friend, get her first drink, whatever would distract her, then he went inside and stepped to the elbow of the bar, keeping the light from the street at his back. He masked himself behind a crowd of office workers and searched the faces.

When he saw that she was with Bullen he couldn't believe his luck. He laughed silently, his mouth wide open, his face creased with glee. The barman looked at him and hesitated. Guys who laughed like that worried him.

Kyle asked for a Southern Comfort, light beer on the side. When the barman came back, he'd gone. The place was crowded with people catching a quick drink before heading home and Kyle wasn't a big man, so it was a few seconds before the barman was able to pick him out again. He was standing close by two guys on bar stools and he'd taken off his long raincoat.

The barman saw the rest in jagged fragments, as if he were watching images flashed onto a screen.

He saw the two drinkers seem to fall away and heard their yells of fear.

He heard the crazy yell, "I'm killing them Evan, killing her, killing them both . . ." and he saw the gun come around as Kyle pulled on the strap and started across the bar to the booth where Bullen and Sonia were sitting.

He saw the man's stance as he swung the gun around, dragging a rope of bullets, not caring who was in the line of fire.

He saw people fall.

He saw himself holding the .38 he kept under the bar, arms straight, lined up dead center on the ugly little bastard's back and firing until the gun was empty.

Kyle wounded seven people in the bar; by some miracle, no one died. In the moment that he'd taken off his coat and stepped forward, Bullen had seen him. Sonia had registered the expression on Bullen's face and began to turn toward the room, but Bullen already had hold of her arm, was already pulling her below the level of the table in the booth and shouting at her, shouting something she couldn't understand. Her face struck the edge of the table as Bullen manhandled her to the floor. She could hear what sounded like a single, sustained explosion, a bedlam, which was the rip of automatic gunfire, people yelling, people screaming.

The noise went on around them. Bullen and Sonia lay in a silence of underground caverns. He was lying on top of her, a shield, and she was motionless. When he finally moved away and crawled out from under the table, Sonia remained where she was. He said, "Sonia," and she didn't answer.

Kyle was belly down on the floor, the gun just out of reach. He was breathing like a swimmer — a gasp, a long pause, then a grunt of exhalation. He lipped up a splash of blood each time.

Bullen said, "Sonia."

She emerged in the moment Kyle died, as if sight of that face was all he'd been waiting for.

Later, I slept at her side like one who has found his heart's ease.

Kyle lifted his head and fixed his gaze on Sonia and took her image away with him.

Sonia talked to the police for three hours. They asked her to call with an address if she planned to leave the city. Bullen was a material witness, no more — a friend of the intended victim. The constituents of Kyle's madness were clear to see: the Duval killings, Sonia's role as principal witness, her face in his mind for months, her name on his lips. No one could quite work out why Kyle should have waited so long to kill her. Psychologists were already busy on the case: Sonia as love object, Sonia as totem of guilt, it was a theorist's dream. The police were even more certain that the original killings were in some way drug-related; they spoke again to relatives of Kelly Duval; they started opening up old wounds . . .

Sonia borrowed an apartment from a friend at the design studio who was going out of town. Bullen moved in with her for three days — long enough for Sonia to decide what she would do. He was staying because no one else could listen to her fear and understand it; because she needed to start her life again, and he was the best person to help her do that.

"Maybe it's easier for you," she said, "it's another country."

He told her about Anne. He said, "It's all risk, whatever you do. The trick isn't making the right choices — it's being able to choose at all."

"Someone I used to work with has a business in San Francisco," Sonia said. "She's looking for a partner. If I sell the apartment and empty my bank account, I can buy in. I hope she still wants that; it's been a while since she asked me."

"A new life," Bullen suggested.

"No, it's the old life but with a better chance, maybe. It's somewhere else. It's what I would have done anyway."

It was their last night together. They had shared a bed, but hadn't made love. Sonia had been crying in her sleep, so Bullen had switched on the light and made some coffee. Now she got up to go to the bathroom, returning to lie on the bed, seeming certain that her nakedness could no longer excite him.

She was still crying gently, as if the dream had welled up again. "Say I meet someone," she said. "I get married, I have kids . . . the wedding, the births, family Christmases — what? — I don't know . . ." She was inventing wildly. "Holidays, Halloween, Thanksgiving suppers, a trip to Europe, a life, a life . . . none of it can cancel out Kyle Bannick. None of it can be bigger than him."

"I could stay longer." He meant a day, two days.

Sonia shook her head. "Separate lives. I have to go forward, you have to go back. I need to begin soon, very soon. The problem is — how."

"Things will change. Everything you've just talked about will happen. You'll be lucky."

Bullen wanted the same thing for both of them: to be lucky. Thinking of Anne, he drew Sonia toward him and stroked her hair.

She said, " *'I slept at her side —'* "

"Things fade," Bullen told her, "things change their meanings."

" *'— like one who has found his heart's ease.'* "

Bullen went to JFK alone.

He bought a postcard of the Chrysler Building at night and took it to a bar on the concourse. He thought that if he managed to drink steadily until the plane was boarding, then follow that with a few more just after takeoff, he might sleep the flight away.

He wrote, "Don't get caught in the cross streets." It meant, "Let's be lucky, let's make it work." Later, he added: "I'm home."

The barman caught his eye and brought the next vodka-tonic. Bullen was beginning to feel good. He would be home a long time before the postcard, but he had already decided it would be best to let Anne make the first move.

We hope you have enjoyed this Large Print book. Other G.K. Hall & Co. or Chivers Press Large Print books are available at your library or directly from the publishers. For more information about current and upcoming titles, please call or write, without obligation, to:

G.K. Hall & Co.
P.O. Box 159
Thorndike, Maine 04986
USA
Tel. (800) 223-6121 (U.S. & Canada)
In Maine call collect: (207) 948-2962

OR

Chivers Press Limited
Windsor Bridge Road
Bath BA2 3AX
England
Tel. (0225) 335336

All our Large Print titles are designed for easy reading, and all our books are made to last.